The Lady and the Mountain Promise

The Mountain Series

Book 4

Misty M. Beller

This book is a work of fiction and any resemblance to persons, living or dead, or places, events or locales is purely coincidental. The characters are the product of the author's imagination and used fictitiously.

Dedication

To my sweet Logan.
You're my pride and joy
and I love you more than you could ever imagine.

In God have I put my trust: I will not be afraid what man can do unto me.

Psalms 56:11 (KJV)

Chapter One

OCTOBER, 1877
BUTTE, MONTANA TERRITORY

I now pronounce you husband and wife. Bryan, you can kiss your bride."

Marcus Sullivan turned his gaze away from the couple, trying not to watch this man he barely knew kiss his baby sister in front of half the town.

It was an honor to officiate over Claire's wedding ceremony, the second one he'd performed in the three months since he'd taken this position at the church in Butte. His church. Correction, God's church. And the flock He'd called Marcus to shepherd. Mining families. Hard-working people, faithful people, the people he felt called to serve.

Once the lovebirds pulled apart, Marcus caught the blush spreading across Claire's face. Something tightened in his chest, but he pushed aside the emotion and sent her a wink. How could he trust her care to another man? Bryan seemed like a good enough fellow, but Claire was his sister.

Inhaling a breath, he raised his eyes to the crowd and motioned toward the happy couple. "I now present to you Mr. and Mrs. Bryan Donaghue."

Cheers and whoops from the surging crowd flooded the small chapel. Marcus stepped back from the clamor.

Music echoed from somewhere to his right, a flowing sound like a brook rushing over stones. A sound so lovely, it pushed back the crowd noise and brought a smile to Marcus's face. He glanced over.

He didn't recognize the woman seated upon the stool. Rich black hair styled in a simple knot, delicate features, dark eyes that were almost haunting. She was the loveliest thing he'd ever seen. Where had Claire found her? And how had he gone three months in this town without ever seeing the mysterious pianist before today?

"Good job, Preacher."

Someone clapped him on the shoulder. Marcus turned. "Ol' Mose. Thank you, sir."

The man, his new grandfather, offered a toothy grin. "Put me in mind o' when ya married yer Gram an' me. Yer a good man."

The man's smile was always infectious. Marcus couldn't help but grin in response. "Thanks. I appreciate it."

The piano music faded, and Marcus glanced back to the woman sitting at the instrument. She started to rise. This was his chance to introduce himself. See if she'd like to play the Sunday morning hymns.

He gave a reciprocal clap to Ol' Mose's wiry shoulder. "If you'll excuse me, I need to catch someone."

"Sure, son."

Marcus swiveled, his foot poised to stride toward the piano, but the woman had disappeared. He glanced into the crowd. She couldn't have strayed far in this mass.

He scanned for anyone with black hair. A few grubby miners, but they sure didn't fit the bill. What color had the woman been wearing? Something dark. Navy? Or it could have been green. Why hadn't he paid closer attention?

Marcus wove through the people, searching for a glimpse of her. A few hands snagged his arm.

"Liked those verses you spoke, Preacher."

"Done good with the weddin', Parson."

He nodded and waved to each person, never stopping his search. As hard as he'd worked these last three months to get to know the folks of this town, a guilty twinge settled in his midsection as he sloughed them off now.

But he needed to find that woman.

He burst through the open back door of the church. Sunlight glared in his eyes. He raised a hand to shadow his face. A crowd milled in the yard, preparing for the celebratory picnic Mama and Aunt Pearl had planned.

No dark-haired woman.

Where could she have gone? The lady couldn't have disappeared into thin air.

"Are you hungry, son?" His father stopped beside him. "I think your Mama's trying to get everyone on the

3

lawn, and I imagine she'd appreciate you shepherding your flock in that direction."

Marcus forced a nod to his father. "Yes, sir."

As disappointment weighed heavily in his chest, he turned to deliver the invitation to the congregation still lingering inside.

THANK GOODNESS she'd slipped out of the church before anyone from the wedding could accost her.

Lilly Arendale settled into the rocking chair and set the wooden runners in motion. The minister's words of hope still echoed through her thoughts. That and the intense expression behind his smile.

She pulled her cloak tighter around her shoulders. Winter nipped at the heels of autumn, making the nights especially cold. Soon, she'd need to start building a fire in the tiny warming stove before they went to bed.

Which meant she'd need to buy firewood. Either buy or gather, but she hardly had time to traipse outside of town with her two-year-old daughter to gather chunks of wood.

After turning up the wick on the lantern, she picked up the leather-bound book and pencil from the table beside her. She stroked a hand over the surface, her fingers finding every groove and indentation in the binding. She opened to the first page. Her own handwriting. *The Musings of Lilly Marie Arendale.*

Flipping faster, she found the first empty page. She'd almost reached the end of the book. A pang tightened her chest. This was one of the few possessions she had left of Pa-pa's. Soon, she'd have to move on to a new volume.

Fitting the pencil between her fingers, she opened her soul and wrote.

To my better self,

Today, I played the pianoforte for the first time since leaving England. It was the most rapturous, heart-rending thing I've done since Pa-pa died. I fingered the cold, ivory keys, heard and felt the familiar melodies soaring in my chest. I think it might have completely broken my heart, had I not sat before so many people.

It was a good thing their eyes were captured by the more beautiful scene of love before them. Claire was a lovely bride with her flashing eyes and the white lace train on her dress.

And the way she looks at her amor. She never gave a thought to music. Most likely did not hear a single note. Yet I am thankful I could add even a small amount of beauty to Claire's special day.

It is my own tiny way of partaking in what will never be.

Dahlia stirred in the bed near the corner of the room and curled in a tighter ball. Lilly closed the book, replaced it on the table, then rose to lay another blanket on her daughter.

As she drew near the bed, blanket in hand, Lilly drank in her daughter's sweet innocence. This precious child. The one solace she'd been granted for the remainder of her days. The one bright flame amidst the darkness.

Lilly settled the extra cover over her daughter, then raised a corner of the covers and slid into her spot next to the child. Together, they would fight against the chill.

Together, they could fight against anything.

Chapter Two

*P*reciate ya stoppin' by, Preacher."

Marcus shook the man's hand as they reached the street in front of the little house. "It was certainly my pleasure." He rested his free hand on his stomach, a little fuller than it had been an hour ago. "My thanks to your wife for her good cooking."

Paul Mason flashed a yellowed smile. "Nothing much better than Lauralee's corned beef and potatoes."

"No argument here." Marcus waved in farewell.

As he strolled down the lane toward his house, his mind drifted back through the visit. The Masons were good, honest folk, just like he'd known back in North Carolina. Despite the rough appearance of this Montana mining town, he'd found a number of these salt-of-the-earth townspeople so far. The kind of people who made it a pleasure to be their pastor.

He'd do his best for them, too. He'd organize games for the kids after services, giving the overworked men and women a chance to relax and enjoy the festivities. And he had plans to invigorate worship as well. Not just sermons, although his head spun every night with God's leading for his messages, but in areas just as likely to touch hearts and change lives. Like the music.

He had to find the lady who'd played piano for Claire's wedding. He'd asked every person he'd met over the last few days if they knew her, but no one had any information to share. If Claire were back from her wedding trip, he could simply ask her. But apparently it wasn't to be that easy. His parents were strangers in town, having traveled from North Carolina for the wedding, and Mama said Claire hadn't mentioned anything about where she'd found the pianist. One of his parishioners said he'd passed the lady on the street before or maybe seen her in the dry goods store, but not a soul knew the woman's name or any way to find her.

How could she be such a mystery? Butte wasn't so big that someone could simply disappear. Especially a woman as beautiful as she.

Marcus reached an intersection and glanced to his right. Gram lived one block over. He should stop by and see how she and Ol' Mose were faring today. When Gramps had died a year and a half ago, then Gram went completely blind last fall, they'd all thought she was in the tail end of her twilight years. Claire had traveled all the way from North

Carolina to the Montana Territory to care for her in what they assumed would be her final days.

A grin pulled at Marcus's mouth. It'd been a bit of a surprise to Claire when she arrived and learned their sassy grandmother had a gentleman caller. They liked Ol' Mose, though. Good thing, too, 'cause one of Gram's first requests when Marcus had arrived in town as the new preacher was for him to perform the wedding ceremony for the two of them.

Now *that* had been a conversation.

Marcus stepped onto the front porch of the little house Gram and Ol' Mose shared when they weren't running freight between Fort Benton and Helena. He tapped on the door. "It's Marcus." With Gram's eyesight gone, he always tried to announce himself right away.

"Come in." Gram's voice held its usual quiver.

Marcus twisted the handle and peeked inside. Ol' Mose and Gram each occupied one of the chairs by the fireplace in the little sitting area. There wasn't a fire in the hearth. Mose looked to be polishing a harness while Gram worked with yarn.

"Come in, Marcus, an' visit with us. Have you had dinner? Let me fix you a plate." Gram set her project aside and started to rise.

"No, thanks. Just finished supper at the Masons'." Marcus grabbed a kitchen chair and carried it over to join the older folks. "Thought I'd stop by and say hi." He settled

9

into the chair, then leaned forward to rest his elbows on his knees.

He nodded toward the leather in Ol' Mose's hands. "Y'all getting ready for a trip?"

The older man sent a fond glance toward Gram. "Yer Gram's got the travelin' itch. Reckon we'll head out the day after tomorry an' run a load."

Marcus swallowed his concern as his gaze traveled between the wiry old man and his sweet little grandmother. He forced a grin onto his face. "You two sure have more get-up-and-go than I do."

Ol' Mose flashed him a toothy grin.

Gram smiled, too, her cloudy eyes staring in his general direction. "How's the sermon coming for Sunday, Marcus. I hate we'll miss it."

"I'll be talking about that passage in Matthew eleven where Jesus tells us to join in His yoke, and we'll find rest."

She nodded. "That's a good one. You're doin' a fine job with the church, Marcus. I'm proud of ya."

Frustration niggled at his gut. "There's still so much more I want to do, not the least of which is provide some music. I can't for the life of me find a pianist. We have that beautiful pianoforte the Bryants ordered, and the only soul in town who can play it has completely disappeared."

The wrinkles on Gram's forehead gathered into twin grooves between her brows. "Who do we have that can play the piano?"

10

Marcus threw up his hands and leaned back in his chair. "There was a lady playing it for Claire's wedding, but I can't find her anywhere. It's a pure mystery."

Gram's lips pursed into such a thin line they were no longer visible. "Who was it Claire said she was trying to have play?" She mumbled the words almost under her breath, then sat up straighter. "Oh. That's right."

Marcus dared not breathe lest he miss the name. When Gram didn't speak, he said, "Well, who is she?"

Gram eased back in her chair. "It was Lilly." A smile played across her face. "Sure did a good job, too, didn't she?"

"Lilly who? Do you know where she lives?" Marcus gripped the seat of his chair and leaned forward.

That thoughtful expression came over Gram's face again. "Don't reckon I know her last name. We just call her Lilly."

"How can I find her, Gram?" Marcus gripped the chair harder, trying to keep his voice from raising.

"Best way'd be to go to Aunt Pearl's, I reckon."

"The café?" Marcus blinked. "You think Aunt Pearl would know how to reach her?"

"That's where Lilly works, honey. In the kitchen." Gram's voice was gentle, as if she were patiently waiting for him to catch up with the conversation.

"She works at the café." Marcus released his grip on the seat and jumped to his feet. He strode across the room,

11

took Gram's face in both of his hands, and planted a kiss on her left cheek. "Thanks, Gram. You're the best."

She patted his hand and chuckled. "I love you, too, Marcus Timothy."

Marcus clapped Ol' Mose's shoulder as he passed, then carried his chair back to the kitchen table. "I'll stop by tomorrow night before y'all head out."

"All right, young feller. Good luck." Ol' Mose raised a hand as Marcus strode to the door.

"WHAT DO YOU mean she won't see me?" Marcus scrubbed a hand through his wavy brown hair, stopping with a handful of it in his grip.

Aunt Pearl braced her arms over her chest like one of the old-time Roman soldiers guarding Jesus's tomb. She wasn't his aunt, nor kin to any person in town, as far as he knew. But everyone called her by the affectionate moniker, and through her good cooking and honest dealings, she'd earned a special place in the hearts of most.

She raised her chin. "Miss Lilly's got a right to decide who she wants ta be social with."

Marcus straightened, taking in a steadying breath. He forced a pleasant smile. "I'm sorry. I shouldn't have come to talk while she's working." He scanned the half-empty dining room of the café. "I only had a simple question, but I can wait until after dining hours."

Aunt Pearl squared her feet and drew her brows into a tight pinch. The woman was more daunting than any Roman soldier. "Preacher, I thought I'd made it clear. Lilly don't want to speak with you. Not now. Not later. Yer outta luck."

He stiffened. What did this bulldog of a woman think he was after? For that matter, what did Lilly think he wanted?

"Aunt Pearl." He kept his tone steady and reasonable. "Perhaps it would help if I tell you what I came to ask Miss...Lilly." It felt so strange to call a woman he hadn't even met by her Christian name. "I want to see if she'd be willing to play the piano for Sunday services. She did an excellent job during Claire's wedding, and we have a need..."

He let his voice drift off as he studied the woman's face. The pinch of her mouth might have lessened a little. Maybe.

"I'll tell her what you asked, Preacher. But I can't promise anything. Lilly likes ta keep to herself most times."

Apparently. He spread his most winning smile for Aunt Pearl. "I appreciate that." He turned and spotted an empty chair right behind him. "I'd be obliged if I could have a bite of whatever sweet your serving tonight."

Her face softened. "It's mincemeat pie tonight. I'll get you a plate."

Less than a minute later, she settled a plate in front of him, close to overflowing with the savory sweet.

"Thanks. This looks mighty good." He raised his fork and hovered over the flaky crust.

"Should be. Your Gram baked it."

He shook his head. "I'm sure it's wonderful then." It was amazing what Gram was still able to do, even in her condition. Baking both the bread and the desserts for the café. Claire had been helping her for the last few months, but now that she was married, would the burden fall back on Gram? What about when Gram was traveling with Ol' Mose? He forced those thoughts from his mind. That was Aunt Pearl's business. He had plenty to do focusing on his own work.

Aunt Pearl headed back toward the kitchen, and Marcus saw his opportunity slipping away. "If you don't mind, can you let Miss Lilly know I'll be out here for a while? Just in case she wants to discuss my request?"

He couldn't be sure, but it sounded like Aunt Pearl *harrumphed* as she disappeared through the dividing curtain.

LILLY PLUNGED the stack of dirty plates into the wash water as her daughter's timid voice murmured from the play area in the back corner of the kitchen. What a blessing that

Dahlia would sit for up to an hour at a time playing with her cloth doll and blocks.

Aunt Pearl swished into the kitchen behind her. "Lilly, hon. The parson said he come by to ask if you'd like to play piano come Sundays. I told him I'd pass along the question."

Lilly's shoulders tensed, and she hunched lower over the soapy water. Just when things were working out. Now that she'd finally formed a safe, comfortable life for her and Dahlia…why this?

Why had she ever agreed to play at Claire's wedding? How could she have ever thought going out amongst all those people was a good idea? She'd planned to slip in, play the songs, then leave the moment the service ended. And that's what she'd done. But she should have known it couldn't be that easy.

A soft hand rested on her back, and every muscle in Lilly's body cringed. She forced herself to take in a long breath. It was only Aunt Pearl.

"Darlin', you know I don't usually mind yer business. An' you'll always have a safe place here, you an' the little 'un both." The hand rubbed slightly, just an inch or two, but the soothing motion pressed against Lilly's defenses. "I think you can trust the preacher, hon. Him bein' Claire's brother an' all. You can tell him 'no' if ya want. But I think it'd be all right to talk to him."

Another gentle stoke on her back. "It's up to you, though. You just let me know if ya need me to pass on any messages."

With a final pat, Aunt Pearl stepped away.

Lilly exhaled a long breath, then gripped the wash rag and rubbed it over the first plate.

"I'm headed back out ta pour more coffee. Lands, if this town don't drink enough to fill the Missouri River."

As Aunt Pearl ducked around the curtain divider, Lilly scrubbed harder on the tin plate. Aunt Pearl thought she should talk with the preacher? A queasy knot started in her stomach. Never. He was a man, and preacher or not, men couldn't be trusted. Not ever.

He'd said he wanted her to play for church. Too bad. She wouldn't be doing that either.

Chapter Three

arcus tossed his hat on the ladder-back chair in his bed chamber and sank on the mattress with a sigh. He propped his elbows on his thighs and let his head sink into his hands.

What had he done wrong? Why wouldn't the woman even talk to him?

Some would consider an invitation to play during worship services an honor. But this woman didn't seem to see it that way. He'd been so sure he could convince her if he'd been allowed to put the request to her in person. But she'd never given him the chance.

Marcus flopped back onto the bed and stared up at the rafters. Perhaps it wasn't God's will that Lilly play at the church. But the nagging in his gut told him otherwise. Or maybe that was his own desire talking. He had to admit he'd found the woman attractive. And intriguing. That was part of the reason he'd been so eager to find her.

Yet other motives played a role as well.

The sound of the piano and a host of voices raised in praise was a sweet melody in the Lord's ears. Music had a way of reaching people. How many times had he been both convicted and exhorted while singing a hymn? He wanted the same for the people in this parish. Of course, they could continue to sing without accompaniment, as they'd been doing. But the richness of adding piano, especially music as beautiful as he'd heard at the wedding, would only enhance the worship. And she was the only one in town who could play.

"Father, if you want me to pursue Miss Lilly's agreement to play for services, please show me what to do."

Marcus sat up, then stood and walked to the washbasin. It'd been a long day. After he ran the dripping cloth over his face, his eyes found the mirror. As they locked there, his mind drifted back to the woman from the café. Lilly. He'd forgotten to ask Aunt Pearl her last name. What was her story? What had brought her to the point where she was so skittish of meeting anyone new?

Or was it just men she didn't like? He propped his hands on the stand. What had she endured to instill such wariness in her? His chest ached as possibilities flew through his mind.

Piano or not, he wanted to reach out to this woman. But how? His gaze flickered to the desk where his sermon notes waited next to his Bible. A note? If he couldn't ask her in person, would she read a note from him instead? It was certainly an unobtrusive way to communicate. If he could just convince Aunt Pearl to pass it along . . .

In two strides, Marcus reached the desk and slid into the ladder back chair. He took a clean sheet of paper, dipped the quill, and set ink to paper.

Give me the words, Lord. This could be his only shot at reaching the woman. He had to get it right.

LILLY RUBBED the moisture from a clean mug and placed it on the shelf with the others. Aunt Pearl plopped another stack of dirty dishes on the work counter beside her and added an additional plate on top.

Dishes. Seemed like that's most of what she did anymore. She enjoyed the cooking part of her duties at Aunt Pearl's Café, but the cleanup she could do without. Of course, it was a minor price to pay for the zealous protection Aunt Pearl provided her and Dahlia.

"Look, Mama."

Lilly glanced at her daughter, sitting at her play area in the corner. The child had her blocks stacked six or seven high, enough that they teetered on the uneven wood floor.

"Crash." Dahlia's little voice rang out a moment before she struck the middle squares, and the tower tumbled into a heap.

Lilly offered a cringing smile as her gaze darted toward the dining room. "Be careful not to make loud noises, honey." Aunt Pearl had been tolerant thus far of Lilly bringing her daughter to the café, but if the child got in the way of business or disturbed the paying customers, Lilly had no illusions of the choice Pearl would have to make.

Turning back to the stack of plates beside her, Lilly pulled the cloth napkin from the top and tossed it in the bucket of soapy water beside the stove, where it joined a myriad of similar cloths. Aunt Pearl believed in the extra touches, like serviettes for her patrons, but they were a chore, always needing to be cleaned.

She grabbed the top plate and lowered it toward the wash water in the sink, but a ruffle of something stopped her mid-air. She raised the plate to peer at the folded paper attached to the tin surface with a drop of grease. It fluttered under her breath.

She reached for the paper, then allowed the plate to sink into the water below. Why did her hand tremble? Flipping it over, she searched for writing that might identify its owner without the need to open the folds.

There. On the underside. In bold ink. *Miss Lilly.*

Her? Lilly's stomach tightened as her fingers fumbled to open the folded piece. Had Aunt Pearl written the note, and it somehow fell from her pocket? But what would Aunt

Pearl need to communicate that couldn't be said in person? Was she telling Lilly she didn't need her anymore? She'd found someone better to cook meals for the café?

Smoothing the creases, Lilly eyed the bold script covering much of the page, then focused on the first words.

Dear Miss Lilly,

Please pardon my use of your Christian name, as I'm not acquainted with your surname. I was hoping for the privilege of asking in person, but perhaps this note will be easier for clear communication.

As I'm sure you're aware, our church was blessed with the gift of a fine pianoforte, the nicest I've seen in a while. It was such a pleasure to hear you bring the keys to life at the wedding held there recently. A pleasure I hope to soon repeat, as we would be honored for you to play a hymn during each of our Sunday services. You would be sharing your great talent with your fellow townspeople as we lift our voices together to worship our great God. Imagine the beautiful sound to the Father's ears.

If you'd like to discuss further, I can be reached at the church most afternoons. Or you're welcome to simply come on Sunday and take your place at the instrument.

I remain your humble and contrite servant,
Rev. Marcus Sullivan

Lilly inhaled a breath, her eyes roaming over the note again. From the Reverend? Warmth slid through her like a rich tea, aromatic and soothing. *Sharing your great talent.*

The way he described the effect of the music—the man had a way with words. That was a rare quality in these rough parts, but one Pa-pa had taught her to admire. In written form, words were jewels, each to be carefully selected and placed for beauty and clarity.

The thud of boots sounded just before Aunt Pearl whisked through the curtain with another tray full of dirty dishes.

Lilly folded the paper quickly and tucked it in her apron bodice. She grabbed the stack of plates from the work counter and submerged them in the wash water just as Aunt Pearl thunked another load in their place.

"Dinin' room's clearin' out. Not many more of these."

Lilly nodded, but even as her hands worked quickly, her mind spun back through the words on the note. Should she respond? Stop at the church and explain why she couldn't agree? But what would she say? That the only way she could keep herself and Dahlia safe was by staying away from people? There were too many men in this town who couldn't be trusted, and she wasn't a good judge of character.

She'd proved that already.

MARCUS SAT in the café, sipping coffee and staring at the curtain blocking his view of the kitchen. Brooding.

Why hadn't she given any kind of response? Of course, he hadn't actually asked her to come out to the dining area to talk to him, but if he made himself available...

The lunch crowd had long since dwindled, and Aunt Pearl would likely kick him out soon for loitering. With a sigh, he pushed the coffee mug away from him, and stood, unfolding his long legs.

"You finally think o' some place better ta hang around than here, Parson?" Aunt Pearl softened the words with a quirk of her mouth.

"Yes, ma'am. Need to finish up some things at the church. I appreciate the extra coffee, though." He offered a grin that he hoped didn't reveal his disappointment.

"Anytime."

Marcus spent the afternoon oiling the tables he'd built for church events, sweeping dust and cobwebs from inside the building, and reading through his sermon notes for the upcoming Sunday.

By evening, though, his stomach growled, and his nerves were tight. He should go back to his little house for dinner. His parents would be there, and Mama always had something simmering on the stove. They only planned to be around for another few weeks before they traveled back to their North Carolina home.

But despite every reason his mind pointed out, his feet carried him to the café.

Aunt Pearl met him at his usual table with a grin and a pot of coffee. "Welcome back. If I didn't 'spect you had other reasons fer hangin' around, I'd think you liked my comp'ny."

He clapped a hand over his heart. "You found me out."

Shooing a hand at him, she turned toward the kitchen. "Food'll be ready a'fore you can shake a stick. It's fried beef and 'taters tonight."

Marcus eased back in his chair and cradled the mug. The food sounded good, but none of it really mattered if he didn't accomplish his mission. He eased in a long breath. No, it wasn't up to him to make this happen. If God wanted Lilly to play piano for the services, He would find a way.

He released the breath.

"Here ya go."

Marcus looked up to thank Aunt Pearl with a smile, then glanced down at the plate. A cloth covered the dish, puckering around the raise lumps of food.

He pulled the fabric off, and his hungry eyes drank in the sight of the steak swimming in juices. The tantalizing aroma of fried beef drew a sharp growl from his midsection. A folded napkin took up a small quarter of the plate. Strange. Aunt Pearl usually kept forks and napkins at each place setting, as she had this time. He'd never received a napkin as part of his meal.

With tentative fingers, he took up the cloth and unfurled it. A folded sheet of paper slipped from the layers and fell onto the table.

Marcus's chest pounded. Did it hold good news? Perhaps she was too shy to speak to him in person. The note had definitely been a good approach. But what if she'd been offended by his forwardness in writing a letter to her? What if this memo was an expression of her displeasure?

His name was written in lovely script on the outside, much nicer than his scrawling print. *Reverend Sullivan.* He fumbled with the paper as his clumsy hands tried to open it.

At last he straightened the paper, his eyes feasting on the words:

Dear Sir,

I am in receipt of your note and I thank you for the honor inherent in your request. As lovely as your piano is, I must respectfully decline your offer.

Sincerely,
L.

Postscript: I thank you for your concern over my surname and propriety, however I give you leave to use my Christian name.

So many emotions assaulted Marcus, it was hard to hone in on just one. But finally he did. And likely the most inconsequential.

I give you leave to use my Christian name. Gentlemen only spoke to ladies by their given name if they were relatives or very close friends of the family. As far as he could tell, he and Lilly weren't anywhere near that footing. About as far as England from the Montana Territory.

So why didn't she want him to know her family name? Was she embarrassed by it? Perhaps her father had been a notorious killer or she had some other reason to regret her title.

But as his mind finally accepted the unlikeliness of that thinking, he was forced to consider the real reason.

She didn't want Marcus to find her.

Surely if he knew her last name, he would be able to ask at the boarding houses and stores in the area. Find out how to reach her.

His shoulders slumped, and he picked up his fork, going through the motions to eat without tasting.

The message of the note was clear, both written and implied. No matter how polite her words, she was not interested in playing hymns for the church service. That was the end of the discussion.

LILLY PRESSED the creases from the pastor's note as she snuggled into her chair that night. With Dahlia asleep, she had a few precious moments to herself.

Had she given the right answer in her response? Would it really do so much harm to play a simple song or two at the beginning of Sunday services? She didn't even have to stay for the sermon. Surely the church people wouldn't cause problems for her.

She straightened her shoulders. What was she thinking? That she would find another tiny congregation like the one they'd left in Derbyshire? Those good people had been the only ones in her life who hadn't ridiculed their unorthodox family. Not her father for taking a Guatemalan wife. Nor her mother for her dark skin and the raven hair she always wore long with only a single comb on the side. No, it would be almost impossible to find another church so welcoming.

And there was too much chance she would meet more of the unsavory kind she'd already experienced in Butte. Playing the piano would make her too vulnerable. Too noticed.

Her eyes found the form of her daughter, sleeping so peacefully in the bed. But as Lilly's fingers crept up to her neck, they slipped under the collar of her night dress, and found the scar she always kept covered.

That scar was for her alone to know. Her warning. The reminder to never again allow herself to be that vulnerable.

Never.

Chapter Four

A s Marcus led the congregation in "Just as I Am" at the end of the service, he tried not to cringe every time his voice drifted off-key. His gaze flickered to the idle piano, but he jerked it back and raised his focus heavenward on the final words of the hymn. "O, Lamb of God, I come, I come."

He breathed a quick prayer of thanks in the silence that lingered, then opened his eyes and smiled at the flock before him. "It was a pleasure to worship with you this morning. And speaking of worship, you may have noticed our shiny new piano sits in want of a pianist." He waved toward the instrument. "If there's any among you who have knowledge of the piano, we would be honored to have you play it for services. Just stop by and see me anytime."

But as he stood by the back door and greeted the exiting people, his spirits dimmed a little more with each encouraging word.

"You're right, Preacher, it sure would be nice fer someone to play that piano up there. It's purty to look at but even purtier to hear, I bet."

Marcus forced a closed-mouth smile. "Yes, it would be nice. Thanks for coming, Mr. Albright, Mrs. Albright."

After he said goodbye to the last of the parishioners, Marcus stepped inside and closed the door behind him. The mid-sized building seemed vast and empty without the people. It held a hint of a musty odor, maybe a bit of the smell from all the humans packed together.

His footsteps echoed on the wooden floor as he strode forward, turned left past the front pew, and settled his hand atop the piano. Its mahogany surface shone, still reflecting the polish he'd applied earlier in the week. He moved around to the front and eased down onto the bench. He'd never played an instrument before. Never known anyone who had a piano. Not even their church back in Charlotte.

With his right index finger, he pressed a key, then another, searching for the opening sound of "Just as I Am."

There. That might be it.

He pressed the key to the left of it. Not right. He went the other way. Yes.

His shoulders eased. He had the first two notes. Maybe this wouldn't be so bad. The third note was easier to find, but it took at least two minutes of pecking to find the fourth. By the time he'd picked out the first line of the song, sweat made his shirt cling to him, and the sounds of the piano notes ran together in his head so he couldn't distinguish right from barely wrong.

He dropped his elbows to the keys in a terrifying clang of notes and settled his head in his hands. "Lord, this doesn't feel right. What am I doing wrong here?"

Several long minutes passed, as his breathing steadied and he listened for the still small voice in his spirit. No resounding message from the Lord pressed him, but a peace gradually took over his soul. Eased his muscles.

At last, he raised his head. And in his heart, he knew what he had to do.

MARCUS SAT on the stoop outside the café's back door, forearms on his knees, watching two squirrels chase each other from tree to tree. A breeze whipped up, piercing his wool shirt. With the sun dipping below the far horizon, the night was growing quite cool. He'd need to drag out his coat soon.

After another hour or so, Marcus's legs had grown as stiff as a mule with joint pain. He'd stood and wandered around the little clearing a few times, but he didn't stray far in case Lilly came out. Something told him she'd scurry away quicker than a mouse with a scrap of food.

The door finally opened, and he jumped to his feet, doffing his hat as he rose.

"Marcus, what in the world?" Claire stood in the door frame, jaw slack and eyes wide.

He motioned for her to come outside.

She darted a glance behind her, then stepped out and shut the door. "What's wrong?" She gripped his arm, panic surging in her voice. "Are Mama and Papa okay? I just saw them this morning."

He waved her worries down and kept his voice low. "Everyone's fine. I didn't realize you were back from your wedding trip yet."

"We arrived late yesterday. Why are you sitting behind the café?" She copied his lowered tone.

He glanced toward the door. Claire could definitely help him convince Miss Lilly. After all, hadn't the woman played for Claire's wedding? And the two had worked together at Aunt Pearl's Café for many months.

"I, um, came to see Miss Lilly."

She arched a brow and raised her hands to her hips. "You did?"

He cleared his throat. "Yes, I wanted to ask if she'd play for services on Sundays."

Claire's eyes narrowed. "How do you know Lilly plays?"

His hands were a bit clammy, so he wiped them on his trousers. "She played for your wedding. Do you think you could ask her for me?"

Her brows shot back up, and she pressed a finger to her chest. "You want *me* to ask? Oh, no, no. Not a chance." She gave her head a hard shake.

"It's all right. I can ask her." That obviously hadn't been the right thing to say. "Do you, um, do you think you could put in a good word for me, though?"

She gave him an impish little smile only a sister could, then patted his arm. "I'm not sure it would help. But you can handle it, Marc. I have faith in you." She pulled her shawl tighter around her shoulders and turned toward the street. "I need to get home now. I told Bryan I'd try to be there before dark, so I'm late."

Marcus watched her retreating figure along the side of the café building. It seemed so strange to see his sister rushing home to a husband. She was barely more than a girl. Well, maybe that wasn't true, but he remembered her in braids and short skirts.

The café door opened again, jerking his attention to the spray of light from inside. A woman's frame was silhouetted there, turned sideways with a large bundle in her arms. She hadn't seen him yet.

She stepped down from the stoop, dropped a bundle to the ground, then pulled the door shut behind her. As she picked up her pack again, adding it to the load still in her arms, her burdens seemed larger than she was. She swayed under the weight.

He stepped forward. "Can I be of help?"

She spun with a little squeal, clutching her bundles tighter and backing away from him.

"It's all right. It's only me, Reverend Sullivan." He held out a placating hand and forced himself to stay put.

She stopped moving, but her tense posture told him she might bolt any minute.

"Who is it, Mama?" A girl's voice sounded from Miss Lilly's arms. A very young voice.

She murmured something, and the bundle shrank closer to her.

Was that *her* child? Was she married then? A weight pressed his shoulders. Perhaps it was her husband who didn't want her playing in church. His chest tightened.

"What do you want?" The woman's voice came out clear and strong, articulate, with a hint of accusation.

Marcus inhaled a steadying breath. "I only hoped for the chance to speak with you. Perhaps I could escort you home while we talk?"

"No. Speak now and be done."

She certainly wasn't as polite in person as she'd been in her letter.

He cleared his throat. "I know you said you don't want to play for services, but I wanted to extend an invitation to come and play the piano at the church any time you'd like."

She nodded, but her face was too shadowed for him to see any expression save the strong jut of her chin.

34

He pushed on. "I didn't realize you had a child." He nodded toward the bundle in her arms. "If you're concerned about her while you play, my mother would be more than thrilled to sit with her." He offered his most charming smile. "Now that Claire's wed, she seems to be even more taken with children."

Lilly didn't respond, and the silence stretched.

"If you'd like me to speak with your husband about it, I'd be happy to." The word *husband* felt like mud on his tongue. Whatever the rapscallion had done to instill so much fear in Lilly, the man should be flogged.

"I'm not married." The words seemed almost vulnerable. Then her chin came up again. "I make my own decisions, and I choose not to play before all those people."

Something about the way she said *all those people* belied her brave front. Her voice held an edge of...fear?

"I... All right." He took a step back, suddenly feeling a strong need to give the woman space. "But the offer to practice stands any time."

She dipped her head. "Thank you, Reverend." Then she turned and strode down the dark alley, not taking the path along the side of the building to the street, as Claire had done.

Marcus watched until the shadows engulfed the woman's lithe form. His chest ached to follow. To protect her from the evils lurking through the town under the shadow of night.

To make things better for this woman he didn't even know.

THE SKIN ON Lilly's shoulders prickled in the night shadows. She hiked Dahlia higher on her hip and scurried faster. Should she step out of the shadows, onto the street where the moon bathed the surface? Or stay on this boardwalk, as hidden as she could be as she dashed past the occasional raucous saloon?

She darted a glance down the gap between two buildings as she passed. Was that a man's shadow? Surely it was only a tree or post, as long and skinny as it was. But it had moved. Or maybe that was a trick of the moon.

"Bumpy, Mama," Dahlia whined in her arms.

"I know, honey. We're almost home." She murmured the words under her breath. Usually Dahlia rested on her shoulder during their walk home and was almost asleep by the time they arrived.

Not tonight, though.

Lilly's skin crawled again. Someone was watching her. She spun around, walking backward for several strides. A shadow moved into the shelter of one of the buildings.

Definitely a man. She whirled back around and strode forward even more quickly.

Could it be the reverend? He'd scared the blood from her showing up behind the café like that, although he'd been quick to explain his presence and had seemed safe enough. But would he follow her like this? Without revealing his presence? The shadow had seemed lankier than the broad-shouldered preacher. Of course, tricks of the moonlight could be deceiving.

She'd almost reached the side street where their little house stood, just three doors down. Then safety.

As she turned right at the corner, she darted another glance behind her.

There he was.

Striding along like he was out seeing the sights. Definitely too skinny to be Reverend Sullivan. But something about that swagger struck a familiar vein in her mind.

She didn't stick around to ponder it.

In less than a minute, she reached her door, pulled the latch string, and stumbled inside. She clutched Dahlia to her chest, almost tripping on her own feet. Her breath came hard as she slammed and braced the door, then staggered forward to the bed in the corner.

"We're home, mija. We're home." She sank onto the bed and rocked her little one, forward and back, struggling to still her racing heart.

To my better self,

It's been two days now since the Reverend stood outside the café door and offered the piano at the church any time I wish to practice. I learned from Claire his name is Marcus. It suits him. A strong name for the man whose broad shoulders remind me of the paintings Pa-pa used to show me of the Roman Gladiators. I can almost imagine him in a leather subligaculum and armor, yet that's not the direction my mind should wander.

Much within me craves to accept his offer and sneak into the church for a few moments of pleasure with that lovely pianoforte. Yet, if I were caught... If he knew I acceded, my resistance would be sliced through. My armor removed, and any further refusals undermined by my weakness. I cannot let that happen.

I wonder if there is a time when I could play undiscovered. I shouldn't even be thinking these thoughts, yet my soul craves the release which music brings. Perhaps early morning?

Lilly closed the leather book and placed it on the little table beside her. With a stretch, she rose and strolled toward the wall where she hung their clothing. Dahlia's precious gowns below, and hers above, draped over a rope strung between two nails. It was a far cry from her elegant wardrobes in England, but it was hers. She answered to no one. Owed nothing that would put her in someone's debt. And that's the only way she would live now.

Propping her right foot on a chair, she raised her skirts to her knee and pulled the Smith and Wesson Model One revolver from the leather strap she'd rigged above her boot. With her woolen stockings, it didn't rub too badly. And after the man who'd followed her home two nights ago, she wasn't taking chances.

Something about him seemed so familiar, but she couldn't place that skinny build. And the more time elapsed, the hazier her memory grew.

No matter, though. Whether she knew the man or not, if his intentions were foul, she wouldn't hesitate to send a bullet through him.

She wouldn't think twice this time.

$$Chapter\ Five$$

*M*arcus breathed in the crisp morning air as he strode along the quiet road toward the church. The homes on his right seemed still and quiet, although, given the fact that it was an hour after dawn, their hush might mean the inhabitants were already off to earn a living.

His mouth formed a tuneless whistle, and he slipped his hands into the pockets of his coat. Mama had promised to finish stitching a scarf before she and Father returned home next week. It had been so nice to have them around, helping him settle into his new home and church. But it would be nice to be on his own again, too. Of course, Claire and Gram would be close by, should he have need of any mothering.

He stopped at the edge of the churchyard to take in the scene. The building was strong and sturdy. Its whitewashed siding sported a new coat of paint, thanks to his father's help. Mama had trimmed the roses climbing the perimeter fence, and he hoped they would be full of blooms come spring.

A sound drifted on the breeze. A melody, flowing and rhythmic, with haunting undertones. He glanced in the direction of town. Was it coming from one of the houses? But how? It wasn't a human voice, but an instrument.

A piano.

His gaze pulled toward the church, awareness settling over him. His feet drove him forward. But when he reached the front porch, he stopped. The music was building now to crescendo with feeling and emotion. If his boots thudded on the wood, would she hear and stop? If he opened the door, would she bolt?

But something in him demanded to see her with his own eyes. Solidify the picture in his mind of her playing such a heart-stirring ballad.

Again, his feet moved before his brain registered the decision, around the corner of the church to the first of the two windows that spanned each side of the building. His chin was level with the base of the window, and his eyes focused on the dim interior.

There she was. He could only see her face, but a flurry of emotions flashed across it as her eyes followed the movement of the keys under her fingers. Those dark flashing eyes. For a moment, they closed as her head rocked to the rolling movement of the song.

He stopped breathing as he watched. She was gorgeous. Even through the glass, and halfway across the church, his eyes tracked the delicate structure of her cheekbones and nose, the way her chin came to a point. So fragile, yet covering an indomitable spirit.

A movement on the floor at the base of the piano caught his attention. A little girl played with blocks. She was young, maybe two years old, possibly younger. She had the same dark hair as her mother, the same delicate features. Her hair fell in a braid down her back, as Lilly's did.

His gaze drifted back to the woman, and he felt a surge of...what? Attraction? Longing? It was both of those, and it was so much more, something he couldn't name. He wanted so much to enter the building. To revel in the music and play with the little waif. But he couldn't interrupt. Couldn't break in on their moment. If he did, instinct told him Lilly would run and never come back.

And so, he watched from a distance.

LILLY CLOSED the café's back door and hiked Dahlia higher on her hip. Her jaw forced itself open as a yawn crept out, but she didn't have a free hand to cover it. At least she was alone here in the back alley, where no one would see her ill manners.

After another long day at the café, her muscles ached, especially her lower back from standing at that stove. It was tempting to let Dahlia walk at least part of the way home, but the child had been dozing on her pallet in the café's kitchen, and now she lay snuggled against Lilly's shoulder. Dahlia never liked to wear shoes, and Lilly didn't usually force her to for the walk home at night. It was easier to carry the child.

The warmth of the small body snuggling into her was a feeling she wouldn't give up, even if her muscles mutinied.

"Home yet?" The little voice at her neck was accompanied by a warm breath.

"In a few minutes, honey."

Shadows in the alley kept them covered, and she could hide from the glaring lights of the few late-night establishments they passed. In the shadows, she could melt into oblivion. But the alley ended, and she was forced to step onto the boardwalk.

As she neared the outskirts of the red light district, she hesitated, as she always did. Should she hurry through? Or turn and take several extra blocks to skirt the area? Her muscles protested louder, making the decision for her.

She marched forward, stepping down to the street to avoid a run-in with any rowdies leaving the saloons.

She'd made it the length of a block when the fine hairs on the back of her neck tingled. *Not again.* She jerked her head first to the left, then the right. Nothing out of place, although the lights flickering inside the Irish Castle beside her made the shadows on the street sway.

Tightening her grip on Dahlia, the skin on her right ankle pricked under the rubbing of the gun strapped to it.

Should she draw it? Have it ready in case the man attacked? She kept moving forward.

By the next cross street, bumps ran the length of her arms and down her back. Someone was definitely watching her.

She paused beside the boardwalk and scanned the shadows. Still nothing.

Except… Was that a man's shadow at the end of the building behind her? It didn't move, but was about the right size for a lanky male.

She propped her boot on the step beside her and slipped her hand under her skirt. With the motion she practiced every night, she flipped the leather strap off with her index finger and withdrew the pistol.

Her traitorous hand shook as she held the gun at her waist, letting the light from the building flash off the metal.

"What are you doing, mama?" Dahlia's sleepy voice.

Lilly boosted the child higher on her hip and started off. "Just had to get something, honey. We're almost home." *But not close enough.*

They were still three blocks from their street. Lilly squared her shoulders and pushed forward. Her ears strained to pick up any unusual sounds around her, but the jaunty music coming from the public house beside her drowned out any other noises. At least this was the last saloon before the scenery faded into shanties and tiny homes, some built onto each other so they shared walls,

44

which probably helped to keep the biting winter wind from sneaking through the cracks between boards.

As the music and laughter faded behind her, another sound caught Lilly's attention. A scuffing sound.

Like footsteps.

She whirled, raising her gun to whatever threat loomed.

A man, not just the shadow of one, slipped into the darkness against the side of the building.

Forcing her fingers to still, she clutched the grip and hooked her thumb on the metal hammer, then pulled. The pistol cocked with a loud click. There was no way the man could have missed the sound.

She swallowed, forcing liquid down her parched throat. "Don't come any closer." Her voice came out stronger than she'd expected, given the fact her legs were quivering.

A faint chuckle drifted over the breeze.

The wash of anger that rushed through her pushed away any fear that tried to linger. No man would have control of her again. And she would certainly not let anyone close enough to endanger her child. Not this shadow. Not now. Not ever.

With renewed determination, she turned back toward her home and stalked forward. She kept a steady ear tuned to any sound behind her, but none drifted through the night air.

As she turned right onto their street, the familiar view of home shone in the moonlight before her. For a moment, her heart stuttered. Was she making a mistake letting the man see where she lived? But if he'd followed her before, as she was sure he had, he already knew. And with a strong metal brace on the door—and the revolver beside her bed— she could protect herself. Couldn't she?

MARCUS GLANCED toward the curtain partitioning off the kitchen as he swallowed another bite of the beef soup. Lilly's stews had developed quite a reputation in town, although they were usually attributed to Aunt Pearl. Claire had let him in on the secret of who really produced all the savory meals from the café's kitchen.

It still astonished him that Lilly could stay so hidden back there. And with a daughter, too. He'd never heard a peep from the child, and Claire and Aunt Pearl were the only women who ever pushed through that dividing curtain. He'd tried to ferret out Lilly's story from Claire, but his sister was tight-lipped for the first time in her life. All she'd told him was that the story was sad. Maybe Claire wasn't privy to all the details.

But Marcus wanted to know. Something inside him craved to learn more about her, almost as much as he yearned to follow God's will for his life and this church.

Aunt Pearl stopped by to fill his mug with fresh coffee. The dark liquid rose halfway up as she poured out the last bit from the pot. "Let me get more for ya, Reverend. Coffee's in high demand tonight."

He shot a glance at the full tables around him. "The café's busy. Is Claire helping you?"

Her mouth pinched. "She asked to take a couple nights off a week. Can't say as I blame her, what with that new husband an' all. I think I'm gonna hafta find more help, though. Gettin' too old ta try ta keep up on my own."

He reared back and eyed her with the hint of a grin. "Why, you don't look much older than Claire. A sight prettier, too, if you don't mind me sayin'."

She shooed him and turned away, but not before he saw a smile pull at her mouth. "Let me get ya more coffee."

Marcus took up his spoon again and inhaled another bite of stew as he watched those around him. Mostly business men, some with their wives. A handful of miners, bachelors he assumed. From what he'd heard, miners with families barely made enough to keep them nourished and clothed. Eating at the café was a luxury they didn't experience.

Food and supplies sure weren't cheap up here in the Montana Territory. He'd noticed that pretty quickly.

A clatter sounded from the kitchen. Then a scream. Marcus's heart jumped in his chest, and he leaped to his feet before he could stop himself.

The voices around him didn't wane. Had he been the only one to hear it? Should he go see if everyone was all right? The kitchen had always been off limits—Aunt Pearl made that clear.

The curtain ruffled, then pulled aside enough for Pearl to peer out. She searched the crowd. When her gaze landed on him, she waved him forward.

Marcus sprinted toward her, brushed aside the curtain, and stepped around it. It took a moment for his eyes to adjust to the cluttered space.

Aunt Pearl and Miss Lilly were bent over something on the floor. A whimpering filled the small space, along with a soothing murmur.

He stepped around them to see what held their attention.

The little girl lay curled in a ball on the floor as her mother dipped her tiny foot in a basin of water. Shriveled, crimson flesh glared up at him, stealing his breath. Tears streamed from the child's eyes as she cowered into Lilly's side.

"Parson, can you fetch the doc?" Aunt Pearl's command jolted him from his stupor. "Dahlia's burned herself good."

"Of course."

"Go out the back."

He spun toward the door, pushed it open, and hit the ground at a sprint. The town had two doctors, Claire's husband, Bryan, and his younger brother, Alex. Neither was

48

likely to be in the clinic at this hour of the evening. He veered in the direction of Bryan and Claire's house at the edge of town. Claire would surely come with her husband, and it would be good for Lilly to have a friend close by.

When he reached the whitewashed cottage Bryan had built, he took the stairs in a single stride and pounded on the door. "Bryan. Claire. Open up." His breaths came hard, and he bent at the waist to gather more air.

As he raised his hand to knock again, a shuffling sounded inside. The door opened, and Bryan's form filled the frame. "What's wrong?"

"Lilly's daughter. Burned herself at the café. Where's Claire?" Marcus still struggled to catch his breath as he peered around the man.

Bryan ducked back inside. "Claire's helping Miriam," he called over his shoulder. "I'm coming now." He reappeared with his doctor's bag in hand. "Let's go."

Marcus led the way as they jogged the blocks to the café. His nerves were a ball of knots by the time they arrived. Bryan seemed familiar with the café as he stepped through the back door.

The two women knelt in the same position Marcus had left them, but Aunt Pearl rose and stepped back when they entered. Bryan took her place, and Marcus moved close enough to see.

"How are you, little flower?" Bryan's words were gentle as he examined the bright red skin on the child's foot.

Marcus couldn't focus on the sight. Not the precious little limb, inflamed and obviously very painful. A sob jerked his attention to the child's tear-filled eyes.

Lilly brushed the girl's hair back from her forehead, soothing with soft words. Her voice was rhythmic, flowing, like the music she'd played the other day. Under the spell of them, his own muscles eased.

Until the child jumped and whimpered.

"I'm sorry, Dahlia," Bryan murmured. "I'm just going to dry it off and put some medicine on, then we'll wrap it so it feels better."

The child didn't answer but caught her bottom lip between her teeth.

Marcus wanted to pace, but that would likely disturb the girl. He really wanted to elbow his way in and help. Do *something*.

Watching the child in so much pain—while he did nothing—was ripping his heart in two.

Chapter Six

After what felt to Marcus like an hour, the doctor finally straightened.

"There now. I know it still hurts, but that will help." The man handed a small bottle to Lilly. "You can give her a capful of this twice a day for the pain. Don't give it any longer than you have to, though."

She took the bottle, peering at the black label with white print. Marcus was too far away to read what it said.

Bryan sat back on his heels and eyed the girl. "Are you starting to feel better, Dahlia?"

She nodded once, and her eyelids drooped a little.

Bryan turned back to Lilly. "Keep it wrapped for a day or two. I'll stop by and check to make sure it's healing nicely. It hasn't blistered, so there shouldn't be much danger if you keep it clean."

The woman nodded. The hint of fear in her eyes gave her a vulnerability Marcus hadn't seen before.

51

Bryan seemed to be taking her measure. "I think it'd be good if you took her home now."

"Of course," Aunt Pearl spoke up. "Y'all go on. That crowd's windin' down out there anyway. Get on with yourselves."

Lilly looked at the woman, a line forming between her dark brows. "Are you sure?"

"Sure, I'm sure."

Bryan started to repack his supplies. "Do you need help getting her home?"

This was his chance. "I'll help." Marcus stepped forward, and all four pairs of eyes turned toward him. "I'll escort them home."

That fear again, stronger now, reflected in Lilly's eyes. Her mouth parted to speak.

"That's a good idea." Aunt Pearl jumped in. "Thank ye, Reverend."

Marcus kept his focus on Lilly. After a second, she closed her mouth, squared her shoulders, and nodded once as she looked down at her daughter. Barely a bob of her chin, but it eased the tension tightening his neck.

"I'll clean the floor, then be ready to go." Lilly's voice was so soft he almost missed it.

When she'd wiped the floor and gathered a small satchel, Lilly gingerly lifted the child in her arms and stood. She turned toward the door, not even looking his direction.

Marcus's brows pinched. "How about if I carry her?"

Lilly halted to fumble with the door latch, but she still didn't give him so much as a glance. "I'm fine."

In two strides, Marcus was by her side, reaching for the latch to stop her efforts. "She's too heavy to carry far." Even though the child was just a waif, it couldn't be easy for this slender woman to carry her past the next building.

Lilly jerked her hand back from the door, even though he hadn't touched her. She spun toward him, fire lighting her eyes.

Marcus gave her his most beseeching look and softened his tone. "Please. Let me help."

Her chin jutted, and she stared at him for a long moment. Then she looked down at her daughter, snuggled in her arms. Lilly's features softened.

"What's her name?"

"Dahlia." The word came out like a prayer in that rhythmic cadence she'd used earlier.

"It's pretty."

"It was my favorite flower." The wistful tone seemed at odds to the fire in her expression only moments before. And was that a hint of a smile on her lips?

But looking at that sweet child, so trusting in her mother's arms, had the power to change anyone.

At last, Lilly peered up at him, almost shyly. "All right." Gently, oh so tenderly, she placed her daughter in his arms. The greatest of gifts.

Dahlia weighed less than he'd expected, and he pulled her close and smiled at the sweet, sleepy face. "Hi,

Dahlia. I'm gonna help you and your mama home, all right?"

She snuggled closer.

A warmth washed through him, bringing a burning sensation to the back of his throat. He cleared it, then looked up at Lilly with a smile. "Ready when you are."

Dusk was just overtaking the town as she led him through the alley. Rows of back doors faced them on either side. Gram's house was a few buildings down on the right, but everything seemed quiet there. At the end of the street, Lilly stepped across the side road and onto a boardwalk.

Marcus took the outside edge, and Lilly finally dropped back to walk beside him, shooting nervous glances at her daughter as they went.

Maybe some conversation would help her feel at ease. "How old is she?"

Lilly darted another glance at Dahlia's drooping eyes. "Two next month."

"A birthday soon, eh?"

A weak pull of Lilly's mouth, which might have been intended as a smile. "Yes."

"Have you worked at the café for long?"

That weak smile straightened into a tight line. "Yes."

"How long?"

"Two and a half years." The words had a bite to them. Time to back off.

"Aunt Pearl seems like a kind woman. I imagine she'd be good to work for."

"Yes, very." That was a better tone. So far, her happy topics seemed to be her daughter and Aunt Pearl.

"Claire likes working at the café, too. I think she's struggling to find balance with her new married life, though."

Lilly's face stayed soft, but she didn't answer.

They'd walked at least half a mile so far, and the scenery seemed to be deteriorating quickly. The Cabbage Patch, Butte's red-light district, loomed ahead. Lilly showed no signs of turning aside. Surely she didn't live here, did she?

Bile roiled in his stomach as he thought about all the ways an unmarried woman might find herself with a child in this part of town. He didn't want to think those things of Lilly.

But no, it wasn't his place to judge, only to help. Still, his spirits sank more the farther they walked. He couldn't bring himself to keep up a conversation.

She didn't stop at the Irish Castle, though. Nor the Spirit of Butte or any of the other saloons, cheap hotels, or brothels. As they passed the last of the bawdy-houses, Lilly's step seemed to move swifter. "Almost there."

Soon, the buildings changed to mostly shacks. Three and four in a cluster, often leaning against each other for support. A stiff wind might do them all in.

Dahlia shifted in his arms, snuggling closer. He tightened his grip on her. The wind picked up now that they were away from the protection of the storefronts.

A couple of blocks later, Lilly turned right down a side street, then pulled up at the second house on the left. "This is ours." Her voice held a hint of pride as she gripped the latch string and pushed open the wooden door.

Marcus couldn't bring himself to follow Lilly inside yet. Instead, he eyed the building. Rickety was a kind word for it. The wooden siding had never been painted and looked to be in the early stages of rotting. The whole thing listed slightly to the left.

A grim knot formed in his gut as he stepped onto the low stoop and confirmed his other suspicions. Only a single layer of boards separated the inside from the biting cold outdoors. The gaps between them must let in enough light to illuminate the room until sundown. It also let in the wind and surely any form of moisture that happened to be falling outside. How could they live like this?

Lilly lifted her daughter from his arms, murmuring gentle words to the child. Her face held a soft glow—pure pleasure—as she pulled Dahlia close. "Let's get you in bed, little one."

She carried her to a mattress in the corner, a size suitable for two people. Clothing hung from pegs on the wall nearby, along with a few gowns draped over the rope hanging between two nails.

Marcus turned his attention away to a less personal part of the one-room shack. A rocking chair sat beside a warming stove on his left. He moved closer and reached a hand close to the heater. Cold.

He grabbed a couple of the smaller logs stacked beside the stove and opened the door to the firebox. Clumps of white ash formed the remnants of a long cold fire. Looks like he'd need matches.

He found the matches and tinder in a small basket and had a fire going within a couple minutes. The pile of firewood stacked beside the stove had dwindled to only three logs, not enough to get them through the night. Marcus brushed off his hands and rose, looking around for Lilly.

She stood at the foot of the bed, motionless except for her dark eyes, which tracked his every movement. The expression on her face took a moment for him to decipher. Wariness. Maybe a hint of curiosity? And something else he couldn't read.

"Is there more wood stacked outside?"

She nodded once and pointed to the right of the cabin. "Around the corner."

He headed toward the door. The burn of her stare followed him until he closed the wobbly door behind him. The firewood was where she'd said, just around the front corner of the house, but it could hardly be called a stack. It didn't rise much taller than his knee, just an uneven assortment of sticks and dead branches, apparently rotten enough to break in two without an ax. The knot in his stomach tightened. Had she gathered these in the woods herself?

When he had both arms loaded with enough wood to see her through the night and morning, the stack at his feet had dwindled substantially. Maybe only enough for one more night.

As he reentered the cabin, Lilly stood by the stove with a pot of something—water for coffee or tea most likely. She stepped back as he neared to drop his load.

He straightened and brushed his hands over the pile. "Anything else I can do while I'm here?" He gave her an easy smile, the one people usually responded to.

"No." The word was swift and clear. "Thank you for...your help." Those last words seemed to require a little more effort. "I can take care of things now."

Why was she so stubbornly independent? Would it be so hard to just say *yes*? Let someone else pick up the slack?

He clamped his jaw against the questions and forced a pleasant expression as he met her gaze. "If there's anything I can do, anytime. Please. I'd like to."

A simple bob of her chin was his only response. She turned back to the pot on the stove. He'd been dismissed.

Marcus turned toward the door, and she didn't follow him. He pulled it open and looked back. "I sure hope Dahlia gets to feeling better soon." No answer. "Y'all have a nice night."

"Thank you." The soft words followed him out.

He stood outside for a moment, breathing in the chilly night air. Darkness had taken over while he'd been inside.

A slight clatter sounded at the door behind him. The sound of metal on metal. A brace to bar the door? At least she had a small measure of protection, although if someone really wanted in, they only had to deliver a few swift kicks to the rotting boards.

He imagined her then, that lovely face, the silky hair. He looked around at the other shanties, then back toward the red light district they'd crossed through to get here. No wonder she carried that attitude with her—the fear and wariness and tension. She might as well have worn a target. What other defense did she have?

He had to do something about her situation, whether she wanted him to or not.

As Marcus strode back through the Cabbage Patch with its raucous music and bright lights, determination steeled within him.

He knew exactly what he would do.

LILLY HIKED Dahlia higher on her hip as they neared their street the following night. The child had been whiny all day due to her burn, and Aunt Pearl had dismissed them early again. With Claire present, she'd assured Lilly the two of them could finish and close the restaurant without a problem during the last hour or so.

A mixture of emotions warred inside. Relief to be able to give Dahlia the attention she needed with her injury. But guilt had warred strong when she'd left the café with work undone. Not to mention a niggle of fear. What if Aunt Pearl decided having a young child about the place was too irritating? Or even too dangerous, after yesterday's disaster.

She couldn't let that happen.

As Lilly turned onto their side street, she heard the pounding of nails—odd this late in the evening. A motion ahead stopped her short and sent her heart racing.

A man. Beside her shanty.

Chapter Seven

*L*illy darted off the street and into the shadows of the quiet shack on the corner. She'd not met the owner of this particular home, but surely they wouldn't mind her taking refuge for a moment.

"Ow, Mama." Dahlia whined again, and Lilly bounced the child on her hip.

"Shh. We have to be quiet for a minute, honey." She fought the urge to clamp a hand over the child's mouth.

Instead she focused on the man outside her cabin. He was moving around on the left side of the building. Working, it looked like. He raised a board to the side, examined it, then swung a hammer, bringing forth the pounding noise she'd first heard.

Familiarity washed through her as she studied the man. Reverend Sullivan. What was he doing here, nailing boards to her cabin?

She squared her shoulders and stepped from the shadows. What right had the man to make changes to her home—her own property—without her permission?

The strike of the hammer drowned out her approach, and she stopped about ten paces behind him. As soon as the pounding stopped, she gathered her nerve.

"Reverend Sullivan. What are you doing to my home?"

He jumped at her words, spinning to face her. A sheepish smile spread over his rugged face. "You startled me."

He must have noticed the fire in her eyes then, because he turned to look at the shanty, stepping backwards. "I was just closing up some cracks between the boards."

She followed his gaze to the siding, eyeing the freshly lumbered wood nailed to the wall at regular intervals. She looked back at him. "Why?"

He shrugged. "Winter's coming. This'll keep you two a lot warmer."

Dahlia whimpered again, and the reverend's gaze softened as he eyed her.

"Hi there, pretty girl. How're you feeling today?" He stepped closer and tweaked Dahlia's hand.

Lilly expected her daughter to cringe the way she did with most strangers. Instead, she stopped whining and allowed a hint of a smile to play at her mouth.

"I need to take Dahlia inside. I'll be back in a minute." Her emotions were in such a whirl, it would take a few moments to collect herself.

The reverend wiped a sleeve across his damp forehead, sweat beading there despite the chilly evening air. "I'm finished with this side anyway. Just need to clean up my tools."

Lilly escaped through her door and eased Dahlia onto the bed. "I'll get you some medicine, honey."

As she poured the dose and helped the child drink it, her thoughts whirled around the man outside and his words. Considering all he'd accomplished, he must have spent all day working on her house. She'd seen the new boards nailed across the front of the shanty, too, and a glance at the right wall showed no cracks. Only the rear wall hadn't been covered. But with another shack built close behind them, wind didn't usually blow in from that direction.

Lilly moved to her warming stove and built a fire. As she piled the sticks, she wondered why had he done it? Did he expect something in return? Men always expected something. She struck the match and lit the kindling, then paused to watch the spark catch and spread to the dried bark and twigs.

Didn't matter what the *good reverend* expected from her. She wasn't giving it. Absolutely not.

She caught her thoughts. The man was a preacher, and Claire's brother, too. Maybe he wanted something entirely different. Hadn't he asked so many times for her to play the piano for services? Was this *encouragement* for her to give in?

She bit her lip as the fire caught hold of the log and the flames flickered steadily. She had to go back out and face him.

Drawing her strength, she sent a smile to her daughter. "I'm going outside for a minute, sweet one. I'll be right back."

No need to worry about the child climbing down from the bed. Her droopy eyelids meant the medicine must already be taking affect. Dahlia stuck her thumb in her mouth and snuggled into the blankets.

A cold breeze struck Lilly as she stepped outside. She'd not felt the rustle of it in the cabin like she usually did. Wrapping her shawl tighter around her shoulders, she moved toward the side of the building and the man who'd worked so hard on it.

He was stacking extra boards close to the base of the wall and didn't seem to notice as she stood at the corner. She took the opportunity to watch him. He wore a long-sleeved green flannel shirt with suspenders but no shirtwaist. Just like a common laborer. Even though the shirt was roomy, the suspenders outlined his muscular shoulders, and his sleeves had been rolled to reveal defined forearms.

The man definitely kept himself in shape, not soft and fleshy like her pastor in Derbyshire had been. And most definitely not balding. Her gaze flicked up to his thick brown hair, trimmed shorter than most men wore theirs. Not slicked down with pomade either. At least not at this point in his workday.

He turned and saw her, his face lighting. "I'm finished here. I hope that helps keep the weather out now." He glanced at the dusky sky. "Looks like it might rain in a bit."

She tightened her lips. As nice as the man seemed, she had to understand his motives. "Why did you do all this?" Maybe not the kindest approach, but she didn't show kindness to men anymore.

He shrugged like he'd done earlier. "I saw the cracks yesterday, and with winter comin' on, figured it would help if I closed them up."

She eyed him. What wasn't he saying?

"Did you do it so I would play at your church?"

Lines creased his brow. "Of course not. We'd love to have you, but whether you play or not is your choice." He motioned toward the wall. "I saw a need here and filled it. That's what God calls us all to do."

That couldn't be his only reason. But the man looked too sincere to be faking.

He reached down for a hat and a burlap sack, then settled the hat on his head. "I'll get out of your way now. Good to see Dahlia's doing better." He stilled, finding her gaze again, his eyes searching. "She is better, right?"

Lilly forced herself not to nibble her lip. "Some. It pains her, though."

65

Sorrow filtered through his amber gaze. "I'll keep praying."

He stepped forward then, tipping his hat as he passed her. The smile that pulled at his mouth started a tiny flutter in her midsection. What was that from?

"Have a good evening."

Something inside her almost called out to him. Almost wanted to stop him from leaving. She could offer him tea.

But she let him go. She watched his long, confident stride as he turned the corner and disappeared from sight.

A wistful longing took root in her chest. Was that…loneliness?

To my better self,

The reverend came again today and covered the remaining cracks on back side of the house. I still don't know how to feel about it. He truly seems to want nothing in return. Is it possible a man would do a kind deed with no expectation of compensation? Do such men exist? Pa-pa would have. And did, so many times. Yet I didn't think there were others like him.

Our woodpile has also been replenished with enough cut wood to last for most of the winter. Not odd sticks like I usually gather, but split logs perfectly sized for the stove. How long must it have taken him to split so much? No wonder the man stays lean and strong.

Another thing that bothers me is the cost of the boards he nailed to the cabin's sides. They were lumber-milled. How much did he spend on such luxuries? More than I could repay should I save all winter, I'm sure.

But I want to repay him. I need to. It irks me to think I'm beholden to a man. Perhaps I could exchange piano playing for his work. Would that be wrong of me? Would I be giving in to his scheme? Yet he looked so sincere when he said he wanted nothing in return. Could that really be true?

"DO YOU SEE the church, honey? We're almost there." Lilly gripped Dahlia's hand as they neared the freshly painted white building. Her insides churned as she strained to hear noise inside. All was quiet, save the chirping of a bird.

"My foot hurts, Mama." Dahlia dragged slower.

"I know, honey. But see? We're here." She didn't usually make Dahlia wear shoes, not at this age anyway. It was easier to carry the child back and forth between the café and home. But the church had been farther, and no child of hers would enter God's house without proper clothing. The poor child, though, with the pain of the stiff leather chapping Dahlia's burn.

Lilly stepped lightly up the stairs and across the wide porch, pulling her daughter with her. Still no sounds from inside. Was it possible the reverend hadn't arrived yet? Claire said the service began at ten o'clock, so she'd come over a half hour early to familiarize herself with the songs. She never imagined she might beat him here.

The hinge on the door didn't creak as she pulled it open and peered inside.

There. On the front row. A pair of broad shoulders hunched, the head of brown hair bowed forward.

"Can we go in?" Dahlia's little voice filled the silence.

The man's head jerked up, eyes wide as he turned to them. For several heartbeats, he stared at her as if trying to decide whether she were real or a mirage.

Then he straightened and rose to his feet, a grin spreading across his features. "Come on in, ladies. I was just...well...come in." He motioned them forward.

Lilly's midsection flipped and fluttered as she tentatively stepped forward. "I thought I would play the piano today. For the service." Why did her voice sound so weak? "Can you tell me the songs so I can practice them?"

His expression changed from pleasant surprise to...wonderment? Awe? Reverence? No word seemed to describe it. He looked almost speechless. The Adam's apple at his throat bobbed. "Uh...I thought *Come Thou Fount of Every Blessing*. Do you know it?"

She thought back through the songs they'd sung in England. That had been one of them, but did she remember the tune enough to pick it out?

He spun around and strode to the piano. "I have a hymnal here. It has the words and notes." With the book in hand, he paused, mid-step. A sheepish expression taking over his face. "Do you play from notes?" Red crept up into his face, splashing his cheeks. He moved toward her again, the book extended. "Here. You can do with it as you wish. If you'd rather we sing a different song, I'm open to anything."

She took the book from him and examined the cover. *Protestant Hymns.*

The reverend bent down in front of Dahlia so he was eye level with her. "And how are you today, Miss Dahlia? You're looking especially lovely. You know what? I found something the other day I bet you'd like. Do you want to come see it?" He held out his hand and waited.

Dahlia studied him for a moment, then released her grip on Lilly and took the Reverend's outstretched hand.

Lilly's heart stuttered. She'd never seen Dahlia accept a person so quickly. Especially a man. The child hadn't even looked at her for permission like she usually did, even with Aunt Pearl and Claire. But Dahlia would be safe with the reverend, as long as they stayed where Lilly could keep an eye on them.

With the hymnal in hand, Lilly moved to the piano. She ran a hand across the smooth mahogany before she removed the cover from the keys. Not a speck of dust anywhere. Who had polished it so fastidiously?

Positioning her fingers on the keys, she eyed her daughter and the pastor. They both crouched over something at the end of a pew. Some kind of paper. Happy murmurings drifted in Dahlia's sweet childish voice.

Lilly started into a few scales. At first, the sounds were choppy under her cold fingers. But the rhythm evened out, and the notes soon began to flow. She played through a quick minuet, then started on a hymn she barely remembered from their church in England. The melody came back to her, though, and she poured herself into it.

At last, she reached for the hymnal and found the page for *Come Thou Fount*. The notes weren't hard, and she soon found herself humming along. It was a rich, flowing melody with words that had the power to haunt.

Jesus sought me when a stranger,
Wandering from the fold of God.

The idea bothered her, and she stopped studying the words. Instead, she focused on the notes and the power of the music. Let it flow through her with cleansing strength.

When she finally drew the song to a close, she looked up to check on Dahlia. Her daughter was sitting in the reverend's lap, chattering on about a paper in her hands. He wasn't watching the child, though. He'd been studying Lilly. His penetrating gaze wasn't harsh, yet it seemed to pierce through the shell she'd worked so hard to grow.

She dropped her focus to the hymnal. "Are there other songs you planned to sing?"

Several beats passed before he answered. "Sometimes we sing *Just as I Am* at the end of the service." The richness in his tone was undermined by a raw quality. As if he, too, were stripped bare, exposed and struggling to cover his emotions.

Lilly swallowed and flipped through the book to find the right page, thankful to have something else to focus on.

This song wasn't familiar to her at all, so she picked out the melody with her right hand first. It was simple, with four easy lines—and another message that she didn't want to hear. She could defend against the words alone. But combined with the music, as the harmony of the chords spoke to her, the words seemed to grow in power. The music penetrated her thoughts.

She ended the song quickly, then flipped the pages back to the first hymn. Without making eye contact, she rose from the piano bench and moved toward the pair sitting on the pew.

The one time she let her gaze flick to the reverend's face, he watched her with the touch of a smile pressing a dimple into one side of his mouth. She looked away and held out a hand to her daughter. "Come on, honey. Let's let the reverend do his work."

"I'd prefer you call me Marcus." His baritone was deep, quiet.

Her eyes darted to his face.

A sheepish tinge took over his mouth, pressing dimples into both cheeks. "After all, you said to call you Lilly. It's only fair."

She pinched her lips against a flush. Yes, she had. As improper as it was, she'd been too afraid to risk giving out her last name. It made her too…identifiable.

At last, she nodded, then reached for the child's hand again. "Come, Dahlia."

Chapter Eight

*P*eople started entering the church soon after, and Lilly parked herself and Dahlia on the corner of the pew closest to the piano. If she could have melted into the wooden seat, she would have gladly done it.

The reverend—Marcus—greeted everyone, his booming voice spreading his quick wit and friendliness throughout the small chapel. If his words could be believed, he really seemed to care about these people. And something in his tone made it hard to suspect him of duplicity.

Lilly's shoulders were rigid, and she dreaded the approach of strangers to *welcome* her. A few smiled and offered greetings from the aisle, but they must have read her desire to be left alone. Wasn't it time for the service to start yet? If she'd had a pocket watch, she would have escaped outside, behind the church, until it was time for her to play.

A woman slid onto the seat beside her and wrapped an arm around Lilly's shoulders. She stiffened, but a sideways glance revealed Claire's smiling face.

Her friend leaned closer to whisper, "I'm so glad you're here."

Relief filtered through Lilly, and she offered as much of a smile as she could. "You, too."

Claire's husband, Doc Bryan, settled beside her, and the couple spent a few minutes talking with Dahlia.

Marcus walked to the front of the church, and quiet eased over the room. He flashed a smile as he greeted the group, a smile that sent a flip through her insides. The man was too handsome to be a preacher. The two realities seemed at odds with each other.

She missed most of what he said during the opening, too caught in her thoughts and perusal of him. But when he spoke her name, her mind jolted to life.

"She's agreed to play for our hymns today, and I think you'll enjoy the treat a great deal."

Lilly took her place at the bench, head ducked under the intensity of dozens of stares. Why had she ever agreed to this? She'd known better. Every muscle in her body ached under the tension, but she started into the introduction to *Come Thou Fount.*

In steady increments, the music took over, performing its soothing ministrations on her soul. The sound of so many voices raised in harmony with the notes amazed her. Awed her. She was tempted to add her own voice to the mix, but instead, she soaked it all in.

"LILLY, YOU HAVE to come see him. I won't take no for an answer."

Lilly eyed Claire as she sat across from her friend at the work table in the café's kitchen. Her kitchen. The kitchen that had offered so much solace and protection these last two years. The lunch crowd had died down, and the two were slicing bread for tonight's meal.

"Miriam came through the birth better than I would have, and that baby boy is the cutest thing I've seen in years." She turned to Dahlia, who was sitting in a chair at the end of the table. "Except for you, sweet thing. He's not quite as cute as you."

That surge of motherly pride swept through Lilly as Dahlia flashed a grin.

Claire turned back to Lilly. "You're cooking chili and beans tonight, right?"

She held out the pause until Lilly finally nodded. Why was Claire so insistent she leave this place of protection to visit a woman she barely knew? Sure, Miriam was Claire's sister-in-law, so she was probably safe. But the last thing Lilly wanted was to struggle for small talk with strangers.

"So put the beans on to simmer, and we'll give Miriam a quick visit. Aunt Pearl will be glad to keep an eye on them, right?" She glanced up as the older woman swept into the room.

"Sure thing, dearie. I saw that baby this mornin', and he's not somethin' you should miss."

Lilly eyed them both. How could she say no to the only two friends she had in the world? "All right."

BABY WILLIAM was worth venturing from the kitchen for.

His features were tiny. So inexplicably perfect. Snuggled in a crocheted blanket in the crook of Lilly's arm, she couldn't take her eyes from the bow-shaped lips, parted slightly as he breathed in his sleep. The little nose, rounded cheeks, and delicate ears.

"Can I touch him, mama?"

Lilly pulled her focus to Dahlia, then pulled the blanket back to uncover a small piece of fuzzy dark hair from the top of William's head. "You can rub him here. He's so soft."

Her daughter breathed a sigh as she stroked the spot.

"Here, Miri, drink some of this tea." Claire carried a tray into the parlor where Lilly, Miriam, and Dahlia sat. She handled the tray with practiced ease after so many months working at the café.

Miriam stretched across a settee and snuggled into a pillow in the crook of its arm. "Thank you."

The woman still looked pale, and no wonder since she'd gone through childbirth only two days before. The memory of Dahlia's birth had begun to fade in Lilly's mind, but she could still call back the long hours of tormented pain.

The front door opened, and Lilly jumped, her grip tightening on the babe. She forced her startled muscles to relax. Little William's face scrunched, protesting against the disruption to his nap.

"Where's my favorite patient?" Doc Alex stepped into the room, and a smile lit his face when his gaze settled on the bundled blanket in her arms. He strode forward but didn't move toward Lilly and the babe. Instead, he veered toward Miriam, then leaned down and placed a lingering kiss directly on her lips.

Lilly looked away, heat soaring up into her cheeks. That was something Pa-Pa would have done to Mama, but she'd never seen another married couple act that way in front of others.

Her gaze rose to another figure who stepped in the doorway. Marcus. Her heart stuttered. The light from behind outlined his silhouette, but she could see enough of his face to know he was staring at her. She wanted to look away, but she couldn't quite force herself to do it.

He stepped forward, closing the door behind him.

"Marcus, what are you doing here?" Claire spoke from the doorway to the kitchen. "I'll put coffee on."

He flicked a glance at his sister. "Thanks." Then his gaze found Lilly again. It roamed down, to the bundle in her arms, then back up to her face as he closed the distance.

When he was just a few feet away, he stopped and crouched on his heels. It looked like he'd come to examine the baby, but his focus turned to Dahlia. "Hey there, sweet one. How are you today?"

She gave him a winning smile, barely laced with shyness. "Good."

"Did you come to help your mama see this new baby?"

She bobbed her pointed chin. "Yes."

"Good. Well, I haven't seen him yet, so maybe you can tell me about him."

He reached a hand and circled her back, then pulled Dahlia toward him. His knees dropped to the floor and he planted her where she could see the baby. "Do you know what his name is?"

She peered over the edge of the blanket at the tiny sleeping form. "Baby William."

"I like that name. What color is his hair?" Marcus leaned forward as he spoke, getting his own look at the baby.

Dahlia peeled the edge of the blanket back where she'd touched his head earlier. "I think it's blue."

Lilly couldn't stop a chuckle as she sent an apologetic glance to Marcus. "We're just learning colors, and blue seems to be her favorite."

A twinkle lit Marcus's eyes as he sent her a conspiratorial grin. "I like blue."

"Can I hold him?" Dahlia looked up at Marcus with round, pleading eyes that were usually hard to resist.

Lilly hurried to answer. "No."

"Maybe—" Marcus cut off the word when he realized she'd spoken, too.

Lilly's heart beat faster as she met his gaze. He wouldn't try to override her decision would he?

Dahlia glanced back and forth between them.

Lilly inhaled to steady her voice. "He's too little still, honey. Maybe when he gets bigger."

Marcus eyed her with soft scrutiny. "Maybe she can sit in my lap while I hold him?"

He sent a glance over his shoulder to where Alex and Miriam watched them. Neither seemed angry, and Alex even wore an amused smile as he shrugged. "Fine by me."

Marcus turned back to her then, looking up from his kneeling position. His face held a mixture of respect and request. He wasn't pushing, just asking.

She looked at her daughter. "I suppose so, but, Dahlia, you have to be very gentle and don't move when you're near him."

Dahlia nodded, those big round eyes filling with excitement.

After Marcus settled himself in the rocking chair with Dahlia on his right knee, Lilly carried the babe toward them. She looked over at Miriam one last time. "Are you sure this is all right?" She knew the fear that could plague a mother's heart over the safety of her child.

But Miriam didn't appear afraid. "Of course." She offered a tired smile. "If he's happy and safe, I'm happy."

As Lilly leaned down to place the baby in the crook of Marcus's left arm, she was closer to him than she'd ever been. His strength seemed to swallow the babe, and she could smell a hint of pine drifting from him. Her gaze wandered traitorously to his face.

She met his gaze there. Rich amber brown eyes, watching her. Softly. So different from any man she'd known. The strength he possessed she'd seen before. But this softness, this earnestness—it was unique to him alone.

Lilly pulled back. Opening herself to any man, even this one, was dangerous.

MARCUS SIPPED his mug of coffee as he strolled toward the church early Saturday morning. He needed to put out tables for the social after church the next day.

And there was always the chance Lilly might come play the piano like she had that one Saturday. She'd not come a second time that he knew of, but since she played for last Sunday's service...he could hope.

As the building came into view, he squinted at it. Something didn't seem right. He lengthened his stride.

The windows.

Both those on the near side of the church sported jagged holes, exaggerated by the reflection of the surrounding trees in the pieces of glass that were left.

He neared the building and started toward the glass, but he stopped himself. If the windows had been broken intentionally, the vandal may still be around. He crept toward the front porch...and stopped.

His pulse notched up as he took in the words carved in the bannister and on the steps. Anger roared through his ears as his gaze lifted to the door.

Whoever did this would pay. And he would do the honors himself. An inkling of guilt crept through his chest at the thought.

Marcus's hands clenched as he moved up the stairs, careful not to step on any of the profanity carved into every single one of them. It was everywhere. In the floor boards, on the door frame.

He breathed hard to keep himself from exploding. *God, why did You let this happen?* How could God have possibly stood by and let His house of worship be vandalized like this?

He gripped the door handle and pushed it open, steeling himself for what he would find. The inside seemed mostly undisturbed, except for the shattered glass littering the floor in front of all four windows.

He blinked to accustom his eyes to the dim interior. What was he missing?

Stepping forward, he swept his gaze across every pew and across the floor. At the front of the church, his focus found the pulpit. Apparently undisturbed. The piano. His chest tightened as he moved closer to examine it. If they'd damaged Lilly's piano, he would tear them apart with his bare hands.

But the instrument didn't appear touched. Its mahogany surface shone from yesterday's oiling. He raised the cover to examine the keys. Pristine.

He let the lid slip back down and sank onto the bench. What now? He propped his head in his hand, clutching his hair as he thought through the destruction outside. Who would have done such a thing? And why? Was someone angry with him? Angry the church was open again? Or could it have been young rowdies, or even old drunkards, out for a perverted *good time*? He thought back to the words he'd read and cringed. Surely no youth would know the meaning of half them.

He had to get rid of those vile words. What if someone came by and read them?

His chest froze. What if Lilly came today, with Dahlia?

He surged to his feet and strode toward the door. He still had some glass paper left from polishing the new picnic tables he'd made. Lord willing, he could remove the worst of it with that.

Chapter Nine

ahlia kept up a steady chatter as they neared the church, and Lilly tried to follow along. But her thoughts constantly strayed to the tall, broad-shouldered preacher who'd manned the pulpit at this very church last Sunday. Would he be there this morning? Probably not. He hadn't been that other Saturday when she'd come to practice. Of course, they were a little later this morning, but...

They passed the final town building, a washhouse, and turned onto the road where the church stood in the distance. Her eyes scanned the structure. A figure knelt on the front porch, his dark clothing outlining him clearly against the white of the deck.

Her heart leapt. Even from this distance, she recognized those broad shoulders.

"Look, honey." She gripped Dahlia's hand tighter to help her make this last stretch. "I see Marcus at the church."

The child's face lifted at the name, just as Lilly's heart did. "I brought Miss Ann to show him. I know he's going to like her." Her daughter clutched the rag doll Aunt Pearl had made her. It had long been a dear friend.

As they entered the church yard, Lilly watched the preacher. What was Marcus doing now? The church fairly gleamed from a fresh coat of paint outside and a thorough polishing inside. It looked like he was scrubbing at something on the porch floor.

When they were a few feet from the steps, Marcus glanced up. Something about his expression didn't look right. Drawn. Tense.

"Look what I brought, Marcus." Dahlia's high-pitched voice filled the air, and he looked at her, his face softening.

"What is it, little bit?" He rose to his feet, his limbs and muscles unfolding as he did. Goodness, he was tall. Moving down the stairs, he stopped before them and leaned down to rest his hands on his thighs. "Let me see."

"It's Miss Ann." Dahlia dipped her chin and held out the doll, pivoting a little as she waited for his response.

He let out a low whistle. "Well, hello, Miss Ann. I'm awfully pleased to meet you." With his thumb and forefinger, he shook the doll's dingy cloth hand. "I'm Marcus."

Dahlia giggled, a sound that rang like music in the air. Lilly couldn't quite bite back her smile.

85

Marcus straightened, meeting Lilly's gaze. The troubled look shadowed his eyes again. "Did you come to play?"

What was wrong with him? Did he not want her there? She forced herself to straighten her shoulders and not bite her lip. "Yes, but I don't have to if it's an inconvenience."

He breathed out a sigh and turned to look back at the church behind him. "I'd love for you to play. We've just had some...damage to the church. I'm working to get it cleaned up, but..." He turned back to meet her gaze. "I'd rather you not see it all."

Lilly's gut tightened. "Damage?" Had someone intentionally vandalized the building? Was no place safe? Were the men even now lurking about? She scanned the open meadow around the building.

Marcus edged closer. "They're gone now. The only things left are some broken glass and words carved in the porch. Everything inside is fine. I almost have the porch done." He stopped the rush of words to swallow, his face losing a bit of color. "The door's going to take a little longer."

She studied him. "What can I do to help?"

His face picked up its ruddiness again. "Nothing. I don't want you around it."

She bent down to Dahlia. "Honey, why don't you sit down under this tree with your bread and apple. All right?"

The child plopped down where she pointed and looked up expectantly. She was always ready for a snack these days. Must be a growing phase.

The heat of Marcus's gaze penetrated the back of her cloak as Lilly settled Dahlia with the food. She straightened to meet his look, then started forward. As much as he'd done for their cabin, she could spend a few hours helping to repair the church.

MARCUS MATCHED her stride across the yard and to the steps. She was a stubborn lady, and the look she'd given him brooked no argument.

She slowed as they took the stairs, her eyes widening. He'd spent a couple hours rubbing out the marks in the wood, so the worst of the words were unreadable. Thank the Lord. It must have been the extent of the damage that shocked her.

The door was another story, though. He'd not started on it yet. So much profanity marred the solid surface of the boards, the thing would most likely need to be replaced.

He stepped forward to open it and hopefully hide the scrawling. Lilly stopped to examine it though.

Even though the awful words weren't his own doing, heat crawled up Marcus's neck while she took it all in. What was he doing letting a lady see these things? He should be protecting her.

She rested a hand on his arm, and her face paled. "Marcus." She breathed the word, the horror of it all playing across her face.

He stepped in front of the door, blocking her from the scene. Pulling her from her trance.

Lilly squared her shoulders, and the shock cleared from her features, leaving behind a guarded expression. "What can I do to help?"

"Nothing."

She glared at him, a look that would have singed a lesser man. But his sister had an expression similar to it, and he'd spent years developing his defenses.

He softened his tone. "I've got the worst of it done. I don't think the door's repairable. I'll need to make a new one."

"What about the inside?"

He glanced through the open doorway. "They didn't touch anything in there. I'm not sure why, but I'm thankful."

She stepped in, her gaze scanning the room. It paused on the shards of glass littering the floor beneath each shattered window. "Do you have a broom?"

His gut fell. He didn't want her working. Not at the church. She labored all the time as it was, both at the café and her house. "I don't want..."

She brought her hand to his forearm again. And this time the touch melted through his shirt. "I want to help."

Those eyes. He was close enough to see the chocolate brown in them, surrounded by the dark that made them look black from a distance. She was almost close enough for him to feel her breath play across his face. She wouldn't be able to feel his, because he'd stopped breathing.

He had to look away before he pulled her close. He forced his gaze from hers, but it simply drifted down to her hand on his arm, despite his efforts to look away. He swallowed. Hard.

She pulled back. Took a step away. "A broom?" Her voice sounded breathy.

Marcus pinched his eyes shut for a second—only a split second, but he used it to send up a desperate prayer for control. A broom. He opened his eyes and looked at the floor. "There's one in the shed. I'll get it."

He loped down the stairs and inhaled for the first time in what felt like an hour as he stepped out of sight around the corner of the church. What was wrong with him? He couldn't feel this way about one of his parishioners. But she'd been standing so close, and when she'd touched him... He needed an ax and wood to split. Or a dunk in a cold river. Something to slow his churning body.

She was beautiful. Stunning. But more than that had his pulse racing and his muscles clamped tight. He wanted to protect her. From the vandalism on the church. From anything that might bring her pain.

That had always been his weakness, protecting those he loved. He held too tightly, even smothered at times. But

Lilly needed protecting. He saw it in the vulnerability that occasionally flashed behind her fierce mask. He'd felt it a few moments ago when they stood in the doorway.

It wasn't a cry for help. Only a tiny glimpse of raw fear. She needed protecting. And he wanted to be the one to do it.

MARCUS WHISTLED an old folk song as he followed the trail along the side of the café toward the back door. Lilly had spent several hours Saturday morning helping clean the damage at the church, then she'd come back yesterday to play for the service. She'd started talking with him, too. Not chattering on like Claire would, but her responses had begun to reveal her history and personality in a way that intrigued him.

Apparently, she'd lived in Derbyshire, England, for over half her life, and she still had family there, although she didn't seem to be close to them. Interesting that her English accent wasn't stronger. Perhaps that had to do with her first nine years spent in Guatemala, and the more recent time in Montana.

Her parents were both deceased, but when she spoke of them, a sweet, affectionate smile touched her mouth. It seemed like she was alone in Butte. How had she come to be here? When his questions had neared recent years of her life, she'd stiffened and changed to one-word answers. Patience. He had to wait until she was ready to talk. When she trusted him.

He stood at the café's back door and hesitated. Was he intruding? Taking liberties just because they'd had a few interactions over the last few days?

But he craved the chance to see Lilly again. He'd not been able to get her out of his head for hours last night. And surely his request would bring joy to Dahlia. She was such a cute little dark-haired angel.

He knuckled a few solid raps on the door. Scuffling sounded inside. Then it opened to reveal the dim interior.

And Lilly. It took several seconds for his eyes to adjust to the poor lighting, and he almost missed the look that flashed across her eyes. Pleasure? Too many shadows to be sure. Probably his wishful thinking.

"Yes?"

The word snapped him from his thoughts. "Hello. I, um, I thought I'd stop by and see if Dahlia wanted to go with me to the livery. To see the horses, and I hear Jackson has a little donkey now, too. I thought she might enjoy it." He paused for breath and forced himself to hold his tongue until she responded.

Her face gave very few of her thoughts away. Indecision, maybe. At least she hadn't spoken an instant no.

"Mama?" A droopy-eyed fairy appeared from behind Lilly's skirts. "Marcus!"

With her rumpled hair and the sleepy smile lighting her face, hearing his name from Dahlia sent a surge of warmth through his chest. "Hi, princess."

"Did you come to see me?" Too precious for words.

He reached forward and tapped her chin. "I sure did."

His gaze wandered up to Lilly's. What had she decided? Surely she could see what a good thing it'd be to get Dahlia out of this dark, crowded kitchen for a few hours. And the child seemed comfortable enough with him.

Lilly's brow creased. "I...I'm not sure she should go alone."

Alone? What was he, stewed tomatoes? But in a flash of vision, he could see the way their reality had been. Lilly had probably rarely left the child with others. That kind of connection wasn't usually healthy sustained over a long period. And it could be very hard to work out of.

"How about if Dahlia and I play here at the café for a while. Then if you get a few slow minutes, we can all walk to the livery."

Her shoulders eased, just a fraction, but he didn't miss it. "All right." She turned back to the stove to stir something in a giant pot.

Marcus honed his focus on Dahlia, still standing in the doorway. "What about you, Dahly-girl. How's Miss Ann today?"

Her face formed a serious expression. "Still sleeping."

Marcus tried to match the look and dropped his voice to a whisper. "Oh. We'd best be quiet then."

She nodded.

"Would you like to ask your mama if it's all right for us to sit on this step in the sunshine? I heard a new story you might like."

As the little fairy tittered away to pull at Lilly's skirts and beg, Marcus pinched his lips. Had he overstepped by asking Dahlia to come outside before clearing it with Lilly? Surely sitting on the stoop in plain view wouldn't hurt anything. And Dahlia needed fresh air and sunshine.

Lilly quietly acquiesced, and he soon had the child snuggled in his lap and listening to the tale of a black-haired pixie who loved to ride her brown and white spotted pony.

It might possibly have been the best moment of his life.

Chapter Ten

I t was heaven.

The warm sunshine bursting through the November chill. The most beautiful woman in the city of Butte—make that prettiest in all the Montana Territory—strolling by his side. And the cutest little waif in his arms, her soft hands wrapped around his neck. This was better than striking it rich in a gold mine any day. If only those other men knew the truth.

"Claire said your parents are leaving for North Carolina this week." Lilly was actually starting to initiate conversations with him, not just answer his questions.

"Yes. Pop's missing his practice back home, I think."

"He's a doctor?"

"Yep. The only one in Charlotte, so far. But he's talking about bringing on another physician to his practice. Claire used to work as his nurse some, but I think he's finally realized things aren't going back to the way they used to be."

"Have they thought about staying in Butte?"

Marcus considered the question. "They haven't mentioned it. They're so settled in Charlotte, I can't imagine them leaving everything."

"Even though their children are here?"

Her tone was so wistful, it made him pause. Was she thinking of her deceased parents? He needed to tread carefully.

"I'm not saying they haven't thought of it. They just haven't talked to me about moving here. But I think it's more than that. They worked for twenty-five years to raise Claire and me. To teach us how to be hard-working, competent adults. Now we've spread our wings. Claire's married a decent chap." He paused to give her a sideways grin. "And I'm where God's called me. The hard work is done for my parents."

She remained quiet, so he took a chance to lighten the mood. "Now when there's grandchildren, that might be a different story."

Those words actually brought a smile to her lips. A small one, tinged with sadness, but still...a smile.

She didn't speak for a few moments. "Do you ever think about going back?"

He shot her a look. "Back to North Carolina?"

Her lips pinched and she bobbed her chin once.

"Not unless God said go. I like it here in Butte. There's so many good people. And still so many that need the Lord." He shrugged, trying to keep his voice casual. "It feels like home."

DAHLIA LOVED the horses at Jackson's Livery, just like Marcus had known she would. And when Zechariah, the donkey, let out a honking bray to greet them, Dahlia clutched tighter to Marcus's neck and giggled. The joyful sound bubbled up warmth in his midsection.

And with Lilly by his side, her quiet presence so strong, he'd never felt so whole—so complete—in his life. He wanted desperately to make this a permanent sensation.

The feeling only grew in his chest as they finished at the livery, said goodbye to Jackson, and strolled toward the café. Dahlia seemed to have worn herself out with the animals and rested against his shoulder.

Lilly didn't say much, but it wasn't the tense, uncomfortable silence of withdrawal. Her face held a softness, almost a quiet happiness, as she strolled along beside him.

Should he say something about his intentions? Now would be an opportune moment. He'd always believed in clear honesty, and he'd never been very patient. Especially when he knew what he wanted.

And this woman... The more time he spent with her, the more his heart opened to her. This feeling of peace. Of rightness when they were together. It was more than attraction, although the Lord knew there was plenty of that. On his side at least. Did she feel the same? She seemed to be settling into his company. And every now and then, she'd look at him in a way that made his heart skip a beat and his breathing hitch.

They were a block away from the café now. If he was going to say something, this was the time.

But she spoke before he could gather his words. "Thank you for the outing today. And for playing with Dahlia earlier. She enjoyed it." A pause. "We both did."

He dared a glance at her face. Softness there, even a sparkle in her dark eyes. Her cheeks had a pinkish glow, although that could be from the cold. Over the last half hour, the temperature seemed to have dropped quickly.

He summoned his courage. "Lilly, I love being with you. With you both. I...I wonder if you'd allow me to court you. Formally." His words were muddling in his mouth. Not coming out the way he'd planned. He forced himself to stop talking and watched her face.

Something flashed through her eyes. Fear? Vulnerability, maybe? And something else. But then that impenetrable mask settled in place, hiding it all.

She started walking again. He hadn't realized when they'd stopped. Lilly didn't speak, and the silence reigned heavy and thick. She strode faster. Trying to outpace him?

"Lilly?" He shouldn't have said it. Shouldn't have rushed her. She'd only just started opening up to him these last few days. "I'm sorry. I shouldn't have spoken yet. I just... I wanted to be honest with you."

They'd reached the back yard of the café, and she spun to face him. "Thank you for your honesty." The words lacked any semblance of warmth, or decoration of any kind. Stark. Clipped.

His chest felt like it might cave in on itself. How could he have been such an imbecile? She'd been wounded severely in her past. He still didn't know the extent of it, but did know how guarded she was. After he'd worked so hard to break through, he'd wrecked it all with his wretched impatience.

Lilly reached for Dahlia, who now slept with her head on his shoulder. He stepped back. "I can lay her down inside."

She spun around without answering and led the way inside to a little pallet of blankets in one corner of the kitchen. Dahlia made a cute little whining noise as he lifted her from his shoulder and settled her on the quilts. One more blow to his collapsing heart.

He straightened and scanned the kitchen. Aunt Pearl wasn't in sight. Lilly stood at the stove, shuffling pans around with her back to him. This was his last chance to salvage it.

Taking a step toward her, he kept his voice gentle. "Lilly, I'm sorry. I shouldn't have said that yet. Please forget about it. I'd still like to be your friend, though. I hope you won't shut me out."

No answer. She stirred one of the pots, the wooden spoon scraping against the cast iron base. Her shoulders formed a rigid line. No way to penetrate that barrier.

He breathed a long sigh and turned to the door.

LILLY SCRUBBED the pot harder as she fought against the thoughts whirling in her head. If only she could keep her focus on the bean residue caked on the iron sides.

Marcus wanted to court her. What had she done? How had she let this man come so close to her? He'd seemed so trustworthy. Was trustworthy. But that didn't mean she should let him so close.

Men did damage. That lesson had been pressed so firmly into her mind, she shouldn't even be having these thoughts.

She poured the last of the rinse water in the pot and swirled it around, then dumped the liquid into the bucket in the sink.

"You girls go on home now. It's gettin' cold out there. Some of the men said it looks like our first snow's acomin' soon." Aunt Pearl placed a solid hand on Lilly's shoulder. "Go on."

Without looking at the woman, Lilly removed her apron and hung it on a nail in the corner. Had Aunt Pearl sensed her unrest? Despite the woman's brusque exterior, she often had a keen way of reading people. "Thanks, Aunt Pearl."

As usual, Lilly had to wake her drowsy daughter to bundle her for the cold outside. This small kitchen stayed constantly warm from the oversize stove, but the weather outside had already chilled when they'd returned from that ill-fated trip to the livery with Marcus. With Dahlia in her arms, a bag of leftover food clutched in one hand, and her revolver in the other, Lilly set out.

The cold smacked her face as she stepped outside. Darkness permeated the air as thick clouds hung low, almost covering the pale moon. This would be her fourth winter in this freezing territory, and she still hadn't come to appreciate the months and months of biting cold.

The shadows hung thick as she scurried through the back alley. Once she reached the boardwalk, light from a few windows lit more of her path. Wind whipped against her in the open space though, piercing her wool cloak as if it were thin cotton.

Would she see the shadow man tonight? Surely the biting cold would keep him away. She simply didn't have the strength to run from him tonight. Didn't have the mental energy to deal with her fear. She was used up.

They'd made it through the first block of saloons in the red light district before that familiar tingle ran up her neck. *No.* She tightened her grip on the revolver and shifted Dahlia to one arm so she'd be ready. Without a backward glance, Lilly picked up the pace. She wasn't about to give this man more attention than absolutely required.

Lilly strained to hear any footsteps, but the sounds from the saloons rang too loud to be sure. The gooseflesh on her arms prickled stronger. Against her will, she glanced back. No one. Nothing except the light dancing from the Irish Castle.

Turning back around, she screamed.

A man loomed in front of her. Not five feet away. His lanky form, the way he stared at her with his face covered in shadow, sent a jolt of fear through her body.

The stranger who'd been following her. Here. Two steps away.

She forced herself not to shrink back. Not to succumb to the terror lighting her veins. Instead, she cocked her revolver. And pointed it.

"Good to see you again, Miss Arendale."

That voice. A fresh wave of shock washed through her. It seized her muscles, even her throat. That voice. That man.

He took a half step forward, washing his face of shadows. That face. Even sunken and hollowed, she'd never forget those thick black brows. The nose that flared at the ends...just like Dahlia's.

Pure, undiluted hatred roared through Lilly. How dare he show his face again? How dare he seek her out?

"What...do...you...want?" The words ground from her like a knife scraping metal. If he came one step closer, she would pull this trigger without a second thought. Her hand shook under the weight of the gun and her fury. Blast her traitor hand.

"Mama?" Dahlia chose the worst possible moment to raise her head from Lilly's shoulder and look around.

The man's beady eyes narrowed as they roamed Dahlia's features. "I thought it would be nice to meet *my daughter*."

Lilly took a step back, tightening her grip on the girl. "You have no right to her." Blood boiled inside her, building speed as it raced through her ears.

"On the contrary." That baritone, a little throaty, sent a wash of terror and memories through her. "I've been keeping my eye on you two. And I think the girl's old enough to meet her papa."

Lilly's whole body shook, and she raised the gun to aim. "Get away from us, or I'll shoot." That icy voice couldn't have come from her quivering mouth.

The man, Barlow, tilted his mouth in a perverted grin. Then he stepped to the side and raised two fingers to his forehead in a salute. "We can meet later if you prefer."

Everything in her demanded she spin around and run as far and fast as she could. Clutch tight to Dahlia and leave the town where this vile man still wandered the streets.

She sent him one more venomous glare. "If you follow me, I won't hesitate to shoot." Clenching her teeth, she turned slowly with her chin high.

At the end of the block, she glanced back for one last look. He still stood there, watching her.

The man who'd ruined her life in one terrible night.

Chapter Eleven

illy marched on, clutching Dahlia with both arms. The shock of seeing that man still had her legs shaking. She was almost back to the café before she realized her surroundings. Where was she going? Back to Aunt Pearl? Lights still shone through the café window. Were there patrons inside lingering over coffee?

Aunt Pearl would take her in, but where would she and Dahlia stay? In the single room above the café? That wouldn't be any worse than their shanty. But if Barlow had been watching her for *two years*, he would know about the café. He would find her there.

She forced herself to keep trudging. Past the café, her usual place of safety. Where else could she and Dahlia go in the middle of the night? She would have to leave town tomorrow. Good thing she always kept her money tucked inside her skirt pocket. It was safer there than left in their shanty while she was gone all day. But her journal... An ache settled into Lilly's chest at the thought of leaving it behind. Maybe she could sneak back in the morning to get it and some clothing before she left.

But where to now? Marcus's earnest expression from earlier flashed through her mind. No. Absolutely no way was she turning to a man for help with this.

What about Claire? She would help, there was no doubt in Lilly's mind. But…would her new husband be angry if Lilly showed up on their doorstep in the middle of the night? No, not Doc Bryan. He was one of the kindest men she'd ever met.

Like Marcus.

She brushed that thought away.

Within minutes, she reached Claire and Bryan's new house on the outskirts of town. Her boots thudded loudly on the wooden porch, especially loud against the stillness of the night in this part of town.

Lilly eased Dahlia down. "Stand up for a minute, honey. You're heavy." If the child grew much more, she'd have to start walking everywhere they went.

She raised her fist to the door and cringed before her knuckles touched it. Was she really going to wake a newly married couple? What if they were *doing something* in there? Warmth blazed up her neck, but Lilly squared her shoulders and gave a firm knock. Doctors were accustomed to people coming with emergencies at all hours, right?

After several minutes, she knocked again. A scuffling sounded inside. Then Doc Bryan's voice. Lilly stepped back and gripped Dahlia's hand.

The door swung open, and a tousled Doc Bryan held a lantern, blinking at her. "Lilly. What's wrong?"

"Is Claire here?" She heard the urgency in her own voice.

He blinked again, then looked back into the room behind him. "Of course." He turned back to her. "Come in, it's freezing out there."

As Lilly entered and her eyes adjusted to the softer lantern light, a movement raised her attention. Claire stepped through an interior door, pulling her dressing gown tight around her.

"Lilly. What's wrong?" She stepped close. "You're freezing. Dahlia, are you cold, too?"

Now that they were out of the wind and she didn't have Dahlia in her arms to share body heat, Lilly's teeth had started to chatter. She clamped her jaw and clutched the child's hand tighter. Her skin was cold, but they could both warm while Lilly spoke with Claire. "We're fine. I just..."

Claire held up a hand. "Let's get you warm first, then we'll talk."

Bryan was already stoking the fire in the large hearth, and Claire scurried to a trunk by the wall, then returned with quilts. "Sit here and wrap this around you both. I'll put some water on for tea." Both Claire and Bryan disappeared through the door to the kitchen.

With Dahlia snuggled in her lap under blankets, Lilly's muscles finally stopped trembling. They were safe for the moment. Claire would keep them for the night, and tomorrow they would find a way out of town. Maybe by stage coach. Even if she had to rent a horse, they were leaving.

At last, Claire settled into a chair across from the settee where Lilly sat. "Now, tell me what's happened."

Lilly glanced down at her daughter. Dahlia's closed eyes and steady breathing signaled she'd already drifted to sleep. The poor child must be exhausted.

If only Lilly could find the gentle peace that glowed from her daughter's features. But instead, her own muscles had begun to tremble again. What was it now? It couldn't be from the cold, because she was much warmer than before. From nerves? Or the coursing anger and fear that had rushed through her over the last hour? Tightening her jaw, she met Claire's gaze. "We need a safe place to stay tonight. I was hoping you wouldn't mind if we slept here. We can bed down on the floor." She nodded toward a bare corner near the fireplace.

"Of course you can stay here. Anytime. As long as you want." Her gaze grew soft and her voice tentative. "Can you tell me what happened? Are you in danger?"

Should she tell the truth? Yes, for Claire to understand why she'd come, she needed to tell what happened tonight. And she could trust Claire.

"There was a man tonight, on our way home..." How much should she say? That he'd been stalking her? That she'd known him from before? That the man wanted to take Dahlia?

"Do you know who he was?" Claire's forehead wrinkled.

"Yes."

Claire's brows drew lower. Confused.

Her single-word response seemed like an ungrateful answer to the woman who'd just agreed to harbor them in her home. Lilly allowed a long breath to escape and started from the beginning. Well, maybe not the very beginning, but from that awful day Pa-pa had died.

It was the first time she'd ever shared the details. How they'd met Mr. Barlow shortly after arriving in Montana. He'd seemed like a kind friend, as one of Pa-pa's business acquaintances, and staying there in the same hotel. How she'd trusted him in her grief.

Until that night...

She didn't go into the details. Not the gags, the bindings, or the sheer terror of what he'd done. The way he'd left her there, tied to the bed while he escaped. She'd spent most of the night trying to get loose, and she'd finally managed it as the rising sun dawned. The blackest night of her life was over, signaling the end of the former Lilly Arendale. She would never again be that innocent girl.

"So what did you do, Lilly? Did the law ever find him?" Claire's gentle prodding forced Lilly from her reflections.

She wanted so badly to close herself away. Forget these memories and hide. But there wasn't much left to tell. She could finish this. She met Claire's gaze. "I never told.

They wouldn't have believed me over him. I used the last of Pa-pa's money to buy our house, and Aunt Pearl took me on at the café. Dahlia and I have done just fine."

Claire leaned forward and squeezed Lilly's shoulder. "You've done remarkable. So what brought you here tonight? Did you see him again?"

"For a few weeks, someone's been following me home at nights. Not every day, but several times. I never got a good look at him before, but tonight he stopped us." The terror crept back into her. "It's him, Claire. That despicable rake. He wants Dahlia, said he's been watching us for a long time. I have to leave town tomorrow, but we couldn't go home tonight. He knows where we live, I'm sure, and he'll do anything. He has no conscience."

Claire's hand tightened on her shoulder. "It's all right, Lilly. You're safe here. You and Dahlia can stay in our extra bedroom."

The band around Dahlia's chest loosened a fraction. They could stay. They'd be safe. For tonight.

"I'll go pour the tea." Claire rose and pulled the tea pot from atop the metal grate beside the fire. She took a mug from a hook by the hearth and poured the steaming brew. The sight sent a familiar feeling through Lilly. Just like they were back in the café, with Claire filling mugs with coffee.

Claire approached Lilly and settled beside her on the settee, not in the chair as she had before. Lilly struggled to pull her hands from under the blanket, then gripped the mug Claire held out. Warmth seeped through her, spreading up her arms. Blessed heat.

Claire settled an arm around Lilly's shoulders, leaning in close in what felt almost like a hug. "I'm so sorry, Lilly." Then she straightened, catching Lilly's gaze. "Do you mind if I tell Bryan? I think he can help us."

Lilly's spine straightened, and she pulled away. *No.* It'd been hard enough to tell Claire. What would Doc Bryan think of her if he knew it all? Of course, he'd helped deliver Dahlia, and she trusted him more than any other man she'd known. "I don't..."

"I don't have to tell him everything, just about the man stalking you. I don't have to tell about how you know him."

That might be all right. Lilly finally nodded. "If you think he can help."

Claire rubbed her back. "Sit here and rest while I go get him. Or do you want to lay Dahlia in the bed?"

Lilly's free hand slipped under the blanket to cuddle her sleeping daughter. Her safe daughter. "She's fine here."

Clair disappeared through a doorway, then murmured voices drifted from it. No words she could distinguish. But honestly, Lilly was too tired to care much what Bryan would think of her. They were safe.

Within minutes, Claire returned, followed by her tall husband. "I think we have the perfect solution." She settled onto the settee beside Lilly again and took the empty mug from her. "You two can go to Leah and Gideon's ranch while we work with the sheriff to find that man. When it's safe, we'll send word for you to come back."

A rush of emotion swept through Lilly, stinging her eyes. "I don't know. I think we just need to leave."

Claire gripped her hand. "You will be leaving, for a time. When it's safe, you can come back and continue your life. Besides, where would you go? Back to your family in England?"

Lilly shook her head hard. "No. They were my father's family. They don't want me. Not with a...child."

A glimmer appeared in Claire's eye, and she squeezed Lilly's hand. "I can't imagine anyone not wanting you. *I* want you. That's why Leah's ranch is the perfect place." She glanced to her husband. "You can take Bryan's horse up first thing in the morning."

Eyeing Lilly and her sleeping daughter, Claire asked. "Do you think you can ride? It will be much harder to get up the mountain with a wagon. And Bryan thinks it'll start snowing by morning. Horseback will be easier."

Exhaustion seemed to be sapping the last of her strength, but Lilly nodded. "Yes. I used to ride with Pa-pa all the time."

Claire's shoulders eased. "Good. Now make a list of everything you need from your house, and Bryan can get it when he fetches Cloud from the livery."

Chapter Twelve

Lilly straightened her weary muscles as she caught sight of a cabin through the trees ahead. They'd made it. Tears burned her eyes from the painful joy of it.

Snow had fallen the last two hours of their trip. Sitting in front of Lilly on the saddle, Dahlia had worn herself out trying to catch the flakes with her hands and tongue. Such innocent delight. Now she lay snuggled against Lilly's chest, lulled to sleep by Cloud's steady gait.

The clearing was quiet except for the relaxing sounds of animals around the barn. A cow's low moo, chickens clucking in a separate pen. Cloud nickered to a group of horses milling in a pen. The cry of a baby drifted from the cabin as Lilly reined to a stop in front of it.

She eased down slowly, one hand on the saddle's horn and the other keeping Dahlia upright. Fire blazed through her legs and ankles as they touched the snowy ground. She bit her lip against a whimper from the pain.

Four hours in the saddle shouldn't have affected her so much, but maybe the cold had numbed her blood flow.

Dahlia whined as Lilly pulled her down. "We're here, muffin. We made it."

The cabin door opened, and a woman a few years older than Lilly peered out. She held herself straight with a bit of a regal bearing, even with an apron wrapped around her waist. Her smile was bright, if a bit curious.

"Hello." The woman's voice was warm, rich. "Come in out of the cold."

Lilly draped Cloud's reins over the hitching post and hiked Dahlia up on her hip. Then she turned to face the woman, nerves churning in her stomach. "Hello. I'm a friend of Claire Donaghue's." She swallowed. Should she say more or just give the woman Claire's letter and let that explain their reason for coming? What a coward she was.

The woman's face lit at Claire's name. "Oh, that's wonderful." She stepped to the side and motioned for Lilly to enter the house. "Please come in. It's freezing out here, and I just put apple tarts in the oven."

The baby's cry sounded from inside the cabin again, and the woman—Leah, she assumed—disappeared into the dimness.

"Mama, I'm cold," Dahlia complained, and her little shoulders started to shiver.

Lilly inhaled a fortifying breath and trudged up the porch steps.

The inside of the cabin was spacious and comfortable—and best of all, warm. The kitchen on the left seemed to be well outfitted, and the sitting area on the right surrounded a massive stone fireplace. Cozy. Two doors lined the back wall, and a ladder between them climbed to a loft above.

"Have a seat by the fire, and I'll bring you snacks. Would you rather coffee or tea?" Leah scurried around the kitchen with a baby on her hip. The little tike looked to be somewhere between six months and a year. She had round, rosy cheeks and held a slice of toast in her hand.

"Tea would be wonderful. Can I help?" With Leah bustling about, it didn't seem right to sit and do nothing.

Leah flashed her a smile. "Please warm yourselves. I'll be over in just a minute."

Lilly settled into an armchair with Dahlia on her lap. She unwrapped the blanket from around her daughter, brushing off loose snow in the process.

Lilly's toes ached as they began to thaw, and Dahlia whined with the same complaint.

Leah carried over a tray and placed it on the side table next to Lilly's chair. "I brought cookies and sourdough toast for you both. I wasn't sure which you'd prefer. Here's tea for you and milk for the child. Is that all right?"

Lilly took the mug and handed a cookie to Dahlia, then tried to summon a thankful smile. "Wonderful, thank you."

The woman settled onto the settee on the other side of the table. "I don't think I've properly introduced myself. I'm Leah Bryant, and this is Emily." She picked up the baby who'd scooted behind her from the kitchen. The child looked like a cherub, with curls in her dark brown hair and dimples on both cheeks.

Lilly met Mrs. Bryant's gaze. Now was the time for explanations. "I'm Lilly, and this is Dahlia. We're friends of Claire's and...she said you might be willing to let us stay with you for a few days." Oh, how embarrassing to assume such an imposition. She reached for Claire's letter from her skirt pocket. "Here. Claire sent this to help explain."

Leah's eyes stayed soft and curious as she took the paper and opened the seal.

As the silence stretched, Lilly tried to read her face. How well did Claire really know this woman? This family? Why had Lilly ever agreed to come here?

As Leah finished reading and then folded the note, Lilly rushed to explain. "I don't have to stay here. We can keep traveling to Helena. I'm sorry I've imposed this much." She motioned toward the tray of refreshments.

Leah placed a hand on Lilly's arm. "Stop. I'm so happy you've come, I can't express it with words."

Lilly dared to meet the woman's gaze, and saw a shimmer there.

"Any friend of Claire's is always welcome in my home. But even if you didn't know her, we so rarely get guests here on the mountain, I'm thrilled to have you."

115

Lilly fought the urge to bite her lip. "Thank you. We can sleep on the floor, and I'll be glad to take over your chores while I'm here."

Leah waved her words away. "If you'll just talk with me and share a little female companionship, I'll be eternally grateful."

She tried not to shrink back into the chair. Talk? She'd rather scrub laundry or cook in a steamy kitchen any day. Straightening, Lilly shifted Dahlia in her lap. "Would you mind if I put the horse in your barn?"

"Of course. Dahlia can stay in here with Emily and me." Leah leaned down so she was on the girl's level. "Would you like to help me put plates on the table? You look like you'd be a great helper."

Dahlia bobbed her pointed chin once, sinking into Lilly's side.

Lilly gave her a pat. "Go ahead, honey. Help Mrs. Bryant."

As Lilly opened the cabin's front door, her gaze took in the snow that fell thicker now. Their tracks were already covered, and there must be at least six or eight inches of white on the ground.

A motion in the distance caught her attention. A man. Riding horseback toward the cabin.

Lilly stepped back inside and shut the door, her heart pounding. "There's a man out there."

Leah approached the window beside the kitchen and peered out. "That's Gideon, my husband. He comes in for

116

lunch most days." Her voice held a joyful lilt that hadn't been there before. "He can take your horse to the barn." She reached for the door. "I'll ask him to."

Lilly stepped aside, but the rapid thump of her pulse didn't let up. Leah had been kind and welcoming, but what would her husband think of a strange woman and child appearing on their doorstep begging for shelter?

She and Dahlia helped Leah set the table and dish out the beef stew and cornbread while they waited for Mr. Bryant to return from the barn. By the time boots finally thudded on the porch, Lilly's stomach was tied in knots.

A giant bear-man appeared in the doorway, a flurry of white falling from him. He stepped inside and closed the door with a stomp, then lowered the fur hood on his coat.

Not a bear-man, but definitely wild-looking. Green eyes flashed from under a shock of dark hair as he took her in. Lilly stood motionless with the coffee pot in hand, as if she were on an auction block, being examined from every angle.

"Gideon, I'd like you to meet Lilly..." Leah's voice faltered. "What did you say your surname was Lilly?"

Now was the moment. Could she trust these people with her identity? She'd come here for refuge, so she had to trust them, right? But giving her last name always felt like such a solid way of identifying herself. It made her traceable. What would they do if she refused to tell it?

She swallowed, then forced out the words. "Arendale. Lilly Arendale."

Leah gave her a warm smile, as if she was proud of Lilly. But she couldn't possibly know how hard that had been.

Leah turned back to her husband. "Lilly and her daughter, Dahlia, are friends of Claire and Bryan. They needed a holiday from town, so I told Lilly she had to stay with us for a few days."

Lilly couldn't help but stare at Leah. That was quite a different spin on their story.

Leah sent her a quick wink as she scooped up little Emily from a blanket on the floor. "Are you hungry, princess? Papa's home, so let's eat."

Without his animal-skin coat, Mr. Bryant didn't look quite as wild as he stepped toward the kitchen table. He moved toward his wife, and Leah raised her face to meet his kiss. Not a quick peck, but a tender meeting of lips and hearts. As they parted, the man leaned down to tickle his daughter's chin. Leah's cheeks had a pretty pink to them as she darted a glance at Lilly.

Lilly tried to look away, but the memory of the kiss played back through her mind. The softness of it, as if Leah's husband thought she was a treasured jewel. What must it be like to be treated so by a man?

Marcus flashed through her thoughts. His broad shoulders and height were similar to Mr. Bryant's, but Marcus had an earnestness in his expressions and in the way he dealt with people. The way he dealt with *her*. For the stretch of a heartbeat, she was thankful she'd be returning to Butte. That she'd see Marcus again.

But no. If Bryan and the sheriff couldn't locate Barlow, she'd not go back. She and Dahlia may still be headed for Helena, or farther if she had to. They'd keep moving until they were safe. Even if that took traveling halfway around the world.

MARCUS WAITED at the café's back door as snow fell around him. He'd just raised his fist to knock again when footsteps sounded inside. His heart thumped faster. Would Lilly speak to him? Or had he forever severed the tender cord of friendship between them?

Aunt Pearl answered, and he gave her his most charming smile. She didn't wait for him to speak, but stepped back toward the stove and stirred something in a pot. "How can I help ye, reverend? Got a lot ta do here."

"Is Lilly around? I hoped to have a quick word with her." He wiped his clammy hands on his trousers.

"Can't see her today." Aunt Pearl turned from the stove and started loading bowls on a tray.

He scanned the room. Where was she? And Dahlia, too? "I know you're busy. Would you be able to ask her if I can come back later this afternoon?"

Aunt Pearl finally stopped and looked at him, propping a hand on her hip. "Can't do that, 'cause she ain't here."

He felt his brow wrinkle. "Is she sick? Or Dahlia?" His pulse raced. Had their outing in the cold yesterday been too much for the child? If he'd endangered her, he'd never forgive himself.

Spinning around, he started to close the door behind him to sprint toward Lilly's shanty.

Aunt Pearl's voice trailed him outside. "Not real sure what's wrong. Claire just came by this morning and said Lilly wouldn't be here for a few days. Got my hands full now, that's fer sure."

Claire knew? Marcus adjusted his direction and sprinted north toward his sister's house. Claire would only be involved if Lilly had come to Bryan for medical care. Something was definitely wrong.

Snow fell thicker now and coated the ground except the deep ruts in the center of the street. As he ran, his mind raced through possibilities. Had Dahlia's burn become badly infected? Maybe even now she lay feverish at the clinic, fighting for her life. Or anything could have happened to Lilly traveling through the Cabbage Patch district after dark. A drunken man might have seen her as an easy target. *Lord God, help her.*

Should he go to the clinic first? But he was already at Claire's home, so he leapt onto the porch and pounded on the door. "Claire!" He thumped it again, and almost turned away before a female voice sounded inside.

The door opened to Claire's pert face, eyebrows raised. She propped a hand on her hip. "You don't like my door, Marcus?"

Impatience flashed through him. "Where's Lilly? Is she all right? And Dahlia?"

Claire grabbed his arm and pulled him inside. "They're fine, Marcus. Come in and catch your breath."

He turned on her, jerking his arm from her grasp. "They're fine? Why isn't Lilly at work?"

"Marcus." Claire's voice held a mixture of patience and reprimand. "Lilly's fine. She just…needed a few days."

A knife to his chest. She needed a few days…away from him. He met Claire's gaze. "Is she at home? I have to talk to her."

"Marcus." Pure frustration in her tone now.

"Claire, I *need* to."

She studied him for a long moment. Then she sighed. "Something frightened her, so she came to us for help. She's fine now. In a safe place until things are better."

He wanted to scream. Turning away from Claire, he ran fingers through his hair and clenched tight. Had he done so much damage, she'd felt she had to escape him? *God, what have I done? I'm so sorry.*

A powerful weight settled over his shoulders, and he slowly turned back to Claire. "Where is she? I *have* to talk with her."

"Marcus."

Enough with his name already. "Please, Claire." He met her eyes and poured every ounce of pleading into his gaze that he could.

Her dark eyes narrowed. "She and Dahlia went to stay with Leah and Gideon for a few days."

They'd gone up into the mountains? He'd never been to the Bryant ranch, but knew it was about a half day's ride over some very steep and winding trails. And in the snow? The weather was probably much worse in the hills.

"Thanks, Claire. If I'm not back in time, post a note at the church saying services will be postponed." He tossed the words over his shoulder as he strode out the door. Then he took the stairs in a leap and sprinted toward the livery.

Chapter Thirteen

"Easy there, boy." Marcus's tightened the reins as his horse stumbled in the almost-knee-deep snow.

They were an hour into the ride, and the snow had grown to over a foot deep, with big flakes still falling all around them. Were Lilly and Dahlia out in this weather? How had they traveled into the mountains? If only he'd asked Claire for more details.

He ached to kick the horse out of its plodding walk, but the snow-covered terrain was too dangerous. According to Jackson's directions, it would be another three hours until he reached the Bryant Ranch. Maybe four at this achingly slow pace. He pulled his wool coat tighter, pressed his hat farther down on his head, and then flexed his fingers in his leather gloves.

The trail crested a hill and dipped down steeply before climbing again. Marcus leaned back in the saddle as the horse descended, helping to balance his weight so the animal could find footing.

Suddenly, the gelding slipped. As if in slow motion, the animal floundered, fighting to keep its footing. It landed hard on its knees, listing to the right, and then falling to its side.

Marcus scrambled to pull his right foot from the stirrup, and barely escaped being trapped under the chestnut gelding's massive side.

The animal scrambled to regain its footing. Marcus rolled away, out of reach of the flaying hooves. Freezing, wet snow touched his neck, sinking below his collar.

Cold.

His breath fled in a gasp as he struggled up to his knees. The icy moisture sank through his trousers. He stumbled to his feet.

The horse stood several paces away, legs braced against the steepness of the hill, and breathing hard.

"You all right, boy?" Marcus shook the last of the snow from his collar, then leaned over, hands on his thighs, to catch his own breath.

A motion flashed in the woods to his right. Marcus and the horse both jumped to alert.

Three deer, about thirty feet away, stood perfectly still, watching them. They were majestic against the background of snow, one with a mid-sized rack of antlers, and all three with patches of white fur at their tails.

The horse snorted, eyeing them with all his attention.

One of the deer leaped backward, and suddenly all three were bounding away.

The gelding pranced a few steps up the hill, tail raised and nostrils flaring.

"Whoa, boy. Easy." Marcus extended his hand and stepped toward the animal. The last thing he needed was a loose horse on his hands.

The animal eyed him, nostrils still wide. When Marcus was a few paces away, it snorted again. Then the gelding turned and bolted up the hill, lunging through the snow.

No. *No, no, no!*

Marcus watched the horse's tail flying high as it crested the ridge and disappeared from sight. Taking his saddle bags and all his supplies with it.

He scrambled to climb the hill behind the animal. Maybe it would run a short distance and stop. The gelding had seemed calm and placid until the deer unnerved it. Surely it wouldn't run far.

When Marcus topped the hill, he stopped to catch his breath and study the scene before him. The horse was just disappearing through the trees, lunging through the snow at a hard canter.

His heart sank to his toes. *No!* He would have fallen to his knees if there hadn't been so much wet, freezing snow on the ground, already soaking through his trousers.

What was he going to do now? Out here in the middle of the mountains with *nothing*. No blankets. No food.

125

No matches. Only the coat on his back and some already damp clothes.

He leaned against a tree for support. "God, what are you doing out here?" The Lord never made a mistake, but this? How could this be right?

Marcus looked down the trail he'd come up. Should he hike back to Butte for a fresh horse? An hour on horseback meant it would probably take two on foot, trudging through the thick snow.

He turned to gaze in the direction he'd been going. Snow piled everywhere, and giant flakes still fell. Were Lilly and Dahlia out in this mess? He hadn't passed any homes in the mountains where they might have taken refuge.

An image seared in his mind of Lilly's willowy frame trudging through knee-deep snow, carrying her tiny daughter. But surely she wasn't on foot.

Still, purpose flooded his chest, and he pushed away from the tree. Onward and upward.

THE SNOW was halfway up Marcus's thighs, with a paper-thin layer of ice on top that broke through with each step. His muscles screamed to rest, but he settled for only a quick break whenever he couldn't force another stride.

He paused to lean against a tree. Dusk was coming quickly, and the walking had been all uphill for a while now.

His stomach rumbled again. At least he'd had the forethought to grab a loaf of bread from home before he'd started out on this trek. Although the single slice he'd eaten before the horse deserted him hadn't stayed with him very long with all this climbing.

How much farther? He scanned the trail in front of him. Darkness limited his vision to shadows after the first twenty feet. It wasn't a road anymore, just a wide path, as far as he could tell. If he had to guess, it was maybe another hour or so further to the Bryant Ranch. He could make it that far. Surely.

It had to have been at least an hour later, with no sign of lights or any civilization that might signal the Bryant ranch. In fact, the trail had narrowed even more, with low branches slapping at him. This couldn't possibly be a wagon road, as Jackson had said.

Marcus paused and gripped a birch tree for support. Had he made a wrong turn? *Lord, help me here.* What was he doing in this place? Stranded in a snowstorm, looking for a woman who didn't want to be found. He should be home in his warm house, spending the last few days with his parents before they returned home.

But an image of Lilly flashed through his mind, when they'd been at the livery and she smiled at Dahlia's reaction to the donkey. He had to find them.

Should he retrace his steps and look for a fork where he might have lost the road? Or keep going in this direction? Neither looked like a good option.

At last, he pushed off the tree that had been bearing his weight and trudged on the direction he'd been going. His eyes kept drifting shut as weariness did its best to take over. At least the snow had stopped falling a while ago.

Something caught Marcus's foot and brought him to his knees. Frigid snow touched his face, shocking him wide awake. He lay planted in the snow, but at least it had been a soft—if wet—landing. He forced his arms and legs to untangle themselves, pushing up to a kneeling position.

What had he tripped over? Marcus worked to clear away the snow and found the scrubby brown branches of a fallen cedar tree. The needles were so thick, the snow had only touched the outer covering. The inner layers looked to be perfectly dry.

Could they possibly be dry enough to catch fire? Heat right now would be almost the best gift God could send. Second only to Lilly.

Marcus pulled off his damp gloves, and tucked them in his waistband to dry. Just a little while longer and, Lord willing, he'd have a warm fire to dry them with. Pulling out his pocket knife, he was, oh, so careful not to let snow fall on the dry branches as he cut them off, one by one.

The ground under the fallen tree was only a little damp, not covered in snow like the rest of it. If he built a platform with some of the larger pieces, he could keep the tinder completely dry. But would the cedar needles be enough to bring a spark to life, if he was finally able to rub one into existence?

Marcus sat up as a memory grabbed him. The tree he leaned against last was a birch tree. Mama always preferred birch kindling because the bark caught fire so easily, even if it was still wet.

Adrenaline finally pumping through his veins again, Marcus retraced his tracks to the birch. He hadn't traveled as far as it had felt like at the time. He peeled sheets of the long bark off until he'd removed everything he could reach. *Lord, please let this work.*

As he circled the tree, his foot struck something hard. Marcus kicked the snow away from it, and the piece shifted under his pressure. It was…a pile of rocks?

Dropping to his haunches, Marcus sorted through them. Why were they stacked around the base of this tree? Some kind of tiny grave? But why way out here? Indians had roamed these mountains for years, and it was said there were still some tribes that traveled through occasionally. But why pile rocks?

One of the stones was darker than the others, and flat on the top and bottom with sharp edges around sides. Marcus's chest began to hammer. Could this be what it looked like? "Oh, Lord, please."

With the dark rock in his grip and the bundle of birch bark in his arms, Marcus stood and traipsed back to his cedar tree. The trail was getting easier between the two areas.

Once he'd finished his platform of dry logs, he laid the bed of kindling inside a tent of larger sticks. Then Marcus tucked several pieces of the birch bark under the edge of the tent. With another prayer, he pulled the knife from his pocket.

He gripped the flint-like rock in his left hand, the knife in his right, then flicked the two hard against each other. A scraping noise sounded, but no spark. He tried again, holding the flint so the two kept contact a little longer. A tiny spark shot from the blade.

Thank you!

The spark died out within a second, but Marcus tried again, aiming the flint so the sparks would fall on the birch bark.

Another spark. It died almost as quickly as the first.

Another and another, some lasting longer, but none took hold of the birch bark. Maybe it was too wet. Mama had always said birch would burn wet or dry, but maybe this had been too saturated by hours of snow.

He sat back and looked around. Maybe if he tried the cedar needles? But if the birch wouldn't catch, surely that wouldn't either. He needed something very flammable—and dry.

He looked down at himself. *Of course.*

Feeling of his clothes, Marcus assessed their dryness. His trousers were damp to his thighs, but the front was dry above that. His shirt wasn't too bad since it'd been somewhat protected by his coat.

He fumbled the buttons on his jacket, then ripped the tail of his shirt from where it tucked in his pants. With shaky hands, he cut several strips of dry cloth from his cotton shirt. If anything would work, this had to be it.

After making a tidy nest of the cloth inside the birch bark, Marcus picked up the flint and knife again.

Five tries and three sparks later, one finally smoldered into the cotton cloth, sending up a plume of smoke. Marcus dropped lower and blew small breaths into it.

The smoking died away.

He wouldn't give up, though. He was too close to a fire. And warmth. And if he could make a way to stay here the rest of the night without freezing to death, he just might be able to find Lilly in the morning. He had to.

WHEN DAWN rose through the trees overhead, Marcus pocketed his knife and the wonderful little black rock God had sent him. Flint. Who would have thought he'd find it up on this mountain? Only by God's provision.

The ashes of his fire lay in a small heap beside the cedar tree he'd spent the night propped against. But he couldn't quite bring himself to scatter the remains of the fire

131

in the snow. He'd worked so hard to build the blaze. And what if he needed to come back to it?

With all the snow around, there wasn't a chance the woods could catch fire. It'd truly been an act of God he'd been able to build the flame he had. Enough to keep him from freezing to death in the night, although he'd only been able to doze a little between feeding the fire.

After rising to his feet, Marcus raised his arms in a long stretch. If only he could find food somewhere. His stomach was gnawing at his backbone, and none too quietly, either. But even if he found berries or was able to catch a squirrel, he wasn't skilled enough in the ways of the mountains to know which flora would be safe to eat, or how to skin the squirrel and separate the meat from the mess. Not unless he was desperate.

So that meant his real job this morning was to reach the Bryant Ranch. If he could get on the correct road, he shouldn't be too far away. Surely only an hour or two.

Marcus took in his surroundings. Trees everywhere. He could still see his tracks to this point from the night before, but they wove around saplings and stout trunks. Certainly not a straight line like a trail or road. Somewhere he'd gotten off track.

He started off following his own steps, keeping his gaze scanning the area so he wouldn't miss the trail again. While he walked, Marcus kept up a steady conversation with the Lord, praying for safety, for guidance, and most especially, for Lilly and Dahlia.

Chapter Fourteen

$\mathcal{I}$ t'd been at least two hours since Marcus had started. Maybe half that since he'd found the road again and turned north toward the Bryant Ranch.

He had to be close.

Occasionally, he'd come across animal tracks. Deer seemed to be the largest, along with lots of smaller forest creatures. The dark line of prints ahead seemed to be another deer, based on the spacing between hooves. Maybe a herd of them as dark as the prints were.

But as he neared, his pulse began to race. Horse tracks. And fresh, too.

He sloughed through the snow and stopped to examine them. The trail of prints seemed to fork here, the tracks coming from the left fork and heading toward the right. He looked around. Could the left fork be the entrance to the Bryant Ranch? This sort of looked the way Jackson had described. As much as his excitement craved following the prints to the right—maybe finding a human being—he had to see if the left trail led to the ranch.

Taking the left, Marcus jogged several steps with high kicks to clear the snow. That was too much work, even in his excitement. His muscles had grown ridiculously weak from lack of food, and he'd long ago stopped being able to feel his toes, which made controlling his feet a little harder.

The trail opened up into a huge clearing and the most beautiful sight he'd seen in days—a cabin, smoke curling from its chimney.

Emotion poured through Marcus, sapping most of his remaining energy. He dropped to his knees as something warm and wet dripped down his face. He'd made it. *Oh, Father, thank You!*

A motion beside the house dragged his attention. A woman.

He forced his focus to clear. That familiar brown cloak. *Lilly!* Marcus struggled to his feet, staggering as he fought to gain his balance. He had to get to her.

"Lilly." He tried to yell across the forty or so feet that separated them, but his voice rasped so much, the words were barely understandable, even to his own ears.

It caught her attention, though, and she looked his way, then lunged through the snow toward the cabin.

She was running from him.

Marcus coughed to clear his throat, then called to her again. He never stopped his forward movement, though. He *had* to talk with her.

This time she stopped, just before she reached the porch stairs. Turning to look at him, she leaned forward, staring hard. "Marcus?"

Her voice was like flowing honey. Warm and sweet.

He'd cut the distance between them in half now, but his strength was quickly waning. He would get to her, though.

Lilly took tentative steps toward him, plowing through the snow with her long skirts. "Marcus? What are you doing here?"

His legs lost strength right before he reached her, and he sank to the ground. She was there. Fitting herself under his shoulder, wrapping an arm around his back, pulling him back up.

"Let's get you inside. You're frozen."

He didn't remember much after that. Not until he found himself in an armchair by a blazing fire, piled with blankets and holding a steaming mug of coffee. His hands shook so much, he'd probably poured half the brew on himself, but it was warm. He breathed in the richness of it.

His stomach took that opportunity to complain again, and he could hear a flurry of feet in another part of the room. But all he could do—all he wanted to do—was soak up this warmth.

"Do you want to trade the coffee for hot gruel?"

He forced his eyes open at the sweet, familiar voice. Lilly. Standing like a dark-haired angel beside him, holding a tray in her hands. Anything she recommended had to be good.

Marcus allowed her to place the coffee on a nearby table then position the tray in his lap.

"Do you think you can spoon it?"

He had to open his eyes again to see her. Why wouldn't they stay that way? She stood there expectantly, waiting for an answer. What was the question again? All he wanted to do right now was sleep.

"Here. Open your mouth, and I'll help."

Marcus didn't even try to open his eyes this time. Just obeyed her direction. A warm, thick mixture landed in his mouth. He savored it as it slid down his throat. Warmth.

"Open again."

He obeyed, relishing again the wonder of warmth and nourishment.

After another bite, he'd established a routine. Open, warmth, swallow, open again.

Gradually, the voracious feeling in his stomach began to dim. His shivers subsided some. And he lost himself in the oblivion of sleep.

"I THINK WE should check his feet for frostbite."

Lilly considered Leah's whispered words as she watched Marcus sleep. Exhaustion radiated from him with every breath. "He looks like he needs the rest. Can we wait until he wakes up?"

"It may be too late to save his toes by then. I'll get some cloths to wrap his feet. Can you take his boots off?"

Leah walked away before Lilly could assemble a response. Remove the man's shoes? Surely she shouldn't do such an intimate thing. Couldn't do it. Could she?

But Marcus certainly wasn't in a condition to perform the task himself. And Leah was right. Already, he could have frostbite beyond what they could cure. How long had he been out there? Surely he hadn't hiked all the way from Butte with only a wool coat and thin leather gloves for protection? Not even a scarf or hat.

She sank to her knees by his feet, gripped the toe and heel of his left boot, and pulled. The shoe wiggled, but not by much. She pulled harder, exerting more effort on the heel than the toe.

Marcus groaned, and she froze, scrutinizing his face. His breathing didn't change, and his eyes remained closed.

She focused her attention on the boot again. Inch by inch, she worked it off until only a stocking remained. Lilly swallowed, then gripped the woven cloth by the toe and pulled.

The surface of his foot glared a scalding red, fading to pale, waxy white on the toes. It didn't look normal at all.

"Here's some warm water to dip it in." Leah kneeled beside Lilly, and pushed the basin where Lilly could place Marcus's foot in it.

Once it was settled in the water, Lilly shifted over to work on the second boot. No matter how much she tried to be gentle, a moan still slipped from Marcus's lips.

"The white may only be frostnip." Leah examined the foot in the water and pressed a finger onto one of the pale toes. "We won't know for sure until they warm."

The right foot looked as bad as the left, and Lilly carefully placed it alongside the other in the warm water.

Leah sat back on her heels. "I wish those trousers weren't so damp." She touched the soggy hem. "But maybe under these blankets and beside the fire they'll dry soon."

The sound of a baby's fussing drifted from the bed chambers. Leah pushed to her feet. "Sounds like someone's awake."

As Leah disappeared through the doorway on the left, Lilly stayed in her position on the floor by Marcus's feet. Dahlia was also taking her morning nap, so for once, there wasn't anything clamoring for her attention. She wrapped her hands around her knees and watched Marcus.

What was he doing up here on the mountain? Had he come for her? That seemed so unlikely, but what other reason would he have to leave town during a snowstorm? And on foot. What had possessed him?

The troubled lines across his forehead started an ache in her chest. What was he worried about? His church? Or maybe the grooves stemmed from exhaustion, or pain as his cold-numbed nerves came back to life.

Whatever the cause, it was hard to see him struggle. This man who worked so hard to bring joy to others. The way he'd taken to Dahlia—and her to him—was remarkable. Did Dahlia sense something trustworthy in him? Or was it just childish innocence? But Dahlia had never been so accepting with anyone else.

Lilly pushed up from the floor and wiped her hands on her apron. She should add more warm water to the basin. And maybe Leah wouldn't mind if she started a stew for lunch. Marcus would need warm broth, along with some hearty meat and potatoes to regain his strength.

SOMEONE was watching him.

As Marcus tried to force his heavy eyelids open, the sensation of another presence settled heavy on him. He finally forced a sliver of daylight through cracked lids. Nothing looked familiar. Opening his eyes wider, he turned his neck to scan the area.

An angelic, dark-haired fairy stood beside him, staring with huge, round eyes.

The weight pressing down on him lightened, and one side of his mouth even pulled in a weak smile. "There's my girl." His voice didn't sound like his own, but it didn't appear to frighten her.

"Hurt?" Dahlia's soft, little-girl voice sounded worried, and a pucker appeared between her dark brows.

Marcus reached to tweak her chin, but blankets held his arms captive. He wiggled a hand out, and instead of her chin, he stroked a strand of long black hair from her forehead. "I'm not hurt, sweetie. Just tired. I think it's time for me to get up, though. Don't you?"

She bobbed her chin in a clear nod.

Marcus chuckled, but it turned into a hacking cough that wracked his chest.

"You're not going anywhere until you eat this." Lilly stood beside her daughter with a steaming tray as the coughs subsided, and Marcus sank back into the chair.

She was beautiful. In the dim light of the cabin, with the fire glowing on her face, the angels themselves couldn't be more glorious. Her long raven braid fell across her shoulder, and the white apron she wore hugged her slender waist.

She stepped closer, and Marcus's mouth grew dry. She was close enough that he could pull her down into a kiss. What a glorious kiss that would be, too. She bent lower. Was she thinking the same? His eyes almost drifted closed, but he couldn't stand to miss anything about this moment.

Something hard and bulky landed in his lap.

Marcus blinked and looked down. A tray sat on the blankets with a bowl of steaming soup, its warmth penetrating the quilts covering his legs.

"That will help you feel better."

Not as good as he'd felt a few moments ago. Marcus swallowed. The broth did look good, though. And its warmth was already seeping through him.

Marcus raised his gaze to meet Lilly's and tried to offer a smile. "Thanks. I'm sorry to show up and then collapse on you. That's not why I came."

She reached for Dahlia and placed her hands on the child's shoulders, almost like a barrier between them. An unconscious movement? Or protection from him?

"Eat now. Talk after that." Lilly's eyes had a bit of the old haunted look that used to be their constant expression. How much damage had he done?

Lilly, Dahlia, and Mrs. Bryant ate at the table, and the latter kept a steady chatter with both Lilly and Dahlia, drawing them out. Despite manners that brought to mind the wealthier families his father had cared for back in Charlotte, Mrs. Bryan had a warmth about her that seemed to relax the atmosphere.

After they finished, the women worked together to clear the table while Dahlia sat on the floor next to Mrs. Bryant's baby. The way Dahlia talked to her and made funny faces so the babe would laugh, it made him want to wrap the little fairy in his arms. She was so precious.

And Lilly. From his vantage point in the chair by the fire, he had his first opportunity to watch her unobstructed. She moved with a lithe grace and perfect posture. Similar to Mrs. Bryant's well-bred carriage, but Lilly's movements were more fluid. She was obviously comfortable in a kitchen, too.

At last, Mrs. Bryant turned from the stove and scanned the kitchen area, then removed her apron. "I think we're all done in here. Dahlia, would you like me to read to you while I rock Emily to sleep?" She didn't look to Lilly for approval, but reached for the child's hand.

Lilly's face seemed to pale some. Or maybe that was the difference in the lighting across the room. He could only hope.

But whether she wanted to talk with him or not, Marcus had things to say. It was time for an apology.

Chapter Fifteen

When the threesome disappeared through a door behind him, a quiet settled over the space, broken only by the crackling of the fire. Lilly picked up a cloth and wiped the table, although she'd already done that at least once.

"Lilly."

She jumped at his voice. Her gaze found his, and he patted the rocking chair beside him. "Will you come sit with me?"

She finished wiping the table, and he worried she'd continue to ignore him. But then she turned toward him, and Marcus's tension eased. She almost tip-toed across the room, her eyes wary as they watched him.

Had he done so much damage with those few words on the way back from the livery? How was he going to make this right? He'd do anything to take away the fear now glittering behind her mask, take her back to the sweet smiles they'd shared while playing with Dahlia.

Lilly perched on the settee across from him, out of reach. Probably best that way.

"I...I came up here to say I'm sorry. I shouldn't have asked what I did." He studied her. Lilly's emotions were hard to read on a good day, but so many times she chose to smother them under that thick mask. Now, two fine lines puckered between her brows. What did that mean?

"What should you not have asked?" Her words came out soft, not laced with anger or fear. At least she was speaking.

Marcus took in a fortifying breath. "I shouldn't have asked to be more than friends. I shouldn't have rushed you. I'm sorry. I didn't mean to scare you. Please know you have nothing to fear from me."

The lines disappeared from her brow, leaving behind clear, smooth skin. Flawless. She drew herself up, taking in a breath and squaring her shoulders. "It did scare me. I...haven't..." She cut herself off and seemed to be contemplating something, then tipped up her chin and started again. "But your words weren't what really frightened me that night."

Now it was his turn to furrow his brow. "What then?"

She held herself perfectly still. "Claire didn't tell you?"

Marcus let out a huff. "She wouldn't say a word. It was like pulling teeth to find out you'd come here." He tossed the quilts aside and scooted forward in his chair. The sight of his bare feet stopped him for a moment. Where had his boots gone?

But then his focus honed in on Lilly. Something about her posture tightened the knot in his gut. He tried to force gentleness into his tone, but his tight muscles made it hard. "What frightened you?"

Her chin quivered once, but then a muscle in her jaw tightened. "A man has been following me home at night."

Marcus gripped the arms of the chair lest he surge to his feet and alarm her. "Who?"

She looked at the floor.

He tried to meet her gaze, but she wouldn't look up. "Lilly, do you know who he is? Did he hurt you?" He wanted with everything in him to take her in his arms and smooth away the terror that man had caused. But something inside told him to give her space. Wait for her. *Give me wisdom, Lord.* He kept a white-knuckled hold on the chair arms.

"He finally showed himself that night. I…knew him from before."

Marcus's insides screamed to react, but he held himself perfectly still. No response. No breathing.

At last, Lilly raised her head, but she looked at the fire in the hearth instead of at him. Her gaze lost itself in the dancing flames. "He was Dahlia's father."

The breath leaked from Marcus. A weight pressed hard on his chest, and he couldn't draw air. Dahlia's father? How? What did that mean? He still didn't know what conditions the child had been conceived under. Didn't want to think about it. He gripped tighter to the chair, digging into the wooden frame under the cloth.

"The last time I saw him, he'd been staying at the same hotel where my father and I were. Then Pa-pa died of the sickness. I was devastated. That man caught me in the hall, but I was too numb to see where he was taking me. Until…it was too late." She released a shuddering breath.

Marcus was beside her before he realized what he'd done. Slipping an arm around her shoulders. Pulling her close.

At first, her muscles held stiff, but then she seemed to crumple. She leaned into him and gripped his shirt as sobs took over her body. He buried his face in her hair as his heart fractured.

He held her for hours. Or maybe only long minutes, but her tears couldn't seem to find an end. How much more could her fragile body withstand? Had she ever truly cried since that awful ordeal? Claire always said tears were healing for a woman. But poor Lilly hadn't had the luxury of healing after what that man had done. Instead, she'd developed the impenetrable mask to cope with the horrors of her past.

Her sobs finally subsided, and she rested against his chest now with only an occasional shuddering sigh. He continued to stroke her back, breathing in the richness of her. The softness.

At last, she straightened and pulled away. He let her go but stayed beside her. Cold seeped in where her warmth had pressed against him, especially with the front of his shirt now damp and salty from her tears. His body missed her contact.

"I'm sorry." She dropped her focus to her lap and wiped her eyes.

"Lilly." He tried to catch her gaze, but she wouldn't look up. He finally cupped her chin, gently prodding her to look at him. When she finally did, his heart nearly cracked at the tears still pooling in her eyes. "I'm sorry, too. But I'm glad you told me."

She sniffed and nodded, dropping her gaze again. "The other night, he said he wants to meet Dahlia. That she's old enough to know her father." She looked at him then, a blaze firing her eyes. "He'll never be her Pa-pa. I won't let him near us again."

Marcus stroked her temple, pushing away stray hairs that clung to her damp cheek. "I won't either."

She stared at him. That haunted look filling every part of her gaze.

"Marcus?" They both jerked at the child's voice behind him.

He pulled his hand from Lilly's cheek and turned to face Dahlia. "There's my ladybug." He forced a smile.

"Will you tell me a story? Miss Leah fell asleep." Her innocent little pixie face tugged at his heart.

He reached down and scooped her up onto his leg. "I suppose I can."

As he started into the story of Noah and the ark, Lilly rose and retreated through one of the doors in the back wall. A bed chamber most likely. His chest tightened as he watched her go. Perhaps she only wanted to freshen up.

But he couldn't shake the feeling she was retreating from him.

LATER THAT AFTERNOON, Lilly stirred the pot of beans at the stove and stared out the window at the world of white. Marcus had spent the afternoon with Dahlia snuggled in his lap. When the child fell asleep, Lilly tried to take her to bed, but he'd given her a besotted smile and said they were both comfortable. There was no need to disturb the little fairy.

She could imagine how Dahlia felt, wrapped in Marcus's strong arms where it felt like nothing could ever hurt her. Lilly allowed her eyes to sink closed as she remembered that feeling. She shouldn't have allowed it. And certainly shouldn't have blubbered all over him. But something about Marcus was different than any person she'd ever known. He was safe. Without a good reason, she knew it in her heart.

That was why she'd told him. Although, it was hard to look at him now that he knew. It'd been so hard to prepare herself for his censure, but he'd needed to know why she wasn't any good for him. She hadn't expected him to be so *nice* about it.

The hairs on Lilly's neck tingled, and she glanced toward the sitting area. Marcus was leaned back in the chair with Dahlia propped on his chest. His head turned toward Lilly as his eyes followed her actions. He gave her a sleepy smile when he realized he'd been caught.

Her heart skittered a beat. "Can I get you something? Tea or coffee?" She kept the words barely above a whisper. Leah was still napping in the bedroom with her babe, and the entire cabin held a homey feeling, almost intimate.

"No. I have everything I need right here." That sleepy smile set off a fluttering in her midsection.

She turned back to the work counter to hide the heat flaming up her neck. Time to make the cornbread.

Lilly barely had the batter mixed when boots thumped on the porch. She jumped to the window and peered sideways through it to get a glimpse of their visitor.

Gideon. He stepped inside, covered in snow and animal skins, as he'd been the day before. As he began to unwrap the layers, he nodded toward her. "Miss Lilly."

Then his gaze caught Marcus, and he paused. "Preacher?"

Marcus leaned forward. "Good to see you, Gideon. I'd stand to greet you, but..." He motioned toward Dahlia's sleeping form.

The mountain man waved his concern away and proceeded to shrug out of his coat. "Don't bother. Just didn't expect to see you there."

Lilly couldn't get a glimpse of the man's face to gauge whether he was angry at all the intruders to his quiet mountain home. She turned back to pour a mug of coffee. Good thing she'd just brewed a fresh pot.

"There you are." Leah's sleepy voice sounded from the bedroom doorway, and she strode toward her husband. He bent down to give her a stirring kiss, similar to the one they'd shared yesterday.

Lilly looked away quickly, but her heart tightened again at the image that replayed through her mind. How much these two loved each other. It was evident in the way Leah looked at him, and the way Gideon treated her.

Marcus joined them at the table for dinner. It was the first time he'd left the sitting area by the fire. She caught him limping as he walked the few steps across the floor. Had the ice done damage to his feet? He'd put his boots back on, and that surely wasn't helping things.

Leah and Gideon plied Marcus with questions about the church as they ate. Well, it was mostly Leah doing the asking, but Gideon seemed interested in what Marcus had to say and made a couple of his own inquiries. The children also kept the meal lively, with Emily fussing and Dahlia not willing to eat unless Lilly fed her.

Lilly was almost relieved when it was over, and Leah took the children in her room to prepare them for bed. She wasn't used to having help with Dahlia's care, but Leah insisted, saying Dahlia was a big help entertaining Emily.

Gideon kept Marcus entertained through the evening, with talk of his ranch and what they could expect through the winter months. Lilly kept an ear tuned to the conversation as she worked in the kitchen, cleaning and kneading bread dough for the next day.

"You think it'd be safe to head back to town tomorrow?"

She tensed at Marcus's question. He was leaving already?

A moment of silence passed. "Doubt it. That pass where you lost your horse gets pretty treacherous. Won't be safe till the weather warms some."

Lilly's muscles eased. He wouldn't be leaving. Not yet. It shouldn't matter so much to her, but it did.

THE NEXT DAY dawned clear and cold.

Lilly was surprised when Marcus asked Gideon if he could help with the barn chores. He must be feeling better. He didn't limp as much this morning, either.

While Lilly cleaned the breakfast dishes, Leah opened a trunk in the corner and pulled out a slew of Gideon's old fur hats and fur-lined gloves. She brought out some buckskin tunics too, but Marcus politely declined.

"My coat'll be fine for the time I'll be outside this morning." Then he flashed that smile that had the power to win anyone over to his way of thinking.

Lilly darted a glance at Gideon, who stood propped against the door frame, watching the scene. His mouth tipped in a sideways grin. He apparently enjoyed watching his wife fuss.

Dahlia whined the entire time Marcus and Gideon were gone, going to the window and watching for them, then wandering around the kitchen and generally getting in the way.

When the door opened and Marcus stepped inside, she squealed and ran to hug his snow-covered legs.

"Here, honey. Let's let Marcus come in and warm himself."

"There's my girl." He shrugged out of his coat and slipped it on the nail, then scooped Dahlia up and whirled her around. Lilly couldn't bring herself to turn away as her daughter giggled and squealed. He made her so happy. Made both of them happy. Too happy, she feared. If she were wise, she'd keep him from getting too close. It would only be harder when they had to leave.

But it was so hard not to let him in.

153

Chapter Sixteen

*L*illy worked in the kitchen for most of the morning while Marcus entertained Dahlia. When Lilly was done with the dishes, she took up some of Leah's mending. Leah was in and out of her bedroom with the baby and seemed content to watch from a distance. Everything about this quiet cabin tucked on the mountain emanated peacefulness. What would it be like to live here always?

About mid-morning, Leah stepped into the room with her little one on her hip. "I'm going to lay down with Emily. Would Dahlia like to come rest with us, too?"

Lilly eyed her daughter, who was studying a picture book with Marcus. "It is time for her nap if you don't mind."

"All righty, up you go." Marcus set the book aside and surged to his feet, lifting Dahlia even higher into the air. She squealed and gripped his neck, then finally released him as he brought her feet back down to the floor. "Take a good nap, sweet one, then we'll play some more."

When Leah's door closed behind them, Marcus turned to face Lilly, catching her watching him. He sent her one of those off-kilter smiles that made her heart skip a beat. She dropped her gaze back to the needle and flannel shirt in her hands.

Marcus's boots thumped on the wooden floor as he took slow, steady steps toward her. "I told Gideon I'd break the ice for the animals in the barn. Would you like to walk with me?"

She raised her gaze. Marcus stood with a hand extended toward her, a soft hopeful smile touching his mouth. She swallowed. She did want to see more of the outside. Even this peaceful cabin could get cramped after a full day inside. And time with Marcus, not having to share his attention with Dahlia…it was too tempting.

"All right."

The corners of his mouth curved up. "Let's get you bundled then."

An intense blast of cold hit her when they stepped outside, and Lilly wrapped her cloak tighter around her.

"Gideon said he thinks a warm spell will come in the next couple days." Marcus gripped her elbow as they stepped down the stairs. "Careful of the ice."

Since Pa-pa died, she'd not had anyone to care whether she slipped on ice or not. Lilly fought a burn at the back of her eyes. Why was she letting her barriers down? Now, when the appearance of Dahlia's father should have had her strengthening those barriers even more.

The thought of that man brought stiffening to her spine, and she pulled in a deep breath and took in the peaceful scene before them. White covered the ground, mostly undisturbed except for paths to each of the outbuildings. Animal sounds drifted from the barn, especially the low moo of a cow.

Marcus chuckled. "Sounds like Bethany's thirsty. Gideon said she likes to complain."

The next half hour passed too quickly. Marcus introduced her to each of the animals and even let her help feed hay to Bethany, the milk cow.

"Have you ever milked one?" He eyed her with raised brows.

"No."

"I can teach you tonight, if you'd like."

Lilly stared at the wide brown and white animal. She'd spent plenty of time with horses at their barn in Derbyshire, but never cows. "I...think I'd like that."

When they left the shelter of the barn, the wind whipped, and she clutched her elbows to hold in as much warmth as she could. Marcus stepped closer and slipped an arm around her shoulders. His warmth eased her shivering. Or maybe it was his nearness. Either way, she couldn't help but lean into him as their steps synchronized.

At the stairs, Marcus's hand slipped from her shoulder to her elbow, and he wrapped his arm around her back as a protective barrier lest she slip. This man made her feel so...cared for.

She stopped on the porch. Something in her dreaded going back in the cabin. She turned to the rail and gazed over the landscape again.

"It's peaceful here, isn't it?" Marcus must have been reading her thoughts.

Lilly nodded. She didn't look at him. But she was far too aware of his nearness, of the brushing of their coats.

After a moment, Marcus spoke again. "Lilly, when the weather warms enough, I'd like you to go back to town with me." He turned to her, his gaze warming the side of her face. "You and Dahlia can stay with Claire until we catch that despoiler. And I promise you...we *will* catch him. I won't let him hurt you, Lilly. I won't let anything hurt you. I make you that promise."

The raw intensity in his voice brought her gaze up. She swallowed. Those eyes. Rich brown with flecks of amber. It was so hard to look at them. Even harder to look away.

His hand cupped her cheek. Where had his glove gone? She closed her eyes against his warmth, then opened them again.

There was magic in him. Magic in the way he made her feel. The way he looked at her.

He was closer now, his face less than a foot from hers. Awareness flickered through Lilly. He was going to kiss her. But his eyes held the question.

He rested his forehead against hers, his breath warming her face. Lilly closed her eyes again, savoring it.

Gathering her courage. She wanted him to kiss her. Part of her wanted it more than her next breath. But could she?

Forcing her eyes open again, she gazed at Marcus, close enough for their breaths to intermingle in a white cloud. The question still in his gaze. With every ounce of courage she possessed, Lilly raised up on her toes and met his mouth with her own.

Sweet bliss.

MARCUS'S EYES drifted closed as he savored the taste of her.

She'd kissed him. A cautious meeting, yet a gift beyond what he'd expected. Beyond what he deserved. He kept it gentle, no matter how much he wanted to deepen the kiss. To truly taste of her. Lilly was too precious to risk frightening. Again.

He pulled back after only a moment and allowed his forehead to rest on hers again, breathing in her sweet rose scent.

With his fingers, he traced the delicate rise of her cheekbones. His thumb worked across her chin, then caressed the fullness of her lips. How quickly she'd become more precious to him than any other person in the world. Than even his own life.

He hated to break the moment with words, but had to say this. Wanted her to know where he stood. His gaze locked with hers. "I've never met anyone like you. And I never thought I could feel this way so quickly."

Her eyes glistened. Was that good or bad?

He pressed on. "I don't want to lose you. I meant what I said about you coming back to Butte with me." He felt her shrink back, and rushed to say more. "But if you aren't ready, I want you to know that I'll do whatever it takes to keep you and Dahlia safe." He brushed a tear from under her eye with his thumb. "Even if that means leaving Butte, I won't leave you."

That was it. He breathed out his spent air. He'd said it. She knew how he felt, and from now on, he'd show her how serious he was about it. His gaze never left Lilly's face as he watched for a reaction.

Her chin quivered almost imperceptibly, and her gaze dipped from his face. She seemed to be looking past him, or perhaps not looking at anything. After a long moment, her lips finally parted. "I'm not sure."

His stomach flipped. Was that bad? It wasn't an outright rejection. Had he really expected her to fling her arms around him and agree to trust her life in his hands? At least she was thinking about it.

She looked up at him again, and the expression in her dark eyes—the uncertainty, maybe a little hesitation—sent a rush of protection through him.

Pulling her close, he pressed a kiss to her forehead and wrapped her in his arms. "We'll figure it out." With her pressed to his chest, her head resting perfectly on his shoulder, and their heartbeats melding, Marcus sent up a prayer. *Show me the way, Lord.*

LILLY SCRUBBED another of the baby's nappies on the washboard as she soaked in the sun's warm rays. The weather had warmed some as Gideon had predicted, and the sun sparkling on the white snow was almost blinding. Still, the warmth of it was worth carrying hot water outside for the laundry instead of staying cooped in the dim cabin.

"Look, mama. It's a snow horse."

Lilly smiled at her daughter and the lumpy, rectangular section of snow. "Have you named it?"

"Snowy."

Dahlia brought another reason to be thankful for the sunshine. Marcus had ridden out with Gideon that morning to help with the livestock, and Dahlia had moped all morning. But now that they were outside, Dahlia's mood had cheered.

He'd certainly won the child's heart. And what of her own?

If she had no concern except her own feelings, that would be an easy question. But there were so many other considerations. There was Marcus himself. With his new church, he needed someone who could be his helpmate, to reach out to people in the community. Someone outgoing. Someone very different from her.

With a sigh, Lilly draped the nappy over the stack of already-clean clothes. She couldn't be what Marcus needed. She wasn't even sure she could be what he wanted.

Of course, he hadn't actually asked her to marry him. He'd said he never thought he could feel this way so quickly. He'd not actually said he loved her. He'd said he wouldn't leave her.

But in her heart, she knew what his words meant. He loved her. He'd meant he wanted to marry her. Marcus was honorable to the core. He simply didn't want to frighten her away. She could tell it in his touch, see it in his eyes.

So where did that leave her?

Even though he'd not spoken the word *marriage*, he had said he would protect her and Dahlia. He'd promised it. And wasn't that what she really wanted? Protection? But could he really do it?

Claire's husband Bryan was supposed to be working with the sheriff to catch Barlow. She had no doubt Marcus would go to whatever lengths were necessary to ensure the man was punished.

But what about others that cropped up in the future? And she had no doubt there would be others. All her life, people had jeered at their family because of her parents' heritage, both in Guatemala and again in England. The cruel

161

tricks and hurtful jabs—could Marcus really protect her and Dahlia from all that?

If he could at least get rid of Barlow, maybe she could stay in Butte. For a while anyway. The only real friends she'd ever had were in this rough mining town. Claire. Aunt Pearl. Marcus.

The cabin door slammed behind her, and Lilly pulled from her reflections, turning to look at the structure.

"Sorry we took so long." Leah had the baby bundled tight in a sling across her front. "Just when I had her ready, we had to change again."

Leah's rueful look brought a smile to Lilly's heart.

"I remember those days. I'm almost done here, though. If you want to take the clean things inside to hang, I'll finish up."

Leah strolled up to the wash tub and stopped. "The sun feels too wonderful to go back inside yet. Let me take a turn washing."

Lilly draped a clean shirt on the stack and stepped back. She dried her hands on her apron. Even with the warm wash water, they'd turned icy.

A sigh drifted from Leah as she scrubbed another shirt. "I've always loved the steady rhythm of washing. It makes for good thinking time."

"Yes."

Leah cut a quick glance at her. Perhaps the simple agreement had been a little too revealing. After a moment, she asked, "Did you get anything worked out during your thinking time?"

Lilly swallowed. That was quite a personal question, but Leah made it sound like the concerns of a caring sister instead of a prying acquaintance. What should she say? Something to put her off? A simple yes? She hadn't really worked anything out. Just mulled through her concerns. Was there a chance Leah could help? Wisdom had seemed to seep from her the few times they'd talked before. And Leah had obviously found happiness in her own marriage.

First Marcus, and now if she shared with Leah… She'd opened up more in the past few days than the past three years. Was she handling things wrong? Truth be told, she was tired of fighting all these battles herself. It was so much easier to let in a few trusted friends who could help.

She inhaled a breath. "I was debating on whether I should go back to Butte with Marcus when the snow melts."

Leah didn't answer right away, but her brow furrowed as she continued to scrub the frilly white article of clothing on her washboard. Her baby fussed in the sling, and Leah straightened to adjust her.

Lilly stepped forward. "Let me take over for a while."

As Lilly settled into her rhythm again, Leah bounced and swayed her little one. At last, she spoke in a quiet voice. "Are you concerned about the dangerous situation in Butte, or are you worried about Marcus?"

This woman was perceptive. But this answer Lilly had worked through. "The situation in Butte. I think I can trust Marcus. I think." It seemed unwise when she voiced the words. Like she was giving up her defenses.

Leah was quiet for a few more moments, then let out a sigh. "I can't tell you what to do, Lilly. But I know the way I feel when I'm with Gideon. I'd rather be near danger and with him than protected and apart from him. I know he would go to the ends of the earth to keep me safe. But there's something else I have to remind myself. Gideon really has no power to protect me. That power is God's, and it requires tenacious faith sometimes. But He will come through for you."

God? That wasn't a notion she was ready to contemplate.

Chapter Seventeen

arcus curled his fingers as he followed Gideon up the porch steps that evening. These fur-lined gloves were miles better than his plain leather pair, but after working all day in the snow, he'd long since lost the feeling in his fingers.

Stepping inside, the blast of heat from the warm cabin soaked over him, quickly followed by a squeal and a blur of black hair as it plastered to his legs. He chuckled. "There's my girl."

He shucked his gloves and worked the buttons on his coat apart as quickly as he could, but Dahlia was already bouncing up and down with her cute little button nose turned up to him.

When he was at last free from the gear, he scooped her up in his arms. "Did you miss me, angel?"

She slipped a soft hand around his neck and nodded her pointed chin in a very solemn gesture. He couldn't resist a tickle under her chin, and she collapsed against him in a giggle.

Marcus's gaze wandered around the room until he found Lilly, standing in her usual spot at the stove, watching him with those intense, dark eyes. That familiar wave of awe struck him, tightening his chest just like it did every time he saw her, no matter how often. She was still the most lovely thing he'd ever seen.

As she stirred something in the frying pan, he met her gaze with a smile. The corners of her mouth tipped slightly, softening her face and fueling his desire. It took everything in him not to stride over and take her in his arms.

She must have read his thoughts, because the flawless bronze skin on her cheeks flushed a pretty pink.

He forced his gaze away, toward the sizzling food on the stove. "Sure smells good in here."

"Fried potatoes and ham with gravy."

His stomach responded with a loud growl, which might possibly have been covered by the sound of the sizzling food. If he were lucky.

The meal passed quickly. Leah asked questions about the cattle and horses, then shared tidbits about their day. The Bryant Ranch had a decent amount of livestock—over a hundred cattle and a dozen breeding horses. Gideon had his hands full, to be sure, but Leah seemed like an avid participant, at least where knowledge and decisions were concerned. With their baby to care for, he doubted she made it out to where the livestock were quartered very often.

When Lilly rose to gather the used dishes, Leah waved her back down. "Lilly, please let me do that tonight. I've been so lazy since you've come, letting you do all the cooking and cleaning. The break's been wonderful, but it's my turn now." She rose with the baby in her arms and moved toward her husband. "Besides, Gideon needs some time with Miss Fussy here." She planted her daughter in his lap, then turned back to reach for the plates in Lilly's hands.

Lilly eyed her for a moment, and something seemed to pass between the women. At last, Lilly's face softened, and she relinquished the stack of plates into Leah's arms. "Just tonight."

It always amazed him how, even with all the words they used, women still seemed to have an unspoken communication style, too. They could have a whole conversation just by looking at each other, and he never could decipher a word.

Marcus pushed back his chair and rose. "I'll head out and take care of the barn chores then."

He glanced at Lilly. Would she want to come along? Gideon had already milked the cow last night, so he'd not had the chance to teach Lilly. But maybe tonight.

But as he watched, she seemed to be having another one of those silent conversations with Leah. What were they plotting now?

At last, Leah turned to him with a smile. "I bet Lilly would like to go to. She was saying earlier how much she enjoys seeing the animals."

167

Lilly didn't quite meet his gaze, but he wasn't about to pass up the offer. "Sounds good."

He helped her on with her cloak. It was such a flimsy thing. When they made it back to Butte, she needed a thick fur-lined coat like the one he'd seen Leah wear. His fingers brushed her shoulders as she slipped into it, sending warmth shooting up his arms.

Lilly was quiet as they walked out. Something was on her mind, he could tell by the tension clinging to her like smoke. But maybe she needed a little more time before she'd be ready to share.

Watching her play with the animals would have been worth paying money to see, as she scratched itchy spots for the horses and cooed soft words to each of them. But when she tried the same with Bethany, the milk cow, she got a long lick across her chin. Lilly darted back and squealed at the slimy moisture, and Marcus couldn't help a chuckle as he strode by with an armload of hay for the horses.

"She likes you."

She glared at him, wiping her chin frantically. "I'm not sure the feeling is mutual."

After dumping his load, he grabbed the clean pail he'd brought from the house and joined Lilly outside Bethany's stall. "Would you like to learn how to milk her?"

Surprise flashed on her face. It was amazing how much more open her expressions were now compared to when he'd first met her. He was probably getting better at reading her, too.

"I...suppose." Something about her response lacked her usual confidence.

Marcus stepped around her to the stall door and let himself in. After he'd secured the cow in front of her fodder, he positioned the stool and bucket. "Bethany's been around for a while, so she knows what to do here. Just run your hand down like this to let her know you're coming, then grip her like so."

The weight of her gaze penetrated his back, warming his neck and making his fingers clumsy. After a few squirts he looked up at her. "Do you want to try?"

After eyeing the cow, she gave a nod and stepped inside. Marcus rose from the stool, but kept his hand on Bethany's hindquarters.

Lilly seated herself with her normal graceful movements, her back erect like a grand lady in a New York parlor.

"Now run your hand along her belly so she knows you're coming."

She followed his prodding and gripped the same part of the udder he'd used. When she squeezed, a few white drops eked out. Her head tilted, and she tried again. Only one drop this time.

Marcus chuckled and bent down to reach around her. "You want to squeeze from the top in a rolling motion at the same time you pull down."

She withdrew her hand, and he showed her the action. He was close enough that the wool of her cloak

169

brushed his jacket front. If she leaned back only a few inches she would sink into his chest. He forced himself to focus on the cow's udder. But he wasn't entirely successful.

"Can I try again?" Lilly's long, slender fingers extended, and he allowed her to take the place of his hand. Her hand fumbled more this time, but she did better with the rolling squeeze, and a tiny stream came out.

"That's it." He placed his hand over hers and helped her with the motion. A larger squirt of milk came this time.

"I'm doing it." The excitement lacing her words sent a pulse through his chest.

Marcus pulled his hand back to let her take over fully, then settled both hands on her shoulders. "You're doing excellent. A born milk maid."

She gave him a sideways glare, and he couldn't stop a chuckle. "Good at everything you touch."

As she kept up the motion, he couldn't quite bring himself to move back. The touch of his hands on her shoulders, even through her cloak, seemed to connect them. His fingers itched to knead the knots from the muscles there, but he kept still. Her rosy scent drifted to him, soothing his senses like a warm blanket on a cold night.

"You can finish feeding the animals if you want. I have things under control here." Lilly's voice held a light touch. Teasing? Or just enjoying her newfound skill? Either way, his close presence must not affect her like her nearness did him. He forced himself to step away.

Marcus had all the animals fed and watered long before Lilly finished the milking, which gave him the chance to stand and watch her. The woman spoke to the cow in soft tones as she worked, the same tones he'd seen her use to soothe Dahlia. It appeared milking had started a tenuous bond between woman and cow.

At last, Lilly straightened and examined the milk in the bucket. "That looks about right. Good girl, Bethany."

After rising, she took up the stool and bucket in each hand and approached Marcus with a pleased smile. Her dark eyes shone in the lantern light. They were enough to blind him for a moment, clearing all thought from his mind and moisture from his mouth.

"Are we finished?" She raised her brows at him.

Umm... He forced his mind to focus. "Yes. I mean...all done." Spending time with this woman was not proving helpful to his mental capacities.

He took the bucket from her, and she dropped the stool in its spot outside the stall. With the lantern in one hand and the pail of milk in the other, he extended an elbow to her. She hesitated for a moment, then took it, slipping her hand around his upper arm. A rush of protectiveness coursed through him.

After he'd paused to latch the barn door behind them, he set the pace for a leisurely stroll back to the house. This outing could drag on for days, as far as he was concerned.

"Marcus?" Lilly's voice seemed hesitate.

His heartbeat picked up pace. "Hmm?"

"When you're ready to go back to Butte, Dahlia and I would like to accompany you."

He stopped mid-stride and turned to look at her. With the almost-full moon, he didn't need the lantern to see the caution shimmering in her eyes. Dropping both the lantern and the bucket, he gripped her waist and spun her around with a laugh. "Yes."

She let out her own breathless giggle. A giggle!

Pulling her close, he breathed in the sharpness of the cold air and the warmth of her body. "I'll protect you, Lilly. I promise."

Her shoulders gave a little quiver. "I hope so."

LESS THAN two days later, Marcus led the way down the muddy mountain trail, with Dahlia snuggled in the saddle in front of him and Lilly's horse trailing behind. Gideon had been kind enough to loan him a mare for the journey back, and Lilly still rode Cloud, Doc Bryan's mount. It would have been nice to drive the women back in a wagon, but Gideon said the trail would be barely passable on horseback, nowhere near ready for wheels and axles.

His mind churned through his plans for Lilly and Dahlia on their return, as it had the last two nights when he'd tried to sleep. He slowed his horse and motioned for Lilly to come up beside him. "I was thinking it would be best for you two to stay with Claire and Bryan until we get things settled. Is that all right with you?"

Lilly nodded. "It will be easier to get to the café from there, too."

Marcus felt his brows furrow. "I don't want you going to the café until we catch that lout. It's too dangerous."

She arched a brow at him, then the little spitfire squared her shoulders and raised her chin. "Aunt Pearl needs me, and I've been away too long already. I'll be safe in the protection of the kitchen."

A vice clamped around Marcus chest. He had to talk her out of this.

"Besides, I have ways to protect myself."

"Ways?" He forced his voice to remain calm, despite the urge to holler the word. What ways had she had when the man had assaulted her three years ago? What ways when the man was stalking her home every night these last weeks?

Something hardened in her eyes, and Lilly reached down toward her stirrup. With the horse between them, he couldn't see what she was doing. When she straightened, the sun glinted off the polished metal barrel of a handgun.

He stared at it, then pushed his gaze up to her face. He closed his open jaw and studied the defiance plastered across her features. Something welled up in his chest then, and he couldn't hold in the chuckle. Dahlia joined him, although she couldn't know what he was laughing at.

Lilly eyed him, almost wounded at first. Then her mouth pulled at the corners, finally stretching into a smile.

When he finally got a handle on himself, he wiped a tear from his eye and sent her a smile. "I guess I should have expected that."

They stopped about an hour later to let Dahlia stretch her legs. As Marcus waited for Lilly to return with the child from a thick stand of trees, his mind worked through the options for allowing Lilly to work at the café in safety.

When both girls shuffled back toward the horses, he eyed Lilly. "I suppose we can make this work, if you let either me or Bryan walk with you to and from the café every time."

She stepped close and met his face with a serene expression. "You haven't stopped worrying about that, have you?"

He pinched his lips together. "I don't want to take any unnecessary chances. Dahlia can stay with Claire while you're gone. Please make sure you keep the kitchen door locked while you're working. Will you promise me?"

Her gaze locked with his, any hint of lightness gone. "I don't want to be a burden, Marcus."

He gripped her shoulders gently, yet firm enough for her to feel the possessiveness that flared through him. "You're definitely not a burden, Lilly. If you don't let me help with this, I'll go mad." One of his hands crept up to her face, brushing the strands of fine black hair from her cheek. "Please."

If Dahlia weren't standing beside them, kicking at the snow, he would have taken Lilly in his arms and kissed her soundly. Enough to drive away any lingering doubts about being a burden. But he wouldn't do that in front of the child. Not until he had the right.

Chapter Eighteen

he sun was partway down the western sky when the trio reined in at Claire's house. Marcus eased down from the horse, careful not to knock Dahlia off as he did. She was bouncing so hard in the saddle, it wouldn't have taken much for her balance to sway.

"We're here!" she squealed, as Marcus helped her soar through the air and land gently on the ground.

When he turned to assist Lilly, she'd already dismounted. She'd proved herself to be a capable horsewoman, although her occasional hesitations told him she was more accustomed to riding sidesaddle than astride.

As they stepped onto the porch, Marcus took in the sights of Butte behind them. It was a good thing Bryan had built this house on the outskirts of town, so they'd not had to ride through busy streets to get here.

Claire greeted them at the door with a smile and ushered everyone inside. "You just missed saying goodbye to Mama and Papa. They left at daylight this morning."

Disappointment stabbed Marcus's chest. He'd not been here to say farewell. And he'd sort of been hoping Pop would help with the search for the man pursuing Lilly. He forced the emotions aside. "Sorry I wasn't here. I'll send them a letter. I brought you some houseguests, little sister." Marcus planted a hand on Claire's shoulder. "Lilly and Dahlia are going to stay with you for a few days."

"If it's all right." Lilly slipped in the qualifier with a darted glance at Claire's face.

Claire responded with a hug for her friend. "I couldn't be happier."

The two women embraced for several moments, and Marcus couldn't see either of their faces. A satisfied warmth flowed through him, though. It was nice to see that his sister and the woman he loved were such good friends.

"Where's Bryan, squirt?"

Claire pulled away and wrinkled her nose at him. "Maybe at the clinic. He had some calls this morning, but he should be done by now."

Marcus's gaze wandered to Lilly, locking with hers as he stepped closer and lowered his voice. "I won't be gone long. Stay in the house, all right?"

She nodded once, a little vulnerability showing in her eyes. "I will."

As Marcus stepped outside and mounted his borrowed horse, Lilly's expression replayed in his mind. *Lord, show me where to find this blackguard.*

"SO YOU HAVEN'T even talked to the sheriff yet?" Marcus clenched and unclenched his fists as he glared at Bryan.

The man returned his stare over the rim of a coffee cup. "He's not been in town. One of the deputies said they expect him back today. Thought I'd ride over to the jail in a bit to chat with the man."

"So what's been done to find this man Barlow?"

Bryan eased into a chair in the little work room at the clinic and pushed another toward Marcus with his boot. "I've gone around to several of the men I trust and given them the description Lilly provided. No one seems to remember the man. 'Course dark hair and brown eyes with a lanky build is kinda common in these parts. The scar in front of his left ear is the only thing that makes him stand out, and a good pair of sideburns could cover that."

Marcus wanted to pace. Wanted to slam his fist on the table. Five days. It'd been five days since Lilly had escaped from town, and almost nothing had been done to apprehend the man. "So what's your plan?" He folded his arms across his chest.

Bryan sighed. "It's a big city, Marcus. There wasn't a lot I could do until the sheriff came back. He has the manpower for a real search, if we can get him to take it on."

178

Marcus tightened his jaw against a tick. "Oh, he will definitely see the need to take it on." Dropping his arms, he spun toward the door. "Are you coming with me?"

"Oh, I'm definitely coming." Bryan's tone was a bit too dry for Marcus's liking.

AS THEY STEPPED up the walkway to the jail, Bryan greeted a deputy descending the stairs. It must be the same man he'd talked to before, because the man said the sheriff had been back in town for barely more than an hour, just long enough to lock up his new prisoner and settle down at the desk with a plate of beefsteak from Aunt Pearl's Café.

When Marcus and Bryan entered the small block building, two deputies and the sheriff were working in the office. All three men nodded at them, and the sheriff brought up a cloth to wipe his bearded face.

"Doc. Preacher. Good to see you both." The sheriff took a swig of coffee and swished it around his mouth. He clunked the mug on the desk and looked up as he swallowed. "What can I do for you?"

Marcus described the thug who'd been following Lilly home at night, and the sheriff's brow furrowed more the longer he spoke.

"You say he stopped and threatened her, too? Did she know the man?"

Marcus darted a glance around the room. He didn't want to tell Lilly's story in front of any more people than he had to. Especially not the two deputies who had turned to listen. "Yes. He had...assaulted her... in the past." He ground out the words in a low voice. "The man has to be found, sheriff. His name is Barlow, and Lilly was able to give a decent description."

The sheriff leaned back in his chair, tapping a finger on his bearded chin. "We can put up some posters, and I can have the boys keep an eye out for him. It's gonna be hard to find one man in all these miners if'n he don't wanna be found."

"But he *has* to be found." Marcus slapped a palm on the front edge of the desk. A hand settled on his shoulder, steadying. He took in a long breath, then met the sheriff's gaze.

The man watched him, a mixture of curiosity and understanding flickering in his eyes. "What is all this to you, preacher?"

Marcus didn't drop his focus from the man. "Lilly and her daughter's life may be at risk here, and I've vowed to protect them. We *have* to find that man."

The sheriff studied him for a few more long moments, then looked over at his men. "Chauncey, you go with these fellows to Miss Lilly. Get her to tell you everything she can about the man. Have her draw a picture if she's any good at that. Harper, round up every available man in town who'll help. Then get the description and spread out. Check every house you can 'afore dark."

A rush of spent air left Marcus in a flurry, almost taking the strength from his legs with it. "Thank you, sir."

MARCUS EXPECTED Lilly to be a little shaken when he appeared at the house with the deputy to speak with her. She wasn't, though. With her chin raised and shoulders squared, she gave a thorough description of the man, both how he'd looked two and a half years ago and how he'd deteriorated into a scrawny shell of a man by the time she'd seen him the week before.

As Marcus stood to the side while they talked, he had to force his fists to unclench. Just hearing about the man made his blood run hot.

But then the thought struck him. Was this really the way he should feel about another human being? Made by God? The man had been a despicable lout with what he'd done, but so many Scriptures warned against judging others.

He turned away from the conversation and stood by the window where he could think. *Lord, am I doing this wrong? How can I not help catch this man? Lilly needs him caught.* A wagon passed by outside the window. Marcus closed his eyes against the distraction.

For man looks at the outward appearance, but the Lord looks at the heart. The verse from First Samuel flickered through his mind. He could easily apply the Scripture to that scoundrel, but what did it say when applied to himself?

Lord, please help the words of my mouth and the meditations of my heart be acceptable to you. Help me to keep the right perspective as we search for him.

"We're headin' out, Parson."

Marcus turned to face the deputy. "Thanks, Mr. Chauncey. I'll be there shortly."

When the door closed behind them, Marcus stepped toward Lilly. "Is there anything you need before I go?"

He'd planned to only ask the question, but the vulnerability in her eyes drew him closer. With his right hand, he cradled her cheek. This would be the perfect moment for a kiss.

"Would you take me to the café?"

Marcus's eyes sank shut, and he dropped his head, letting it hang limp from his neck. "Lilly." He dragged out the word, then raised his face to look at her. "Tomorrow. I'll come in the morning to walk with you. Will that work?"

The corners of her eyes crinkled. "That will work."

He lowered his mouth for a kiss then, soft and gentle, laced with a promise. Oh, she was so sweet. But he forced himself to pull back, then fought to control his breathing. Now wasn't the time.

As he took in one final gaze, he asked, "Where's Dahlia?"

"Sleeping. That ride wore her out." Her lips curved in the hint of a smile.

Those lips. He turned away. "I'll be back to check on you after dark."

MARCUS SCANNED the street, the boardwalk, and inside the buildings. Anywhere a man could hide. He tugged Lilly's elbow closer to him. Having her out in the open like this had his stomach tied up in knots.

From the moment Marcus had awoken this morning, something had felt off. But who was he kidding? Nothing about his life these days was even close to normal.

The search posse hadn't found any sign of Barlow's whereabouts the day before. A few merchants thought they might have seen him during the last few months, but they had no idea where to find him. Sheriff Timber had needed his deputies for other duties today, but Marcus and a few of the men planned to take up the search where they'd left off.

"This way." Lilly stepped into an alley, and Marcus almost pulled her back until he realized they were beside the café. He wasn't paying as much attention as he'd thought.

Lilly padded to the back door and slipped it open. Marcus stayed close behind.

Aunt Pearl turned from the stove, her expression blank for a moment before her face lit like a lantern in a dark closet. "My Lilly, how are you, girl?" She clutched Lilly's head and drew it down to plant a kiss on her forehead, then wrapped her in a tight hug. "Ye had me worried, dearie."

After a moment, Aunt Pearl drew back and held Lilly's face in her hands, studying her. No words passed, but it seemed to be another of those silent conversations Lilly was so good at.

Finally, Lilly stepped back and reached for her apron. "What are we serving today?"

Marcus eased a step back. He wasn't needed any longer. He should leave and do something useful, like hunting down a rapscallion.

Lilly must have sensed his retreat, for she turned toward him and offered a soft curving of her lips. A smile. It lit his chest like a sunrise.

In two steps he was in front of her, only inches separating them. He forced himself not to touch her, though. It'd be too easy to take her in his arms and kiss the breath from her. "Don't leave until I come back for you, all right?"

Her eyes shone as she met his gaze. "All right."

"And if something happens that even slightly scares you, tell Aunt Pearl to send for me. All right?"

One side of her mouth pulled up. "I'll be fine, Marcus."

"Promise me."

"I promise."

He let the air seep from his lungs as he summoned the strength to turn away. But there was one more thing. "Lilly."

"Yes?"

"I love you."

Her eyes widened, but he didn't wait for a response. He leaned in for a quick, gentle kiss, then turned and marched out the door.

Chapter Nineteen

The rich, spicy scent of cinnamon and apples permeated the air as Claire stepped to the cook stove and lowered the oven door. Four pies sizzled from the metal rack, perfectly browned. Dried apple pies were always a favorite with the café's customers, especially in the winter when fruit pies were harder to come by.

Gram usually did the baking for the café from her own home when she was in town, but she and Ol' Mose had headed out for another trip yesterday while the weather was still warm and the snow melting. It was nice to have something to keep her busy while her new husband was out on doctoring calls.

With those pies on the cooling rack and another four in the oven, Claire closed the door and wiped her hands on her apron. Dahlia should wake from her nap soon. Poor child must be exhausted from all her travels. She'd slept almost an hour and a half already. It was nice to have a little voice around the house, even if it belonged to her friend's child. But someday... Someday, she and Bryan would have their own little voices running through the rooms and slamming doors.

Claire softened her step as she crept to the door of the room Lilly and her daughter shared. No sleeping sounds drifted through the wood, so she turned the knob quietly and peered inside.

The bed lay empty.

Claire scanned the room. Perhaps the child had climbed down and started playing. Her pulse sped up as she circled the room, even bending down to peer under the bed. Nothing. She whirled to the wardrobe and opened the oak door. Nothing save a single long dress.

"Dahlia?" Her voice quivered as her gaze swept the room again. It hooked on a flutter at the window. The pale blue calico curtain swayed as though a breeze shifted it from the outside.

"Dahlia?" The word came out high-pitched. Claire raced to the window, her fingers confirming her fear. Why was it open? Tearing the curtains aside, she pushed her upper body through the wide opening and scanned the empty yard. *No!*

"Dahlia!" Claire screamed the word as she wiggled and contorted her body to fit through the open window frame. As soon as she cleared the sash, she jumped the five or six feet to the ground.

Where now? Surely the child couldn't open the window and jump from that height on her own. And the window had definitely been closed when she'd drawn the curtain for Dahlia's nap.

Her heartbeat pounded in her ears as she raced toward the back of the house. Before she assumed the worst and alerted everyone, she had to make sure the child wasn't simply hiding.

"Dahlia? Come here, sweetie!"

Claire circled all four sides of the house, then vaulted up the front steps and plunged through the door.

"Dahlia!"

Deadly silence met her cry. Claire pinched her eyes shut. She had to get Marcus. Bryan. But first...her chest ached to think of it...she had to tell Lilly.

Claire took off for the café at a run, but when she caught a glimpse of Alex, Bryan's brother, striding down Elm Street, she veered his direction.

"Alex. Lilly's daughter's missing. I think someone's taken her." Claire's lungs heaved as she struggled for breath.

Alex turned with wide eyes. "Missing?"

She recounted her search in quick sentences. Alex had been part of the manhunt the day before, so his suspicions quickly flew to where hers had.

"I have to go tell Lilly," she said. "Do you know where Marcus is?" She'd caught her breath now, and with it, a renewed fervor to accomplish her mission.

"I'll find him, then we'll start tracking the man. Hopefully, he left a clue near the house."

A KNOCK RADIATED through the café's back door, jerking Lilly's attention from the stove. "Who's there?" Her pulse thumped through her chest.

"It's Claire."

Lilly's gut tightened. Claire was supposed to be at home with Dahlia. Had she brought the child with her? Maybe Dahlia had been upset when she woke to find Lilly gone. This was the first time she'd left her daughter in someone else's care.

She jerked the door open, trying to summon a smile for her worried child.

Claire stood alone. And the expression on her face sent shivers of fear through Lilly.

"What's wrong?" Lilly's hand crept up to find her mouth.

"It's Dahlia." Claire's voice cracked. "She's missing."

The words struck Lilly like an avalanche, knocking her backward. "What? Where?" She couldn't bring her mind to formulate more words. She gripped the edge of the table. The rough, wooden underside dug into her skin.

"I'm so sorry, Lilly." Claire took a step forward, then hesitated. "I went in to check on her while she napped, and the bed was empty. The window was open. I looked everywhere, but I think someone must have taken her. Alex went to find Marcus, and they're going to track him."

Lilly tightened her grip on the table as her legs wobbled. This couldn't be happening. Her body flushed hot, and bumps broke out across her arms. She had to pull herself together. Had to find her baby. "Where...? What...?"

Inhaling a deep breath, she pressed her eyes shut. *God, if You're there, please save my baby.* She released the breath, then straightened and looked at Claire. "I have to find her."

"Let me tell Aunt Pearl, then I'll walk with you back to the house."

But she didn't wait for Claire. Snatching off her apron, Lilly leaped across the threshold and ran.

MARCUS SEETHED as he raced toward Claire's house.

How could he have let this happen? He'd promised Lilly. And now that disreputable cad had stolen Dahlia. His sweet, adorable Dahlia. The image of her pixie face swam in his vision, but he pushed his legs harder, faster.

Claire's house loomed ahead, and a figure stood by the side window. Lilly. Her tall, willowy form pierced his chest. He'd failed her. Would she ever forgive him? Not that he'd ever forgive himself.

He dropped to a walk as he neared her, his breaths coming in short heaves. She didn't look up. Did he want her to? No. Yes. No, he couldn't look at the torture in her eyes.

But then she did look up. Her eyes were wells of grief. "Dahlia."

In three steps he was by her side. She catapulted into his arms, and he wrapped her tight.

"I'm sorry. So sorry." His vision grew blurry, but he clutched tighter. How had he let her down so completely, this woman he loved? And why didn't she hate him for it?

After a few moments, Lilly pulled back, swiping at tears with her wrists. "These are his tracks." Sniffing, she motioned toward the ground under the window.

Marcus dropped to his haunches in front of them, and Alex stepped forward to peer over his shoulder.

"Definitely a man's boots. You can see where he stood to open the window, and here's where he dropped down as he was leaving." Alex pointed to each set of tracks.

Marcus's mind wouldn't focus, but he reined it in like a ranch horse dragging a roped calf. He needed all his concentration to find this man.

They followed the tracks to the street, but the prints quickly blended with a plethora of man, hoof, and wheel marks. Slush from the melted snow had made the road a muddy mess.

Marcus straightened and ran a hand through his unruly hair. "Alex, round up as many men as you can. I'll get the sheriff."

"And I'll start looking for him."

Marcus whirled on Lilly. "No. Stay at Claire's house, and don't leave for any reason. Keep your gun out, and

191

don't unlock the doors or windows unless you know it's one of us."

Lilly's chin jutted. "I'm going to find my daughter."

He inhaled a steadying breath. "You might be his next target. We can't risk that. I'll get half the town looking for Dahlia. We'll find her." His voice grew hoarse on the last sentence, and he willed her to believe him. Yet how could she? He'd already broken his most important promise.

He'd have to show her.

Claire stepped forward and wrapped an arm around Lilly's shoulders. "Come inside, honey. Our work will be prayer."

NUMBNESS SANK over Lilly like a morning mist hanging thick in a valley. Claire led her inside and settled her on a settee by the fire. "Let me brew some tea and pull the pies from the oven."

As her only friend walked away, Lilly dropped her face in her hands and took in long shaky breaths. Each one pierced her heart, like a knife chipping away at a log wall.

Where was Dahlia now? What was that man doing to her?

Her shoulders began to shudder as thick sobs built in her gut and clawed their way out. Pain so deep, it ripped huge chunks from her heart as it fought for escape.

Hands slipped around her shoulders, gripping with a gentle firmness.

But they didn't stop the purging of her soul as the sobs wracked her body. Lilly fought for breath, but part of her wanted to stop breathing. Whatever it took to escape this physical torture. Escape the thought of her baby at the hands of that vile demon.

The pain carried on, consuming her. No tears. Just this thick, shuddering ache. Her misery was too deep for tears. At last, her body began to quiet, and her quivering lessened.

She became aware of Claire speaking a steady stream of words beside her. Praying?

Lilly rubbed her eyes with the heels of her palms then rested her face there again. "What do I do, Claire?" As if her friend would have the answers. But she wasn't really asking Claire.

"We have to put Dahlia in God's hands. He's the only One who can help her."

A bitter, mirthless laugh escaped Lilly's lips. "Why would I expect Him to help now? He's not been there before when I needed Him."

"Oh, Lilly." Claire pulled her closer, resting her cheek on Lilly's shoulder. "He loves you more than you can imagine. I can't explain why those terrible things happened to you. This is a wicked, fallen world. But He's stronger than the world. He wants to be your strength. He loves you and Dahlia more than you can imagine."

Moisture stung Lilly's eyes. *Now* she was going to cry? She tried to swallow the tears back, but they rushed anyway. How could she think of putting her trust in a God who had let so many dreadful things happen?

For two and a half years now, she'd refused to trust anyone. She'd finally lowered her barriers enough to let in Marcus. Yet he'd not been enough. He'd certainly done the best he could—was still doing it. But he was only one man. He wasn't all-powerful.

But God was. If only He could be relied on to use that power for good. If only He cared enough to save her *before* the terrible things happened. Putting her life in His hands was too much risk.

"In God have I put my trust. I will not be afraid what man can do unto me."

Lilly glanced up at Claire's words.

Her friend gave a sad half-smile. "One of my favorite psalms. It's true though, Lilly. God is trustworthy. You can rely on Him, even if everyone else fails. The last verse in that chapter says, 'For thou hast delivered my soul from death. Wilt not thou deliver my feet from falling, that I may walk before God in the light of the living?' I love that promise."

A high-pitched whine sounded from the kitchen, and Claire rose to her feet. "I'll pour the tea."

Lilly hugged her arms around her chest. *God, I don't know if You care, but my daughter's out there. Alone and scared. Save her. Please.*

Chapter Twenty

*I*f we see her, we'll sure come tell the sheriff."

Marcus turned away as Alex bid the sleepy man farewell. He couldn't quite pull the slump out of his shoulders. They'd only covered half their assigned territory, and there'd been no sign of Dahlia yet.

"Marcus, I think we should stop for the night." Alex fell into step beside him. "We're getting people out of bed, and it's too dark to do a thorough search. The rest of the men stopped hours ago when dark set in. Let's get some sleep, and we'll start again at daylight with the others."

Marcus didn't halt his marching as they neared the next house. Another shanty. Was that all this town held? At least this section seemed to be families, not roustabouts or seedy-looking bachelors. Which meant they probably *were* waking the children with their search. He glanced at the moon. It must be close to midnight. But then an image passed through his mind of Dahlia, huddled in a cold, dark corner.

He had to find her.

A hand gripped Marcus's shoulder. "We're not doing a thorough search with it so late. You'll be worth more to Dahlia if you're fresh and people let you in to check every room. Besides, I'm sure it would help Lilly if you stop by and fill her in on what's been done so far."

Lilly. He'd left her alone all afternoon. Not that she'd be eager to see him without Dahlia in his arms. But still, he owed her an update. It was the least he could do.

The weary walk back to Claire's house might have taken hours. His mind scanned through the areas they'd searched. The people they'd questioned. None seemed especially sinister, and none matched Lilly's description of Barlow. The rest of the men searching had checked in every few hours as their paths crossed.

One or two of the townspeople they'd questioned had thought they might've seen someone matching Barlow's description in the last few weeks, but none could give any idea of his whereabouts or living conditions.

How could a man disappear so thoroughly, even in a city the size of Butte?

At Claire's door, Alex tapped lightly. The wood jerked open to reveal Lilly's drawn face.

Alex mumbled something as he stepped inside, leaving Marcus standing before her, flayed by her penetrating stare.

Lines spanned her forehead. Shadows from the lantern pressed dark impressions under her eyes. Her hands balled into fists gripping her apron.

"What news?"

His gaze found her eyes, pulled there against his will. "Nothing yet. We've had two dozen men searching, covered about half the town. We'll all start again at daylight."

Her shoulders sagged as he spoke, and she turned away, back inside the house. His chest couldn't have fractured more completely if she'd plunged a cleaver into it.

"Lilly."

She froze at his voice.

Marcus couldn't quite stop himself from stepping forward and laying a hand on her shoulder. "We'll find her, Lilly. I promise."

Her shoulders stiffened. "I hope so." Then she slipped from his grasp and escaped toward the kitchen, where the murmur of voices drifted in the night air.

His head drooped, and he sagged against the door frame. *God, why haven't we found her? I have to find her.*

Footsteps sounded inside, and Marcus raised his head enough to see who approached. Claire.

"Come in and have some tea," she said. "We thought it might be a good idea to pray before everyone heads home." She wrapped a hand around his upper arm.

"Everyone?" He didn't have the strength left to face people tonight.

"Well, mostly just Miriam and Alex and the baby."

197

Summoning his strength with an inhale, Marcus followed his sister through the parlor and into the kitchen. A handful of people sat around the table. Bryan. Alex holding his infant son. Miriam with an arm tucked around Lilly. Claire took the chair on Lilly's other side and tugged Marcus down between her and Bryan.

She scooted a mug in front of him, then scanned the faces around the table. "I'm sure we've all been praying through the afternoon, but we thought it would be good to join together for a moment." His bossy little sister, never afraid to take the lead.

Claire reached under the table and gripped his hand. "Would someone like to start? Then we can take turns as your heart leads."

Marcus swallowed. He was the reverend in town. Always the one who led prayers and kept God in the center of the conversation. Yet he had nothing for these people. Completely dry.

"I'll start."

Thank the Lord for Bryan. Claire really had married a good man.

Marcus bowed his head as his brother-in-law's deep baritone rumbled through the room. His prayer was simple. Not wordy, just like the man. A simple expression of trust that God would lead them to the child. A request for guidance.

When Bryan's voice drifted away, Miriam spoke up, raising her plea for Dahlia's safety and peace during the ordeal. Next came Alex, then Claire. The common theme across each petition reigned strong—prayer for God's guidance and intervention in the situation.

The words sank around Marcus's heart like a millstone, weighing him down. What an idiot he'd been. From that first promise he'd made Lilly, up on the mountain, he'd carried the weight of her safety on *his* shoulders. As if *he* had any real power to control what happened around her and Dahlia. He'd gone about town on a crusade to save the women he loved by his own efforts. As if *he* were the one all-knowing and omnipotent, who knew this precise moment where that sweet child was hidden away.

Dropping his head, Marcus squeezed his eyes shut. *God, I'm so sorry.* Words didn't seem adequate to express the depth of his remorse. How could he have fallen into such a trap of self-importance? *I'm sorry, Father. Forgive me.*

With his head bent low, the weight gradually fell away from his shoulders. Marcus breathed in the sweet aroma of humility. And forgiveness.

LILLY COULDN'T BREATHE when Claire led her back to the bedroom she and Dahlia had shared. Her baby.

Claire took her hand and pulled her down to sit on the bed.

"Have a sip of tea, Lilly. And breathe."

The warm solidity of a porcelain mug touched her palm, and Lilly wrapped her hands around it.

"Drink."

Lilly glanced at Claire's face. Tender. Earnest. She took a sip.

"Is there anything I can do to help you sleep?"

She pinched her lips together. "I don't want to sleep." Not when Dahlia was out in the cold. Hungry. With that...man. Steeling her jaw, she forced her mind not to think of the possibilities.

"We'll keep praying, Lilly. God will lead the men to her. I know it."

Lilly swallowed.

Claire rose and placed a kiss on her forehead. "Lie down now. You'll need rest for tomorrow."

As Claire's footsteps padded away and the door clicked behind her, Lilly stared at the wood paneling on the wall across the room. Claire and the others seemed so certain God would fix this. That God was caring for Dahlia even now. How could they believe so steadfastly? And did they really believe? Or were their prayers merely desperate words to make them feel better?

She dropped her face into both hands. Her heart wanted to believe. Wanted to trust in someone other than herself, for she'd failed Dahlia so miserably to this point. But did God really care?

"God." The whisper leaked from her throat with raw anguish. "If You're trustworthy, if You care, bring my daughter back to me. Please. You can have anything You want from me, if You'll just bring her back."

MARCUS BLINKED scratchy eyes in the darkness and listened. Sounds drifted from another room, dishes clanging, voices murmuring. And the rich aromas of coffee and fried ham. Light glowed from the crack under the door. Where was he?

He sat up, focusing his gaze around him. Claire and Bryan's parlor. The awful truth of it all crashed around him as he rubbed his forehead and lumbered to his feet. Dahlia was out there somewhere. They had to start looking again.

He'd slept in his clothes on a pallet in the corner, easier than traipsing home and back again. As he pulled on his boots, Marcus sent up a prayer for guidance in the search.

The kitchen door opened, spilling light into his dark room. Claire's profile outlined in the open frame. "I thought I heard you up. Coffee's on and Bryan's almost ready to head out with you."

Marcus straightened and followed her toward the smells. His stomach let loose a loud rumble. He blinked at the flood of light and stopped in the doorway.

Lilly stood at the stove, her long black braid swinging halfway down her back as she worked. She turned at his entrance, and the deep shadows under her dark eyes speared him. Had she slept at all?

Every instinct in him craved to wrap her in his arms and rub away the pain and despair. But he had to tread carefully. He skirted the table to stand beside her.

Ham and potatoes sizzled in the frying pan, and she kept her focus there as she turned them with a fork. They stood, side by side, for long minutes. What could he say? He had no words of comfort. Nothing he hadn't already said.

His body craved contact with hers, yet he couldn't pull her into his arms. Especially not with Claire scurrying around between the counter and table behind them. So he settled for brushing his fingers across the back of her arm, just above her elbow.

She didn't stiffen, so he used his thumb to apply gentle, steady strokes. Was it his imagination or did she lean into him?

"I'm going to check on Bryan."

Marcus glanced back at Claire and nodded. Giving them time alone? He'd take it.

Quiet settled over the room, save the sizzle of food in the pan. And a sniff from Lilly.

Was she crying? He leaned forward to glimpse her face, and the moisture running down it. That was the last straw. Marcus reached both hands around her and pulled her close to his chest. She sank into him.

His eyes drifted closed as he wrapped one hand around her waist and the other around her shoulders, breathing in the aroma that was uniquely hers. A sob shook her back, and he stroked her arm, rubbing circles against the sleeve of her dress. "We're going to find her, Lilly. God will lead us to her."

She didn't answer, but her fingers slid across his chest, gripping his shirt with both fists.

Lord, give her peace.

For several long minutes he held her while shudders shook her body every so often. Marcus infused into her every bit of strength and reassurance he possessed.

At last, she leaned back to look up at him, wiping the dampness from her cheeks as she sniffed. "I'm sorry."

He loosened his grip a tiny bit, but not enough for her to pull away. "I'm sorry, too." He brought the hand that held her shoulders around to wipe away the moisture from her temple. Now was the time. He needed to tell her. "I realized last night I've made a mistake. I was relying on myself to take care of you and Dahlia. I'm sorry I did that, Lilly. He's the only One who can do it. He knows where she is."

She nibbled her lip, twin lines forming across her brow, and her gaze lingered somewhere around his chin. What was going through that mind of hers?

When she didn't speak, he said, "I'm praying hard He'll lead us to her today."

Lilly raised her focus to his eyes. "I hope so."

Something lingered in her gaze. A tiny shoot of faith. Hesitant. But enough to leave Marcus with the feeling that the outcome of this search may have more of an impact on her relationship with the Almighty than any other event in her life could.

Marcus leaned forward and pressed a kiss to her forehead as he squeezed his eyes shut. *She's yours, Lord. Please show her Your faithfulness.*

Chapter Twenty-One

Bryan eyed the shanty snugged in between two saloons, as the deputy, Chauncey, approached the tilting door. They were deep in the heart of the Cabbage Patch, where most of the residents had either left for the mines or were sleeping off the night's activities. As a doctor, Bryan had been all through this section over the past couple years. Seemed like these fellows needed patching more than most. He couldn't remember who occupied this particular place, though.

Chauncey's knock yielded no response, so the man gripped the door and eased it open. Not even a latch to hold the thing shut, and at least one of the leather hinges had worn in two.

"Anyone here?" The deputy had perfected the authoritative tone a man of the law needed when dealing with these ruffians. He peered inside, then glanced back at Bryan. "Don't see anyone."

Bryan motioned him in, then grabbed the door and propped it open. This tiny shack wouldn't take long to search.

While Bryan eyed the scant possessions inside, a noise drifted to him. Was that a child whimpering? It might have been the wind, but the hairs on his arms tingled at the sound. Either way, it was coming from outside, behind the cabin.

He spun for the door. "I'm going to check out back."

Chauncey mumbled something, but Bryan didn't stop to catch the words. There was a narrow opening along one side of the shack, enough for a man to scoot sideways between it and the saloon on the right.

With his coat on, it was a tight fit, but he finally slipped out the other end. A sea of shacks greeted him, like disorderly gravestones in a cemetery.

A sound pulled his attention to his left. There, curled into the corner of the shanty and the opposite saloon, sat a tiny figure. Only a sliver of pale skin and wide eyes peered out from under a mass of tangled, dark hair.

Dahlia.

The fear emanating from her eyes and her cowed posture clutched at his chest. The child looked like she might bolt any minute.

Bryan lowered to his haunches. "Dahlia? It's me, Doc Bryan. I sure am glad to find you. Can I take you back to your mama?" He held out his hand.

She nodded, not saying a word, but unwrapped herself and started to stand.

He eased closer and extended his hand for her to take it. The child hesitated, but finally, she slipped her tiny fingers into his palm.

They pressed through the crack between the buildings, and Chauncey greeted him the moment Bryan stepped onto the boardwalk. "Found her huddled in a corner back there. No sight of anyone else around."

Bryan turned to Dahlia and extended both hands. Standing with her arms wrapped around herself, she looked like she might blow away in a stiff wind. She stepped closer and allowed him to pick her up. Tiny little waif.

Chauncey tried to talk to the little girl, but Dahlia hid her face in Bryan's neck. Not that Bryan could blame her. The man had a shock of curly red hair and beard that made a person have to look twice.

Bryan turned to face the deputy. "I'll take her to her mother. Can you let the others know? Start with Marcus down in the southeast quadrant. Once I get her settled, I'll come back and help search for the man."

They parted, and Bryan made long strides toward home. Miss Lilly had looked two shades darker than death that morning, and he could hardly blame her with her daughter in the hands of that despoiler. Marcus had looked a sight better than last night, but the man held too much of the weight of the kidnapping on his own shoulders.

As he neared the house, he rubbed the child's back. She hadn't moved much as they traveled, probably finally collapsed into sleep. Who knew how much, if any, she'd had last night? "We're here, little flower. Your mama's gonna be so glad to see you."

A whimper greeted his words.

He hadn't taken three strides across the porch before the front door jerked open.

"Dahlia?" Lilly's voice was almost frantic.

The child jerked upright and turned. "Mama?"

Lilly took her daughter in her arms, tears and laughter spilling from her face. Little Dahlia cried, too, and clutched her mother like she'd never let go.

Bryan stared at the scene, then found his wife's teary features just beyond them.

Claire stood behind Lilly, a soft smile lighting her features as she watched the pair. Then her gaze wandered up to his. That look she gave, like he'd just saved the town from an army of ten thousand. He could get used to his woman watching him like that.

She slipped around Lilly, who wasn't paying a bit of attention to either of them, and slid under Bryan's arm. He wrapped her tight, savoring the feel of her. It still seemed too good to be true that this woman not only loved him, but was *his*.

Pounding footsteps echoed from the road, and they both turned to look. Marcus, disheveled and drawn, closed the distance with long running strides.

MARCUS'S PULSE RACED as he neared the house. The image of Lilly came clearer, clutching the most precious bundle he could imagine.

He checked himself as he pounded up the steps. This was Lilly's moment with her daughter. Not his to intrude on. But she turned to him, eyes wet and red-rimmed, but the most beautiful smile shining from her face.

He was by her side then, wrapping his arms around both his girls.

Dahlia squirmed to look at him. "Marcus?"

"There's our little princess." He tried to smile through the tears that blurred his vision. He wanted to say more, but too much clogged his throat to speak.

A hand touched his back, as Claire scooted by them. "You all must be starved. I'll make sandwiches."

Marcus looked up at Bryan, but kept one arm wrapped around Lilly. So many questions to ask. But he couldn't say anything in front of Lilly and Dahlia. Especially not Dahlia. The quicker she could forget about the whole ordeal, the better.

He pressed Lilly's waist. "Let's get you inside. I bet Dahlia needs to eat."

Lilly sniffed, wrapping her daughter tight for one more squeeze.

Once Marcus had Lilly in a chair at the kitchen, her daughter snuggled close in her lap, and Claire scurrying around to lay out milk and biscuits, Marcus dragged Bryan back to the parlor.

He leveled his gaze on the man. "Where was she?"

"Tucked in a corner behind the shanty that butts up against The Spirit of Butte."

Marcus cringed. Right in the heart of the red light. "Any sign of the man?"

Bryan shook his head. "I didn't wander around to look, but Chauncey was gonna take a group back and start searching the area."

"Is she hurt?" He steeled himself against the answer. *Lord, please don't let her be hurt.*

"I didn't do a full examination, but there weren't any obvious injuries. Seemed more cold and scared than anything."

Marcus sucked in a long breath. His sweet little pixie. He sought Bryan's gaze. "How do you think she got away from him?"

Bryan shrugged. "Been ponderin' that, but I don't have an answer."

Running his hand through his unruly hair, Marcus turned toward the kitchen door. "Let me make sure these two are settled, then we can head back out."

"Marcus?"

210

He turned back at the word. Bryan's mouth was pinched, like he wasn't quite sure he should share his thoughts.

"What is it?"

"I think it might be a good idea to bring the child with us. She can probably take us straight to the place he kept her. If the man's already high-tailed it, we may never find his trail. This way, we could at least have a start."

Marcus was already shaking his head. "No." *No, no, no.*

"It might be a good plan."

He whirled at the soft female voice behind him. Lilly. How could she even entertain the idea?

She met his gaze. "I'll ask if she thinks she can do it." She must have read the absolute refusal on his face. "The man has to be caught, Marcus. We can't live with him out there."

Conflict wrenched his emotions. She was right, they couldn't live with the shadow of fear that Barlow would strike at any time. As long as the man was loose, there was always that chance.

But to endanger Dahlia again to catch him? To expose her to the memories he only wanted her to forget?

And Lilly. He had no misguided notions that she'd let him take the child without staying by her daughter's side every step of the way. Could he really expose her to the danger if they found the man?

Cast thy burden upon the Lord, and He shall sustain thee. He shall never suffer the righteous to be moved. The verse flittered through his mind, bringing a touch of peace with it.

All right, Father. Please keep them safe.

With a long exhale, Marcus nodded. "All right."

LILLY CLUTCHED her daughter tight as they walked. Marcus didn't stray far from her side, especially as Bryan led them deeper into the red light district. These roads were far too familiar. It wasn't much farther to her own house, maybe a quarter of a mile. Had that low-life resided so close to her treasured hideaway all this time?

She soaked in the sweet little-girl scent Dahlia hadn't lost, even in the trauma from the last day. God had brought her back. Safe. She owed the Almighty a long talk as soon as this was over. *Thank You, Lord.* The simple prayer would have to do for now, but she meant it with every fiber of her being.

Bryan pulled to a stop, then pointed to a tiny opening between the buildings. "I found her back here."

The men struggled through the crack, but Lilly was able to squeeze through without a problem, even with Dahlia pressed against her. The crevice opened to a multitude of wooden structures, most of them shanties, but a

212

few rough-looking businesses with haphazard signs advertising wares and services.

"She was curled up right there." Bryan pointed to the back corner of the shack where it met another building. Then he brushed the back of Dahlia's hair. "Weren't you, little one?"

Lilly crouched down to the ground and pulled Dahlia away enough so she could see her face. "Do you remember being here, honey?"

The child looked around, then slipped a thumb in her mouth and sank against Lilly. "Uh-huh."

"Do you remember where you came from? Where did that bad man take you?" She almost held her breath. Would Dahlia understand? Maybe she'd been so lost, she wouldn't be able to remember.

Dahlia was quiet for a moment, then looked around. "That way." She pointed south.

Lilly's heart pounded. "Good job."

She helped Dahlia stand, then rose and gripped her daughter's hand. "Can you show me?"

A red-haired man approached from the north and spoke with Bryan—the deputy who'd taken her description of Barlow. But she ignored him as Dahlia began to lead her.

Marcus stayed close, not taking his hand from her. He kept either touching her elbow or the small of her back, depending on which way Dahlia pulled her. His presence cloaked her in the warmth of security. She wasn't alone in this. No matter what they faced, Marcus would be with her.

Dahlia led them down the alley for a few minutes, then paused. She glanced around, her little eyes squinting. Had she lost her direction? Finally, she pointed between two shacks. "I think I came through there."

Marcus signaled the men who'd trailed them—the deputy and some others. "Search the area," he murmured just loud enough for the little crowd to hear.

Lilly pressed forward as Dahlia led her, and Marcus took Lilly's other hand in his. When they stepped onto another narrow street, Dahlia stopped.

Cowering into Lilly's skirts, she slipped her thumb into her mouth again. That was a habit they'd been working hard to get rid of, but if it helped her cope now, they'd deal with it another day.

Lilly bent down to eye level with her daughter. "Do you remember where he took you?"

Dahlia eyed her with an uncertain expression. "Somewhere around here, I think."

She couldn't help but pull her daughter close for a hug. "Good job, honey. You did really good." She glanced up at Marcus. Would it be enough?

He nodded as if he understood the question, then ran a hand over Dahlia's stringy, black hair. When this was all said and done, the child needed a bath and clean clothes.

Men around them filtered in and out of shacks, barking comments and commands as they searched. Marcus stayed with her, the three of them an island amongst all the activity.

214

A shout echoed from a shanty three doors down and drew Marcus's attention.

Lilly stared at the open doorway of the little building. What had the man said?

Bryan appeared in the door frame, his eyes finding Marcus. "Chauncey, you better come in here." But his gaze never left Marcus. Telegraphing some kind of message?

Marcus moved forward, jogging toward the shack as other men swarmed in.

Lilly scooped up her daughter and followed. Bryan's reaction hadn't sounded like the man was there. Just some kind of evidence. Something inside pulled her toward the scene.

Chapter Twenty-Two

*P*repare yourself, man."

Marcus stepped over the threshold as his brother-in-law's words drifted back to him. Chauncey was close on his heels and barked for the rest of the men to stay outside.

The shack was dark, and it took a moment for Marcus's eyes to adjust. He followed the curve of Bryan's outstretched finger to a shadowy mass on the floor by the stove.

Marcus's heart seized. It couldn't be.

As he stepped closer, the outline of a man's contorted body took shape. A lanky form, emanating a rancid, coppery smell, almost like the singeing of iron at the smithy's forge.

Chauncey slipped past him and approached the man on the floor. Bending low, he rolled the figure onto its back. "He's dead. Looks like a bullet in the chest."

Marcus's throat constricted. "Is it...?" His mind wouldn't formulate the rest of his question.

"Matches the description of Barlow." Chauncey touched the man's face, turning it sideways. "Has a scar on his cheek under the beard."

The deputy rose to his feet and eyed Marcus. "Since she's here, I'd like the woman to identify him. We can cover everything but his face for her to see."

"No." The word was out before Marcus's mind had even processed the question. Under no condition would he allow Lilly to be traumatized any further by this man.

"I think it'd be wise," Chauncey said. "This could be another drunken miner for all we know. The description wasn't very unique."

"I'll do it."

Marcus spun to face her, pressing himself toward the open door frame. "Lilly, no." She stood beside the steps, Dahlia's hand still clutched in her own. They were both at an angle where they couldn't have seen the corpse.

"Marcus." Her word came out long and deliberate. "I need to know it's the right man."

The air whooshed out of him like a mule kick to his gut. Why did she keep doing this? Putting herself in situations he wanted her to stay far away from? "Lilly…"

"Perhaps Bryan can stay with Dahlia out here?"

At least she hadn't proposed *he* stay outside with the child. Marcus slowly swiveled to face the men inside the shack.

"I'll go out with her." Bryan was already striding past him.

217

Chauncey had found a blanket somewhere and flicked it into the air. He allowed it to settle across the corpse on the floor.

"Make sure *nothing* of the wound is visible."

The deputy nodded, kneeling to adjust the dead man's head. "Bring her on in."

LILLY BARELY BREATHED as she followed Marcus into the dim cabin. The pungent, coppery smell of the place tightened her stomach.

Her eyes roamed to the deputy, then drifted down to the mass of blanket on the floor. Her gaze slid from one side of the form to the other, finally finding a shock of dark hair protruding from the left end.

She pressed past Marcus to get a closer look.

The man's eyes were closed, but the face was undeniable. She swallowed down the bile that rose in her throat.

A hand closed around her waist, pulling her into a strong, comforting grip. She leaned into Marcus, but couldn't take her eyes off the man who'd haunted her nightmares for years.

"Is it him, ma'am?"

She nodded, but her focus wouldn't move. Barlow's eyes were closed, as if he slept and would awaken any moment to attack her. His scruffy, drawn face looked so different than when she'd first met him with Pa-pa at the hotel. Then he'd looked almost respectable. But now...there was no doubt the man was vile.

It was good his eyes were closed and the week-old beard covered his face. They masked the shape of his eyes, the flare of his nose, the point of his chin, so that any resemblance her daughter had to this man was lost.

She turned away. She'd suffered enough at his hands, and he'd not get the satisfaction of another moment of her life.

Lilly gripped Marcus's elbow as they exited the shack, the deputy close on their heels. Outside, Lilly's gaze found Dahlia and she closed the distance between them, scooping her daughter up into a hug. She squeezed her eyes shut as she breathed deeply, drawing in strength.

A throat cleared behind her.

With effort, Lilly forced her eyes open and swiveled to face the deputy. Marcus's steadying hand settled at her back.

"If you don't mind, ma'am, I'd like to ask the girl how she got away. And if she saw anyone else fightin' with Barlow."

Would this nightmare never end? After the blackguard was finally dead, they still had to be traumatized by dragging up memories of him? She opened her mouth to object, but the deputy spoke again.

"It'd help us know if he had a partner we need ta chase down." The lawman cleared his throat and glanced down at his mud-caked boots.

She raised her chin, forcing in a calming breath. He was trying to help. If Dahlia could answer a couple questions, maybe this would all be over.

Squaring her shoulders, she leaned back to make eye contact with her daughter. "Honey, can you tell me about the man who took you to that cabin? Was there someone else with him?"

Dahlia slipped her thumb in her mouth and shook her head.

"So it was just you and the man?"

The child nodded.

"Did he talk to you?"

"A little. But then he coughed a lot and didn't talk anymore."

Lilly struggled to fit this new piece of information into the picture in her head. "Was he sick?"

Her daughter shrugged.

She tried asking a different way. "Did he lay in bed a lot?"

Dahlia pulled her thumb from her mouth. "I was tired, but then a loud bang woke me up. The man was sleeping on the floor, but I couldn't wake him up. So I left. I wanted to find Mama." She shrank into Lilly's arms, and Lilly squeezed tightly.

"It's all right, honey. I'm so glad you found me."

The image that formed in Lilly's mind now looked nothing like the earlier one. Had Barlow killed himself? Or had another man sneaked in while Dahlia was sleeping? It would be fine with her if they never found out, but would this information be enough to satisfy the deputy? She glanced at him.

He nodded, his lips forming a grim line under his red beard. "I'm still not sure if it was a suicide or a murder, but it sounds like there wasn't another man who stayed with them. I suppose we can let it be."

Relief washed through Lilly as she pressed a kiss to her daughter's hair. "Thank you."

They walked back to Claire's house in silence. Beside Lilly, Marcus carried Dahlia, who'd fallen asleep on his shoulder. If it weren't for his hand on Lilly's elbow, guiding her, she wasn't sure she'd have made it to their destination.

She would have expected thoughts to whirl in her mind, but none came. Her eyes merely stared ahead, although she couldn't have said what they passed or where they were going.

Was this normal? Every muscle and joint in her body required so much effort to move, unyielding under the weight pressing on her.

At Claire's house, Marcus released her arm long enough to open the door, then guided her inside.

Claire met them in the parlor and took Lilly's hand to help her into the kitchen. "Lilly, why don't you sit and have a cup of tea. Marcus can lay Dahlia down for a nap."

She shook her head, fighting the pull of Claire's hand toward the table. "No. I'll lie down with her."

Claire didn't object but scurried around Marcus as he lay Dahlia in the bed, then stretched a quilt atop her.

Lilly could only stand and watch, like she were an invisible flying creature, hovering somewhere above the scene.

Marcus touched her arm. "Do you need anything else?"

He was so gentle, she forced herself to look at him. Kindness radiated from his eyes. Something else, too, but she couldn't examine it right now.

"No. Thank you."

The Adam's apple at his throat bobbed, and he stayed there watching her for another moment.

"Try to get some rest."

She looked back at Dahlia and nodded.

And then they were gone, the only sound left in the room being the steady in and out of Dahlia's breathing.

Lilly's legs began to quiver. She reached for the bed and sank onto it. Why was she falling apart now? After the awful ordeal was over?

She pressed her thumb and forefinger against her eyes, relishing the burn. She had to process what had happened.

Her head popped up, and she glanced around the room. Her journal. She'd had Doc Bryan retrieve it from her house before she and Dahlia left for the mountains, but she'd not touched it in all these days.

Now was the time. She dropped to her knees by the flour sack in the corner, then rummaged inside. Writing had always helped her sort feelings and find her true self. She needed that now more than anything.

With the book and a pencil in hand, she scooted back against the side of the bed. Enough light filtered through the sheer curtains over the window to make this the best spot. Without reading through any of her earlier entries, Lilly found the first blank page and raised her pencil.

To my better self,

I don't know what to think or what to say. Barlow is dead. I've seen him with my own eyes. My Dahlia is returned to me. Even now I watch her steady, even breathing as she sleeps. Marcus has been my rock through it all.

Yet why is my heart still troubled?

I prayed last night. Really prayed, that if God cared, he would bring Dahlia back to me. And He did. So what does that mean for me? I want so badly to believe that He cares. That I might be more to him than a single careless thought at my birth. But can I really possess that kind of faith? It scares me. Maybe more than I can overcome.

Yet I made a promise. Not in words, but in my heart. I promised that if God brought my daughter back to me, I would give Him a chance. But can I really do it?

She laid the pencil in the center crease of the book and stared up toward the light from the window.

Could she be brave enough to trust? It wasn't a choice she would consider half-heartedly. No, if she made the decision to relinquish control of her life, she *would not* rescind without just cause. She would keep her promise.

Lilly's eyes sank closed, and she rested her head against the bedding behind her. "God, I promised." Her whisper sank into the quiet of the room. "I give you my trust. Here and now. Please don't fail me."

As she lay propped against the bed, drawing in one breath at a time, the weariness and fear slowly dripped from her like ice cracking and melting under the sun's glow. The peace left behind by the warmth filled every part of her.

It was her last coherent thought.

LATER THAT EVENING, Marcus sipped coffee from the steaming mug as he sat in Claire's parlor and reread the last few verses in Matthew chapter eleven. *Come to Me, all ye that labour and are heavy laden, and I will give you rest.* What a promise that was. One he still needed a reminder of, apparently.

A soft scuffling brought his attention up. Lilly's beautiful frame stood in the doorway, her long, dark braid laying across her shoulder.

"I didn't think you'd still be here." Her voice was groggy from sleep. Precious.

He patted the settee beside him. "Join me?"

She padded over to sit down. She left several inches between them, but Marcus slipped his hand behind her and pulled her close.

Lilly sank into him, resting her head against his shoulder. He breathed in the rosy scent of her. With his arm still behind her shoulders, he brushed the hair from her cheek with his fingers. So soft. Everything about her. How much she'd changed from the ramrod-stiff loner he'd first met.

"I didn't think you'd still be here." She repeated her statement, softer this time.

"I went to check on things at the church, but I wanted to be here when you woke."

She raised her head to look at him. "The church. Oh, Marcus. You missed the service last week. I've kept you away. I'm sorry."

He lightly pressed her head back to his shoulder. "No need to be sorry. Claire posted a notice while we were gone, and I'll be there tomorrow to resume services."

"Is that what you're working on?" She nodded toward the open Bible in his lap.

"Mm-hmmm." He leaned his cheek against the softness of her hair. "I thought I'd talk about how much easier things are when we give our cares into the Lord's hands."

She was quiet for a moment. Should he say more? Or let it go?

"I did that today." Her words were so quiet it took him a moment to decipher them.

Then he straightened. "You did?"

She raised hesitant eyes to him. "Yes. I promised Him last night that if He brought Dahlia back I would give Him another chance. I had to keep my promise."

Exhilaration sluiced through Marcus. He set his coffee mug on the side table and wrapped both arms around Lilly, pulling her even closer. "I can't tell you how happy that makes me." The back of his throat burned. "You won't regret it."

Her head pressed against his chest, and her words almost drowned in the cloth of his shirt. "I hope not. I do feel...lighter."

As Marcus held this woman he loved more than anything else on earth, the words to a Psalm rang from his heart. *Many, O Lord my God, are Thy wonderful works.*

Chapter Twenty-Three

I think you've worn her out."

Marcus eased Dahlia's sleeping form onto the blanket as Lilly's words drifted over his shoulder. It'd been a full morning for the little pixie, with the church service, then an afternoon picnic in the grassy area behind the church. The two of them had played hide-and-seek—apparently Dahlia's first time—and then romped around the field with her riding pickaback. Now that he thought about it, a nap in the sunshine might be just the thing.

He flopped to the ground beside Dahlia and stretched out on his back as Lilly spread a second blanket over her daughter. "Isn't the weather wonderful?"

Marcus squinted up at the sun. "A warm spell in December. Reminds me of North Carolina."

Lilly returned to her spot on the blanket and eyed him. "Do you miss it?"

He turned to his side and propped himself up on an elbow. "You've asked me that before."

She dropped her gaze. "I...guess I keep wondering if you'll be leaving."

This woman. How could she possibly think he'd want to leave all that God had given him here? Slowly, so she could see the firm intent in his face, Marcus raised to a sitting position. Then up to his knees until he knelt right in front of her. With both hands, Marcus cupped her face.

Lilly's dark, luminous eyes grew wide.

"I want you to hear me, Lilly, because I mean every single word. I will *not* be leaving you. Not for any reason in my control." He brought his face closer to hers and rested his forehead against her soft skin.

"Marcus." The ruffle on her blouse rose and fell with her every breath.

Slowly enough to savor the nearness, he lowered his mouth. Closer. Her breath touched his skin, and he inhaled deeply. Closer. He touched her lips with his own.

Oh, sweetness.

She didn't pull away, and he angled his head to deepen the kiss, closing his eyes to infuse every bit of love he had into the action. She responded, her hands slipping up to his collar, pulling him closer.

Something unleashed inside him, and he groaned, dragging her onto his lap. Closer. Deeper. He ran his hands down her back, planting one hand at the deepest part of the curve, while the other slid upward. His fingers plunged into her hair, its softness fueling his desire.

A sound drifted from Lilly, plunging a single prickle of awareness through the tempo of his racing pulse.

Marcus stilled. *Oh, Lord. It's too much.* With every ounce of strength in his body, he pulled away, allowing cool air to touch his face where Lilly had moments before.

He didn't stray far, just tilted away enough so he could soak in the beauty of her face. He slid his hand from her hair to her cheek. "So beautiful."

Her dark eyes shimmered, drawing him back in. But he couldn't. Not yet.

Marcus pulled back, putting more than a foot between them. He reached for both of Lilly's hands.

A question played across her face. Maybe a little wariness?

He pushed forward.

"Lilly, I hadn't meant to do this yet. I thought you might need more time, but…I can't wait any longer." Those weren't the words he'd planned. Inhaling a deep breath, he tried again. "What I mean is…will you marry me? I want you to be my wife. And Dahlia my little girl." He let out the breath and studied her reaction. Had he gone too far?

A flurry of emotions crossed her face, melding together until he couldn't decipher any of them. She didn't speak.

He rubbed his thumbs across the backs of her hands. "If you're not ready yet, I understand. You can have time. I'll wait until you're ready." Now he was rambling. He pinched his mouth shut.

Lilly's gaze met his, shimmering sorrow. Sorrow? His chest ached. That wasn't the emotion he'd wanted to inspire at all.

"Marcus, I... I don't think I'm what you need. I wouldn't make a good minister's wife." Her voice seemed so quiet in the expanse of space around them.

His heart squeezed even tighter. How could she think so little of herself? If only she could see what he did. He squeezed her left hand and released the other to bring his palm back up to her face. "You're perfect, Lilly. Your strength and calm. Your caring. Everything about you is exactly what I need. You balance me. I'm impulsive and sometimes a little too pushy. I feel too deeply. But being around you helps to level me." He brought her hand to his mouth and pressed a kiss to her fingers. "You're perfect in every way."

Her mouth quivered, and a breath shuddered her shoulders. "Are you sure you want me?" Those eyes, shimmering now with a yearning he was more than happy to fill.

"More than anything in the world." He leaned forward and planted a gentle kiss on her mouth. A promise.

Chapter Twenty-Four

I can't go in there." Lilly stared through the crack in the church doorway at all the people filling the seats inside. Her pulse raced through her chest, louder than the harmonica drifting through the rafters inside. If she walked in there, every eye would be on her.

"You can do it, Lilly." Claire kept a firm hand across Lilly's shoulders. "All you have to do is focus on Marcus."

"But there are too many people." Hadn't she said a simple wedding? With only their close friends? Perspiration dampened the skin under her chemise. What had Marcus been thinking to invite all these people? She twisted a handful of the pale blue silk of her skirt.

Miriam reached forward to loosen her grip and take her hand. "You're beautiful. That gown fits you far better than it ever did me. You have Leah's height and bearing, I'm so glad she passed it on to me so I can give it to you."

Lilly glanced down at the fitted bodice with the tiny buttons marching down the front. The sleeves and gathered edges of the skirt had been stitched with an eggshell-colored embroidered crepe. The gown truly was lovely. She'd not worn anything as regal since she'd left England. What would Marcus think of it?

She glanced toward the newly-hung church door. He was in there. Waiting for her. She couldn't disappoint him. Not Marcus.

"Are we gonna go inside, Mama?" Dahlia tugged on Lilly's skirt, pulling her attention down.

Lilly inhaled a breath, then forced a shaky smile for her daughter. "Yes, honey. Marcus is waiting for us."

"Let's go then." Dahlia reached toward the door and would have pulled it open and charged through if Lilly hadn't grabbed the child's shoulder.

"Wait a minute. We'll walk together."

Claire rubbed a gentle hand across her shoulder. "It's going to be fine."

Lilly forced herself to breathe. Breath in, breath out. In, out. *Lord, I could use some help with this.* She squeezed her eyes shut for the quick prayer, then opened them and reached for the door.

On the simple strains of the harmonica, Lilly gripped Dahlia's hand and stepped into the room. The tingles of dozens of stares pricked her arms, but she kept her chin resolutely forward. She could do this.

And then her gaze snagged on Marcus and left her breathless.

Marcus. With his broad shoulders and square jaw, and the way his thick brown hair never quite stayed contained. So much like the man. Sometimes a little impulsive, but always with a heart so full of caring. This man loved her. The thought still filled her with awe and a warmth that sank through every part of her.

He watched her, as every step she took drew her closer. Close enough to see his eyes now, and the shimmer that washed them both. Marcus loved her. He'd proved it with every action, every word. And now, she was about to become his, truly and forever.

His gaze flickered down to Dahlia when they stopped before him. A smile pulled at his lips, and he reached forward and flicked her chin.

Lilly leaned down to her daughter. "Go sit with Aunt Pearl now, all right?"

The child darted to the front row and wriggled onto the pew beside the older woman.

Lilly turned back to Marcus, catching his eye with a shy smile. He reached for her hand, and for a moment, Lilly wished she didn't have on the lovely kid leather gloves Claire had loaned her. Her skin ached to feel the warmth of Marcus, his touch. But he wove his fingers through hers, and together, they turned to face the minister.

Marcus had been elated when the pastor from Helena had agreed to come and perform the ceremony. Sheriff

Timber was a licensed justice of the peace and could have filled the role without concern, yet having their wedding officiated by a man of God, here in the church where they would serve Him together—that had been so important to Lilly. And Marcus had readily obliged, looking more than a little relieved.

The reverend was speaking, and she forced her attention on him.

"Marcus Joseph Sullivan, do you take Lilly Marie Arendale to be your wedded wife, to live together in marriage? Do you promise to love her, comfort her, honor and keep her for better or worse, for richer or poorer, in sickness and health, and forsaking all others, be faithful only to her, for as long as you both shall live?"

She couldn't quite meet Marcus's gaze, but she could feel the heat of his stare.

"I promise."

With a whoosh, the air left her, and she was lost in the brown depths of his eyes. Marcus.

"Miss Arendale, do you take Reverend Sullivan to be your wedded husband..."

She focused on Marcus while the pastor continued, but she took in each word he spoke, pressing it deep in her heart to retrieve later.

When the minister finished speaking, she took a breath and smiled at the man she loved. "I promise."

Epilogue

TEN MONTHS LATER

L illy winced against the screams reverberating through the house. Under her hand, the muscles snaking down Marcus's arm tightened as he clenched and unclenched his fists. She stroked his tanned skin with her thumb.

"Something's wrong in there." He gripped the bottom edge of the settee and pushed himself up to pace the length of floor in front of the fireplace.

She nibbled her lip against a smile as her tall, muscular husband fretted like a mare being weaned from her colt.

Another cry rent the air, stealing any humor from Lilly's chest. *Had* something gone wrong with Claire's birthing? Surely with two doctors attending her, not to mention Miriam, who was practically a nurse, they must have things well in hand.

235

An urge in Lilly's chest propelled her to her own feet.

Marcus whirled at her movement, then his shoulders collapsed, and he scrubbed a hand through his thick brown locks. Lilly closed the distance between them and wrapped her arms around his waist. He closed her in, gripping her shoulders with a fierceness that almost took her breath. Literally.

"Claire's in good hands," she said. "I'm sure we'll hear a baby cry any minute."

He relaxed his grip and kneaded the muscles in her back. Lilly inhaled deeply, soaking in the strength and rich, masculine aroma of him. This wonderful man—God's blessing for her. With his propensity to love so deeply, so...fiercely. How had she ever deserved him? *Thank You for Your grace, Father.*

She leaned back to share her thoughts, but a knock on the door stopped her words. She raised a brow at Marcus, but his were scrunched in confusion, too.

Lilly pulled from her husband's arms and stepped toward the door. "I hope it's not someone in need of a doctor. I don't think Bryan's in any condition to be left alone with the delivery of his child."

When she pulled Claire's front door open, a young woman stood on the porch. A rather elegant woman in a lovely hunter green traveling gown, perfectly fitted and trimmed with so many laces and gathers, like a fashion plate from Godey's Lady's Book. A sheer lace veil hung from the tiny matching bowler hat perched atop her complexly braided coif.

"Hello." The debutante dipped into a half-curtsey, then rose to meet Lilly's gaze. "I'm looking for my brothers, Bryan and Alex Donaghue." Her focus wandered from Lilly to Marcus, who'd taken his place behind her. "I was told one of them lived here."

Lilly blinked, then snapped her jaw shut. *This* was their sister? When Bryan said his baby sister Cathleen was coming for a visit over the winter, she'd pictured a quiet, mousey type, maybe a little homely.

"Of course. Yes." She took a step back and motioned for the woman to enter. "This is Bryan and Claire's home. But I'm afraid—"

Her explanation was shortened by another intense screech from the bedroom. Lilly's heart jumped into her throat, but she forced a deep breath.

The other woman's eyes grew round as Golden Eagles, and her white-gloved hand crept up to cover the "O" of her mouth. "What? Who?"

"It's Claire, Bryan's wife. Their child..." Lilly paused as the lusty wail of a baby drifted from the back room.

If it were possible, the lady's eyes grew even larger, at least to the size of silver dollars now. Her hand lowered as a wide smile bloomed, highlighting the loveliness of her features. "Oh, my."

The door to the bed chamber opened, drawing all three pairs of eyes. Alex appeared, wiping his hands on a cloth. After closing the door behind him, his gaze found Marcus first, with a lopsided grin. "Claire came through it admirably. Mother and daughter are doing just fine. Wish I could say the same for Bryan."

Lilly let out a gasp. *A girl.*

A squeal from the door brought Alex's attention. The look on his face when he first saw his sister sent a surge of warmth through Lilly's chest. Utter delight.

"Cathy, you're here." He lunged toward her, and the young lady met him half way, swinging up in a flurry of skirts as he swung her around.

When she landed, she stepped back, a grip on each of his arms. "You look good, Alex. Did I hear my niece is born?"

He darted a glance back toward the bedroom door. "Miri's cleaning her now. I'll tell Bryan you're here."

As he slipped back into the other room, the young woman turned to Lilly and Marcus. "I'm sorry for my ill manners. I'm Cathleen Donaghue."

"Of course." Lilly stepped forward and extended her hand. "I'm Lilly Sullivan and this"—she motioned behind her—"is my husband, Marcus, Claire's brother."

The girl clasped Lilly's hand with a curious expression lighting her eyes. "Yes. I've heard of you both in letters. It's a pleasure to make your acquaintance."

"We heard you were coming," Lilly said, "but didn't expect you for another week at least."

She shrugged. "I left a few days early. Mum wanted to write, but I would have arrived at the same time as the letter, so..." The jaunty twinkle in her eye displayed a striking resemblance to Alex.

As if summoned by the thought, the bedroom door pushed open, and Doc Alex leaned into the room. "Claire says for you all to come see the wee one."

Marcus covered the room in four quick strides. Lilly's stomach clenched as she fell into step behind her husband. The poor man had been uncharacteristically quiet since Miss Donaghue entered. That must be a sign his worry for Claire still lingered.

By the time Lilly entered the bed chamber, Marcus was already by Claire's side, hovering close as they talked. With Bryan on the opposite side of the bed, the two men looked like twin palace guards.

Lilly bit back a smile as she sidled next to Marcus and leaned over to see the baby bundled in Claire's arms. "Oh..." She could only breathe the word.

The infant's features were even smaller than she'd expected. She had Claire's tiny china doll chin. And those eyes—even gray-blue, they held the same round intensity as her mother's striking brown ones. Of course, Claire's eyes had closed to half-mast as she reclined into the pillows.

"I'll get you some tea and bread, Claire. I'm sure you need to eat before you rest."

"Miriam went to get it." Claire gave an exhausted half-smile, then she glanced over to peer at the commotion in the doorway.

Bryan had skirted the bed to grip his sister in a tight clutch, then held her back to examine her. "You look good, little bit. Come meet Claire and the new one."

Lilly leaned into Marcus as they watched the introductions, and he slipped his hand around her waist, drawing her closer. Who would have thought two years ago she would be surrounded by so many friends, friends as dear as any family? God had blessed her with so many gifts. It turned out He was trustworthy after all.

Her gaze took in the babe again, resting with steady breaths in her mother's arms.

One day, would that be Lilly in the bed holding their own babe? Marcus adored Dahlia, and the girl returned the sentiment, but Lilly wanted so much to give him a child of his own flesh and blood. A fourth to make their family complete.

Something prickled against the flesh of her neck, and Lilly's gaze tracked up to see Marcus watching her. Those eyes. That off-kilter smile. He was so good at speaking volumes with only a single look. And this look held nothing but love.

Love and a promise.

Did you enjoy this book? I hope so!
Would you take a quick minute to leave a review?
http://www.amazon.com/dp/B011GC7VHA
It doesn't have to be long. Just a sentence or two telling what
you liked about the story!

About the Author

Misty M. Beller writes romantic mountain stories, set on the 1800s frontier and woven with the truth of God's love.

She was raised on a farm in South Carolina, so her Southern roots run deep. Growing up, her family was close, and they continue to keep that priority today. Her husband and children now add another dimension to her life, keeping her both grounded and crazy.

God has placed a desire in Misty's heart to combine her love for Christian fiction and the simpler ranch life, writing historical novels that display God's abundant love through the twists and turns in the lives of her characters.

Sign up for e-mail updates when future books are available!
www.MistyMBeller.com

Don't miss the other books by

Misty M. Beller

The Mountain Series
The Lady and the Mountain Man
The Lady and the Mountain Doctor
The Lady and the Mountain Fire
The Lady and the Mountain Promise
The Lady and the Mountain Call
This Treacherous Journey
This Wilderness Journey
This Freedom Journey (novella)
This Courageous Journey
This Homeward Journey
This Daring Journey
This Healing Journey

Texas Rancher Trilogy
The Rancher Takes a Cook
The Ranger Takes a Bride
The Rancher Takes a Cowgirl

Wyoming Mountain Tales
A Pony Express Romance
A Rocky Mountain Romance
A Sweetwater River Romance
A Mountain Christmas Romance

Hearts of Montana
Hope's Highest Mountain
Love's Mountain Quest
Faith's Mountain Home

Call of the Rockies
Freedom in the Mountain Wind
Hope in the Mountain River
Light in the Mountain Sky

CPSIA information can be obtained
at www.ICGtesting.com
Printed in the USA
LVHW050832130321
681184LV00006B/51

Wellness Coaching for
Lasting Lifestyle Change

Wellness Coaching for
Lasting Lifestyle Change

Michael Arloski, Ph.D., PCC

WHOLE PERSON ASSOCIATES
Duluth, Minnesota

Whole Person Associates, Inc.
210 West Michigan
Duluth, MN 55802-1908   218-727-0500
E-mail: books@wholeperson.com
Web site: http://www.wholeperson.com

Wellness Coaching for Lasting Lifestyle Change

Printed in the United States of America

10   9   8   7   6   5   4   3   2   1

Editors: Peg Johnson, Robin McAllister
Art Director: Joy Dey

Library of Congress Control Number: 2006940524
ISBN-13   978-1-57025-221-1
ISBN   1-57025-221-1

WHOLE PERSON ASSOCIATES
210 West Michigan
Duluth, MN 55802-1908

Contents

Chapter I

Toward a Psychology of Wellness 1

Chapter 2

Grounded In Wellness: Basic Wellness Principles . . 11

Chapter 7

Charting the Course of Change: Wellness Mapping 360° Part I 85

Chapter 8

Charting the Course of Change: Wellness Mapping 360° Part II. **117**

Chapter 9

Choosing, Living, Loving, Being: Coaching The Strategic, Lifestyle, Interpersonal, and Intrapersonal Aspects of Effective Change. . . 161

Chapter 10

Health and Medical Coaching—
Coaching People with Health Challenges 191

Chapter 11

Wellness Coaching In Action 213

Acknowledgements

Through the process of creating this book one concept emerged as paramount in importance . . . connectedness. This book happened because of not only my individual effort, but because of the connections to and with many others. In the present moment my wife, Deborah, has been, and remains a continual support both as my work partner, and my loving life partner. The love and support of family and friends and their continual efforts to maintain connection was also critical through this time.

As I wrote I felt like I was often casting nets back into my past to connect and draw to me learnings that I had experienced earlier and needed to remember now. I acknowledge all those learning gifts that I was given by clients, students, teachers, professors, colleagues, authors, and people I have met around the world.

I am very grateful for the experiences of encounter, gestalt, mind-body awareness and humanistic psychology that I gained at Bowling Green State University from psychologists Melvin Foulds and James Guinan. Those mind and heart-opening experiences helped equip me to connect with others better than I ever had. I also acknowledge a deep gratitude to John Mould, a student of Fritz Perls, my supervisor and mentor for years, who profoundly helped me deepen my psychotherapeutic skills.

Since 1979 I have also enjoyed a sustaining connection that has taken the form of belief in me and my work. John (Jack) Travis and Don Ardell, both pioneers in the wellness field, have continually been there with encouragement, professional stimulation and support. I am also grateful to The National Wellness Institute and Conference, their present staff and board, and their previous directors, Linda Newcomb and Linda Chapin, for their continued belief in me and my work. I also wish to thank Patrick Williams, founder of The Institute For Life

Coach Training, for the work we have done together and a wonderful friendship.

Lastly, I acknowledge the shaping and molding that my connections with those I have been especially close to has had over the years. Friends, loved ones, and especially my parents, Anna Merle Arloski, and Joseph John Arloski. I was very fortunate to never doubt their love for even one moment in my life. I dedicate this book to them and their memory.

—Michael Arloski, Ph.D., PCC
November, 2006

Prologue

On the steep hillside where I grew up in eastern Ohio, overlooking the Ohio River, I used to sit on a sandstone boulder and reflect. I would contemplate my young life, and enjoy the shade of the two hundred year old oak tree beside me. Being reflective has been a blessing and a curse all my life, but all in all it has served me well.

In the mid 1970s I began to reflect, as did many of us in the field of behavioral health, on the irony of a nation where the majority of health problems were preventable, and where abundance had spawned our greatest health challenges. We were gathering evidence and awareness that what not only was killing us, but limiting the length and quality of our lives was, in fact, our own choices. All around us we saw health risks being ignored and the consequences being suffered. Obesity, smoking, stress and other factors related to the way we, as a culture, were living were being discovered to be the deadly carriers of our collective "dis-ease".

The fledgling wellness field had begun to grow and capture a lot of excitement and imagination. In 1979 I attended my first National Wellness Conference at the University of Stevens Point, Wisconsin. There I was surrounded by other reflective souls who were not only wondering about these questions of irony and puzzlement, they were implementing ideas of what to do about it! In that wellness milieu I discovered a subculture of like-minded people who were not only studying wellness and lifestyle improvement as an academic subject, they were living it! Living well was, and is, fun!

A flood of health information began to pour forth about our lifestyles and ways to live healthier. You could hardly pick up a magazine or newspaper that didn't have an article about cholesterol or exercise in it. The jogging craze had become the running craze, more young people were backpacking and bicycling than ever before. The public became more and more savvy in the ways of wellness, yet, to our amazement, the health of our nation did not seem to improve that much.

The question for reflection that I have found the most fascinating and the most challenging, is this: *What keeps people from doing what they know they need to do for themselves?* Despite great health information there is still great struggle, for many people, in consistently making the real behavioral changes that create and maintain a healthier lifestyle.

As a behavioral scientist I thought I was a pretty easy teach. Just show me the data that indicates a health risk and I'll believe you and change my behavior to come in line with what is best for my health. Right? Well...that was easy in some areas of my life, and a lot more challenging in others. Exercising and eating right seemed no problem. Taking time to relax, be in nature and spend time with my family...no problem. Get my needs met in the most important intimate relationship in my life...that was a much greater challenge! There is no denying that living well means attending to every area of our lives, especially the ones that are not easy. From my own experience, and the experience of my colleagues, friends, students and clients, I saw that improving one's lifestyle was as much psychology as it was physiology.

My deep interest in biofeedback and behavioral health, as well as Eastern philosophy and spiritual practices, had shown me the potential of our own choices. Through the subtle processes of EEG, EMG and thermal biofeedback, meditative practices, etc., my colleagues and I, in many disciplines, saw how people could exercise influence on parts of the nervous system commonly held to be beyond our conscious control. Through effortless effort people could learn to slow their heart rate, lower their blood pressure, relax their muscles, and even dilate the blood vessels in their extremities. Surely we were discovering, or in some cases re-discovering, new and age-old secrets of how to truly gain conscious control of our lives.

Perhaps some of my interest in approaches that we use in the field of coaching today began in the behavioral medicine and stress-related disorders work that I did for two decades after graduate school. Like coaching, there was an emphasis on awareness, tracking, practicing various relaxation techniques, and reporting in to be held accountable for progress. The results were very measurable, and for the most part, extremely successful!

Clients who had experienced little, if any, success with conventional medicine were finally able to reduce or prevent their headaches, calm their digestive systems, conquer insomnia, minimize anxiety, and more. Central to the approach was educating clients about their challenges (many had no idea how a migraine headache came about or functioned, even after years of treatment) and empowering them to take charge of their own health. Seeing them tap into their own potential for self-regulation was extremely rewarding.

Working with individuals who were motivated to practice relaxation by the positive pay-off of pain reduction, increased sleep, and noticeable improvement in their lives was one thing. Helping people to adopt new behaviors and make it a regular part of their lifestyles was a bigger challenge. When I stepped beyond the treatment-oriented world of behavioral medicine and into the bigger world of wellness, the answers became much more elusive.

Inspired and educated by that 1979 wellness conference, our campus medical director and I brought the wellness concept to Miami University's campus in Oxford, Ohio. We focused on the residence hall system and introduced a health risk assessment and a wellness-environment residence hall program. I began teaching undergrad and graduate classes in wellness and soon began presenting regularly at The National Wellness Conference.

As anyone who works with campus wellness knows, combating the immortality mentality of undergraduates is challenging to say the least! Yet, by inspiring personal growth as well as personal responsibility, and fostering a residential environment with healthy, wellness-oriented norms, we experienced some success.

At the same time my love for the natural world helped me see the connections between lifestyle and environment. I began writing and presenting about the environmental dimension of wellness, helping people see how their own behavioral choices affected not only their own health, but the health of the planet. Contact with the natural world also has a positive effect on our mind, body and spirit. Nancy Rehe and I, at the urging of the president of the Global Tomorrow Coalition, founded a non-profit organization to further these environmental wellness goals.

My attraction to psychology, even as a freshman in college, had always been to the humanistic aspects of the field. The work of Abraham Maslow, Fritz Perls, Carl Rogers, Virginia Satir and others was my earliest draw to wellness as they wrote about self-actualization. In the mid-1990s I discovered that a whole new profession that embraced many of the principles of holism, self-actualization and human potential was developing. The field of personal and professional coaching was getting off the ground and I jumped on board.

Here was an approach to working with people that was about possibilities, not pathology. Here was an approach that held the client to be whole and complete, as they were, right before you. Here was an approach that fostered insight and integration, and then asked the client, "OK, so how can you apply that to your life?"

As I received training in coaching I enjoyed the differences between it and counseling. I saw the value of both, and will always be a powerful advocate of counseling and therapy when it is the method of choice, because I know it works. I deepened my work in coaching and became the Director of Wellness Coaching for The Institute For Life Coach Training.

The blending of wellness and coaching was a natural extension of who I am, and who I had become. For all of our efforts at influencing groups to become healthier through influencing their norms, through wellness education, through incentives and promotions, we saw some success, but many in the wellness and healthcare fields felt disappointment.

Today, with the outrageous (but unfortunately accurate) statistics telling us of epidemic levels of obesity, diabetes, heart disease, and more, combined with the once-again increasing costs of healthcare, solutions are desperately sought. Perhaps the time has come to work on wellness one person at a time.

Wellness professionals are not typically educated in all the interpersonal skills that it takes to work one-on-one. Counselors and others who begin training in the field of coaching may be familiar with holistic health, but are usually not aware of the principles and methods of lifestyle change developed by the wellness profession/industry.

Fritz Perls loved to play on the words of Sigmund Freud about dreams. Freud said that dreams were the "royal road to the unconscious." Perls liked to say that dreams were the "royal road to integration." Perhaps our dream here is one of integration. Perhaps our dream is to develop a new profession that integrates the best of wellness and coaching. Perhaps our dream is to develop qualified professionals who can be the allies that people have long needed to make lasting lifestyle behavioral change.

Introduction

Imagine you are a person who is ready to change your life. Imagine that you want to feel fulfilled in some areas that now seem wanting, or even empty. While certain dimensions of your life are satisfying, even rich, others are a source of frustration at best, and increasing illness and loss at worst.

Imagine that you have expended, over the years, great energy to change and to grow. You have succeeded in some areas but other areas feel like boggy swamps where your progress is like walking knee-to thigh-deep in failure, sadness, regret and perhaps even self-loathing.

Others have tried to help. At times you reached out to them and got information and treatment that kept you going. They may have given you all manner of advice and criticism while imploring and cheering you on. All the motivation seemed based on their own agendas for your life. Despite their efforts, and yours to work with them, you once again feel like you are essentially alone and still bogged down in that swamp.

Now imagine that you begin talking with someone who approaches the process of helping you in an entirely different way. They listen to you—truly listen—not just waiting for their turn to talk. You feel they hear and understand you. Rather than stand above you they stand beside you and with you as an ally. Their agenda is your agenda.

This person does not live with you or work with you, they work for you. You employ them to help you find your way through that swamp that impedes your progress. They require you to look into yourself, to acknowledge your strengths and build upon them in order to confront your fears. They ask questions not so much to gain information, as to require you to seek answers from within yourself, to benefit yourself.

They come equipped with tools that help you take stock of your life and with effective methods for change. They acknowledge that you are ready to make those changes and they ask your permission to delve deeper and push you further. You are treated with respect and compassion, while you are confronted and challenged to do your best. When you make a commitment for action, they help you hold yourself accountable so that you will accomplish your goals in the time frame you allocate.

This person goes beyond gathering information and stresses motivation, helping you find within yourself the motivation needed to initiate, sustain and maintain change. They are there to celebrate your success with you. They are your coach.

Lifestyle Change

Over half of what affects your health is your choice of lifestyle. The way you live your life largely determines the level of health with which you get to experience your life. Perhaps this awareness comes slowly, over years of self-awareness and learning about health and wellness and perhaps it comes quickly, in that teachable moment when you receive a diagnosis or in some way encountered a health challenge.

Most of us have had the experience of being diagnosed and treated or have been to a health-educator who implored us to change our lifestyle behavior. This often magnifies our problems and our own sense of failure. These solitary efforts at change are not easy. To quote Pat Williams, the founder of the Institute for Life Coach Training, "If you could have done it by yourself, you probably would have done it by now." There is the growing awareness that people need an ally to work with, and that wellness is a very individual and personal issue.

Worldwide there is tremendous interest in living happier, healthier lifestyles. Wellness products and services are among the fastest growing economic areas. People are fascinated with spas and magazines that promote living a more simple and healthy lifestyle. The popularity of classes in yoga, Pilates, Tai-Chi, and related methods are at an all-time high. Restaurant menus offer more healthy, lower-carbohydrate, lower-fat, and vegetarian options. Paul Zane Pilzer's book *The Wellness Revolution*, calls wellness "the next trillion-dollar industry."

Simultaneous with this vigorous interest in wellness is our awareness that the cost of healthcare, in the United States in particular, is spiraling out of sight. Managed care momentarily reduced healthcare costs for employers by restricting access to needed healthcare. It did nothing to increase wellness. Now, statistically, we are seeing the resumption of the same trajectory of healthcare cost increases. The 2004 and 2005 surveys of the CEOs of America's Fortune 500 Companies revealed that the number one threat to company profitability is healthcare costs. As automaker giant General Motors struggles and lays off record numbers of employees, healthcare costs add about $1,300 to the cost of every car and truck GM makes in the United States.

If, as we believe in the healthcare and wellness fields, over half of what determines our health is lifestyle choices, then implementing effective ways of changing lifestyle behavior is paramount. Millions of people are interested in improving their overall wellness.

Yet, more and better health information is not enough. Spending a day or a week at a spa, while enjoyable and perhaps even helpful, does not usually effect a lasting change in lifestyle habits. The process of changing human behavior is complex. Slowly, we are looking to those who have studied human behavior, lifestyle and wellness, for the answers. Many effective methods have been discovered and now they need to be implemented so more people can enjoy better lives.

Coaching

The field of personal and professional coaching is well established and is growing worldwide. The International Coaching Federation, which sets standards of certification, provides professional development and education in the field, holds annual conferences in the United States, Europe and Australia/Asia. Coaches now work with business executives, managers, small business owners and entrepreneurs, career professionals, artists, parents, students, families, and more to help fulfill a wide variety of missions and objectives. The coach approach has been found valuable not only to one's business and career, but to develop leadership, deepen character, and help people become the architects of healthy, rewarding lives.

Drawing upon the roots of counseling and psychotherapy, management and human development, the coaching profession saw rapid growth in the early 1990s. (For an excellent review see "The History and Evolution of Life Coaching," chapter two, in *Therapist As Life Coach* by Williams and Davis). What evolved was a realization that much of the work being done in coaching was life coaching. Often one's effectiveness and success at work stemmed not from knowing how to do the job better, but from working with the person's belief systems (especially beliefs about themselves), their interpersonal relationships, and their way of living—their lifestyle.

People found that having an ally who could engage them in possibility thinking, hold them accountable to complete their plans and challenge them to be their very best resulted in real growth, real movement, and often, career/business success as well.

As a coaching and wellness professional, I saw the natural fit and the alliance that needed to be created between the fields. It was like knowing two very different people in a small town who cared deeply—passionately—about the same area of interest, but who would walk obliviously past each other day after day. It seemed obvious to everyone else that they would have a great deal to give to each other. I saw the connections and similarity and have worked to introduce wellness to coaching.

Coaching, at its very foundation, is wellness oriented. Coaching holds the client to be a whole individual, responsible for his or her own choices. According to the Coaches Training Institute, "coaching is a powerful alliance designed to forward and enhance the lifelong process of human learning, effectiveness, and fulfillment." Work is done looking at the client's entire life.

As I wrote about wellness coaching and began presenting about the subject, I discovered a few pioneers out there who, like me, had a long-time interest and/or background in health and wellness, and were purposely applying the skills of coaching to helping people with health and lifestyle goals. The fledgling specialty of wellness coaching had taken flight.

Taking Wellness One-On-One

I regularly found myself talking with health educators, nurses, and various wellness professionals who were becoming discouraged at the ineffectiveness of their efforts to help people live more wellness-oriented lifestyles. The nurses would say "I tell them exactly what they need to do, and they (the clients/patients) don't do it!" The health educators would add "We do great programs in health promotion and have wonderful facilities available, yet so many of the people who really need to use the facilities and make changes in their lives never do!"

These wellness professionals also talk about how, increasingly, they were being asked to work individually with employees who were at high health risk. They found that the same prescribe and treat and educate and implore methods they used with large groups showed little or, at best, sporadic success. Their years of professional schooling and training had never included the training in interpersonal skills that are needed when working one-on-one.

Discovering coaching skills, for these professionals, was a true deliverance. Even health professionals whose contact with clients was limited to fifteen minutes at a time found tremendous value in applying the skills of coaching to their work.

Today wellness coaching is finding application in hospitals, clinical practices, company wellness programs, retreat centers, spas and with the individual consumer. In the larger picture there is a shift occurring towards individualizing wellness. Using sophisticated wellness assessments and possessing improved one-on-one skills helps us create realistic wellness plans for individuals. We are better able to serve the health and well being of people who want (and often need) to benefit from lifestyle improvement.

I think we are on the verge of a major
paradigm shift in promoting health and wellness driven
by coaching. Coaching provides a positive connection—a
supportive relationship—between the coach and the person
who wants to make a change. That connection empowers
the person being coached to recognize and draw on his or
her own innate ability and resources to make lasting
changes for better health and well-being.

—Anne Helmke
Member Services Team Leader
National Wellness Institute, Stevens Point, WI

Mapping The Course

The intention of this book is to create a resource that helps people create lasting lifestyle change through the process of wellness coaching. While there will be some lifestyle improvement information contained in this work, the emphasis is not how to be well, but rather on how to work as a professional ally with people who do want to be well.

As in any journey, we want to begin by becoming well-oriented and well-grounded in where we are, who we are, and what we want to do. We will begin with a foundation in some of the best theoretical concepts about how people change their behavior. This is based on the humanistic contributions of Abraham Maslow and adapted to use in wellness coaching.

We will then ground ourselves in an understanding of the wellness principles essential to working with lifestyle improvement. Drawing upon some of the classic contributions of pioneers and leaders in the wellness field will prepare you to venture further into the integration of wellness and coaching.

The trend is moving toward the individualization of wellness and the current models for wellness work are shifting. In applying the coach approach to the wellness field, you will discover a process for taking wellness one-on-one and the benefits of acquiring such skills.

Then it is time to lift your pack, put on your walking shoes, roll up your sleeves and begin your exploration of just what wellness coaching is, what skills are involved, how to learn them, and how to use them. We will thoroughly cover these skills and provide you with tools and resources for further learning and your application of what you have learned.

From this new vista, further down the trail, we'll look out at how the field of wellness coaching is being applied by fellow travelers who are out there contributing to the field and helping people around the world to be well.

This journey doesn't have an "X" on the map where the trail ends, instead, we'll take a good look at what lies ahead and do our best to speculate on what might be around the next bend, or at least, what we'd love to see there.

Happy trails!

Chapter 1

Toward a Psychology of Wellness

If you have built castles in the air your work
need not be lost; that is where they should be.
Now put the foundations under them.

—Henry David Thoreau

The lifework of psychologist Abraham Maslow, was in many ways, the foundation that allowed the concept of wellness to be built. The cornerstone was the posit that human beings have within them an "inner nature" that is continually striving in a positive way to actualize their true potential. Early on in *Toward A Psychology Of Being,* 1962, Maslow outlined principles of self-actualization theory that sound like the predecessors of modern behavioral medicine. He spoke of the importance of encouraging this inner nature, this essential core of the person to guide our lives, thus allowing us to "grow healthy, fruitful, and happy." (p. 4) If denied or suppressed, the lack of expression of this inner nature, he argued, leads to sickness.

Just as we see the striving of individuals towards healthier wellness lifestyles, we see this inner striving for the maximization of potential in action. Even the challenges that people face, in their efforts to be well, are addressed by Maslow. "This inner nature is not strong and overpowering and unmistakable like the instincts of animals. It is weak and delicate and subtle and easily overcome by habit, cultural pressure, and wrong attitudes towards it." (p. 4) When we look at behavioral lifestyle change, the challenges of habit, peer health group norms and cognitive structures resemble closely what Maslow referenced.

1

So much of the discouragement in people's attempts at lifestyle change could be lessened if we saw the structure inside all of us that cheers on healthy behavior as more delicate and subtle. While he described it as weak, Maslow goes on to say that it "rarely disappears in the normal person—perhaps not even in the sick person. Even though denied, it persists underground forever pressing for actualization." (p. 4)

Inside all of us is this fragile warrior or warrioress for good. Though easily beaten down by greater odds, it always re-emerges to pull us back on course towards health and well-being just as surely as we strive to align our eyes level with the horizon.

Abraham Maslow was not one to deny the realities of this world or sugarcoat our human history. The oldest of seven children born to Russian Jewish parents who immigrated to the United States around the beginning of the twentieth century, Maslow knew a hard life growing up in Brooklyn, New York. Urged by his parents to seek a better life through education, Abraham eventually got his doctorate in psychology. Working under Kurt Goldstein, he was introduced to the concept of self-actualization, which he developed into one of the quintessential theories of human motivation.

Maslow saw that our suffering and challenges serve to bring out greater strengths. He spoke of the "necessity of discipline, deprivation, frustration, pain, and tragedy. To the extent that these experiences reveal and foster and fulfill our inner nature, to that extent they are desirable experiences . . . The person who hasn't conquered, withstood and overcome continues to feel doubtful that he could." (p.4)

Sometimes called the father of American Humanism, Maslow inspired other famous leaders in psychology to develop therapeutic methods and approaches to self-actualization that founded the human potential movement. People like Carl Rogers, Virginia Satir and Frederick Perls grounded much of their work in Maslow's principals. Much of the groundwork for today's therapeutic, counseling and coaching methodologies are rooted in these contributions.

A key part of the human potential movement was the body-mind or whole-person approach to human behavior. It became more and more apparent that self-actualization was not just an intellectual or cognitive activity. Mind, body, spirit and environment were all considered in the equation that eventually manifested itself in people looking for ways to improve the quality of their lives—their lifestyle.

In the mid to late 1970s all of this combined with increasing evidence and awareness that how we live our lives is a huge determinant of not only our happiness and well-being, but also of our physical health. John W. Travis, M.D. and Don Ardell, Ph.D. began writing about the concept of wellness in ways that helped us all question our lifestyle status quo, and increase our conscious awareness.

In the years since then, we have seen the field of wellness go through a slow, but steady, metamorphosis. The field revolved through focus on health-risk reduction, peer health norms, reducing health-care costs, physical fitness, diet, stress management, and other facets of lifestyle. Wellness has now come full circle, exploring all aspects of being well.

The wellness continuum that Travis developed positions the field of wellness with an eventual goal of self-actualization. As Travis states in *The Wellness Workbook,* 3rd Ed. "The Illness-Wellness Continuum . . . was a melding of the health risk continuum created by Lewis Robbins, MD, MPH (founder of the Health Risk Appraisal) and Abraham Maslow's concept of self-actualization." (Travis, p. xix)

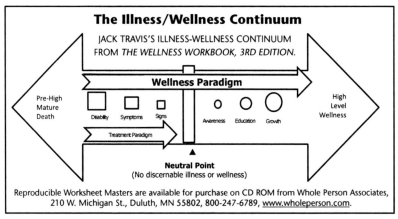

FIGURE 1.1

Don Ardell refers to this as high level wellness and contends, like Travis, that health is not the mere absence of illness, but a continual striving to live a life that is full, meaningful, zestful and exuberant. (Ardell, p. 7)

> **The eventual goal of wellness** is the actualization of one's true psychophysical/spiritual potential. Wellness is Maslow's notion of self-actualization, carried to its natural extension as growth towards the full integration of mind, body, spirit and environment.

This end point is not really an end. It is not perfection. Better than a continuum in this case is a spiral model, continually cycling through the ebb and flow of life towards higher levels of wellness.

> *Self-actualization is the intrinsic growth of what is already in the organism, or more accurately, of what the organism is.*
>
> —Abraham Maslow

Deficiency Needs/Being Needs

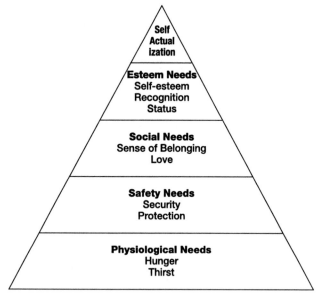

FIGURE 1.2

When we look at Maslow's hierarchy of needs, FIGURE 1.2, through a wellness lens, we see some very familiar terms. Each of his levels of needs correlate with principles most wellness theorists value also.

Maslow's Term	Correlating Wellness Term
Self-actualization	High Level Wellness
Esteem Needs	Adequate Self-esteem
Belonging Needs	Inclusion/Community/Peer Health Norms/Spiritual
Safety Needs	Community/Family/Self-sufficiency
Physiological Needs	Nutrition/Movement/Breathing

Deficiency Needs

Maslow held that part of being a living organism was that our deficiency needs took precedent in our motivation for behavior. Building from a physiological base, we have to survive first and breathing, drinking, and eating always will come first. When deficiency needs are not met we do not function well, and we eventually become ill or die. This applies not only to the obvious situations of suffocation, dehydration and starvation, but also to the somewhat higher (yet still deficiency-based) needs of safety, belongingness, and esteem. When these needs are not met, Maslow argued, we see the rise of psychopathology.

Aberrant behavior and neurosis comes from unmet needs. Using the term illness in both the physical and mental sense he saw a need as a deficiency need, as a basic need or instinct if:

1. Its absence breeds illness
2. Its presence prevents illness
3. Its restoration cures illness
4. Under certain (very complex) free choice situations, it is preferred by the deprived person over other satisfactions
5. It is found to be inactive, at a low ebb, or functionally absent in the healthy person

When we look at the lifestyle of a person we see aspects of it that work their way up through the entire needs triangle. When someone attempts to improve their lifestyle they attempt to meet these needs increasingly effective ways.

Let's use eating as an example. We can eat a very inadequate diet and survive. Sometimes we have to, sometimes it is all we know, and sometimes we know better, yet we eat in ways that don't really serve our health well. The physical need is being met, but, in the long run, how healthy is the way it is being met? Is it really working for us?

Another example would be movement. The human body was born to move! Exercise physiologists and personal trainers will be quick to tell you that it is our lack of movement (or our repetitive isolated and limited movements) that get us in trouble. We literally have a need to move! Our modern world's increasingly sedentary lifestyle is now seen as one of our greatest health risks.

We can take any one of these needs, which all correlate with some dimension of wellness, and overlay them onto the Illness/Wellness Continuum.

When we coach someone towards higher levels of wellness we are, in fact, helping them discover increasingly effective ways of getting their basic needs met. Thomas Leonard, the founder of Coach University and one of the pioneers of the coaching movement, often exhorted coaches to help their clients to do two things: eliminate tolerations from their lives, and meet their needs. Leonard believed that people who acknowledge their wide range of needs and consciously go about meeting them here and now (not waiting until after retirement, etc.), are happier, healthier and more successful.

Being Needs

As renowned lecturer Leo Buscallia reminds us, it's important to be a "human being" instead of a "human doing"! When we feel sated, safe, included, good about ourselves, etc. what is next? Fortunately the field of wellness has long recognized that being truly well is not just about doing OK, or just getting by, but rather, about maximizing human potential.

As seen in Figure 1.3, we can take any dimension of wellness into the realm of being needs where we are engaged in a behavior not just to meet needs, but for higher purposes. We dance because we like to, because it is an expression of who we are. We cast flies to trout, or chuck pork-rind to bass, not just to bring fish home to eat, but for many other reasons, perhaps even to relax to the point where we are actually meditating. (Shhhh! Don't let that secret out!)

Some of our behavior is overtly purposed to explore the spiritual, to transcend our everyday existence, and seek connection with something greater than we are. The monk or nun comes easily to mind, but to one degree or another, this is a realm that we all explore in our own way, in our own time.

Indeed, we see Jack Travis' Wellness Energy System model and Wellness Wheel containing twelve dimensions of wellness, two of them being "Transcending" and "Finding Meaning." Much of the writing of Don Ardell in recent years has focused on the vital nature of finding meaning and purpose in our lives, and how central this is to our own pursuit of higher levels of wellness.

Maslow believed that we naturally seek growth, that it is, given the satiation of the deficiency needs, as powerful as the force that turns barren land eventually into climax forest. This point of view sees humankind as naturally good, and given the right environmental support, continually drawn toward the light.

Keys To Wellness

Maslow was, however, quick to point out that our movement towards growth is not so simple. Here the field of wellness and the field of coaching need to study his writings. If growth is so wonderful what holds people back? What keeps us from progressing smoothly to higher levels of growth and wellness? Why is the growth process often painful?

This is where Maslow reminds us of the power of unmet deficiency needs, "of the attractions of safety and security, of the functions of defense and protection against pain, fear, loss and threat and of the need for courage in order to grow ahead." (p. 46)

Inside us are two sets of forces, one that clings to safety and defensiveness out of fear, and one that urges us towards wholeness and full expression of our true selves.

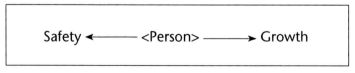

Safety ◄——— <Person> ———► Growth

(MASLOW, P. 46)

7

One part of us is afraid to take chances, afraid to bother the status quo, afraid to move! Another part is driven by a nagging sense of feeling unfulfilled, that our lives will be incomplete unless we express ourselves in some important (to us) way.

In cognitive psychology and in coaching, we often talk about the effect of the inner critic or gremlin on our lives. Here is the continual advocate for safety and the status quo. Here is fear personified, in the sense of the things we say to ourselves that hold us back.

This fear, this need for safety, is not a rational fear—that kind of need for safety we might simply call good judgment. Standing a hundred feet above a lake we might conclude "The cliff is too high above the water, I'm not jumping off!" That is rational fear. The kind of fear our inner critic arouses is based on "False Evidence Appearing Real."

There are certainly attractions to hold to the *status quo*, or even regress when we are under stress. The couch beckons when we are lethargic, not only when we are fatigued. What tastes better than salty, greasy and sweet? Maslow goes on to acknowledge that beyond simple need-reduction there is a hedonic factor. Empty calories taste good!

Knowingly or not, we have been employing some of Maslow's theories in our wellness promotion efforts over the years. When he recommends what we see in Figure 1.3, we can see how this schema has been advocated.

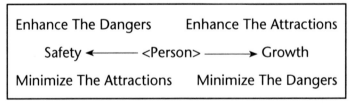

FIGURE 1.3 (MASLOW, P. 47)

Health education efforts have exposed the dangers of smoking, sedentary living, etc. Public health efforts have made smoking in public places sometimes inconvenient, and sometimes illegal! We have attempted to enhance the dangers and minimize the attractions of unhealthy behaviors. We have also done our best to make wellness more attractive and appear less dangerous. Yet Maslow says, "safety needs are pre-potent over growth needs." (p. 47)

He notes that "growth forward customarily takes place in little steps, and each step forward is made possible by the feeling of being safe, of operating out into the unknown from a safe home port, of daring because retreat is possible." (p. 47) Yet, what of the outstanding individuals who risk it all, who truly jump from the eagle's nest on untried wings, fall like a stone, and then soar? What conditions need to be present for such risk taking? Of what does that home port need to be composed psychologically?

Being Centered

Let's borrow a metaphor from the martial arts. Perhaps the home port is equivalent to being centered. Being centered is not just a matter of working our internal gyroscope until we are in physical balance. That might be step number one, but there is much more.

When martial artists assume a physically centered stance, they must also center themselves mentally. They do so by focusing on a spot just below the naval, but mid-way between back and belly. They focus on their breath and its rhythm. Their eyes take in their whole field of view at once. On a less conscious but extremely important level they tap into the confidence they have in what they have learned about how to move. They are confident they can move to defend themselves. They feel connected to their vital energy system (the same energy system science has verified through the study of acupuncture, etc.). Their body has been programmed with a set of movements and responses. They know what they can do and have confidence in it. If they are, in fact, a highly skilled martial artist, in the middle of all of this, they are able to relax and move out of conscious awareness.

If they achieve this centered state there is no room for fear. If they let fear creep in, even in the form of expectation of outcome or assumptions of any kind, their probability of remaining safe decreases.

In the much more expansive experience of living our daily lives, rather than meeting a specific physical challenge, how can we apply this notion of being centered, and how do we need to expand it? By exploring what it means for each of us to be centered in our lives we discover what allows us to feel safe enough to grow and move forward towards self-actualization and high-level wellness.

When we consciously seek to meet our needs, when we live our lives in balance, and are true to ourselves, we create that centered life, that safe home port from which to venture out. Clearly much of our most significant growth comes from that venturing out into the unknown. The goal of a life in balance does not mean anxiously attempting to even out everything in our existence. Perhaps living in balance is what allows us to risk, to go the extra mile, to reach summits we never thought we could climb.

The part of us that clings to the safety end of Maslow's continuum can masquerade as a real wellness lifestyle advocate. Under the guise of "balance" it can cause us to walk on eggshells, fearful of not getting enough sleep, of getting hurt or of missing a meal, when the risks are really not that great. Indeed much of our growth comes from experiences on that uncomfortable edge where growth really happens. Real growth may occur when we take the risk of assertively saying no to an unreasonable demand; by pushing through exhaustion and finishing a canoe portage; by steadfastly facing a fear with a loved one; by reaching down deep enough to learn the courage we actually do possess.

Abraham Maslow took on the daunting task of presenting a new theory of human motivation. As challenging as that was, he was up to the task. Here we are considering a less pervasive explanation of human behavior. Perhaps in looking at how can we help people feel safe enough to grow we will find answers to our vexing question about why people don't do what they know they need to do for themselves.

I am convinced that much of what we now call psychology is the study of the tricks we use to avoid the anxiety of absolute novelty by making believe the future will be like the past.

—**Abraham Maslow,** *Toward A Psychology of Being*

Chapter 2

Grounded In Wellness: Basic Wellness Principles

The concept of total wellness recognizes that our every thought, word and behavior affects our greater health and well-being. And we, in turn, are affected not only emotionally but also physically and spiritually.

—Greg Anderson

There is a maxim that says if you really want to learn something, teach it! I've certainly found this adage to be true. Through the years I have taught graduate and undergraduate courses on wellness, lead workshops and retreats, made presentations on wellness and coaching skills, and taught classes about wellness coaching. I've found it essential to help students of all kinds to begin with a solid foundation in what wellness really is, and I've learned from them what is needed.

There is great confusion and even disparity about what wellness is and what the term means. In my wellness coaching classes I found that most students thought they knew what wellness was—and some did. Others knew a lot about holistic health, but little about wellness. Even the wellness professionals in my classes often lacked some of the basic long-accepted concepts vital to an understanding of wellness.

When I keynoted the ISPA-Europe Conference (International Spa Association) I was amazed to talk with so many people who felt they were working in the center of the wellness field, yet had never heard of many of the authors and organizations that I thought were as central to wellness as Freud is to psychiatry.

A physician at the same conference delivered an excellent Power Point presentation entitled "What is Wellness?" Noting his own incredulity, he showed a slide featuring a German wellness product—Wellness-brand horse hoof balm! Using this balm on the hooves of a horse purported to prevent splitting of the hooves, so I guess that made it a wellness product. Any product that assists a person or an animal to become well can, evidently, be called a wellness product.

Indeed, the toothpaste is out of the tube on defining wellness, and we are never getting it back in. That gives all the more reason to present here some basic principles and concepts that the profession of wellness has developed over the last thirty-five years or so.

What Is Wellness?

The Elusive Definition

In 2004, psychologist Judd Allen, Ph.D., a board member of the National Wellness Institute, surveyed a number of experts in the wellness field to get input regarding a definition of wellness. From that survey he concluded that there appears to be general agreement that:

- Wellness is a conscious, self-directed and evolving process of achieving full potential.
- Wellness is multi-dimensional and holistic (encompassing such factors as lifestyle, mental and spiritual well-being and the environment).
- Wellness is positive and affirming.

It is difficult to differentiate wellness from other disciplines, because wellness can be useful in nearly every human endeavor. Wellness is being applied in related fields, such as health promotion and holistic health. We can assess the degree to which wellness is incorporated into a particular approach or program by asking:

- Does this help people achieve their full potential?
- Does this recognize and address the whole person in all of

his or her dimensions?

- Does this affirm and mobilize people's positive qualities and strengths?

Allen stated "We [The National Wellness Institute] have adopted the following definition: Wellness is a process of becoming aware of and making choices toward a more successful existence."

This definition agrees with the input received in the survey's responses from experts in the field of wellness. Some of the survey remarks are below:

- Wellness is a choice, a way of life, a process, an efficient channeling of energy, an integration of mind, body, spirit and a loving acceptance of self. —John Travis

- What are the defining characteristics of wellness? Key components for me include: recognition of the holistic nature of health and wellness; a focus on optimal wellbeing for each individual; attention to and integration of many dimensions of health and wellbeing; individual and community responsibility for 'choosing' to be healthy and the creation and maintenance of healthy environments; and encouraging and supporting others in the pursuit of high-level wellness. Wellness is not focused on the diagnosis and treatment of illness; rather, the goal is helping each individual and community achieve the highest level of health possible. Figuring out how to motivate people to change their behaviors and engage in long-lasting healthy behavior patterns is a crucial and perhaps unique dimension of the wellness effort.—Dennis Elsenrath

- It is a positive approach that implies self motivated action. It implies the application of knowledge and information. Facts alone do not lead to a wellness life.—Bill Hetler

- Being all that you can be. Should we use a phrase that has been worn out by the U.S. Military? Even if it works perfectly? Probably not. Somewhere between self-actualization and Being All That You Can Be must lay a phrase that will say the same thing but be at least somewhat unique.— Irv Moore

- The defining characteristics of a wellness lifestyle/mindset are a strong sense of personal responsibility, exceptional physical fitness due to a disciplined commitment to regular/vigorous exercise and sound diet, a positive outlook and a devotion to and capacity for critical thinking, joy in life and openness to new discoveries about the meaning and purposes of life.—Don Ardell

Wellness is the experience of living life with high levels of awareness, conscious choice, self-acceptance, interconnectedness, love, meaning and purpose. Wellness is the individual's life journey (and our society's larger task) of taking Abraham Maslow's concept of Self-Actualization and applying it to mind, body, spirit and our interconnectedness with other people and our environment.

Defining Wellness Coaching

Psychology is the study of behavior. Psychotherapy is the process of applying the principles of psychology to help people change their behavior. Likewise we might say that wellness is everything about living well in a very conscious way. Wellness programming and wellness coaching are about helping people to improve their lifestyle behavior.

Wellness coaching is a very new field. As it emerges and the world discovers the value of it, it will continue to define and re-define itself. What is clear is that wellness coaching is the application of the principles and processes of professional life coaching to the goals of lifestyle improvement for higher levels of wellness. It is an alliance between a professional coach and a person (or persons) who, through the benefit of that relationship, seeks lasting, lifestyle behavioral change.

Taking Stock

One of the simplest ways to get an overall picture of a person's wellness is to simply ask them to rate their level of satisfaction in each of several areas of their life. Most people can give you (and themselves) a fairly accurate picture of the overall picture of wellness this way.

. . . the preventative posture is defensive and largely reactive. That is, it is designed to protect you against illness or disease; wellness, on the other hand, achieves the same end by advocating health enrichment, or health promotion, and life enhancement.

—Don Ardell, *High Level Wellness*

The Wheel of Life

As you look at the lines that you have drawn across each area of wellness in your life, imagine that the rim of the wheel is no longer the outer line of the circle itself, but this new set of lines now forms the new rim of your wheel of life. How well does your wheel roll?

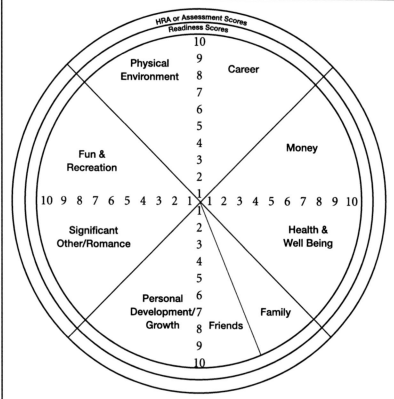

The Wheel of Life in Coaching

- Rank your level of satisfaction in each area of your life.
- The closer you are to 10, the more fulfilled you feel. Once you have marked your number in each area, connect each number forming a new outside perimeter for your circle.
- How smooth or bumpy is your life?
- Are there areas of your life that need attention?
- What areas of your life are you willing to address now, soon, later?

Reproducible Worksheet Masters are available for purchase on CD ROM from Whole Person Associates, 210 W. Michigan St., Duluth, MN 55802, 800-247-6789, www.wholeperson.com.

FIGURE 2.1

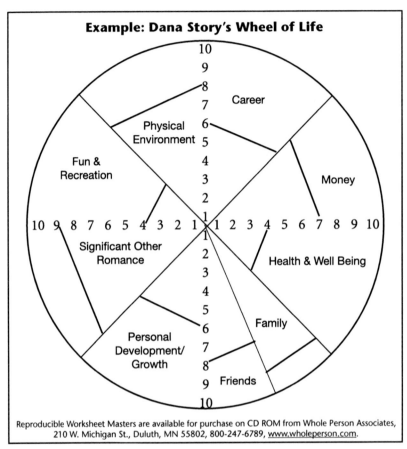

Example: Dana Story's Wheel of Life

Reproducible Worksheet Masters are available for purchase on CD ROM from Whole Person Associates, 210 W. Michigan St., Duluth, MN 55802, 800-247-6789, www.wholeperson.com.

FIGURE 2.2

The nine sections in the Wheel of Life represent balance. Dana Story ranked her level of satisfaction in each life area by marking the number and drawing a line in each section to create a new outer edge of the wheel. The new perimeter of the circle represents her actual Wheel of Life. How bumpy would the ride be if this were a real wheel?

The satisfaction rating, 1-10, in each area reflects the level of *fulfillment* in that area. The shape of the new wheel, with it's new rim, represents *balance* in life. Both are important. I once had a workshop participant ask, "Well I've put down a five in everything, so my wheel rolls just fine! Is that good?" After a room full of laughter settled down, I responded that while he seemed to understand balance, that the fulfillment piece showed need of some work!

Don Ardell likes to say that while we seek "high level wellness," which is much preferable to "low-level worseness," we should never settle for "mid-level mediocrity."

COACHING NOTE

This straightforward Wheel of Life exercise can effectively get a person started on the foundational task of taking stock of their own wellness picture. As a coach you can use this to initiate conversations with prospective clients and to form part of the initial, foundational work you do with your clients.

The Illness/Wellness Continuum

As we saw earlier, the goals of high level wellness and self-actualization are at one end of this continuum, and premature death at the other extreme. There is much more to be gained by a thorough understanding of the Illness/Wellness Continuum.

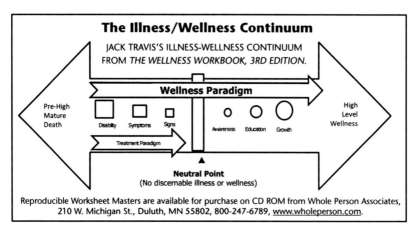

FIGURE 2.3

Wellness is not simply the lack of a disease process or simply the absence of illness. Just as there are degrees of illness, there are degrees of wellness. Wellness, like the way Maslow speaks of self-actualization, is not a static state. It may be counter-theoretical; in fact, to speak in terms of being able to pinpoint one's level of wellness, for it is a fluid, ever-changing process rather than a score or end state.

As we see in the treatment paradigm, however, it is clear that treatment is finished when the person reaches a state of no discernable illness. Treatment is complete and the person usually no longer receives any more services.

Wellness may, at times, actually come into the picture before treatment is finished. There is overlap here more than a quick glance at the model might reveal. For example we are finding great benefit in pre- and post-surgical health education, as well as in pre- and post-birth education. The processes of awareness, education, and growth may, in fact, begin before treatment is finished. Among these processes we would include wellness coaching.

Travis and Regina Ryan (co-authors of *The Wellness Workbook*) realized that it is important to also apply the continuum to include those individuals facing health challenges. They readily admit the limitations of a one-dimensional model and now contend that the key factor may not be where a person is physically on the continuum (they could be physically disabled, sick or even in the process of dying), but *which way are they facing*. Are they facing towards high-level wellness with a healthy, positive attitude and a rich spiritual life, or are they facing towards premature death. In this vein, a physically fit marathon winner could be facing premature death, if that person experienced extreme anxiety and strivings for perfection.

> *The good life is a process, not a state of being.*
> *It is a direction not a destination.*
>
> —**Carl Rogers,** *On Becoming A Person*

Dimensions of Wellness:
Models, Models, Models

The most common misconception about wellness is that it is physical fitness alone, or perhaps physical fitness coupled with nutritional awareness. Diet and exercise/wellness brochures showing pictures of people on treadmills or eating healthy food are mostly what we see.

Wellness (like coaching) is about the whole person and all aspects of their lives. While physical fitness and nutrition are very important, they are only two of the dimensions of wellness. The paradox of any holistic concept is that to be inclusive enough, and to really understand it, we usually have to break it down into its component parts. The gestalt maxim that the whole is greater than the sum of its parts is quite true. Every aspect of our lives affects every other part. An emotional conflict at home will affect our day at work and may even contribute to a headache or some such symptom showing up. An improvement in our diet may result in more sustainable energy all day long, or a better night's sleep.

To ground you in some dimensional models of wellness we have included three of the best known.

Ardell's Model

At the core of Don Ardell's model is *self-responsibility*. As we will explore later in more detail, *you* are primarily responsible for your own health. In his ground-breaking 1977 book, *High Level Wellness: An Alternative to Doctors, Drugs and Disease*, Ardell contends that "The single greatest cause of unhealth in this nation is that most Americans neglect, and surrender to others, responsibility for their own health." (p. 102) Ardell emphasizes that taking personal responsibility for our *choices* is critical in every aspect of our lives. Taking responsibility for our feelings, what we say to ourselves and where we are in our lives is also seen as key to this, and points the way to more effective methods to motivate ourselves to pursue and maintain a more wellness-oriented lifestyle.

Ardell's Model

Self-responsibility
Nutritional Awareness
Stress Management
Physical Fitness
Environmental Sensitivity

FIGURE 2.4

The dimensions of physical fitness, stress management and nutritional awareness are forthright enough, but a word needs to be said

19

about environmental sensitivity. The environment in which we live can either enhance or limit our health and well-being. Ardell sees environmental sensitivity as having three aspects: physical, social and personal. This covers many influences in our lives, from pollution and toxins in our air, water, soil, home and work interiors, and the ergonomics of our workstations.

There are the negative factors that weigh in like noise pollution and heavy metals in drinking water. However there are also ways to affect and interact with our environment to enhance our wellness. Personal growth through contact with the natural world has been the keystone of many organizations developing tomorrow's leaders. From corporate leadership retreats, Outward Bound classes, scouting, and spa nature programs, to spiritual retreats and Native American vision quests, reconnecting with nature is seen as a way to deepen our sense of self and to develop character and purpose. Consciously creating home and work environments that sooth instead of stress the body and mind also contribute to our higher levels of wellness.

COACHING NOTE

Using Ardell's Model in Wellness Coaching

Ardell's tenet of self-responsibility is a concept key to coaching. My own experience is that until a coaching client accepts responsibility for where they are in their life, including their own health, there is little movement towards improvement. When blame and victimhood are shed, when the client accepts responsibility for his or her own choices, real progress happens. A person may be feeling "stuck" in a job or career that does not serve them well, but when they accept the fact that they have chosen that job or career and they continue to choose to stay with it, they no longer feel trapped by it. A paradoxical sense of freedom emerges and they know they can now make life and health-affirming choices.

This may sound harsh for the person facing particular health challenges, but it applies there too. While one does not "choose" to have diabetes, and there is nothing to be gained by living out one's days regretting all the ways one increased their health risks by years of poor diet and sedentary living, a person can choose the attitude and the way they live with diabetes. Coaching the person with a health challenge requires a thorough exploration of the attitude the client has toward their challenge. The key is helping the client determine what they are responsible for, and helping them to empower themselves to take the action they can for their recovery and the very best life possible.

In coaching you might use Ardell's five dimensions as a way to explore specific areas in a client's life. Stress management, physical fitness and nutritional awareness goals are particularly good candidates. The dimension of environmental sensitivity can be creatively explored and may yield new ideas that help in the other dimensions as well. Increased awareness of one's environment and the effect it has upon one's health can lead to decisions to modify the environment (home improvement, new office lighting, sound proofing, etc.), or even move to a new location. Such decisions can be processed effectively in coaching.

Hetler's Model

Bill Hetler, M.D., Co-founder of The National Wellness Institute developed a comprehensive and inclusive model that looks at wellness in terms of six dimensions:

FIGURE 2.5

Since its inception in 1976 Hetler's model has served as one of most common ways to allocate resources for wellness programs. It has been expanded into ten dimensions in TestWell, the assessment instrument developed by the National Wellness Institute (NWI).

1. Physical	6. Intellectual
2. Sexuality	7. Safety
3. Nutrition	8. Occupational
4. Emotional	9. Environment
5. Self Care	10. Spirituality

COACHING NOTE

Using Hetler's Model in Coaching

Wellness coaches may find that using either the six or ten dimensional model of wellness is a very straightforward way to help clients organize their thinking and create a wellness plan that covers each dimension in some way. Using the TestWell instrument as a pre and post instrument (or at intervals during coaching) can serve as a way to stay on track with wellness plan goals. An advantage is that most people can identify what elements of their life fit into each dimension without having to learn any theory.

Travis' Model

In the third edition of The Wellness Workbook (2004), Jack Travis and Regina Ryan elaborate on the Twelve Dimensional Model of wellness that Travis developed. A detailed understanding of each of these dimensions and their interrelationship is best found in the Wellness Workbook itself, but here we will look at some advantages that the model holds for wellness coaches.

Travis' model is based on a theory of energy and energy flow. He sees the dimensions of Eating, Breathing, and Sensing as the way we take energy into the body/mind, and the remaining nine dimensions as ways we transform energy and put it out into the universe.

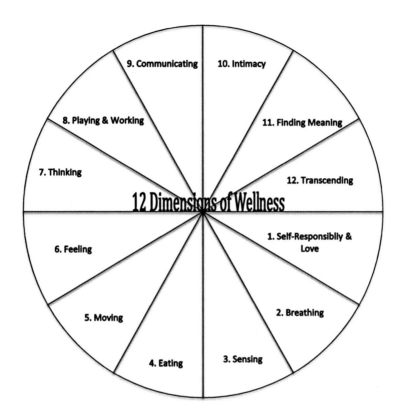

FIGURE 2.6
JOHN W. TRAVIS, MD, MPH 1976, 2004 & HEALTHWORLD ONLINE, INC.

Looking At Each Dimension

1. Self-Responsibility and Love. As a wellness coach you may find your clients make their best progress when they realize they are primarily responsible for their own health. When they take ownership for it they begin to make progress. We look at how loving the person is toward themselves and how connected they feel towards the world around them.

2. Breathing. Coaching about breathing might include not only helping your client to increase their awareness of their own breathing, but also to help them see how easily they are breathing in life. The dimension of breathing looks at the way we either block or allow energy to flow into us, and can be used to help someone find ways to relax.

3. Sensing. Wellness is about conscious living. A great way to increase awareness is through sensory awareness. "Lose your mind, and come to your senses!" is the famous quote by gestalt therapist Fritz Perls. Exploring this dimension can help clients to balance out their intellectual tendencies by becoming more aware of their bodies and what can be learned from them.

4. Eating. There is a distinct advantage to talking with clients about "eating" as opposed to using the trigger word "diet" or "nutrition." This term allows for easy exploration of the role that eating plays in your client's life. Not only is it about what we eat, but how, when, and even why! It can be about how a person digests or takes in their world —what is said to them and what they say to themselves.

5. Moving. When we speak about moving with our clients we avoid the sometimes heavily loaded trigger word exercise. Speaking about movement allows the client to see all their movement in perspective and not just the time they spend working out. Now the client can see such acts as dancing, stair climbing, parking as far away as possible and walking, as movement that can help their health. This expansive notion allows for creative wellness plans that may work where exercise programs have failed before.

6. Feeling. This dimension drives home the fundamental importance of the emotional components of wellness and opens this area up to exploration through coaching.

7. Thinking. This dimension helps clients to understand how thoughts are intertwined and interrelated with feelings and health. Much of the coaching process is about assisting clients to explore the beliefs they hold about themselves and the world. The coach helps clients to examine the thinking that limits them and make new conscious choices.

8. Playing and Working. The coaching process can help clients explore how conscious they are about this dual dimension and how in balance it is for them. A frequent goal of wellness coaching is to increase fun, recreation (re-creation!) and joy in a person's life.

9. Communication. This dimension is a life skill that can either facilitate a smooth journey or bog it down with one conflict or heartache after another. This dimension reminds us that wellness coaching is not just about diet and exercise, but about our ease of connection with others and the integrity of our relationship with ourselves.

10. Intimacy. This dimension allows clients to explore (if they so choose) a dimension of healthy living that is often ignored. Travis takes an approach that sees human sexuality as another form of life energy. There is no judgment here about how it is expressed, but rather an emphasis on flow instead of blockage. The wellness coach, with the client's permission, can help a person explore ways to increase the satisfaction with the way sexuality is expressed in their life.

11. Finding Meaning. Living a life with meaning and purpose is central to many definitions of wellness. Exploring this dimension can be foundational to making change in any other dimension of living.

12. Transcending. This dimension of wellness may seem esoteric, but it is surprising how often it strikes a respondent chord in clients. The quest to bring one's life into balance by exploring the transcendent side is an ancient endeavor that still speaks to the soul. Again, this dimension can be foundational to other dimensions.

The Iceberg Model of Health and Disease

The Iceberg Model of Health and Disease is a concept that Travis developed that can be helpful in looking at what contributes to the creation of the state of health that is observable. Like the iceberg, we only see the tip of the entire situation. Three-fourths of it lies beneath the surface. Travis sees our state of health as being built upon a foundation of greater and greater breadth and depth. The deepest (therefore the most out of our awareness) and broadest level is what he calls the Spiritual/Being/Meaning Realm. Layered on the spiritual level is the Cultural/Psychological/Motivational Level, and then just below the surface, the Lifestyle/Behavioral Level. Built upon these three subsurface layers is what we see as our state of health.

The Iceberg Model

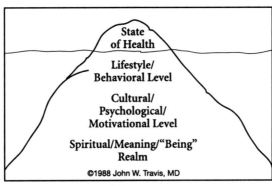

FIGURE 2.7

COACHING NOTE

Using Travis' Model in Coaching

As you coach your client keep in mind that the lifestyle behaviors you and your client are working with have more beneath them. Shifting one's lifestyle without addressing the underlying values, motivations, and philosophical foundations may not allow a person to make a congruent shift and may result in only temporary behavioral change. You may not need to journey to "the depths" with your client for these shifts to occur, but be prepared to help them look deeper into themselves in a variety of ways.

Michael Arloski's Ten Tenets of Wellness

The Encarta World English Dictionary defines a tenet as "any of a set of established and fundamental beliefs." When I originally developed the "Ten Tenets of Wellness" in the early 1990s, I sought not to so much establish a model of wellness, as to set forth fundamental principles of how people can and do change their lifestyle behavior, and what holds them back.

Tenet 1. Wellness is a holistic concept. Anything short of that is incomplete and ultimately ineffective. We need to look at the whole person and create programs (and coach) for the mind, body, spirit, and environment. Just picking the dimension of wellness that you like and minimizing the others doesn't work in the long run.

> **COACHING NOTE**
>
> **An exercise in holism**
>
> Using "The Wheel of Life" that we referred to earlier, fill in your levels of satisfaction and consider what areas of your life you may have been ignoring. Make a commitment to explore and/or take action in one of those areas in the next week.

Tenet 2. Self-esteem is a critical factor in change. Wellness is caring enough about yourself to take stock of your life, make the necessary changes and find the support to maintain your motivation. Heal the wounds. Find what is holding you back from feeling good about yourself and work through the blocks, not around them.

Everything we do comes either from love or from fear. Where do your wellness lifestyle efforts come from? For many of us, change requires the hard, roll up the sleeves, work of facing our fears and healing old wounds from our experience growing up in our families of origin and our peer group and community. Positive affirmations, or self-statements, are excellent, but need to be coupled with this type of life-long self-reflective work.

> **COACHING NOTE**
>
> **An exercise in self-esteem**
>
> Identify one negative message you frequently say to yourself ("You're so stupid!" "You'll never amount to anything.," etc.). Relax for a minute or two with your eyes closed. Think of the negative message, and say out loud in a shout "Who says?" Notice who flashes into your mind, a parent, teacher, one-time peer? See with whom you have some unfinished business to deal with.

Tenet 3. Positive peer health norms encourage wellness lifestyle changes. Who we surround ourselves with either helps us stretch our wings and soar, or clips them again and again. Norms are the patterns of behavior that we are surrounded with in our society, our culture, sub-cultures, work-places, neighborhoods, and families. Mutually beneficial relationships with friends, lovers, family and colleagues who care about us as people are what we need to seek and create in our lives. Rather than being threatened by our personal growth, they support it. Do your friends (partners, etc.) bring out your OK or NOT OK feelings? Giving and receiving strokes are what it's all about. Friends keep friends well.

> **COACHING NOTE**
>
> **An exercise in positive peer health norms**
>
> List who has joined your inner circle of supportive friends in the last ten years. Give thanks, or grieve and get busy making new friends!

Tenet 4. Conscious living means becoming aware of all the choices we have and acting on them. Break out of the trance! Conscious living involves a realization that we don't have to run our lives on automatic pilot. We can turn off the television (remember TV stands for time vacuum), read labels, turn off the lawn sprinklers when we have enough rain, notice how our food tastes, and notice how tense and contracted we are when we drive fifteen mph over the speed limit. Consciously work on relationships, life goals, and maximize our potential.

> **COACHING NOTE**
>
> **An exercise in conscious living**
>
> For three workdays in a row minimize your attachment to the world of the media. No radio, television, internet, newspaper, or magazines. See what you become aware of about yourself and the world around you.

Tenet 5. A sense of connectedness grounds us in our lives. We are all of one heart. Consciously expanding our web of interconnectedness to other people, other species, the earth and to something greater, may be one of the most powerful acts we can take for being well. Allowing ourselves to move beyond fear and connect with others, to reduce our sense of isolation, can vault us forward in succeeding at lasting lifestyle change. There is a huge difference between **I-llness** and **We-llness**.

Much of this sense of connection can also come out of the land we live on. By identifying with where we live and getting to know the plants, animals, weather patterns, water sources and the landscape itself, we develop not only a love for it, but feel that love returned. Through our commitment to our place on earth we value and protect our environment by the way we live our lives, and by how we speak at the ballot box. Through our contact with the natural world we experience a solid sense of belonging, peace and harmony.

Theologian Matthew Fox likes to say that we can relate to the earth in any of three ways. We can exploit it, recreate on it, or we can be in awe of it. I believe it is within a sense of awe that our potential for growth and healing is multiplied. From such a state of wonder it is easy to see all other species as relatives. The Lakota close every prayer with "Mitakaue Oyasin"—For all my relations.

COACHING NOTE

An exercise in connectedness

Spend twenty minutes in a "natural" area just listening to every sound you hear. Locate origins of the sounds. Identify patterns. Try it with your eyes closed part of the time. Cup your hands behind your ears and try it. Be aware of your responses.

Tenet 6. We are primarily responsible for our health. There are the risk factors of genetics, toxic environments and the like, but our emotional and lifestyle choices determine our health and wellbeing more than anything else. As much as we'd like to cling to blame and copouts, we must be honest with ourselves. The benefit is the empowerment that this realization gives us.

One path out of passivity and illness is to realize what you can do to boost your immune system. Stress, fatigue and poor diet have a tremendous influence on our body's ability to resist illness and disease. Many people report excessive stress and chronic sleep deprivation.

COACHING NOTE

An exercise in health responsibility

To take charge of your own health and boost your immune system, follow the usual wellness advice and live a well-balanced healthy lifestyle but, more specifically, experiment with getting more rest, and practicing some established form of relaxation training.

Tenet 7. Increased self-sufficiency gives the confidence and power that overshadows fear. The Australian aboriginal people say that when a person cannot walk out onto the land and feed, clothe and shelter themselves adequately, a deep primal fear grips their soul. Recognizing our interconnectedness, we grow tremendously when we can care for ourselves on many different levels. Skills, information and tools that enable us to choose our food wisely (or even grow it ourselves); become more competent at our career; adjust the shifter on our bicycle; take a hike into a wilderness area; or bake bread from scratch all increase our self-respect and self-confidence. We need to learn these skills and teach them to others, especially to our children.

COACHING NOTE

An exercise in self-sufficiency

Identify some skill you want to learn that would make your life easier, more economical, or more fun, if you possessed that skill (baking, doing something mechanical, or performing an outdoors skill) Locate a person who you can learn that skill from and arrange an exchange of knowledge, skill, time, or some other way to barter a reciprocal arrangement you both like.

Tenet 8. Time spent alone helps us to get to know ourselves better. As much as we all need time with others, we all need time apart. *Solo time*, especially in the natural world, helps us relax, deconstruct, and get beyond the distractions of modern life that prevent us from really knowing ourselves. There are some powerful reasons that people from all around the world spend time alone (usually in a wilderness setting) in order to gain vision about the direction and meaning in their lives.

COACHING NOTE

An exercise in solo time

Find a partner who shares your desire to spend one full day in "solo time." Locate a nearby natural area where you both feel safe and where you would enjoy spending the day. Pick a day with a relatively good weather forecast. Take a whistle with you, appropriate clothing, rain-gear, etc. Bring plenty of water, but no food unless you have a special dietary consideration. Do not bring anything to read, or anything with which to write. When you arrive at the area you should both select a small area(a maximum of ten to fifteen yards in diameter) where you would like to spend 5-8 hrs. alone. Your site should be close enough for your partner to hear your whistle easily, but far enough away that you can have complete privacy. Taking

---

opposite sides of the same hilltop ridge works very well for this. Reunite at a prearranged time. Spend your time in contemplation and awareness of everything around you. This is a journey into inner and outer nature. Reflect and write about your experience afterwards if you like.

The goal here is not endurance. Bail out if you have a nasty change in weather or feel ill. You can always reschedule. Though the process of solo time is not physically demanding, you need to be your own judge, or you should seek your physician's advice, if you have health concerns.

Tenet 9. You don't have to be perfect to be well. Extreme perfectionism is a shame-based process that feeds a really negative view of ourselves. Workaholism, anorexia, and other addictive behaviors can result. Wellness does not mean swearing off hot-fudge sundaes. It just means not bs-ing yourself about when you last had one! Whenever our healthy habits move from being positive addictions to being compulsive behavior that works against us, we're usually the last ones to know. Often extreme behavior is a way to distract yourself from some other issue that needs your attention.

COACHING NOTE

An exercise in letting go of perfection

Get a gauge on your diet, exercise and other behaviors. Read several sources and see what the experts recommend. Check your program out with a qualified local resource such as a nutritionist, exercise professional or other specialist, then experiment with a free day once a week. If you are the sort of person who can handle it, take one day a week where you give yourself permission to eat anything that you want and medically can have. Remember: ONE day a week!

Tenet 10. Play! We all need to lighten up and not take ourselves (and wellness) too seriously. Remember the lessons of the coyote and be playful, even ornery in a non-malicious way. Let the child within out to play. Give yourself permission.

The work hard, play hard philosophy does little to help us maintain the balance needed for a healthy life. Psychophysiology works twenty four hours a day, every day (not just on weekends). Integrate a healthy sense of humor and play into the workplace. Make sure your yang equals your yin!

COACHING NOTE

An exercise in play

List several of your favorite play activities that you either do, or did at one time in your life. Now, think about when you last engaged in each of these activities. Celebrate or contemplate what you've (temporarily) let go of in your life. Have fun reclaiming it!

Even with these tenets there is no concrete wellness formula. You have to discover what works for you. Take them not as rules, but as modern folklore gathered by one who has walked the wellness way for a few years.

COACHING NOTE

Using The Ten Tenets In Coaching

The "Ten Tenets" serve you, the wellness coach, by first of all giving you a fundamental set of principles to help you understand what drives lifestyle change. These tenets attempt to answer the vexing and recurring question "Why don't people do what they know they need to do for themselves?"

Secondly: you can use the tenets as a reference for what you explore in coaching. Ask powerful questions that help your clients consider how well connected they are to their world, how can they feel better about themselves by in some small way becoming more self-sufficient, etc.

Thirdly: you can share the Ten Tenets of Wellness with your client. Give them a copy of it to read and explore it together. Ask them which of the exercises they might find of value as they explore and experiment within their lives.

You can also attract clients to your coaching by presenting The Ten Tenets and sharing these fundamental principles with your audience. Ask them to identify one or two of the tenets that really seemed to have a message for them in their lives right now.

There are as many reasons for running as there are days in the year, years in my life. But mostly I run because I am an animal and a child, an artist and a saint. So, too, are you. Find your own play, your own self-renewing compulsion, and you will become the person you are meant to be.

—George Sheehan

Chapter 3

Taking Wellness One-On-One:
Changing the Health Promotion Model from Large Groups to Individuals

The People Of The Waterfall, A Folklore Tale

There once was a village of people who lived at the base of a huge waterfall by a lovely river. Life was good until one day a stranger was washed over the falls and plummeted to the rocky cauldron of foaming water beneath it.

The people were alarmed and immediately sent two of their best swimmers out to rescue the person. With much effort the person was dragged ashore and the people succeeded in reviving him.

Before long another stranger was washed over the falls and again a rescue team was sent into the dangerous waters. As they worked on reviving the person they decided to station a rescue boat and a lifeline by the base of the falls.

As time passed, strangers continued to be washed over the waterfall and rescue efforts increased. Soon a small building was erected with emergency supplies and designated people were constantly on call for more rescues.

The number of strangers being washed over the fall continued to increase. Soon the people constructed a small hospital at the base of the falls and built a fine rescue boat with full-time emergency rescue workers to staff it.

The people were perplexed but continued to respond to the demands of the victims of the waterfall. They built an even bigger hospital and started to build a whole fleet of rescue boats, when, at long last, someone asked . . ."Why don't we go upstream and see why these people are falling in?"

Preventive Health

There is obvious wisdom in going upstream and doing something about the source of a problem. In our modern world systems bound to the reactive and remedial are being overwhelmed. Sometimes underfunding keeps the current system on the edge and sometimes the lure of greater financial rewards supports the *status quo*. There is definitely a great deal of money to be made in surgery, pharmaceuticals and other remedial products and services. Prevention is a less profitable area. Despite all that we know about what someone needs to do to stay healthy, the U.S. federal health care dollar spends ninety-five cents to remediate problems and only five cents to prevent them from occurring.

We all remember hygiene in our health classes in school. The early days of health education seemed more about cutting those toe-nails in a straight, not curved line than in teaching us about safe sex or how to reduce some more virulent health risks. Although I seem to have had it pounded into my head that a diet composed primarily of highly polished white rice would give me beriberi, I do not remember being taught what a good diet was!

Much of the research that we now take for granted had not been done until the 1970s. Not until the famous Framingham studies of the fifties and sixties did we know that there was a real link between smoking and lung disease, or between our diet and heart disease. Disease avoidance or keeping disease away was the picture of what it meant to be healthy.

In 1961 a little book called *High Level Wellness* was written by Halbert L. Dunn. It was never a bestseller, but it did resonate with a few forward-thinking people in the health-related fields. The revolutionary thing about Dunn's view of health was that he presented it as more than simply the absence of illness. He posited that health and wellbeing were a matter of mind, body and spirit. It was a matter of the whole human being and their personal, social, and physical environment. He described a state of being vitally alive and dubbed it "wellness."

Wellness Full Circle

The field of work that we came to call wellness emerged in the mid-1970's from the body of work by John Travis, Don Ardell, Robert Allen, Bill Hetler and others. They infused the much-neglected area of preventative health with psychological principles of behavioral and development change.

Epidemiology also spurred on some of the first wellness work, largely through the actuarial tables of insurance companies. Cause of death statistics yielded more questions than answers and a great deal of speculation that many factors other than medical were impacting our health.

Studying the relationship between health and behavior yielded the concept that our lifestyle choices affect our health in profound ways. The field of wellness began with looking at health-risk behavior and tackled the challenge of helping our society reduce its health risks. Smoking cessation and weight control were at the forefront of this early effort with many of the fear-based programs intending to scare people into quitting smoking and reducing their weight. The emphasis was on reducing health risk factors and thereby reducing health related problems. Out of the movement came the health risk appraisals or assessments (HRAs) created to formally measure a person's health risk.

Over the years, more health correlations were made and we began to look at stress reduction, healthier interpersonal relationships, career satisfaction and other aspects of a person's life in order to get a complete picture of their health and well-being. Various models of wellness emerged and the value of concepts like "meaning and purpose" in life became recognized as central. The personal growth movement of the late sixties and early seventies spurred on the wellness movement and validated its base in the concept of personal growth, development and self-actualization.

In 1975, a physician who wanted to do more than just treat illness established the first wellness resource center (not a clinic). Jack Travis, developed a Marin County, California center to work with individuals who truly wanted to be well. Offering programs that helped people learn skills for well-being, it went light years beyond what we learned in health class. In addition to some of the expected how to be well information on better ways to exercise and eat, the Wellness

Resource Center emphasized the psychological as well. The Center placed emphasis on identifying and removing emotional barriers to being well, improving communication skills, enhancing creativity and learning deep relaxation techniques. And, in very coach-like fashion, it asked clients (not patients) to look at envisioning desired outcomes and taking full responsibility for their own health and wellbeing.

Travis' center worked with individuals to help them learn how to take charge of their own lives. The Center's clients worked with the early version of The Wellness Inventory (developed by Travis), as well as a Health Risk Appraisal and then created a plan for how to really live well. After the evaluation stage, clients enrolled in individual sessions with counselors and joined a lifestyle evolution group to help them learn the basics of wellness.

The Wellness Resource Center did not last many years though, and the center model did not catch fire. Companies looked to insurance and managed care as the answers. With the costs of health care beginning to rise, corporations began to look seriously upstream. Companies such as Progressive Insurance, Campbell Soup, Bayer, IBM, Coors, and others, looked to the growing field of health education and health promotion for wellness help.

Psychologist Robert Allen pioneered examining how health norms of the people we live and work with affect our health. In the workplace, programs were developed to influence the culture of the work environment. Many companies invested in physical fitness facilities for employees. Health-risk assessments were used on a broad scale. The emphasis was moved to health education and affecting large groups of people through classes, incentive programs, and various wellness health promotion efforts.

This was a step in the right direction and yet today health educators have found that in addition to the educative-classes-and-promotion approach, they are increasingly expected to work with individuals. Sometimes they have the skills to do so, other times they apply the training they know and attempt to simply educate the individual, hoping it will result in behavioral change. It often does not. Wellness is also becoming more consumer-driven. There is an increasing demand by individuals, outside of the workplace, for alliances that can help them, once and for all, be successful in changing their lifestyle behavior.

Many in the wellness field feel they been successful in some ways, and unsuccessful in others. Our culture-wide, society-wide or company-wide health promotion efforts have not been able to adequately improve the health of our country. There is encouragement instead of discouragement when we take wellness one-on-one. The new trend in wellness is helping improve the health of our world, one person at a time. It seems we are best served to come full circle to an individualized approach to wellness.

Individualizing Wellness:
The Coach Approach to Lifestyle Change

The wellness field has grown and been around for approximately thirty years. Changing the health behavior of the world has been a challenge, to say the least. In the United States, Canada, Europe, Australia, some parts of Asia and South America, the health efforts have been vigorous. In other areas the primary factor in overall health is not lifestyle, but living conditions, and there, wellness faces more unique challenges.

Throughout the thirty-year effort we discovered many approaches that worked and some that did not. Central to it all is a change in basic mindset that the approach to individual wellness has been based on.

Prescribe and Treat

As I began training wellness coaches and teaching coaching skills to wellness professionals, my students often reported that behavior change was so puzzling to them. "I tell them what to do, and they don't do it!" was often the exasperated cry.

Much of wellness is steeped in the great medical tradition. At times wellness professionals are working in medical clinics. Many times they are themselves nurses, therapists, or others trained in the medical model. That mindset is prescribe and treat, or diagnose, prescribe and treat. It is a mindset that was designed for remedial care. It is a mindset that works well in medical cases, and especially well when there is no behavioral compliance required by the patient.

In recent years we have seen the medical field extremely frustrated by the lack of patient compliance even with pharmaceutical prescriptions, much less behavioral directions from the doctor to alter one's lifestyle. Half the battle, they will tell you, in treating a newly diagnosed diabetic, is getting them to comply with directions for their own self-testing, diet, exercise and self-administration of treatment.

Unless there is no behavioral component to the treatment that requires the patient to follow-through in any way, the prescribe and treat method can be replete with difficulty. Just telling people what to do doesn't work well. The inherent authority of medical personnel just doesn't carry the same weight it used to. Although there may be acquiescence in the medical office, things may be quite different when the patient is on his/her own. Culture, lack of money, time limitations, access to conflicting information on the internet, all play a role that is not addressed in the current prescribe and treat system. When wellness work is carried out with this same prescriptive and admonishing approach we see results only when the client is truly ready and open to making the changes prescribed.

The National Pharmaceutical Council, an industry research organization, estimates that non-compliance with medication adds over one billion dollars annually to the U.S. health care system. Filling a pharmaceutical prescription and then remembering and taking the medicine prescribed properly are all behavioral acts. Add to this the lifestyle prescriptions to change one's diet, exercise more and manage stress better, and we see that the issue of patient/client compliance is truly a critical behavioral health issue.

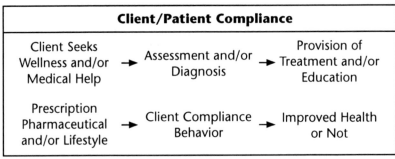

Client/Patient Compliance		
Client Seeks Wellness and/or Medical Help →	Assessment and/or Diagnosis →	Provision of Treatment and/or Education
Prescription Pharmaceutical and/or Lifestyle →	Client Compliance Behavior →	Improved Health or Not

FIGURE 3.1

Whether applied to a treatment situation or to a wellness/health education situation, the final goal of improved health and wellbeing will only be reached if the flow is completed and there is client compliance. Success hinges on this crucial stage; if the client does not complete the process, all the previous efforts are to no avail.

There are treatment situations where the treatment provided immediately is sufficient. Administration of an appropriate medication may do the job, if the job is small enough. However, there is usually some kind of procedure that the patient needs to follow. That is where compliance comes in. So, as physiological as medicine is, its success is often determined by the psychological aspects. In the field of behavioral medicine we have come to say that there is nothing physiological, only psycho-physiological. We have come to realize that there is no separation between a person's mind and body. They work together and impact each other.

The other contradiction is that a prescribe and treat approach to wellness assumes that there is something wrong with the person. This seems to make the assumption that the wellness professional knows more about the client's body than the person consulting with them. The "I'm going to figure out what's wrong with you and tell you what to do about it" approach does not engage the person in his or her own wellness process. It operates on the illness side of the Illness/Wellness Continuum and still calls it wellness.

Many wellness professionals are simply doing what they have been taught. Some students from the medical field have told me how they have been taught ways to cut off the input of the patient in order to save time and get to the diagnosis and prescription more quickly. Time is limited and emotional connection is discouraged. Wellness coaching is not medical interviewing.

Educate and Implore

Wellness professionals don't always take a medical approach. Some are trained as health educators. Being educators, they want to educate! The vast majority of wellness and health promotion is done in the belief that providing people with the best possible health information will result in improved health.

Certainly the importance of good, accurate health information cannot be criticized. We have seen great strides in public health since we begin teaching people to wash their hands (especially surgeons!) and not to sneeze on one another. We take it for granted today, but these simple maxims were not common practice only a hundred years ago. Establishing the link between smoking and a whole list of deadly diseases and getting the word out about it is just one example of heroic public health education. Did you know that smoking is banned in public places in the entire Republic of Ireland?

There are those rare occasions when just the right information hits at just the right time. I experienced this when I read an alarming article on feedlot-raised beef. That was over fifteen years ago and I haven't eaten beef since. However, when it comes to lifestyle behavioral change, information alone is insufficient most of the time.

All too often the health educator provides great information and delivers it in friendly, caring and often creative, ways to the person. Yet, there is often no change in behavior. The health educator implores the person to use this great information and change. Still, there may be no change in behavior.

Health educators are trained to conduct classes and do health promotion. Weight-loss classes are often just that—classes. The educator educates and there is hope that the students will take the information presented and transform their lives.

When the educative approach is attempted in a one-on-one situation, educate and implore just isn't enough. I would say that every one of the health educators I have worked with have been sincere about their job and have given it their very best effort. In fact, they often tell me that before they discovered the coach-approach, they thought that the more they talked (and provided great information) the better job they were doing. They truly wanted to give as much as possible to their client. Yet in retrospect, they realized how they often had overwhelmed their clients with information and left them in dazed confusion. Often there was no implementation of any of the great information that had been provided.

> *To hold and fill to overflowing*
> *is not as good as to stop in time.*
> *Sharpen a sword-edge to its very sharpest,*
> *And the edge will not last long.*
> *Withdraw as soon as your work is done.*
> *Such is Heaven's Way.*
>
> –Lao Tzu

Advocate and Inspire

With the recognition that so much of health and wellbeing is behavioral, we are at long last, acknowledging the need for a third professional to enter the scene. Joining the valued treatment providers and the health educators is the wellness coach. Taking a different stance than even the counselor or psychologist, who are still in the realm of treatment, the wellness coach is there to be an advocate for the client's health and wellbeing, to inspire and support their growth and development.

Operating with a mindset that is fundamentally different, the wellness coach is there to stand by the client, to stand with them, and stand next to them as a guide. Living in Colorado for many years, and exploring mountains around the world, I enjoy using the metaphor of the coach being like a mountain guide.

Mountain guides do not climb mountains for people. Nothing is accomplished, really, if you hire me as your mountain guide and pay me merely to plant your flag on the summit while you sip martinis and observe me through a telescope down at the lodge.

As your guide, I help you plan the climb. We assess your readiness for the climb, examine what you have and what you need in equipment and resources. Together we determine a route to take. We plan how long the journey will take and allow for elements we can't control, be it the weather or a family crisis. We examine what your personal goals are. Are you a peak-bagger, or more into the sheer experience of the high country? We get clear on what a successful and fulfilling climb will be for you.

Mountain guides do not make people climb mountains. The motivation for the climb has to be within the climber. During times of discouragement I may lend support, or even challenge you to reach a little deeper for strength I know you have. I also know that your chances of success are far greater if your motivation is internal. You WANT to climb this mountain! You are excited about it, and you anticipate that the journey will in itself be a large part of the pleasure of the experience. It works best when it is not fear-based motivation. You are not climbing the mountain because you are afraid what will happen if you don't!

Most importantly, your chances of success are far greater just because you aren't doing it alone. Knowing that I am there with you on the journey shifts your entire mental approach. You push through the temptation to turn back prematurely (as you may have done so often in the past) as you look over at me climbing beside you. You know

41

I will hold you accountable to yourself to do what you said you have come to do. You also know that you retain your freedom, and if you choose to turn back you will not be criticized for it. When we do summit, it is your flag that is planted, not mine, for this was your journey. It was you and the mountain. Your coach was like a good solid rope—a support.

The Mindset Shift—Being an Ally

The wellness professional sees everything new as if through a different lens once they make the mindset shift to that of an ally. Doing so may not be easy. In addition to the sheer power of habit, there may be some attraction remaining to the older models. Look inside and ask if you are ready to become an ally to your patient/client instead of a teacher or medical authority. Some people have higher needs for control than others. Being a wellness ally requires letting go of those needs for control and distance.

Another part of the mindset shift is a shift in responsibility. As an ally you work with a person to make their own changes. They, not you, are ultimately responsible for changing their own behavior. In fact, part of the coach approach is supporting the client's acceptance of more and more responsibility for their own health and their own life. To do anything else encourages a co-dependency that works against the client, not for them.

Shifting the emphasis from education and provision of services to the role of an ally is indeed a different role. The services we provide are actions done with the client, not to them or for them. At first it may seem that we aren't doing enough for the client, but as we see them grow and change, we realize that our alliance is making a truly significant difference.

Four Cornerstones of Coaching

One of the most beautiful alignments of wellness and coaching is in the "cornerstones of coaching" set forth in the book *Co-Active Coaching* by coach education pioneers Laura Whitworth, Henry Kimsey-House and Phil Sandahl.

Cornerstone One: Clients are naturally creative, resourceful and whole. The wellness approach and the coaching approach both see the client as OK the way they are, nothing to be fixed, nothing to be treated. The client is whole and complete, just they way they are, and the coach accepts them as such. That is not to say that real health challenges are ignored. However, the person with the health challenge is seen as OK, as a resourceful, creative and complete human being who wants to grow. The leg may be broken, but the person is not!

This mindset shift becomes operational in many ways. When you adopt the mindset of the wellness ally your interaction with your client or patient changes on a number of levels.

- Intention shifts. We are all masters of perceiving, largely through non-verbal communication, and perhaps on other perceptual levels harder to study, the intention of people we are communicating with. What is the intention of the healthcare provider who is providing treatment? Hopefully to heal, but even that can come across as fixing, as a judgment that there is something wrong with the patient that needs fixing. This is the most common doctor-patient agreement—just give me a pill and send me home. However, the patient is now asking to be part of healing process and is not seeking to be fixed. So there needs to be a new intention. Now the client is looking for an ally who respects his/her own ability to help him/herself, and needs what that alliance can provide to ensure success.

- Closeness shifts. When we meet a client as an ally we sit beside them, not above them, and we work at the development of trust. We are open to more closeness than before. We demonstrate this openness to our client and present an invitation to trust and to deepen our experience of each other in our professional relationship. Many a student of medicine, nursing and therapy got the advice I received my sophomore year as a psychology major from a veteran professor and clinician. "Don't get too close to your patients!" There are some legitimate reasons for therapeutic distance. Clinical judgment can be impaired by personal feelings. Burnout prevention may require the art of compassionate detachment. The beauty of this different coaching position is that we are not sitting in clinical judgment we are free to be a professional ally.

- Clients have the answers: Another way the coaching field acknowledges the nature of this alliance is with the pearl of wisdom that "The client has the answers, the coach has the questions." We are engaged in a process to help clients find their own answers that they really do have within themselves. We don't motivate anyone! We help them find (gain access to) the motivation they have within themselves.

To work from this perspective requires us, as the wellness ally, to let go of the expert role. As a consultant it can feel very good to provide the kind of information a client finds helpful. At times, the coach can do this. We can direct a client to a resource that may help them or even make a specific suggestion. In the coach approach, though, we always ask the client for their permission, and we check out their desire. "Would you like to hear a suggestion I have about that?" We then offer our suggestion for the client to decide to accept or reject. Contrast that with the professional who is working in the role of expert and telling a person directly what they should do.

To let go of the expert role may require some work on our own self-confidence. It is easy to over-work, over-provide and over-educate (all called over-talking!) when inside we doubt ourselves. Clinging to that white uniform and the expert role we distance and protect ourselves, staying on what we might call the helpful offensive when working with a client.

To be present, to be dancing in the moment as we like to call it in coaching, we are required to be more centered about who we are and comfortable with just that. Many times as a coach I urge them to ask themselves "Who do I need to be?" instead of "What do I need to do?" The same is true for the wellness ally. Who do you need to be? What aspects of your character needs to show up, to be present, as you work with your client to serve them best in a coach-like way?

Cornerstone Two: Coaching addresses the client's whole life. In my first group teleconference call that introduced me further to the field of coaching, our host was drawing upon his extensive CEO business background for examples. Speaking for myself and several other therapists on the call, I asked what did we non-business background people have to bring to coaching. He laughed and said "You know, I'll tell you all something. All, yes, all of the business coaching I've done, at some point became life coaching." He went on to tell us—and I learned over the years that it was absolutely true—it wasn't lack of information that kept the business person from being more successful, it was their own personal characteristics, self-defeating behaviors, limiting self-beliefs and interpersonal skills (or the lack thereof) that determined their success. In wellness coaching, the same principle is true.

> *Tug on anything at all and you'll find it connected to everything else in the universe.*
>
> —John Muir

When we really look at health and wellness, the atomistic, bio-medical model only takes us so far. The great rise of integrative health-care can largely attribute its powerful emergence to the fact that it focuses on the whole person. When we look at lifestyle improvement we quickly realize that it is a holistic concept. The sedentary, over-weight client doesn't need just another prescription for a 1500 calorie diet, they need to look at how they are living their life, how they feel about themselves, where the support in their life comes from, and much more. They are not a person in isolation. They are part of other systems we know as family, workplace and community.

In wellness coaching we help our clients assess their wellness by looking at all aspects of their lives, three hundred and sixty degrees. A narrow behavioral approach to changing individual behaviors proves to be quite myopic when it comes to helping people with real lifestyle change. We identify areas for exploration, and sometimes it is surprising where the real benefits come from and where the keys to change are found.

Cornerstone Three: The agenda comes from the client. The coaching model thoroughly embraces the idea of operating in what is basically a client-centered way. Like the counseling approach developed by Carl Rogers, we stay with the client and go where they lead. As we apply this to wellness coaching we see that it is, again, a mindset shift from the medical or treatment model. It is even different than an approach a business consultant might take (the consultant knows best).

It may be very apparent to the wellness professional that the person they are talking with needs to quit smoking, exercise more, manage their stress better or find more supportive relationships. When the wellness professional takes this assessment and shoves it at the client as a recommendation it is very easy for it to be perceived as a prescription, or worse, as a judgment. This person doesn't feel like an ally. Clients are often resistant to such an approach and most often will comply while in the conversation and then not follow through, or will even drop out of participation.

The wellness coach may ask "What do you want to do? What are you ready to do?" In the coach approach we trust in the wisdom of the client and support them in what they are ready to work on. Nothing succeeds like success. Once the client experiences success in the first wellness goal they work on, they are more ready, willing and able to tackle another goal that they may gain even more benefit from.

> *Always remember that you are absolutely unique.*
> *Just like everyone else.*
>
> **–Margaret Mead**

Clients have friends and family who want to help, but they all have their own agenda. Family members may want the best for the client, but they would like it to look a certain way.

- Don't rock the boat.

- Don't be too assertive, we like having you do everything for us!

- Go out more, but not with him or her!

- Take time to have fun, but not too much time because we really need you to make more money.

- Take care of yourself, but oh, please don't cut down on the overtime you are doing for us.

One of the most refreshing things about coaching is that clients get to talk about their lives with someone who doesn't have to live with them or work with them, or even be related to them! Yes! The only agenda is the client's agenda!

When a wellness coach co-creates a wellness plan with a client, it is just that, co-creation. A plan is crafted together from the agenda the client sets. That's not to say the coach might not challenge the client to go for more, or coach them to attempt less. Like an athletic coach who believes in the ability of a player to perform better, the wellness coach might challenge the client to stretch themselves a bit. The coach may, on the other hand, see that more is being bitten off than is likely to be chewed and rather than creating a setup for failure may suggest taking on less. When all is said and done, the client remains behind the wheel—steering their life toward higher levels of wellness.

Cornerstone Four: The relationship is a designed alliance. Very consciously the coach and the client fashion a professional relationship that is a custom fit, instead of a one-size-fits-all treatment or education program. The goal is to create a relationship that matches the role of the coach with the kind of coaching the client needs. In the very first session, once it is clear that coaching is what the client wants, the first work of the new alliance is to create itself, and to do so in a conscious and unique way.

I often start a discovery session (the first session with a new client) by asking "What is the best way for me to coach you?" Often clients are not shy about telling me! Sometimes they really need an explanation of what the choices are and all the different ways that coaching can look. We all need accountability, but how much and in what manner? Are you a client who works best with a light rein or with really firm deadlines?

Agreements are created, not only about the more interpersonal aspects of working together, but the concrete and practical as well. Coaching agreements spell out fees, policies, etc. in real detail so everyone is clear.

With this new mindset and reliance on these cornerstones you are being more coach-like, and have a new way to interact with your clients. When you give your client an ally instead of an expert, and then stand with them, and stand by them through the change process, the client feels the support needed to succeed.

A safe and courageous space for change must be, by definition, a place where the truth can be told. It is a place where clients can tell the whole truth about what they have done (and not done) without worrying about looking good. This is an environment without judgment. And it is a place where the coach expects the truth from the client because there is no consequence of truth other than growth and learning.

—L. Whitworth, H. Kimsey-House, P. Sandahl
Co-Active Coaching

Chapter 4

Seven Steps to Lasting Lifestyle Change: Lifestyle Improvement Model

What is the most rigorous law of our being? Growth.
No smallest atom of our moral, mental, or physical structure
can stand still a year. It grows—it must grow;
nothing can prevent it.

—Mark Twain

There are many wonderful books available which tell us how to be well. They are great resources and more information is always valuable. What I am striving to do in this book, however, is to provide more in the way of exploring how we change our lifestyle. This involves behavior change. This is a territory worth exploring because is seems to be grounded where the trails are faint and elusive. Many a journey into this realm comes to a halt and the person turns around, retraces their steps and goes back where they came from. What blocks us from really getting far enough down that trail towards wellness to realize success? How do we block ourselves? What keeps us stuck at the trailhead, maintaining a lifestyle that at the minimum is keeping us from realizing our fullest potential, or, at it's worst, is killing us? What intrigues us about exploring this trail leading off over some hill and into the unknown? What motivates us to start the journey of a thousand miles with our first step? These are questions that have always fascinated me.

Present Lifestyle

We always begin the journey where we are, in the present. We review our present lifestyle to see what it looks like and how it is being maintained. Our current lifestyle is always maintained by some combination of habit, comfort, fear and reinforcement. While one could argue that there are many ways that these elements overlap and combine, let's look at each separately.

Many of the habits with which we live our lives are efficient ways of behaving, serving us well and saving us time and energy. I brush my teeth pretty much the same way, the same times of day, without a whole lot of thought. My dental hygienist might show me a better way of brushing my teeth, but chances are good that I will just continue in my old habitual way unless I engage is some kind of real change process. Other habits may be quite neutral or may have a severe negative impact on our level of wellness. At the very least, one of the most insidious aspects of habit is that it dulls our awareness. When I drive to work the same way everyday I may notice less about the world around me than when I vary the route. Noticing less about the world around us contributes less to our growth and the enjoyment of our experience. Noticing less may mean a traffic wreck. Today it is the driver running the stoplight in front of us and in ancient times it was the growl of the saber-tooth tiger. Awareness is one of the keys to our survival, and also one of the keys to our living a delightful life! When I am more aware I notice the beauty of the world as well as the dangers. I notice the flowers beside the sidewalk as well as the crack that may trip me.

Habits can be so ingrained that even when we identify them for change, the process is not easy. Most people have a pretty good idea of some important changes they would like to make in their lifestyle. The power of habit often keeps them stuck. They make up their minds to change a behavior and then criticize themselves harshly when sheer will power isn't enough to overcome a long-standing and deeply rooted habit. We'll explore how to work through and change a habit later in this book.

"I'm into creature comforts!" a friend of mine used to say. His idea of a great lifestyle was richly marbled steaks, good aged scotch, a plush lounge chair and satellite television. As you might expect, since this was his way of living on a regular basis, not just an occasional enjoyment, he was overweight, in very poor physical condition, and while he certainly knew how to relax, his health was walking a very thin line. This fellow was an extreme case, but we all know how many of our lifestyle choices are swayed by what simply gives us the most comfort. The lure of the couch can be powerful, as can the comfort that comes from foods that remind us of home, warmth and relaxation. While there is nothing wrong with comfort—in fact some people need to seek much more of it in their self-denying lives—balance is really the goal. Unfortunately, the habitual need for comfort can keep us stuck in very unhealthy lifestyles.

Change creates loss. Even if the change is positive, we have to let go of something. Fear of change is fear of loss and fear that we may not be able to adapt to the changing environment. There seems to be a little voice inside all of us that shouts "Status quo!" and fights change with tooth and nail. The more a person lives in fear the smaller they make their world. People reduce their options and choices in order to stay safe. They pass judgments on others to eliminate having to deal with them and perhaps encounter the forces of change. We fear failure and we fear success.

For many people lifestyle improvement is an area where they have already experienced the pain of many failures. Usually alone, they have tried to quit smoking, lose weight, be more intimate in close relationships, etc., and their efforts have only seemed to cause pain. Why try again? Discouragement feeds the fear and unfortunately there is much in the world around us that reinforces a very unhealthy lifestyle. Our peer group or family may exhibit unhealthy habits and find connection with us through these habits. It's hard to be the only person in a work group who brings their own bag lunch when everyone else takes a break together at the fast-food restaurant. It's tough for the college student to have just a couple of beers at the binge-drinking party. Why get out and hike or bike on the weekend when everyone else in the family is into movies, video games and television?

Beyond peer norms, however, is the phenomenal impact of a culture where gigantic profits are made from the promotion of unhealthy living. Mass media constantly challenges our efforts at a healthy lifestyle with billions of dollars of advertising promoting industrialized food, gas-guzzling pollution-mobiles, sugar-loaded beverages, and the message that materialism is the way to true happiness. A quick review of Eric Schlosser's book *Fast Food Nation*, or Morgan Spurlock's film *Super-size Me* will raise awareness of how the simple goal of greater profitability has cast human health aside.

The bottom line is that these forces in our society do have an impact on us, even though we all certainly have the ability to make our own choices. Free will may be a reality, but all that we have learned from social psychology would argue that it's not that simple.

The Desire to Change

When a wellness professional sees all the factors at work to hold a person's present lifestyle in stagnation, how can they hope to assist people to change? One of the continually remarkable and fascinating things about human beings is our desire to set out for the great unknown. Despite a dozen reasons to stay where we are, time and time again, we search for a better life and make our attempts at growth and change. What moves or motivates this desire for change? Love and fear are primary motivators. We are either moving towards something or away from something.

Psychiatrist Gerry Jampolsky (*Love Is Letting Go of Fear*) has long shared the wisdom from *A Course In Miracles*, that everything we do comes either from love or from fear. When we apply this to the lifestyle change arena we see that fear is motivating us not into fight or flight but into freeze or flight. Just like a rabbit in the brush as the hunter comes near, we might find that our fear causes us to become immobilized. We may fear the diagnosis, so we never go in for the exam! However, when we flush into flight, it is fear motivating us to take action. As Bill Cosby said in a comedy routine about the grim subject of cancer, "I figure if I don't go in and get the exam then the doctor can't tell me I've got it, and if he doesn't tell me that I've got it...then I ain't got it!"

A good wellness assessment tool may alert us to risks that are shortening the chances for us to have a long and healthy life. A new diagnosis or health incident may alarm us and motivate change. We may act out of fear of death or a life of disability. At the same time our motivation for change may come out of love of self.

It may be the love that we have for ourselves that motivates our desire to maintain life and health. It may be the love that we have for others who love and care about us. Many people quit smoking either to help their children avoid second-hand smoke, or out of a pledge they make to themselves to be around longer for those children or grandchildren.

Fear is often a great springboard for change. It can jolt us into taking action. Sustaining that action, however, is where fear begins to lose its effectiveness. One of the primary reasons for having a wellness coach is to succeed in lifestyle change where the client may have failed (perhaps repeatedly) in the past. When we look for change that lasts, when we look for the motivation to carry the person through the replacement of negative health habits with positive ones, we need to look to love. We will cover the motivational aspects of how to do this later in this book, but clearly self-esteem, self-love, is a well to be tapped to sustain our desire for change. Tapping into the innate self-loving forces that strive for self-actualization accesses a powerful energy that fuels change.

Seven Steps for Lasting Lifestyle Improvement

The pursuit of higher levels of wellness can take many forms. When we look at ways that wellness professionals and wellness coaches can help people in this process, this is one model to consider.

Seven Steps for Lasting Lifestyle Improvement

1. Assessment

In any change process it is important for a person to assess where they are and what they want to accomplish. Self-assessment, feedback from others, and evaluation tools all can help determine the current level of functioning in different areas or life dimensions. Looking at the whole person, the coach determines the client's readiness to change specific behaviors and assists him/her to set a direction.

We all need to develop the ability to observe ourselves. Taking stock of our wellness through some kind of thorough review process increases our self awareness and helps us determine areas to focus on. Again, some of the irony in wellness is that, for such a holistic concept, where we realize that every aspect of our lives is inextricably linked to every other aspect, we need to break it down into pieces we can work with. Mind, body, spirit and environment all benefit from examination.

As a coach you ask your clients questions with a specific purpose. Rather than gathering data for a diagnosis, you are instead posing questions that help your clients dig down and gain insights into how and why they do things. In your initial work with clients much can be gained by a supportive and patient exploration, in conversational form, of clients' current life and lifestyle. Avoid why questions and explore the what and the how of the client's life. Help them to put descriptions of their experiences into words. In doing so, your clients are required to observe, review, synthesize, and communicate about their experience in a way that is very different from just thinking about it to themselves. Realizations may emerge for your clients during this time and you can help to capture and work them into an effective wellness plan.

Wellness assessment tools provide valuable feedback for clients and often get at areas that might otherwise be ignored. Health risk assessments (HRA's), instruments like The Wellness Inventory, and Test Well help the client expand their awareness of how they are functioning in the life dimension areas included in the specific HRA.

As the work of James Prochaska, et. al. in *Changing For Good* reminds us, people don't change until they are ready to. A key part of the assessment phase of this model is helping your clients to realize which stage of change they are in with regard to each behavior they would like to improve, and how they currently define improvement.

2. Foundational Work On Self

Before any goal setting can be truly effective, action must be taken to increase awareness of self on environmental, interpersonal, intrapersonal, and spiritual levels. Exploration of various wellness teachings and systems are beneficial and may be carried out during this step.

It is tempting to simplify wellness work into a system of identifying something to work on, setting a goal and following up on progress. Sometimes this is adequate. When we look at how often lifestyle change efforts fail, perhaps we need to help the client dig a little deeper.

The original concept of wellness was rooted in the model of personal growth. When we help clients become excited about their own personal growth process the motivation for wellness becomes much more intrinsic. Supporting clients in their journey of self-exploration, and giving them permission and encouragement to do so helps access this internal drive to actualize potential and engage in change.

Foundational work on one's self requires a good, hard look at one's life, not just one's lifestyle. Values may need to be clarified. Time set aside for introspection and reflection may yield a more accurate vision of the changes that are really important for this person at this time in their life.

3. Setting the Focus
Desired outcomes become clear from the foundational work areas that a client wants focus on. Wellness action steps are developed that are designed to move clients toward the desired outcomes in these areas of focus.

Combining the information from the assessment phase with the realizations and insights of the foundational work on self, the coach helps clients to determine what they are ready, willing, and able to work on now and in the near future. A wellness plan is co-created. All the exploration and steps are brought together into this wellness plan.

Conscious awareness is what distinguishes a wellness lifestyle. It is with conscious awareness and thoughtfulness that a step-by-step plan is forged. Together the client and coach ask "Where do we want to go? How will we know when we've arrived?"

The wellness plan is an agreement for action. As the wellness plan is put into effect, agreements are formed about accountability. One of the real strengths of the coach approach is the way in which it helps a client hold themselves accountable to themselves. No more empty self-promises. Effective wellness coaching accountability is escape-proof.

4. Working Through Habit + Environmental Support
Old habits are overcome through repeated, patient and persistent action. When no longer desired habits re-emerge they are accepted as evidence of their truly habitual nature and discouragement is avoided. During this phase a person needs to develop a supportive environment

for lifestyle change to occur. We need peer health norms that support healthy changes, such as alliances with friends and wellness professionals support consistent action for healthy change.

As your wellness coaching client begins the actual process of behavioral change they are soon confronted with the power of habit. Lifestyles are defined by habit. The less awareness a person has, the greater the habitual power of the behavior will have over them. Most clients vow to change a certain behavior and when it re-emerges they blame themselves and make it a matter of lacking will power or strength of character. The wellness coach can truly serve their client well by reminding them of the true nature of habitual behavior and encouraging them to accept this and celebrate their success in noticing and catching the old behavior.

Friends do keep friends healthy. By strategizing with you, the wellness coach, your client can consciously seek out more and more environmental support for their wellness efforts.

5. Initial Behavioral Change

When we see initial success it is accepted and celebrated and not minimized. Seen as *initial* success, it is also recognized that more work remains. As resistance patterns emerge they are noted and addressed but not focused on endlessly.

Many clients tend to discount or minimize their successes. Sometimes, without a wellness ally, they don't even recognize when they have made progress. Especially early in the behavioral change process, it is paramount to identify successes and to celebrate and reinforce them.

Experiencing initial change in a particular behavior is often something the client has experienced before, but which did not last. Alone, it is easy to see some progress and then to revert back to old patterns and discouragement, even abandonment of all efforts at the desired change. Here you can play a vital role by not only keeping your client on task through accountability and support, but by helping them become conscious of their experience of the process. This is the time to tweak the wellness plan. Resistance patterns need to be identified and examined and the goals may need to be re-evaluated and perhaps re-adjusted.

6. Deeper Work On Self

Higher levels of self-awareness, fear and resistances are explored in this phase. The spiritual elements and emotional issues become primary. Systems of exploration learned earlier are used as tools to find the answers that come from inside rather than outside.

Experiencing change, even positive change, can bring up fear. Changes in lifestyle ripple through our lives affecting our relationships with others and engaging issues not previously thought about. A client who decides to drink less and less often must now deal with his or her drinking buddies who want to continue to party hard and often. A positive increase in setting boundaries and saying no to people can have totally unpredicted reactions by others. You may not be acting like the person people learned to care about or used to play with. Sometimes it brings up emotional closeness issues or trust and loss issues that may require reaching deeper inside to find the courage to maintain the changes.

Knee-deep in the change process, clients sometimes exhibit self-defeating behavior based on self-limiting beliefs about themselves and the world around them. The inner-critic absolutely abhors change and at this stage usually floods the client with all the lies they are willing to listen to about themselves. This is often been the place where discouragement takes over and previous wellness efforts were abandoned.

When this happens, the coach helps clients as they take their journey into the heart of self. If clients choose to explore old wounds and to do some deep healing, then a referral to psychotherapy is more in order than coaching. Coaching can go on simultaneously during therapy to continue progress on lifestyle improvement goals. The coach can continue to be an ally as the client searches for the answers that lie within.

7. Lasting Behavioral/Lifestyle Change

In this phase centering practices solidify and help maintain lifestyle improvements. Clients experience and enjoy good health and celebrate in joyous action. The lifestyle change has taken hold and the benefits of the change are the motivation. It has become part of the current lifestyle habits of the client. Periodic re-assessment maintains awareness and identifies new areas for attention. Alliances with friends and wellness professionals support the continuation of healthy lifestyle behavior.

Success is experienced and now the work is one of maintaining the successful change. As Prochaska points out in his Stages of Change model, until the new behaviors become almost automatic, the job is not done. Addiction models have taught us about relapse and there is a wellness equivalent. Now, the wellness coach helps reinforce the success and creates strategies with the client to maintain it. Self-efficacy feelings have to be high and alliances with others at home and work solid to assure that the changes will endure. Connectedness and social support now ensure lasting success. Agreements for periodic re-assessments will help keep the client vigilant and identify newly emerging areas to work on.

Personal growth has no end point. While coaching may be over, the client is encouraged to see their life as a continually evolving adventure.

The journey into self-love and self-acceptance must begin with self-examination . . . until you take the journey of self-reflection, it is almost impossible to grow or learn in life.

—**Iyanla Van Zant**, *Until Today*

Chapter 5

Becoming a Wellness Coach

So, faith is no more than the willingness and bravery to enter
and ride the stream. The mystery is that taking the risk to
be so immersed in our moment of living in itself joins us
with everything larger than us. And what is compassion but
entering the stream of another without losing yourself?

—**Mark Nepo,** *The Book of Awakening*

The helping professions attract wonderful people who are committed to serving others and making the world a better place. As interests and talents combine with what people believe about themselves and their own life circumstances, career directions develop. Some become social workers, some nurses, physicians, counselors, psychologists, and therapists of many varieties. A few even become wellness educators. For the most part though, wellness is not so much a profession as it is a way to practice one's profession.

The recently birthed profession of coaching sprang from the marriage of the business world and the world of psychology, counseling, etc. Coaching, and life coaching in particular, brought with it a set of competencies that are proving valuable throughout not only the business world, but the helping professions as well. When people graduate from reputable coach training schools, they gain expertise based on some of the most effective and cutting edge knowledge in the areas of communication, problem solving, creativity, conflict resolution and more.

Who Become Wellness Coaches

Wellness coaches seem to emerge from two primary sources; coaches who are drawn to wellness, and wellness professionals who are drawn to coaching. Life coaches discover that they can combine long-standing personal and professional interests in wellness and/or holistic health with the skills of their coaching training. Despite their own backgrounds in coaching and perhaps even in therapy, they may or may not be familiar with many of the concepts that have been developed by the wellness field and the related professions. The challenge is to learn what wellness truly is and the key concepts that form the basis of effective lifestyle behavioral change. Understanding wellness theories, assessments, and foundational concepts, such as readiness for change theory, are extremely helpful to the life coach.

For the wellness professional the challenge is learning one-on-one skills and how to apply them in their wellness work. While they may be very familiar with wellness and lifestyle improvement concepts and principles, their academic and on-the-job training is usually devoid of interpersonal skills work. If they did receive any client interview training, it may have been from the medical treatment model orientation of diagnostic data gathering. The skills of coaching open their eyes to a whole new world of interaction with their clients/patients.

Many wellness professionals decide to combine the mindset shift and skills of coaching with their existing wellness work. One example would be physical fitness trainers who add coaching to the fitness training work that they do. Such a person may or may not actually practice as a "wellness coach," but may simply be more "coach-like" in the way they do their work. This can be a very valuable shift for the wellness educator, the nurse practitioner, the diabetes educator, etc., as they interact with patients/clients in a more effective and productive way.

Some wellness professionals decide to complete training as a professional coach and either establish their own independent work, or function as a wellness coach within an existing organizational setting. Theirs is a more complete shift in professions and their work helping people make lasting lifestyle change now operates more completely from a coaching foundation.

. . . character transforms while persona copes.

—Kevin Cashman
(*Leadership From The Inside Out*)

What Makes a Good Coach

Williams and Davis, in their book, *Therapist As Life Coach*, list twenty characteristics that people who are drawn to coaching tend to have.

1. They are well adjusted and constantly seek personal improvement or development.
2. They have a lightness of being and *joi de vivre*.
3. They are passionate about "growing" as people.
4. They understand the distinction and balance between *being* and *doing*.
5. They are able to suspend judgment and stay open-minded.
6. They are risk-takers willing to get out of their own comfort zones.
7. They are entrepreneurial—even if they do not have great business skills they are visionaries, able to see the big picture and reinvent themselves and their business to meet current trends.
8. They want to have a life as well as a business.
9. They have a worldview and a more global vision.
10. They are naturally motivational and optimistic.
11. They are great listeners who are able to empathize with their clients.
12. They are mentally healthy and resilient when life knocks them down.
13. Their focus is on developing the future, not fixing the past.
14. They are able to collaborate and partner with their clients, shedding the "expert" role.
15. They have a willingness to believe in the brilliance or potential for greatness in all people.
16. They look at possibilities instead of problems and causes.
17. They exude confidence, even when unsure.
18. They present as authentic and genuine, with high integrity.

19. They are willing to say, "I don't know," and explore where and how to learn what is needed.

20. They enjoy what they do and are enthusiastic and passionate about life.

While wellness coaches may, or may not, have as many entrepreneurial and business-oriented tendencies, they do share these 20 characteristics, plus ten more:

1. They are committed to living the healthiest lifestyle possible.

2. They have fairly low needs for control.

3. They tend to be very centered emotionally and calm in a crisis.

4. They are patient, but not indulgent or enabling with their clients.

5. They tend to see patterns and be good systems thinkers.

6. They love to strategize and develop new ways to do things.

7. They believe that mind, body, spirit and environment all contribute to health and wellbeing.

8. They embrace challenges instead of fearing them.

9. They are perpetually curious about life in general and human behavior in particular.

10. They are life-long learners.

Getting Professional Training to Be a Coach

Learning to be more coach-like in the wellness work you do can be achieved best from direct training in coaching skills. The excitement about wellness coaching as a model for individualizing wellness services is driving some folks to just jump headlong into attempting one-on-one work after having just read a book and few articles. Winging it will only go so far, and the danger is that the newly self-proclaimed coach (or dubbed to be such by the organization) will not have the theoretical background, awareness of when to refer to treatment, and the actual powerful communication skills that are the foundation of coaching. These coaches may have more difficulty staying in the coach mindset and continue to revert back to the old models of prescribe and treat or educate and implore. Some wellness veterans who have been doing one-on-one work for years may benefit tremendously from discovering how the profession of coaching can hone their skills and give them an even more effective mindset and background.

Nothing beats live training with a qualified and experienced wellness coach/trainer and many trainers travel internationally. Teleconference courses in coaching are a close second. Many in the coaching profession feel that the highly interpersonal/interactive skills of coaching cannot and should not be attempted with solely online (computer based) learning. This is not a matter of studying data. It is learning both shifts in mindset and actual interactive skills that require practice, demonstration and feedback.

When a wellness professional wants to go in the direction of becoming qualified as a professional coach, seeking out training from recognized and certified schools is best. The first criterion would be looking for a coach training school that is certified by the International Coaching Federation (ICF). Meeting the rigorous standards of the ICF requires that a school offer quality courses taught by qualified and competent instructors. It is quality assurance that the student will receive the education they are promised and a certification that has respect. Equivalent certifications can be found offered in countries other than the United States. Though the ICF is indeed international, you may find other quality standard measures in your country.

With today's sophisticated world-wide communication systems, it is quite possible to receive coach training via teleconference calls from anywhere in the world. These may require some very early morning or late night calls from your time zone, however! You may also be able to enlist a mentor coach to provide individualized coach training.

Look for Wellness Coach Training

While some coaching schools offer a good life coach training program, not all may contain actual training in the specialty of wellness coach training. Missing from their programs may be emphasis on how to adapt coaching to the area of lifestyle behavioral change, and the theoretical and practical information from the wellness and health promotion fields that are essential to effective wellness coaching. Look for programs that offer you either complete training in wellness coaching or include a firm foundation in life coaching and also train specifically in wellness coaching as a specialty area.

Your Personal Wellness Foundation

Your credibility as a wellness coach depends to a great extent upon your dedication to your own wellness. This is truly an area where you must walk your talk. That doesn't mean you have already achieved physical, mental/emotional and spiritual perfection, or complete self-actualization. It means you are dedicated to working on improving your lifestyle, your health and wellbeing, and in the process of self-actualization. This will be quite evident and very inspiring to your clients.

There are a number of great rationales for continual work on your own Personal Wellness Foundation (PWF).

1. Doing so lends credibility and integrity to your work.
2. Your level of empathy and understanding is increased.
3. You will prevent burnout.
4. You continue to learn as both a provider and a consumer of wellness.

Your ability to appropriately self-disclose about your own wellness journey can be a real asset to the client's coaching experience. The worst coaching comes from someone who comes across, as "the way it is for me is the way it is for everyone." However, judicious and strategic use of self-disclosure builds trust. It conveys empathy by revealing that you have had (or have) your challenges too. Again, you are the ally, not the expert.

Any time you have an opportunity to make a difference
in this world and you don't, then you are
wasting your time on Earth.

—**Roberto Clemente**

My Own Story

Like many people I would experience muscle tension headaches from the tight muscles in my back. For many years my massage therapist, chiropractors and other had told me that strength training would help my occasional but persistent back problems immensely. However, I did not like strength training. I hated calisthenics. I was into aerobic conditioning and flexibility training through running, Yoga and Tai Chi. I was turned off by pumping iron.

I was well into my coaching career and a friend of mine and I were in the habit of meeting often at a local bagel shop. Before my eyes I watched him transform from a middle-aged guy with a pot belly into this amazingly strong, lean and vibrant man! I was intrigued to say the least. We had often talked about his career and family life challenges but his wellness lifestyle was an extremely positive factor that helped everything else in his life. He shared with me what he was doing to be suddenly so fit. He was following a well-structured diet and exercise program that was well researched and seemed to have a lot of validity to it. I was very curious.

I had coached many people who had engaged in one form or another of structured fitness/diet programs. Some programs were quite pre-packaged, others were self-administered following a book's instructions. I had never done any kind of program like that myself.

In my mid-fifties I embarked on unknown territory. With my friend's guidance, I began the same program. I bought the book and the accompanying materials. I began planning everything I ate and, most importantly, recorded everything that I actually did eat, six days a week. I began working out six days a week. My friend knew a lot about proper lifting technique and helped me to follow the program and include, for the first time, strength training into my exercise regiment. I stuck to it, and because of that, it worked!

Benefits for Me and For My Clients

The first one to benefit from the experience was me! I felt great! My energy level was much more constant throughout the day. I felt good about myself for losing ten pounds that all seemed to have been located around my waist, and certainly felt more attractive. I was clearly stronger and able to hike, paddle a canoe and lift portage loads easier. I also had to sheepishly admit that what the chiropractors and massage therapists had been telling me for years was true...strength training helped my back tremendously. I went through my first totally headache-free month in many years.

The others who benefited from my experience were my clients and students of wellness and wellness coaching. Before the new program I had been living a pretty good wellness lifestyle, exercising fairly regularly, but I had never engaged in any kind of a structured program.

Empathy for my clients who struggle with fitness programs and diets reached a new high. Suddenly I understood more from direct experience than I had been able to comprehend before. I knew that the experience of each of my clients was uniquely their own, but now I had more of a foothold in their world. It taught me many things about what that experience is like, and it taught me several principles that work to help someone lose weight and be fit.

Conscious Awareness Works

I realized that the awareness process of planning meals and then recording them was key. Unplanned meals for me had a tendency to be something quick and easy like white spaghetti pasta and bottled sauce, or a run to a restaurant. Planned meals were balanced, and more in line with things I really did like to eat. Recording them kept me honest, and kept the plan working.

Recording workouts in detail also helped me both stay regular and learn about this area of fitness that was new to me—strength training. I used solid principles from exercise physiology to guide my workouts and increased weights slowly, relying greatly on the principal of muscle development through adequate rest for the muscle groups affected.

Self-Perception

Probably the most powerful thing that the experience taught me came from the photographs. The program recommended that I take photographs of myself, just in a swimsuit, before the program, and afterwards. Mug shots of front, side and back views were brutally honest. I felt so bad about the digital pics that I took that I buried them somewhere in my computer where they would never show up accidentally on the screen.

When the ten weeks were up I took the second set of photos and examined them. I was disappointed in my results. Even though I had lost ten pounds, and more importantly, had lost almost ten per cent of my body fat, I still looked fat and out of shape. I was discouraged.

I looked for the before pictures and couldn't un-earth them from the depths of my hard drive. Having only the after pictures to look at, I focused in on the gut that was still there, the arms that had not transformed into guns, etc. Then, I finally found the before pictures and put them up side by side with the after pictures on my computer screen. My jaw dropped in astonishment. There was tremendous improvement evident.

Evident? It was obvious! I did look better. My back showed a lot of improvement, shifting from a weak looking structure holding up fairly broad shoulders, to a strong and healthy looking back. My gut was still there, but it had slimmed down! I realized how incredibly subjective the whole body image and self-perception experience is and how it can affect one's feelings. Of course I had worked over the years with many clients who struggled with these issues, but now I experienced first hand, what it was like. Looking in the mirror is ridiculous. We may as well look in a mirror at a carnival funhouse. Only when I had the objectivity of a camera lens did I see my improvement. No wonder my clients are so often discouraged, even when they do make progress!

Insuring Your Own Personal Wellness Foundation

Contrary to what one might imagine, not everyone who becomes a wellness coaching student is in stellar physical condition and optimal health. Not everyone in the wellness field runs marathons, meditates daily, eats a perfect diet, and climbs mountains on the weekends. We all tend, like our clients, to be incredibly—human! Our own wellness journeys teach us much that we can then apply to our coaching, but first of all they serve us ourselves.

Here are some quick guidelines for working on your own Personal Wellness Foundation.

1. Read and apply "The Ten Tenets of Wellness" to your own life. This sums up the basic principles for living your life well.

2. Work with a coach. This seems obvious, but it is important to not only buy into this concept and learn from it, but to

benefit from it as well.

3. Value every aspect of your life: mind, body, spirit and environment. Many of us have learned to only value intellectual development. Embrace the aspect that you have been neglecting most.

4. Make sure your movement (exercise) includes all three areas: endurance, strength and flexibility. Do the things that challenge you, and that you tend to avoid.

5. Pay attention to current research and decide what to apply from it to your own life. Remember how the food pyramid has been recently turned upside down?

6. Increase connectedness in your life, in every way possible. Lubricate existing connections to friends, family and neighbors. If you are self-employed this is especially critical.

7. Make it about your personal growth! Get excited about continuing to grow as a person and much of the motivation to be well in every aspect of your life will follow.

8. Practice extreme self care. Enough with the taking care of everyone else to the exclusion of yourself! Others benefit the most from a healthy and happy you!

9. Write it down. Maintain a personal wellness journal, and use methods that allows you to keep track of your wellness efforts.

10. Move your body outdoors whenever possible. Make the natural world your ally.

11. Discover what centers you in your life and do more of it on a regular basis, be it reading, dancing, connecting with friends, gardening, hiking or other activity.

12. Remember you are not your work.

> *It is the call to service, giving our life over to something larger than ourselves, the call to become what we were meant to become – the call to achieve our vital design.*
>
> **—Joe Jaworski**
> *Synchronicity—The Inner Path of Leadership*

Chapter 6

Creating the Alliance:
Let the Coaching Begin!

*I have seen that in any great undertaking it is not enough
for a man to depend simply upon himself.*

—**Lone Man** (Isna-la-wica)—Teton Sioux

Lone Man was a Teton Sioux who fought with Sitting Bull at the battle of Little Big Horn against Custer. His historical quote is ironic for a man of his name, yet it holds great wisdom. For a woman or man to simply depend upon themselves sounds ideal in many cultures. Self-sufficiency is a praiseworthy strength and I even include the concept in my "Ten Tenets of Wellness." Yet when we are faced with a truly great undertaking isn't it time for wisdom over strength alone? Today we would call it "working smarter, not harder."

Lone Man never considered taking on the Seventh Cavalry alone. When many of us attempt significant lifestyle change where we have failed before, it feels like the odds of success are about the same? It is a time for an ally, someone to help us move forward in a way we have not tried before.

Getting Clear On Coaching

One of the first tasks in wellness coaching is getting completely clear with your client about coaching and making sure it is a good fit for them. This might be done through an informal chat where you explain what coaching—and wellness coaching in particular—is and what it can do for a client. During this conversation you explore and really listen to the needs that your potential client has for services. Is coaching the right service for them at this time? If so, are you the right coach for them? If not you, then who might be? It's certainly about getting a good match formed where the client feels like they will be well served and progression towards their goals can be assured. A free mini-coaching session can be performed with the client at this time to give them a taste of what coaching is and contrast it with other helping experiences they have had.

If the client has come to see you in another capacity that you perform (wellness educator, nurse, fitness trainer, etc.), then introducing wellness coaching as another service that you can offer to help the client also requires clarity. Seek a mutual agreement that derives from the client understanding of what coaching is, how it works, and what it can do for them. Distinguish between the services that are part of your other role and the services of your coaching role. This is especially important when your non-coaching role is treatment or consultation oriented. When wellness professionals become more coach-like, they no longer just enroll, inform and educate their clients, they take the journey with them, by their sides. They accompany the client as their professional ally.

When you step into the role of coach and co-create an alliance to work together, the client needs to be aware of, and in agreement with, their own role as coachee. Especially in the area of wellness coaching you may find your clients, who are looking for ways to improve their lifestyle, still want you to take primary responsibility for this task. They may still be operating on the prescribe and treat mindset that they are used to, and that you have worked hard to shift out of.

Who's Responsible for What?

One of the absolute best questions to pose to a coaching client is "Who's responsible for what?" This is a great question for the client who is working through a conflict in the workplace, and an excellent question for all sorts of partners (business, marital, etc.) to be clear on. It is also a key question for wellness coaching.

One of the benefits of the coach approach that wellness professionals get really excited about is that it shifts responsibility for their own health and wellbeing back onto the client. Wellness professionals suddenly feel free of the burden of having to come up with all the answers for their client. By requiring their client to make their own effort coaches are not shirking their work and the client will benefit more from that approach. They've even learned how to deal with the clients who cry "Just tell me what to do!" by honoring their frustration, patiently explaining the benefits of an approach where the client finds their own answers and elaborating on how the coach can, and will, be of support.

Gaining buy-in from your client around the concept of self-responsibility for their own health may not be an overnight accomplishment. It is not about who's to blame for the state of one's health, but it is about the client's acceptance of responsibility for shifting their present lifestyle in such a way as to improve their health and reduce their risks. When clients give up the stance of the victim and embrace their own power to improve their lives, real progress begins.

You can pave the way towards such full acceptance of responsibility by working out with the client, in very concrete terms, who's responsible for what in the coaching alliance. Most coaches use agreement forms that spell out the details of the coaching arrangements. Appointment times, cancellation policies, fees and other details, are all spelled out in writing. As we'll see in later chapters, the coach also works with the client and their challenges and goals around the concept of accountability in a system of very clear agreements. (See the appendix)

We make all sorts of assumptions because we don't have the courage to ask questions.

—**Don Miguel Ruiz,** *The Four Agreements*

Agreements vs. Expectations

To be more coach-like when working with clients, be aware of which agreements have been made (and which have not), and be very aware of what expectations are being operated upon.

- Expectations are much like assumptions. We expect (assume) that Larry will know the right thing to do. We expect (assume) that Mary knows how she is supposed to follow up after our meeting.

- Expectations are much like wishing and hoping. We hope that Larry does his job the way we instructed him.

- Unmet expectations are very disappointing. The more we expect, the more we may be disappointed.

- Unmet expectations are very hard to confront. Failure to communicate the expectation properly will most likely result in someone being blamed instead of real responsibility being taken.

- Agreements clarify the question of "Who's responsible for what?"

- Agreements need to be fashioned continually even when it seems laborious to do so. Writing them down may help.

- Agreements work best when they are "true agreements," that is, the agreement is reached mutually.

- Broken agreements are easy to confront. "I thought we had an agreement that you would do_____ by_____."

- Clearly-stated agreements that seem impossible to meet can be re-negotiated with more ease than expectations or ambiguous agreements.

Expect nothing. Be prepared for anything.

—Samurai saying

"Expect nothing. Be prepared for anything." This does not mean expect nothing to happen. It means do not have any expectations. It means to expect only what is agreed upon to happen. Approach each person and each situation without assumptions or expectations. Make clear agreements.

Thomas Leonard was fond of saying: "Give up all hope . . . but have faith." Wishing and hoping don't get the job done. Faith in yourself and others (who have earned your trust) and, perhaps in, shall we say, "something greater" does work!

Permission

The coach is aware of what a coaching relationship needs to look like. The client may not be as familiar with it. To proceed and attain agreements as a coach you need to operate using the process of permission over and over again. Whitworth, et.al., call permission the heart of the intake session. They see all actions being filtered through this process, which continually honors the client. Doing so helps the client realize that they are the ones in charge and that you are working for them. Clients learn their role is not that of student or unquestioning patient, but rather as decision maker, the captain of their soul and master of their fate.

Coaching language is permeated with permission. Continually ask your client "May I ask about . . . ?" "Can we explore this further?" "Would you like to look deeper into this area, or not?" "May I make a suggestion?" "Would you like to hear about some resources I know of in this area?" Permission continually honors the client and their own ability to help themselves. It also really helps you to stay within the mindset of ally, not expert.

The Foundation Session: Two Time-Tracks for Wellness Coaching

Much of the literature on coaching and psychotherapy is written based on the private practice or clinic model of lengthy appointments. The "fifty minute hour" of counseling and therapy is quite standard. In coaching most scenarios describe a one or two hour foundation session, followed by either half-hour appointments (most commonly on a weekly or four-a-month basis), or even hour-long appointments.

Wellness coaches who either have their own business, or are working with organizations as an out-sourced wellness coach may work on the same time model. There are some situations where an on-staff wellness coach may have this much time available to work with clients, but not often. Frequently either the wellness professional doing wellness coaching as part of what they do or the wellness coach in a corporate or healthcare setting has a very brief amount of time with their client. Fifteen to twenty minutes may be the maximum contact time they get with a client at any one time. To honor the reality of these two different time situations, I will present two different approaches to working with wellness coaching clients. There is much overlap in the models because the basic concepts used in both are the same. Time availability and how to focus the coaching quickly are the main differences.

Sample Agreement

Name _____

Address _____

Phone # _____

Email _____

Initial term _____ months   From _____ Through _____

This fee is $ _____ per month and my method of payment will be _____

Session day: _____ Session time: _____ Session length: _____ Sessions per month: _____

Referred by: _____

Other: _____

Protocol: 1. Client calls the coach at the schedule time.

                 2. Client pays coaching fees in advance.

                 3. Client pays for long-distance charges, if any.

1. As a client, I understand and agree that I am fully responsible for my well-being during my coaching class, including my choices and decisions. I am aware that I can choose to discontinue coaching at any time. I recognize that coaching is not psychotherapy and that professional referrals will be given if needed.
2. I understand that "life coaching" is a relationship I have with my coach that is designed to facilitate the creations/development of personal, professional or business goals and to develop and carry out a strategy/plan for achieving those goals.
3. I understand that life coaching is a comprehensive process that may involve all areas of my life, including work, finances, health, relationships, education and recreation. I acknowledge that deciding how to handle these issues and implement my choices is exclusively my responsibility.
4. I understand that life coaching does not treat mental disorders as defined by the American Psychiatric Association. I understand that life coaching is not a substitute for counseling, psychotherapy, psychoanalysis, mental health care or substance abuse treatment; and I will not use it in place of any form of therapy.
5. I promise that if I am currently in therapy or otherwise under the care of a mental health professional, that I have consulted with this person regarding the advisability of working with a life coach and that this person is aware of my decision to proceed with the life coaching relationship.
6. I understand that information will be held as confidential unless I state otherwise in writing, except as required by law.
7. I understand that certain topics may be anonymously share with other life-coaching professionals for training OR consultation purposes.
8. I understand that life coaching is not to be used in lieu of professional advice. I will seek professional guidance for legal, medical, financial, business, spiritual or other matters. I understand that all decisions in these areas are exclusively mine and I acknowledge that my decisions and my actions regarding them are my responsibility.

I have read and agree to the above.

_____   _____
Client Signature   Date

Reproducible Worksheet Masters are available for purchase on CD ROM from Whole Person Associates, 210 W. Michigan St., Duluth, MN 55802, 800-247-6789, www.wholeperson.com.

FIGURE 6.1

Sample Client Policies and Procedures

Welcome to coaching as my client. I look forward to working with you. There are a few guidelines that I expect clients to maintain in order for the relationship to work. If you have any questions, please call me.

Fee	Clients pay me on time unless prior arrangement has been made. Payment may be made by check or credit card.
Procedure	My clients call on time. Come to the call with updates, progress, and current challenges. Let me know what you want to work on, and be ready to be coached. Make copies of the enclosed client prep form and fax or e-mail a completed form before each call. The agenda is client-generated and coach-supported.
Calls	Our agreement includes a set amount of calls. If you or I are on vacation, we spend more time before you/I leave and after you/I return.
Changes	My clients give me 24 hours notice if they have to cancel or reschedule a call. If you have an emergency, we will work around it. Otherwise, a missed call is not made up.
Extra Time	You may call between sessions if you need "spot coaching", have a problem, or can't wait to share a win with me. (You can also fax or e-mail me.) I enjoy delivering this extra level of service. I do not bill for additional time of this type, but I ask that you please keep the extra calls to five or ten minutes. When you leave a message, let me know if you want a call back or if you are just sharing.
Problems	I want you to be satisfied with our relationship. If I ever say or do something that upsets you or doesn't feel right, please bring it up. I promise to do what is necessary for your satisfaction.
A Must	It is necessary for the client to implement the coaching for it to be a success. You have hired a coach to help you do things differently. If you choose to not use the coaching and keep doing what you have always done, you will get the results you have always received.

Reproducible Worksheet Masters are available for purchase on CD ROM from Whole Person Associates, 210 W. Michigan St., Duluth, MN 55802, 800-247-6789, www.wholeperson.com.

FIGURE 6.2

Track One—The Conventional Time Coaching Model

Once you have established clear agreements about your coaching it's time to launch the coaching process through your Foundation Session. Intake sounds too clinical for the first coaching meeting. In this session you are building the alliance together by laying the foundation of your professional relationship together. Some coaches call this the exploration or discovery session.

The Foundation Session Is About:

- Listening deeply to the client's story and honoring it through acknowledgement.
- Grounding the coach in the world of the client.
- Building trust.
- Determining what works best for coaching this particular client.

- Getting clear on what the client is asking for in the coaching relationship.

- Evaluating the client's readiness for change on key areas they want to work on.

- Co-creating an initial wellness plan based on areas of focus and readiness.

- Getting the client started with initial action-steps for which they are prepared.

The ideal format is for the coach to have the client complete a welcome packet (see appendix) and perhaps a wellness assessment tool as well (online or paper). The coach and client then schedule either two contiguous hours for the foundation session, or two one-hour appointments within the first one or two weeks to go over the information you have gathered and do the foundational work.

The foundation session should have a comfortable flow to it where the coach and client are meeting each other as equals and getting acquainted. Differing in intent from a casual or even business-like connection, the wellness coaching relationship is started with the conscious intention that it be an alliance designed to help the client improve their lifestyle.

Foundation Session Road Map
Within the flow of interaction the coach follows a road map that makes sure important processes are completed. While you might create your own content to such a map, certain areas need to be considered. These would include:

- *Connect with your client.* Relate with genuineness, honesty and sincerity.

- *Get on the same page.* Inquire about the best way to coach this person. Offer them choices and options. Help them see what coaching entails and what might work best with them.

- *Begin your exploration together.* Ask directly what they would like to focus on in coaching.

- *Get a horizon-to-horizon view.* Use a simple tool like The Wheel of Life to help the client get a complete view of balance and fulfillment in their entire life.

- *Clarify values.* Through questions, conversation, and possibly exercises, help the client to clarify what is important to them, what gives them meaning and purpose in life.

- *Take stock.* Help the client to recognize and acknowledge strengths they possess and where they receive support for a healthier way of living. What are they aware of (both within themselves, and in their environment) that is working for them and against themselves? How ready are they for change?

- *Co-create an initial wellness plan.* Strategize with the client to set up areas of focus: initial goals that are specific, practical, inspirational, realistic and obtainable (the SPIRO model). Agree upon action steps that the client is ready to initiate. Agree upon criteria that will allow for recognition of when the client has achieved those goals.

- *Secure an agreement* of accountability.

- *Leave the client knowing* exactly what to do next, and exactly how to prepare for the next session.

- *Leave them with an inquiry*—something to ponder about themselves and their way of living.

Track Two—The Limited Time Coaching Model

In the situation where a wellness professional is individualizing the wellness services that they provide through using wellness coaching and/or wellness coaching skills, time is often limited. Some common scenarios may look like this:

- An employee is given a wellness/health assessment (usually an HRA—health risk assessment), and a follow-up session is provided. The wellness professional usually has somewhere between 15 and 55 minutes with this person, with 20-30 minutes being most common.

- An employee is attracted to wellness coaching services that are offered as an aspect of a larger wellness program offered by their employer. These are usually time limited and often focused on specific challenges.

- An employee may be referred for wellness coaching by the medical/health program of the organization, but the system only allows for very brief sessions.

In the role of the wellness professional you are faced with many of the same tasks outlined above, connecting with the client, building trust, etc. Your real challenge is that you need to do this in much less time, and yet still be effective.

A Key Skill From Coaching For Time Limited Wellness Coaching: Laser Coaching

The profession of coaching has developed some skills that are more central to personal coaching and serve this time-limited situation well. Thomas Leonard, a founder of the coaching movement, liked to urge coaches to use laser coaching. The key here is for you to maintain empathy and compassion, and yet cut through the client's story and maintain laser-like focus without any distracting tangents being allowed. The more masterful coach can acknowledge the client's experience and help them feel heard, yet will continually guide the client to stay on the subject at hand, get to the point (which can be fact or feeling), and help the client assess what action they are ready to take (or not).

Often the content of the client's story is not as important as how they felt about it, or what they have concluded about it in their lives. There may be a very long and drawn out story about how someone became overweight that a client feels compelled to share. Your client may actually not feel so much of a need to share it anymore (having done so with many others before you), but may assume that you want to hear the entire tale. You may have to interrupt this process and, after acknowledging their experience and its importance to them, urge them to move ahead in the story to the most recent chapters. Let them know that you really care about how their experience is affecting them now. Ask powerful questions that help them focus on what is important in the present.

In the field of Gestalt therapy the emphasis is not on the past, but on the here and now. Borrowing from this way of working with people, we help our clients to presentify their experience. We acknowledge that we cannot do a thing about the past, what happened was real, and the key is how the person feels about it, how it affects them, and what they are aware of about it in the present.

Forgiveness is giving up all hope for a better past.

—Jack Kornfield

The Foundation Session (Time-Limited Model) Is About:

- Showing evidence that you are listening to the client's story and honoring it through acknowledgement.

- Grounding (the coach) in the world of the client.

- Building trust quickly and genuinely.

- Determining what works best for coaching this particular client.

- Clearly establishing what the client is asking for in the coaching relationship.

- Conveying to the client what the coaching relationship can look like, given the time- limited nature of this specific coaching situation.

- Evaluating the client's readiness for change on the key area they want to work on.

- Co-creating an initial wellness plan based on areas of focus and readiness for change.

- Getting the client started with initial action-steps for which they are prepared.

As you can see, much of the same work needs to be done, but in a much shorter time frame. The reality is that the same degree of depth and even accuracy about what really needs to be worked on will be less likely to be accomplished. This is one of the trade-offs that comes with the time-limited territory. It is not a true substitute for the broader and deeper work that the conventional coaching model will bring.

Foundation Session Road Map—Time Limited Model

- *Connect with your client.* Relate with genuineness, honesty and sincerity.

- *Give the client a quick introduction* to the structure of your time together and how it can/will be used. Share the responsibility for keeping track of the time during the session.

- *Begin your exploration together.* Ask directly what they would like to focus on in the session.

- *Bring the session into focus.* If they have completed a tool like an HRA, begin to review it. Start by asking what the experience of taking it was like. ** Get welcome packet and basic assessment information online or by fax prior to the foundational session to save time and allow you time to review before the session.*

- *Take stock.* Help the client to recognize and acknowledge strengths they possess and where they receive support for a healthier way of living. What are they aware of (both within themselves, and in their environment) that is working for them and against themselves? How ready are they for change?

- *Make it more coach-like.* Explain to the client how you can be more of a coach with them, instead of only providing treatment or education, and what that can look like.

- *Co-create an initial wellness plan.* Strategize with the client to set up areas of focus, initial goals that are specific, practical, inspirational, realistic and obtainable (the SPIRO model). Agree upon action steps that the client is ready to initiate. Agree upon criteria that will allow for recognition of when the client has achieved those goals.

- *Secure an agreement* of accountability.

- *Leave the client knowing* exactly what to do next, and exactly how to prepare for the next session and securing a time for that to happen.

- *Leave them with an inquiry*—something to ponder about themselves and their way of living.

Trust

What allows a client to walk into a room, or pick up a phone, and start trusting someone? Establishing trust is central to the coaching relationship. As a wellness coach, what do you have going for you, to help establish trust from the beginning? What do you have to do to earn and grow that trust?

> *Trust men and they will be true to you; treat them greatly,*
> *and they will show themselves great.*

—**Ralph Waldo Emerson**

Trust is often difficult to wrap one's arms around. What is it really? How can we define it? Merriam-Webster's Dictionary defines it as "assured reliance on the character, strength, or truth of someone or something." The question now becomes what is present in the character of someone that allows us to assign that assured reliance? One way of breaking it down is to look for the consistent presence of integrity, competence and compassion.

As a wellness coach you first convey integrity by simply being who you are. Don Miguel Ruiz (*The Four Agreements*) calls it "being impeccable with your word." You speak the truth, you say what you mean, and mean what you say. You are reliable and predictable. You can be counted on. You are the ally you purport to be.

You also convey integrity by your level of professionalism. Your clients will be more likely to trust a healthcare professional (the good side of the "white coat effect"), and a truly professional coach who comes across as well trained and preferably is certified in that training. Integrity is also implied by the coach handling their business in a professional business-like way with a business-like (yet caring) appearance.

Competence will also show through in the actions of the well-trained and professional coach. When coaches demonstrate the competencies listed by the ICF as central to the profession of coaching (see appendix), clients know they are in good hands and trust increases as the relationship goes on.

Compassion is the heart and soul of coaching. It is a human being-to-human being experience of acceptance, caring and understanding. Even if we do not agree with the other person's actions, we accept them and reach within ourselves to attempt to understand the other person's experience. Compassion is complete when we find a way to convey it to the other person.

For someone who must struggle to share compassion with others, choosing coaching profession is about the most incongruent career fit there is. If we are not being compassionate, are we being judgmental? It is hard to tread some kind of neutral space between the two. Empathy and compassion is how we move out of judgment. They are how we train our psyche to avoid being judgmental.

When we come into contact with the other person, our thoughts and actions should express our mind of compassion, even if that person says and does things that are not easy to accept. We practice in this way until we see clearly that our love is not contingent upon the other person being lovable.

—**Thich Nhat Hanh**

Everyone has trust issues. We cannot control, and are not responsible for the trust issues of others that make forming an alliance more challenging. All we can do is live our lives as the kind of person others can put their trust in. Trust is partly about doing (our consistent and reliable actions), but largely about being. The more we coach from the centered place of who we truly are, the more trustworthy we appear.

Foundational Coaching Skills

You have a client who is seeking ways to improve their life and their lifestyle. You've connected and co-created a coaching alliance that has you both excited about change. Now what do you do?

You are making good use of your basic coaching skills and you have taken it one step further into the realm of wellness coaching. Our purpose here is not to duplicate the already great training that is out there on basic coaching skills. Understanding and developing competency in the ICF Coaching Core Competencies (see appendix) are critical to the development of a professional coach. On the foundational level though, because of its importance, I would like to share more on the importance of listening.

Giving Evidence Of Listening

Seek first to understand, then to be understood.

—**Stephen Covey**

A central part of the training that anyone in any kind of human service receives is about the importance of listening. In the conflict training that I developed twenty years ago, I saw how vital it is that people in conflict feel they are truly being heard. A perception that they are being dismissed or not really being listened to, escalates the conflict. People speak louder (as though you truly are not hearing the sounds they are making), get angrier, and move closer to violence. When people feel they are being heard, they calm down, speak softer and are more reasonable. The conflict usually de-escalates. When people talk about their health and wellbeing, really personal and vital topics for them, you need to listen with professional skill.

When we need to tell our story, we want to be heard and we want to know that we are being heard. When my dog, or a deer I see in the woods listens to sounds I am making I can tell because their ears move. Since it would be possible for me to sit in front of you motionless and speechless, and yet have my ears work perfectly, taking in every sound you make, how do you know that I am really listening? There is much more to listening than having my ear drums vibrate with your sound waves. Am I getting it? Am I understanding and comprehending what you are saying? How do you know that you are, in fact, making a connection? Well, I have to give you evidence that I really am listening.

Giving evidence is about observable behavior. Your client needs to be able to see and hear evidence that you are not only absorbing sounds, you are really hearing them. We do this in two primary ways, non-verbal and verbal behavior.

Evidence of effective listening non-verbal behaviors include good eye contact, appropriate and naturally changing facial expression, open posture and natural, relaxed movement. During a face-to-face, rather than teleconference coaching session, you have the opportunity to build trust and faith with your client by evidencing good non-verbal coaching listening behavior. It's your chance to show them that you are really with them.

The words you say that can be transcribed on paper are your vocal behavior. The rest is non-verbal. Make good use of your voice to engender trust, sincerity, self-disclosure, and commitment. If you tend to have a soft voice, this is a time to pump up the volume. If you tend to be loud, use your voice volume very, very consciously. Tone, inflection, accentuation, and that elusive conveyance of sincerity, are all key to demonstrating that you are really with your client every step of the way.

Verbal Evidence of Listening

When I reiterate to you the essence of what you just said, then you know that I am listening to you well. The good ol' basic coaching skills of paraphrasing, reflection of feeling, and summarization really shine here. Using them shows your client that you are tracking well with them. You give evidence that you not only are hearing the words correctly, but that you get the meaning, the feeling, of what your client is saying. As simple as this sounds, it is of paramount importance. Listening on many levels and doing it well, then giving evidence to your client that this is what you are doing, builds the coaching alliance perhaps better than anything else. Continuing to give this evidence continues and deepens the relationship and the effectiveness of the coaching.

> *The Great Good Spirit gave us two ears and one mouth so*
> *we would listen twice as much as we speak.*

> —**Shawnee** (Native American) saying

Chapter 7

Charting the Course of Change: Wellness Mapping 360°

The most fundamental aggression to ourselves, the most fundamental harm we can do to ourselves, is to remain ignorant by not having the courage and the respect to look at ourselves honestly and gently.

—Pema Chodrin
When Things Fall Apart

Wellness coaches help their clients to see their health and wellbeing as part of an infinite and incredibly interconnected web. Our wellness is determined not just by ideas we have, or information we are aware of, but by every aspect of that web. When we tug on one strand, the vibration is felt in the entire web.

I often explain to my new clients that during the course of our coaching we will at times roll up our sleeves and put our elbows on the table and really focus on one particular thing. At other times, we will shove ourselves away from the table and go out and get into a hot-air balloon, where we will rise up into the sky and look at their life from horizon to horizon, three hundred and sixty degrees.

In the medical model it is easy to slip into an analytic, atomistic, sequential process that narrows down a wealth of information into a diagnosis. Conventional medicine today is starting to realize that mere symptom reduction diagnosis and treatment are inadequate. The tremendous surge in the use of integrative medicine approaches in Europe, North America and elsewhere, is evidence that the public sees increasing value in methods that work with the whole person. Since wellness is a holistic concept, wellness coaching, by its very definition is holistic.

In the next chapters we will look at ways to help our clients improve their lifestyle behavior by fashioning a path through the huge landscape of wellness and health. To guide them and you on that journey we have developed a process or a model of wellness coaching we call Wellness Mapping 360°©. *(You can find more about this model and how to become a Wellness Mapping 360° coach at the end of this book.)*

Wellness Mapping 360°

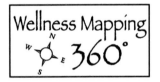

Assessment & Exploration

Never assume the obvious is true.

—William Safire

Sometimes our clients know exactly what they want to work on, and sometimes getting clear about it is your starting point. Remember the "You Are Here" marks on maps in downtown areas or shopping malls? Every journey has to start from somewhere, but some of our clients come to us precisely because they know a journey is needed, but they really aren't sure what port they are setting sail from. To begin our voyage of discovery and exploration of wellness, we have to be very clear about where we are from the start.

Groundedness

In many spiritual traditions the purpose of ceremony is to ground you and orient you so that you have a solid sense of where you are to begin your journey to higher places. The coaching relationship itself helps to do this. As your client tells you their story, answers your powerful questions, and completes your assessment instruments, they do so only partly to provide you with information. They do so to hear themselves, and sometimes they are surprised at what they discover themselves saying. The foundation session(s) helps them organize their thinking and helps them review and take stock of their lives. This grounds them in the present moment, taking the focus off the desired outcome that perhaps brought them through the coaching door and brings them to the here and now

Coaches believe their clients. When your client speaks you are there to listen and work with them, not to judge them. Since you are not in a treatment situation, you are not there to "figure out what is really going on." Your job is not to dig for the truth. It is to create the container in which the client feels safe enough to reveal the truth, to you, and to themselves.

In therapy I would often find clients would come in with what I called an "admission ticket." Their "ticket" was some sort of issue that was less fearful to discuss. As trust was developed they often felt safe enough to talk about the more serious, underlying issue. In coaching I don't sit in suspicion. I do, however, never make an assumption that what I've heard is the entire story. Likewise, I never assume that every molehill is yearning to become a mountain.

The Value of Self-exploration

Requests from clients need to be taken at face value. If your client says they are here to lose weight, here's the diet, here's the exercise program, let's go, what are you to do? They just might be so ready to change that all they need is some of the support and accountability aspects of coaching. They may also be doing what they think they should do, or what they have always done before (and usually failed at). You don't want to throw cold water on their enthusiasm, but you might also invite them to take a good look at where they are right now before they launch into their program.

The wellness journey, or quest, begins like any other classic quest, with self-knowledge. The coaching process can be the rare oasis where the client has complete permission to take a deeper look at their self. The style of wellness coaching that I teach emphasizes motivation, not information. Many of your clients will have a fair to excellent understanding about what they need to do to be well. Helping them understand their own motivation, and the lack thereof, is a true value the coach can offer.

It may be very tempting to stay in the diagnose and treat mindset and quickly set up a behavioral coach-knows-best program. When we remind ourselves to stay in the coaching mindset of the wellness ally, we shift into a mode of facilitation and allowing, of assisting our client on their journey.

Allow your client adequate time, to the degree you can, to tell their story. You are not there to be therapist-like or priest-like, but instead to be a witness. Your professional level of listening, your very genuine and human compassion, your challenging coach nature, will help them feel acknowledged, validated and whole. The bonus for your client is that this very basic human process helps them fight their own inner critic, their own demons, that have been sabotaging their previous attempts at lifestyle change. This strengthening process is like getting in shape physically before you head off to climb the 14,000 foot peak.

We shall not cease from exploration and the end of all our exploring will be to arrive where we started . . . and know the place for the first time.

—T.S. Eliot

Tools for Exploration

Part of the power of coaching is that it does not just take place for one fifty-minute hour a week. It is an ongoing process for the client beyond the time in person or on the phone with the coach. Encourage your client to explore themselves in greater breath and depth by using a number of other tools.

1. Journaling. When you sit around and think you engage in one type of cognitive process. When you speak with me you engage in yet another cognitive process. When you sit down and write, you engage in still another cognitive process. Why not use all three?

Encourage your client to journal in a way that fits for them. Secure a commitment from them (if they are up for it) as to how many times a week they will journal. Usually a commitment to write every single day is a set-up for self-failure. Committing to only once or twice a week probably deserves a challenge from the coach to examine what they truly would benefit most from.

2. Solo Time. If your client seems to have little time to reflect, perhaps they need to literally get away from it all. There is a rich tradition through history and all around the world that encourages the seeking soul to spend some time alone and away from business-as-usual. Christ's forty days in the wilderness, the Australian Bushman's walk about, the Native American vision quest, are all examples of processes that call upon solo time for insight, and often, breakthroughs.

There are profound guided experiences that your client might want to sign on for (see resources section). There are also ways in which a client may want to engineer some time away from work/home that are safe, and practical for them. Coach them through the process of planning and carrying out such a personal self-exploration process. (See "Living the Ten Tenets of Wellness" in the resources section.)

3. Bibliocoaching. What we used to call bibliotherapy now serves us in the personal growth arena as well. Coach your client through the process of selecting and following through on reading (yes, there's the value of a coach!), several titles that match their interest and the questions they hold for themselves. Sometimes good books on the very process of change, such as *Who Moved My Cheese*, can contain great insights. I find myself making extraordinary use of the Don Miguel Ruiz book *The Four Agreements*.

Some books may be more for wellness information, but in this exploration phase, books that point the way into self-exploration/self-discovery are very valuable. Ask permission to make suggestions if your client has no idea of where to start, or sit down and do some exploration online with them.

4. Life Review. Another tool to offer is the life review process. You might start with a time-line of the client's life that indicates from the date of birth onward, the significant events in the client's life. Make a yearly indicator across the timeline to the present, leaving the end open for the future. Then have your client enter on the timeline the events that occurred in their life at the time they happened. Ask them to write down what they learned from going through the experiences.

- How did you grow from it?

- What ways of living and coping did you adopt from it?

- Was your adopted behavior something that worked then, but doesn't serve you now?

Don't get into the paralysis of analysis. Support them in avoiding self-criticism and regret. Focus on how the person became who they are and how it affects them in the present moment.

Richard Bach in his little classic *Illusions* likes to say that everything we experience in life is either something we are learning from, or something we are just enjoying! Help your client in their exploration process realize what they are continuing to learn.

5. Quieting Practice. The process of change and self-exploration, insight and understanding requires patience. Sometimes it is like the old Japanese rice farmer story. The farmer was so anxious to have his fields produce a harvest that at night he would go out and pull on the rice stalks to try to make them grow faster! Sometimes we too are tempted to pull on the rice stalks at night in the hopes that they will grow faster but must realize that all we can do is be aware and believe in self and the world. You can be at peace if you have done everything possible to reach your goal in the moment.

You might ask permission and suggest to your client that they experiment with simply sitting and spending ten or fifteen minutes a day doing nothing. If they already practice some form of prayer or meditation that produces a sense of stillness encourage them to use it. What works here is not a reflective self-questioning process, which is intellectual and keeps us psycho-physiologically active. Just have the person be with a simple emptying of the mind.

If the sitting meditation style doesn't work well for your client, encourage them to spend fifteen minutes a day walking alone in silence, while letting thoughts come in and then evaporate. Have them focus on their breathing and their steps. Yoga, Tai Chi, and other quieting practices may be of interest to your client. Support their exploration.

The important thing here is that the quieting practice not be just another thing to do. It needs to be effortless effort. It is a clearing of the mind so that the work done later will be fresher and more focused.

Don't just do something! Sit there!

—Old Zen saying

6. The Welcome Packet. Your client welcome packet (see appendix) should contain powerful, thought-provoking questions well beyond just assembling informational data. Ask your new client what their dreams are! Ask them what they know they must complete in this lifetime to feel fulfilled. Experiment with creating your own welcome packet that is just the right length, not too long and laborious, not too brief and inadequate.

If your client skipped over the more reflective questions in your welcome packet, explore their experience with them. "Tell me about the questions you chose not to answer." You may help them to slow down a minute and realize something about themselves. Are they in just so big of a hurry in life that they felt they couldn't slow down and reflect for a moment? What are they afraid of? Help them find out.

If your client is willing, obtain an agreement to complete the more reflective questions. Explain to them the benefits of doing so for both you and themselves. Set up a good way to hold them accountable for completion.

Laying the Foundation for Coaching

As your coach, it's important for me to understand how you view the world in general, yourself, your family and your job or career. Each person comes from a unique place in their thinking and in the way they interact with the world around them.

Answering these questions clearly and thoughtfully, will serve both you and me. You may find that they help you clarify perceptions about yourself and the direction of your life. These are "pondering" type questions, designed to stimulate your thinking in a way that will make our work together more productive. Take your time answering them. If they are not complete by our first (foundation) session, just bring what you have completed and finish the rest later. These answers will be treated with complete professional confidentiality.

Occupation / nature of business: _____

Employers or Business Name: _____

Date of birth: _____ Marital status_____

Do you have children? _____ Do your children live with you? _____

Coaching

1. What do want to get from the coaching relationship?_____
_____
_____

2. What is the "best" way for me to coach you most effectively, what tips would you give to me about what would work best? _____
_____
_____

3. Do you have any apprehension or preconceived ideas of coaching? _____
_____
_____

Job / Career

1. What do you want from your job / career? _____
_____
_____

2. What projects or tasks are you involved in currently or regularly?_____
_____
_____

Reproducible Worksheet Masters are available for purchase on CD ROM from Whole Person Associates, 210 W. Michigan St., Duluth, MN 55802, 800-247-6789, www.wholeperson.com.

FIGURE 7.1

Wellness Assessments

Knowing is not enough; we must apply.
Willing is not enough; we must do.

—Johann Wolfgang von Goethe

As we start our lifestyle change journey, a more thorough inventory of our current condition and equipment might be wise. Wellness assessments can help us in ways that our reflective dialogue with our clients does not reach.

Wellness assessments allow us to get more of an actual measurement of where we are to start with, our baseline. Knowing truly where we are, we can measure later to see what progress is made. It's kind of like taking GPS coordinates, or working with our compass to locate where we truly are on the map to start with.

Wellness assessments give our clients feedback on a number of variables that are very relevant and often critical to their health. Wellness assessments often ask questions that would never occur to the client, or even the coach to ask. While more personal questions seem inappropriate early on in a conversation, an inventory can be more forthright.

You would never want to ask your client one hundred questions in one session. However, a wellness assessment can do just that, especially when it is in the convenient form of an online inventory that can be partially completed, cached, and then finished later.

A comprehensive wellness assessment can also be a great learning experience for your client. Some assessments teach as they assess. Clients can increase awareness and gain insight. In addition to feedback, the client also learns what behaviors are associated with good health and which ones with higher risks. Sometimes change can result from the awareness gained from taking the inventory alone.

When we have this baseline information to start with, it is possible to use the assessment instruments again at a later date to chart and measure progress. This is very helpful to the client, and leads to the measurable results we are seeking for them. In situations where an employer is funding the coaching work being done, measurable outcomes (still following rules of confidentiality) are vital.

Simple Wellness Assessments: Tools of Elicitation

Sometimes in finding our way we don't need a highly technical topographic map, we can get started very well with a simple sketch on a piece of paper. The assessment component of wellness coaching is not about pathological diagnosis, it is about increasing awareness. Here we find or create anew, tools that help us elicit from the client, for their own use, information that would not have been discovered otherwise. "Whatever works!" might be the motto here.

The Wheel of Life

A real stand-by of the wellness coach is the Wheel of Life tool. This simple pie-chart approach for rating your own level of satisfaction in eight to nine areas of your life is not to be underestimated. I've been amazed at how startled a person can be once they see how out of balance their life really is when they look at it both graphically and holistically.

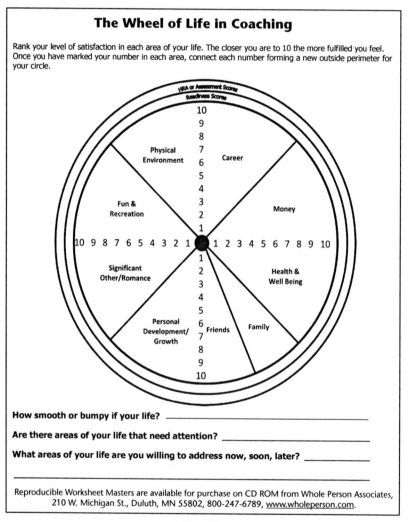

The Wheel of Life in Coaching

Rank your level of satisfaction in each area of your life. The closer you are to 10 the more fulfilled you feel. Once you have marked your number in each area, connect each number forming a new outside perimeter for your circle.

How smooth or bumpy if your life? _____

Are there areas of your life that need attention? _____

What areas of your life are you willing to address now, soon, later? _____

Reproducible Worksheet Masters are available for purchase on CD ROM from Whole Person Associates, 210 W. Michigan St., Duluth, MN 55802, 800-247-6789, www.wholeperson.com.

FIGURE 7.2

Working With The Wheel of Life

Ask your client to mark their level of satisfaction in each dimension of their life. Have them draw a line across each section at their point of satisfaction. Their Wheel of Life should become a circle with a jagged outside edge that reflects the client's satisfaction with their life.

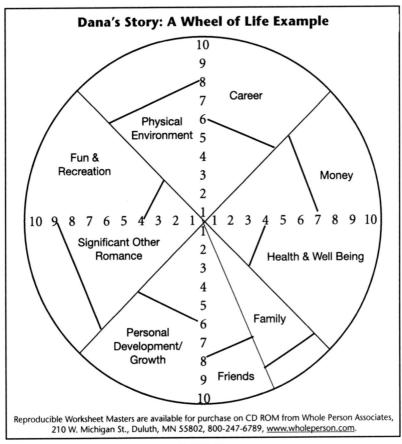

Dana's Story: A Wheel of Life Example

Reproducible Worksheet Masters are available for purchase on CD ROM from Whole Person Associates, 210 W. Michigan St., Duluth, MN 55802, 800-247-6789, www.wholeperson.com.

FIGURE 7.3

Instruct them to reflect on each area. Remind your client that only they define satisfaction. The challenge here is to see the glass half-full, but to not minimize a lack of satisfaction or fulfillment in any area. Reassure them that you will keep their responses entirely confidential.

You can also customize your own wheel of life to cover the eight or nine dimensions of life that you believe are important to living a wellness lifestyle. Here are the nine dimensions that I utilize in the

Wellness Mapping 360° Wheel of Life and the questions you might ask as you coach your client through the results.

Career

1. How fulfilling is your career? Are you content? Is it a good fit for you?

2. On a scale of 1–10 (1 = the least, 10 = the most) how motivated are you to change or develop this aspect of your life?

3. If you are up for some improvement, what is one small action you can take this week to either find out more about changing in this area, or to actually make a small behavioral change?

Money

1. Describe the stress (if any) that you experience around the issue of money. Describe your "relationship" with money (stable, unpredictable, volatile, rewarding, frustrating, etc.) . . . elaborate.

2. On a scale of 1–10 (1 = the least, 10 = the most) how motivated are you to change or develop this aspect of your life?

3. If you are up for some improvement, what is one small action you can take this week to either find out more about changing in this area, or to actually make a small behavioral change?

Health/Wellbeing

1. Describe any health challenges that you currently face. Describe any particular joys you experience about your health. Describe the level of health you want to experience five years from now.

2. On a scale of 1–10 (1 = the least, 10 = the most) how motivated are you to change or develop this aspect of your life?

3. If you are up for some improvement, what is one small action you can take this week to either find out more about changing in this area, or to actually make a small behavioral change?

Family Relationships

1. How fulfilling is your relationship with your own

immediate family and/or your family of origin? How satisfied are you with the level of closeness and support that you feel between yourself and others in the family. Are you able to get many of your needs met through your family?

2. On a scale of 1–10 (1 = the least, 10 = the most) how motivated are you to change or develop this aspect of your life?

3. If you are up for some improvement, what is one small action you can take this week to either find out more about changing in this area, or to actually make a small behavioral change?

Friends

1. Friendship is about both quality and quantity. Do you have enough friends, and close enough friends to meet your needs? Have you created any new friendships in the last two years?

2. On a scale of 1–10 (1 = the least, 10 = the most) how motivated are you to change or develop this aspect of your life?

3. If you are up for some improvement, what is one small action you can take this week to either find out more about changing in this area, or to actually make a small behavioral change?

Personal Growth/Development

1. Do you invest enough time, energy and money in your own personal growth and development, including spiritual development?

2. On a scale of 1–10 (1 = the least, 10 = the most) how motivated are you to change or develop this aspect of your life?

3. If you are up for some improvement, what is one small action you can take this week to either find out more about changing in this area, or to actually make a small behavioral change?

Significant Other/Romance

1. Are you at peace with this aspect of your life? If this is still an active part of your life, are your needs getting met well in this area?

2. On a scale of 1–10 (1 = the least, 10 = the most) how motivated are you to change or develop this aspect of your life?

3. If you are up for some improvement, what is one small action you can take this week to either find out more about changing in this area, or to actually make a small behavioral change?

Fun & Recreation

1. Do you invest enough time, energy and money, in having fun and re-creating yourself? Do you allow yourself to adequately value this way of re-energizing and re-vitalizing yourself?

2. On a scale of 1–10 (1 = the least, 10 = the most) how motivated are you to change or develop this aspect of your life?

3. If you are up for some improvement, what is one small action you can take this week to either find out more about changing in this area, or to actually make a small behavioral change?

Environment

1. How satisfied are you with the home, neighborhood, workplace, and surrounding landscape/environment where you live? Does is contribute well to your quality of life, or challenge it?

2. On a scale of 1–10 (1 = the least, 10 = the most) how motivated are you to change or develop this aspect of your life?

3. If you are up for some improvement, what is one small action you can take this week to either find out more about changing in this area, or to actually make a small behavioral change?

Balance and Fulfillment for Your Client

As you go over the completed wheel of life with your client, you will be helping them see how balanced and fulfilling their lives are. The level of satisfaction in each area (1-10) is their level of fulfillment in that area. The relationship between all of the dimensions and levels of satisfaction displays the reality of balance in their lives. Ask them to answer the question "How well does your wheel roll?"

As we said earlier, suggest to your client that they look at their wheel in the following way. Instead of imagining that this pie chart is a wheel with the outer rim being the pie chart outer circle, have them imagine that the rim of the wheel is really the "rim" they have drawn with their combined satisfaction ratings. Most people find that their ride is not as smooth as they thought or desire! A high rating in several areas and low ratings in others makes the wheel go "ka-womp, ka-womp" down the street of life.

The Pie-Chart Advantage

You could ask your client to list their rating of satisfaction on several dimensions of wellness/life in a vertical list. While you both would probably gain some valuable information to work with, you would lose a couple of distinct advantages the circle offers.

The circular pie chart helps the client see each dimension equally. Vertical lists inevitably engender a rank-ordering of their content, implying that number one is more important than number two, etc. The pie-chart allows the client to assign his or her own level of value to each area.

COACHING NOTE

The reason the Wheel of Life I use has nine dimensions instead of the eight that would maintain a nice symmetry is worth noting. In other wheel of life tools I've seen, the dimensions of family and friends are often combined. As I worked with clients this combination of friends & family often puzzled them. Frequently I got ratings in the 4-6 range. When I would enquire about this I often got responses like "Well, my friends are awesome, a ten, and my family is awful, a zero, so that's a five, right?" When I broke the nice symmetry of the chart and separated out these two areas I got the real story. I found this especially valuable because understanding the client's support system (and lack thereof) is critical in helping them make lasting lifestyle change. So—nine dimensions. It works.

The wheel approach uses the power of a strong visual graphic to engage different parts of the brain and help the client see relationships between dimensions. You may be able to effectively engage your client in an exploration of how their career satisfaction is indeed related to the level of satisfaction they experience in family, money, fun and recreation.

Uses of The Wheel of Life

The Wheel of Life is a great tool to include in a client welcome packet. It can allow you to have a solid starting place in your foundation session. Before launching into each dimension I always ask the client to tell me about their experience in completing the wheel. What was it like? How did they feel during and after completing it? What did they realize or become aware of by completing it?

You can also use the Wheel of Life in other settings such as workshops, or even at booths at health expos. It's a quick and easy tool to complete and can stimulate curiosity about one's wellness. I even had one client begin coaching with me after he approached me following a workshop with his Wheel of Life of in hand and merely stated "My wheel won't roll!"

The Wheel of Life is a great health promotion and education tool. What I like about it is that it really points your services (or that of your program's) in the direction of individualizing wellness. It shows your client (or employees) that their own evaluation of satisfaction in these areas is quite valid as an important aspect of their health and wellbeing. Yes, blood pressure numbers are important, but so is satisfaction with one's life.

Make Your Own Wheel of Life

Try adapting this pie format to the particular focus that your coaching client might need. Perhaps you have a client who is focusing on physical fitness. A quick snapshot of their satisfaction in this area can be obtained, with more accuracy and detail, by using a Wheel of Life modified for this purpose.

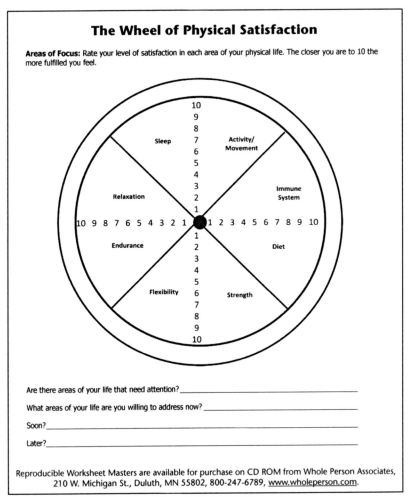

The Wheel of Physical Satisfaction

Areas of Focus: Rate your level of satisfaction in each area of your physical life. The closer you are to 10 the more fulfilled you feel.

Are there areas of your life that need attention?_____

What areas of your life are you willing to address now? _____

Soon?_____

Later?_____

Reproducible Worksheet Masters are available for purchase on CD ROM from Whole Person Associates, 210 W. Michigan St., Duluth, MN 55802, 800-247-6789, www.wholeperson.com.

FIGURE 7.4

By working with this wheel (Figure 7.4) we help our client see that physical fitness, and their satisfaction with it, is not a simple all-or-nothing concept. When asking a client how satisfied are they with their general physical fitness you may trigger a different story in every person. For some clients the question will translate into "So! Just how fat are you?," and all the self-judgment that is carried with that question. Looking at physical fitness from an eight dimensional perspective (as in the wheel above) gives the client the message that there is more to physical fitness than just strength, or waistline measurements. It also allows the client and coach to see ways to co-create a wellness plan that will really get at the specific areas where there is the least satisfaction.

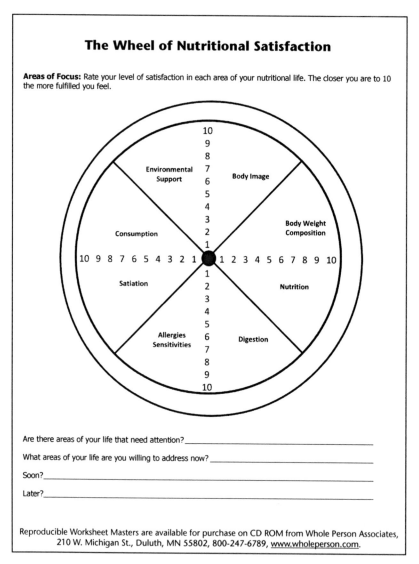

FIGURE 7.5

The Wellness Continuum
As a Wellness Mapping 360° Tool

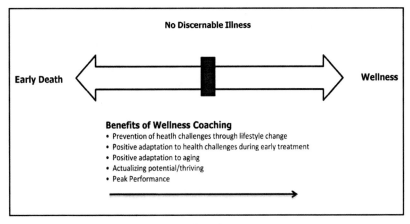

FIGURE 7.6

As we learned in an earlier chapter, the Illness/Wellness Continuum has tremendous value as a concept to help people understand what wellness is and isn't, and to help people see how treatment and wellness are related. Let me show you how we have developed the Illness/Wellness Continuum further as a tool to work with whatever dimension of wellness you might like.

The Illness/Wellness Continuum is connected to Travis's 12 Dimensional Model of Wellness. This unique way of looking at wellness forms the structure of the Wellness Inventory (which we will explore in depth later) and has the following dimensions:

1. Self Responsibility and Love
2. Breathing
3. Sensing
4. Eating
5. Moving
6. Feeling
7. Thinking
8. Playing/Working
9. Communicating
10. Sex
11. Finding Meaning
12. Transcending

With Dr. Travis's encouragement, I've applied this continuum concept to each of these twelve dimensions and discovered a valuable tool. By plotting any of the twelve dimensions on a continuum that holds the illness/wellness concept, we have a tool where the client can rate himself or herself on this continuum. By recognizing where they are functioning on the continuum they can plot themselves and see where they have to go to make progress and live a healthier life.

The different levels on the continuum help the client understand the meaning on both the illness and wellness sides. The continuum again emphasizes that any dimension of wellness is a dynamic concept where we are all in continual movement and growth. The illness side of the continuum also acknowledges that a person can be functioning in ways that are either true health challenges, or behaviorally work against the person's well being. The wellness side of the continuum acknowledges that a person can be functioning in ways that promote health even when they are recovering from illness.

Physicians and healthcare providers who refer to wellness coaches can find value in these continuums. The referring professional might rank where they see their patient functioning and this could supplement the treatment program (especially the behavioral and lifestyle aspects) they recommend.

Formal Wellness Assessments

HRAs

Wellness programs found in corporations, hospitals, fitness centers, etc.are often built around the most basic of wellness assessments, the Health Risk Assessment, or HRA. Developed early in the wellness movement, HRAs are still in widespread use today. Over thirty HRAs are on the market aiming to help individuals and organizations reduce health risks by identifying the correlations between behavior and health for each individual.

The idea is to increase awareness in the participant of the lifestyle behaviors they perform that increase their risk of illness and premature death. Due to years of research, it is now easy for us to conclude that the more someone smokes tobacco, the greater the health risk they experience. It's all probabilities, but the message is clear: behave in these ways and you increase your risks and may not live as long; behave in these ways and you decrease your risks and may even live longer. HRAs have become more sophisticated than the early models that pioneered the field. They look at more than just smoking, drinking, and seat belt usage. Many of the risk factors are associated with coronary heart disease and cancer. Some include the risks of unsafe sex being practiced in the age of HIV/AIDS. Some look at the more psychological side of health.

HRAs are used primarily as feedback devices for the people who take them. The key to their effectiveness is the nature and quality of that feedback. Increasingly online-based, HRAs are often providing extensive links to support resources that provide the client with tons of health information and even tools for tracking their own lifestyle change attempts. Better HRAs have built into them some form of change readiness scale (e.g. Prochaska, et.al.), or if not, change readiness may be assessed in feedback sessions through direct questioning.

One of the most common scenarios is for a company to require some or all of their employees to take an HRA, usually online, but paper and pencil HRAs are available too and then are machine scored. The employee/client is then given feedback in a number of ways that range from low to higher effectiveness.

1. The client may simply be mailed the results, or be able to see themonline with instructions written as to what the results mean.

2. The client is set up with a telephone appointment with someone who spends 15-20 minutes on the phone going over the results with the employee. This person may have training that ranges from minimal to very good. In a good system these people are typically some type of health specialist, such as LPNs, fitness specialists, or trained health coaches.

3. Another step up is when HRAs are combined with the gathering of biometric data (actual measurements such as blood pressure, blood work results, BMI, etc.) taken by health specialists, and then either a telephone or, better still, live appointment, is made to review and interpret the results and answer questions.

4. If the program is fairly comprehensive and woven into the larger employee health benefits resources, the assessment

may result in a referral to an Employee Assistance Program (EAP), an employee's clinic, a physician, etc. Here, an employee may get valuable help or medical intervention for a condition that was going undiagnosed and untreated.

5. In the best programs, at least a taste of what we might call more complete wellness coaching takes place. If the educator interpreting the results is a trained wellness coach, the results may go to a different level. Even in a system where time is severely limited, the coach approach may allow the client to build some trust with the wellness coach, and determine a direction of focus. After a brief exploration with the coach listening on a professional level, the coach helps the client leave with a sense of ownership of their health, what they want to work on, and a system of accountability regarding it.

6. The system may opt for some participants (perhaps especially those at high risk) to have follow-up sessions based on the results. Even brief (ten-minute) follow-up phone calls every quarter and regular e-mails can have some effectiveness.

The Down Side of HRAs

Some critics of Health Risk Assessments point out that there are disadvantages to HRA usage. When the first bit of feedback you receive about your health is what age you are predicted to die, it may be hard to hear! Not all HRAs hit you with this message first, but a criticism of HRAs is that they can tend to paint a picture of morbidity and the postponement of the inevitable. While some see this as merely a dose of reality therapy for us all, others would argue that it is a poor motivator. Do we change our health behavior out of fear alone? Can we be scared straight into buckling that seat belt, and eating our high-fiber vegetables?

One would think that an employee required to take an HRA would be happy that they are getting a free health assessment that is designed to help them be healthy and recognize ways to improve their health. However, in an organization where trust is an issue, and where there is fear that one's job may be in jeopardy if one's health is anything but excellent, how honest will answers be? How reliable is the HRA if an employee is telling management what they want to hear?

Coaching With HRAs

A challenge for the wellness coach working with a client who has just taken an HRA is to maintain the wellness coaching mindset of advocate and inspire. The temptation with the diagnostic nature of the HRA is to shift into the diagnose and treat model and start prescribing to the client instead of remaining their ally. Instruments that point out the client's risky behaviors may come across as judgments about the behavior. It is easy for some clients to feel like they are wrong and not OK. The coach's task is to be aware of this possibility and help the client see that the instrument is not so personal. Certain behaviors are statistically correlated with increased incidence of illness, injury and other negative results, and it's recommended that you behave this other way instead, and that's all that is being said.

For many wellness coaches the HRA is a standard tool that is part of the system they work in. For the solo wellness coach, who is in business for themselves, the HRA is another instrument to consider and to know how to use. You may find that you like to have it as an option, and discover that with certain clients it really provides something that they are looking for, and something that will fit in with what motivates them to change.

TestWell

The TestWell program (www.testwell.org) is an online assessment tool based on the six-dimensional model of wellness put forth by wellness pioneer Bill Hetler, M.D. While containing an HRA, TestWell also offers a self-educative device, the Holistic Lifestyle Questionnaire (HLQ), that helps your client discover how the choices they make each day affect their overall health. By participating in this assessment process they also learn how they can make positive changes to improve their lifestyle. Because the instrument is taken online, accessibility is easy and feedback is immediate. Paper and pencil versions are also available.

FIGURE 7.7

With TestWell your client explores and then gets feedback on ten areas of their life:

1. Physical Activity
2. Nutrition
3. Self Care
4. Safety
5. Social and Environmental Wellness
6. Emotional Wellness and Sexuality
7. Emotional Management
8. Occupational Wellness
9. Intellectual Wellness
10. Spirituality and Values

Feedback comes in the form of numerical scores and bar graph charts. Individuals get their own scores and their scores compared with those of either the group they have taken the instrument with (i.e. all the employees of a department), or the average scores of all who have taken the instrument. The administrator of the instrument (in this case you, the coach) can go online and look at answers to specific questions to pinpoint why a client scored low in a particular dimension of wellness.

The TestWell HRA highlights the positive areas of your client's lifestyle, which are reducing their health risks. It then briefly goes over general results, nutritional results, and height and weight results. HRA resources are recommended and accessible.

The Behavior Change Guide is a very useful tool that comes with the TestWell results. Ideal for the coach and client to work together on, it is a very straightforward step-by-step process of stating behaviors, readiness for change, benefits of changing, setting goals, strategizing, setting up support and tracking behavior. It also includes a behavior change contract and a behavior-tracking chart. This can become a key component of the wellness plan that coach and client co-create.

This instrument works well for people who don't have a very broad or well-defined view of wellness. It can create a "whole" picture of what a healthy wellness lifestyle entails. TestWell introduces people to what wellness is as it sets the language, categories and values that help define what you, the wellness coach are going to be talking about with your client.

The Wellness Inventory

The Wellness Inventory (WI) was the first true wellness assessment instrument created. It was developed initially in 1976 by John W. Travis, M.D. Jim Strohecker through HealthWorld Online (www.my-wellnesstest.com) developed the extensive online delivery system it is today.

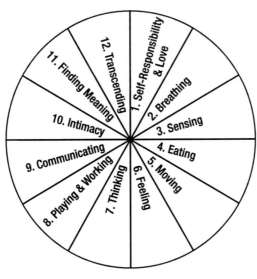

FIGURE 7.8

109

The WI conceives of wellness in a 12-dimensional model (wellness energy system) that gives an inclusive and unique view of what healthy wellness lifestyles include.

1. Self-Responsibility and Love
2. Breathing (and relaxing)
3. Sensing
4. Eating
5. Moving
6. Feeling
7. Thinking
8. Playing and Working
9. Communicating
10. Intimacy and Sex
11. Finding Meaning
12. Transcending

In *The Wellness Workbook* (Travis & Ryan), Travis elaborates on each of these dimensions. For the wellness coach there are some immediate advantages to this unusual way of looking at wellness. Instead of confronting your client with the topic of exercise, which I find many clients to be almost phobic about, you can talk about movement in their lives. Instead of diet, you speak about eating and it can open up a broader exploration of the role that eating and food plays in their life.

The inclusion of dimensions such as feeling, thinking, communicating and intimacy & sex opens up the more mental/emotional sides of wellness and reinforces that wellness is much more than just diet and exercise. The dimensions of finding meaning and transcendence open up the philosophical and the spiritual areas for exploration. Using Travis's energy model you can see how self-responsibility & love provides the foundation for a wellness, breathing, sensing and eating are our primary ways of taking in energy, and the remaining eight dimensions are ways we output energy.

Taking the WI is a very self-educative wellness experience. All the questions are stated in positive statement terms. An example is "I recognize that responsibility for my health lies within me, rather than with an outside authority." The client then answers each item by indicating how true it is for them (Yes/Always/Usually, Often, Sometimes/Maybe, Occasionally, or No/Never/Hardly Ever). They are then immediately asked how satisfied they are with their response. The content of the items themselves is a tutorial on factors involved in living a wellness lifestyle. Your client can also click on any topic and find a complete description of it, and can also access further resources and information on each area in the resource section.

The WI is actually set up online as a one-year wellness and lifestyle change program.

Step 1—Assessment: Complete a whole person assessment in the 12 dimensions of wellness and lifestyle.

Step 2—Scores: Receive Wellness & Satisfaction Scores in each section. Discover where you are most motivated to change.

Step 3—Personal Wellness Plan: Create 3-5 wellness action steps in the areas you are most motivated to change.

Step 4—Tools to Help You Reach Your Goals: Utilize tools to help you follow your wellness plan and meet your goals.

Step 5—Supporting Ongoing Wellness: Re-assess in six months and monitor your progress. Optional wellness coaching.

Common to online inventories, the administrator (in this case the coach) has confidentially protected access to scores so they can review the WI results with their client, even telephonically by looking at the same online screens at the same time. Like TestWell, group analysis data and customization of demographic data questions is also available.

One of the best features of the WI is the Satisfaction Scores. The key in the Satisfaction Score is that the client is not being asked how truthfully they answered the item, but how satisfied are they with their answer being what it was. For example if the item was: "My daily activities include at least 15 minutes of vigorous physical effort.," and I respond to the question how true is that for me, and I answer, "Occasionally," I may be very dissatisfied that this is true in my life.

The Satisfaction Scores yield one of the most thorough readiness for change scores possible concerning lifestyle behavior. As you work with your client on these satisfaction scores you can immediately examine the low satisfaction scores and explore how your client feels about these and see if any of these dimensions are important for inclusion in the wellness plan that your client wants to work on. Likewise, you may see an area where the overall score is low, but the satisfaction score is moderately high. This would identify an area of wellness where, though the client would benefit from improving that area in their life, they are either not interested in doing so, or just not ready.

You might have your client complete the built-in wellness planning process and go over it together with them. Ask them in detail about it and look for ways to strategize with them to make it operational and build in the accountability they desire regarding their plan.

Physiological Measures

One concrete advantage that wellness coaching enjoys is that some of its more important outcomes are quite measurable. While we can probably never really pinpoint the variable(s) responsible for a shift in the physiological functioning of our client, we can often look for physical changes that can be measured. A decrease in blood pressure, an improvement in blood-work measures, an increase in endurance, a reduction in percentage of body fat, more hours of restful sleep, are all benchmarks that progress is being made.

The realm of taking some of the more sophisticated physiological measures falls into the world of treatment where the coach becomes an ally to the healthcare specialist. Anyone can step on the scale, move the notch on the belt, or time their assent of a steep nearby hill, but the professional work of coaching lies somewhere between simple self-observations and the more medically oriented work.

Let the nurse practitioner take your client's blood pressure. Work with your client's M.D. and the treatment program they have prescribed. Be a coach about it. Work as your client's coach and not their healthcare provider. Stick with your effective and vital role of helping your client with the behavioral aspects of medical compliance. Help your client actually do what their treatment program directs them to do with their lifestyle.

Combining wellness inventories and/or HRAs with actual physiological measurements, or biometric data, is a powerful method. It gives your client an accurate picture of where they are. When their LDL cholesterol score is compared with the healthier range that is expected, they know what they need to shoot for. You are there to help them with the lifestyle component of making that happen.

One of the most common physiological goals is to attain a healthy weight. A few words here are important. In working with individuals seeking a healthier weight, a common error is to look solely at pounds/ kilos lost. It is misleading because when your client begins to exercise, they are increasing muscle mass. This is good, but muscle weighs more than fat! The Body Mass Index, or BMI, is an approximation based upon finding your height and weight on a chart and seeing how you stack up. Differences in body type are not factored in well, nor are health conditions that affect overall height (such as scoliosis, etc.). While the BMI has contributed greatly to research, the wellness coach has to use it with caution.

Percent body fat is often held by exercise physiologists to be the single best measurement to take to show healthy body composition change. Have your client get a good measurement from a personal fitness trainer, an exercise physiologist, or someone trained in the how to of this process. There are now at least four different ways to ascertain percentage of body fat.

Because fat floats taking body weight under water is probably the most accurate measurement! Some health clubs have monthly hydrostatic weigh-ins at their swimming pools. There are electronic devices on the market now that resemble a simple set of bathroom scales, but electrically measure bio impedance through the body and calculate percent body fat that way.

A much more convenient method is the simple circumference measuring methods like the one developed by the U.S. Navy, however this seems to fall victim to all the problems that the BMI does. Much more accurate and almost as easy to do are the skin-fold caliper measurements. When taken by a trained specialist, the Academy of Sports Medicine says these methods are 98% accurate. The central challenge with results of any assessment you work with is helping your client to determine what their goals should be. What is the ideal percentage of body fat for them? Perhaps a better question is "What is the most healthy body composition for me?" Individual factors abound. Is your client a sedentary couch potato, a competitive weight lifter or a long-distance runner?

The effective wellness coach helps their client work with physical measurements, but helps them put it all in the context of their overall health and wellness goals. The measurements can provide helpful benchmarks of progress, or reminders of extra effort required along the way.

Coach First, Measure Second

A word to the wise . . . If you are like many health educators, who typically begin an initial session with a client by taking physical measurements such as weight, height, waist circumference, etc., you might consider not taking any measurements at the first contact. While your client may expect this, give them the unexpected! Talk to them. Coach them with great listening. Hear their story. Coach them with powerful questions that help them to explore what their weight issue means to them. Explore all their tried and failed experiences. Ask how they hope this one will be different.

When we take biometric data upon first contact it can feel like we are judging the person. It may feel like we are evaluating what is wrong with them. It can put them through a process that reminds them of numerous times in the past where they have felt ashamed. In the coach mindset, as opposed to the medical mindset, we are here to form an alliance for change with them, not to provide treatment. Set the tone by being their coach first!

> *There is a human striving for self-transcendence. It's part of what makes us human. With all of our flaws we want to go a little bit further than we've gone before and maybe even further than anyone else has gone before.*

> —**George B. Leonard**

Chapter 8

Charting the Course of Change: Wellness Mapping 360°

Human life is a journey whose end is not in sight.
Searching, longing and questioning is in our DNA. Who we
are and what we will become is determined by the questions
that animate us, and by those we refuse to ask. Your
questions are your quest. As you ask, so shall you be.

—Sam Keen

The Personal Map or Plan

You've assisted your wellness coaching client to take stock of their life and identify where they want to go. Together you've set a firm foundation place to start from and helped them to see what some of their strengths and challenges are. You've established an alliance with them so they know they don't have to take this journey alone. Now is the time to create the map.

Co-creating the Wellness Plan

To insure commitment and motivation, let the development of a wellness plan be a process of co-creation that gives your client a clear map to follow. Stay in the coach mindset of advocate and inspire. It may seem so absolutely obvious that your client needs _____! In reality, if your client did in fact do blank, everything might work out just fine. The prescribe-and treat-approach may seductively appear to be much more time efficient. You might think that you could just write up a great plan for your client, like a prescription, and expect that they would thankfully take it and implement it. Your client may even be pleading for you to "Just tell me what to do!" Your challenge, as a coach, especially if you have a healthcare background, is not to create a treatment plan.

One of the real advantages of wellness coaching is that it is different than what your client has tried before. Wellness coaching is different because the client takes responsibility for their own health and wellness and because they improve their lives themselves. Chances are great that your client will have already been there and done that with prescriptive approaches. They've had books, talk-show celebrities on TV, healthcare professionals, gym teachers, friends, parents and others recommend, cajole, intimidate, frighten, shame, manipulate and lovingly urge them to change by telling them what to do. Yet here they are, still stuck.

All these other people have stood at the bottom of the mountain and told the person how to climb it. They've recommended a route, told them what equipment to carry, patted them on the back and wished them well. The wellness coach goes up on the mountain with their client. The coach doesn't climb the mountain for the client, they serve as a guide for them.

You can offer a framework for creating a wellness map to help your client get started. They will be the one completing the framework, filling in the blanks. Your coaching skills can come forth and help them with strategizing, prioritizing, challenging, encouraging and acknowledging. You can help the person to dis-invite their inner critic or gremlin from participating in the creation of their plan. That same gremlin loves to discourage the person or build in self-defeating components to keep them from changing and instead cling to the comfort of the *status quo*. Help them identify gremlin talk and keep it out of the wellness plan.

Make your approach to wellness planning growth oriented. Instead of a wellness plan consider calling it a wellness growth plan. When your client sees the connection between being well and his or her own personal growth, motivation will be even stronger. Actualizing potential in all dimensions of a person's life as defined by that person, is the ultimate wellness process.

Drawing The Map—The Essential Components of the Wellness Plan

When you look at many general wellness plans you often find various prescriptive formulas for being healthy and well. Eat this, exercise this way, get more sleep, etc. In wellness coaching, the customized wellness plan is really a map or a tool that helps your client to:

- Find their way by identifying specifically how they want to work on improving their lifestyle

- Set up ways to measure and track progress

- Secure adequate support

- Identify outcomes so they know when they have arrived at their destination.

From the world of coaching we may discover various action plans. Some of these models may work fine with wellness coaching, however we need to be careful not to emphasize an action-only approach. Motivation, blocks to completion, support resources all deserve consideration as well. Wellness coaching is about lifestyle improvement – lifestyle change and maintaining that positive change. The wellness growth plan looks at the questions of "How can I grow further, and actualize more of my potential?" "How can I improve myself in these ways?"

Wellness plans can be very simple, even focused on one goal at a time. On the other extreme they can become so complex and inclusive that they become cumbersome and are often totally abandoned. Your coaching challenge is to work with your client to strike a balance that is effective and suits them best. We do know that success promotes success. For some clients the baby steps approach works best; others are ready to make huge strides!

Here is the Wellness Mapping 360° approach to creating the wellness plan: the Wellness Map.

1. Vision: the clients larger, over-arching image of themselves functioning at their best and living life at its fullest. An inspirational statement of what that would look like for them.

2. Areas of Focus: for maximum success, prioritize this to no more than five areas, and make those areas the ones where there is the greatest readiness for change. Lifestyle prescriptions from healthcare providers and results/feedback from wellness assessment instruments can also factor into the prioritizing process.

For each Area of Focus:

- **Desires:** What do you want?
  In the client's own words, what are the stated desires for this area of focus? This is good to state as both an immediate goal (e.g. lose ten pounds) and a longer-term, more motivational goal (e.g. I want to climb a 14,000 foot/4,267meter peak this summer).

- **Current Location:** Where are you currently?
  Current status of the area of focus the client wants to work on. For example, current percent body fat; hours of sleep/night; 1–10 scale self-ratings of situations or levels of conditioning, etc.

- **Destination:** Where do you want to go? Who do you want to become?
  What that will look like, stated specifically and as measurably as possible.

- **Committed Course:** What are you, the client, making a commitment to do?
  The action steps involved, stated very specifically. Through coaching the client arrives at success-insuring action strategies that are challenging yet attainable.

- **Challenges:** What are you up against?
  What obstacles are in the way? What blocks your path? It is important to speak about blocks in the language of "challenges" instead of "problems."

- **Strategies To Meet The Challenges:** Ways to overcome the hurdles that are blocking you presently.
  Co-Create strategies to adjust and to bend without breaking from the commitments made in the plan. For example: when under a work deadline I will make my exercise session briefer, but not skip it.

3. Sources of Support—Who can go on this journey with you, to help you out? State specifically who/what are your sources of support, encouragement, and accountability as you follow your wellness map into new territory? Encourage your client to think outside their typical or normal set of family and friends.

I have never been lost, but I will admit to being confused for several weeks.

—Daniel Boone

My Wellness Map–
Life Vision and Focus Tool

Wellness Mapping
360°

Name: _____

1. Life Vision – Either on your own or working with your coach, arrive at a statement that sums up your idea of what it would look like to be living your life to the fullest and functioning at your best. Be realistic and yet, inspiring!

My Life's Wellness Vision:

_____
_____
_____

2. Current Life Status: Summarize what your current life is like. Do not be discouraged or judgmental with yourself – just be honest.

_____
_____

- Take a deep breath, relax and ask yourself "What would have to change for me to achieve my life vision?"

_____
_____
_____

3. Areas of Focus: To make my life vision a reality I choose to focus on the following areas of my life. For maximum success, prioritize no more than five areas and make those areas the ones you are most ready to address. Suggested lifestyle improvements from healthcare providers and results from wellness assessments or health risk assessments can also be listed. You might want to work together with your coach to determine these areas.

1. _____
2. _____
3. _____
4. _____
5. _____

Reproducible Worksheet Masters are available for purchase on CD ROM from Whole Person Associates, 210 W. Michigan St., Duluth, MN 55802, 800-247-6789, www.wholeperson.com.

Wellness Map— Areas of Focus, Page 1

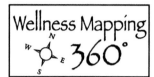

Name _____

Area of Focus One - To make my vision real I want to focus on the following area.

Choose an area from #3 of the Life Vision and Focus Page that you are most ready to work on or because you feel you need it the most, or because it is easy and you just want to get the ball rolling.

Focus area: _____

A. Desires: *What do you want or how would you like it to be?* Write in your own words, "What are your stated desires for this area of focus in your life?

This is good to state in both an immediate action your want to see happen (for example, I want to lose ten pounds) and in a longer-term, more motivational action (for example, I want to be able to go on a very physically active vacation this summer).

_____

_____

_____

B. Current Location: *Where do you see yourself currently in this area of your life?* Right now this is where I'm at regarding this area of focus:

(List whatever describes your present situation. For example you could list your current percent body fat; number of hours of sleep/night; 1-10 scale self-ratings of situations or levels of conditioning, etc.)

_____

_____

_____

C. The Path: *What do you need to do?* What do you need to do or what needs to change in your life for you to realize your desire for this area in your life? Describe what needs to change in this area of your life for you to attain your desires. State the changes needed as specifically as you can.

_____

_____

_____

Wellness Map— Areas of Focus, Page 2

Name _____

D. Committed Course: *What are you making a commitment to do?* Work with your coach to create realistic and attainable action steps that will move you towards the desired outcome for your chosen life area. Choose an initial step to make that will get you moving. Like a map, chart your coarse to your chosen change. Once again being specific is important. Write down what you will do, when it will be completed by, and how you will communicate the accomplishment to your coach. Work with your coach to arrive at strategies that are challenging enough without being too much.

What you will do	Duration	When	Check-in method
Step 1.			
Step 2.			
Step 3.			

E. Challenges: *What are you up against?* List what obstacles are in your way or what you believe could prevent you from reaching your desired destination.

_____

_____

F. Strategies To Meet The Challenges: *Ways to overcome the hurdles.* With your coach develop strategies that you can use to make adjustments in your life to overcome or get around things that hold you back from your committed course of action. (For example: when under a work deadline I will make my exercise session briefer, but not skip it.)

_____

_____

_____

G. Sources of Support - *Who can share this journey with you or support your journey?* State specifically who or what your sources of support, encouragement, and accountability are as you follow this area of focus on your wellness map into new territory?

_____

_____

_____

Reproducible Worksheet Masters are available for purchase on CD ROM from Whole Person Associates, 210 W. Michigan St., Duluth, MN 55802, 800-247-6789, www.wholeperson.com.

Readiness for Change— Prochaska's Model

Part of selecting the Areas of Focus for the Wellness Map is best done through putting readiness for change theory into practice. The coach unfamiliar with this concept would profit greatly from studying it.

A foundational concept that is used pervasively in the wellness field, is the readiness for change work of James Prochaska and his associates, John Norcross, and Carlo Diclemente (*Changing For Good*). Used by thousands of addiction treatment programs and wellness programs world wide, Prochaska's work has had a profound impact. Deceptively simple at first, Prochaska reminds us that people don't change until they are ready to. While this seems absurdly obvious, when you examine most healthcare or treatment programs, you see that the healthcare provider often demands change immediately. The coach can also make this mistake.

Change is not controlled by a toggle switch that flicks on or off just because we—the healthcare provider, or the coach—see the need for change. Even if the client intellectually sees the need for change too, will it automatically happen? In fact, a real caution for coaches is not to rush to action. Many coaches are trained to respond quickly to their client's insightful statement with "So! What are you going to do about it?" When we rush to action in the arena of the lifestyle change process we are often sabotaging success and the client's ability to gain true insight.

When we plug the readiness for change theory into our coaching we can see that a client moves through the six stages that Prochaska outlines.

1. **Pre-contemplation.** The client is unaware and isn't concerned.

2. **Contemplation.** Client becomes aware and begins to consider change.

3. **Preparation.** Client begins exploring change possibilities (looks for resources, accessibility, affordability, etc.).

4. **Action.** Client takes action for change.

5. **Maintenance.** Client works at maintaining the change.

6. **Termination.** The new behavior is now a part of their life.

The wellness coaching client can be at a different stage of readiness in each specific behavior we look at. Just because someone is ready to exercise doesn't mean they are ready to quit smoking. We move and grow sequentially but not necessarily evenly.

All too often we approach results in lifestyle change in an all-or-nothing manner. It is easy to conclude that our coaching failed if we don't see the person quickly succeed in accomplishing their lifestyle change and health goals. When we plug in the stages of change approach we may see that many times we are doing our coaching job very well when we help a person to simply advance along this change process. The client who is oblivious about their sedentary lifestyle, becomes aware of it, and merely begins to search out information about movement is, in fact, being quite successful at making progress in lifestyle change. Sometimes masterful coaching has taken place when we help a client move up one or two stages in this change process. Results need to be measured in the light of movement toward the goal or lifestyle change. The client and those administering a wellness coaching program need to be aware of the cycle of change and its specific use in lifestyle change.

Prochaska has found that this six-stage model is, in fact, a spiral model. People cycle and recycle through it. Perhaps someone contemplates beginning a program of recreating more with their children and prepares for it by buying some sporting equipment. Then their child cancels out of the outing by opting to go to an event with their own friends. The parent is disheartened and gives up trying to connect with their child, slipping back into contemplation, or even pre-contemplation. Perhaps they see their coach, realize it doesn't serve them to take the "rejection" so personally, and follows through with a wonderful time spent enjoying that planned for activity with their child at a later date.

Prochaska's Stages of Change and Coaching

The work of Prochaska and his associates is a deep and powerful resource. His trans-theoretical model of change matches therapeutic interventions with the appropriate stage of readiness for change.

Here is an overview of ways to adapt the Stages of Change Theory to coaching.

1. Pre-contemplation. The person has no thought of changing, now or later. Others who care about them may repeatedly urge them to take action to improve their lives, but at this stage, they are truly deaf to their pleas. This is not resistance, just complete lack of awareness.

> **COACHING NOTE**
> The initial exploration and assessment phase of coaching can often help a person to shake out of this lack of awareness about a particular behavior or behaviors. Use of informal and formal wellness assessments often jog the person into awareness.

2. Contemplation. The person is thinking about changing—considering it, but can be quite ambivalent. "When in doubt, don't act." Introspection about why one follows a bad habit, what its payoff is. Bringing both the rational mind and the emotions into play helps to move the client to the next step.

> **COACHING NOTE**
> The contemplator can often stay here forever weighing the pros and cons. The coach approach helps the person examine how their current behavior is working for them, or against them. It offers them an ally—the coach—to help them move forward. The ultimately critical area of motivation, both internal and external is explored.

3. Preparation. Getting ready to change. Gathering information about topics and/or resources (Is there a pool/yoga class/hiking trail/bike path nearby?) Some preparatory steps might include: removing temptations, planning how action will be taken and arranging support and understanding from family, friends, perhaps a support group. When arranging substitutes for the missed habit or activity or substance, beware of substituting a new problem (over-eating, over-spending) for the old.

> **COACHING NOTE**
> Helping a client move from contemplation to preparation can be a huge accomplishment. Many times we feel we fail when we can't

> get a contemplator to jump into action. The new action can be the preparatory steps of gaining information, etc. Agreements to do so can be developed in the coaching process and methods of accountability set up so follow through is maximized by the client.

4. Action. The stage most of us picture, actual practice of the new way of being.

> **COACHING NOTE**
> The coach is in the ideal position to insure that the action taken is one that the client feels is entirely congruent with who they are, and how ready for change they are. Coaches can challenge the forever-preparing client to take action at a level they believe will work and then be a strong support during the process. Coaching accountability methods insure greater follow through. When the client fails to follow through, exploration of motivation can be of vital importance.

5. Maintenance. The actual process of maintaining the action that has been taken. Remembering that the Stages of Change Model is a *spiral* model—people frequently attempt a change, and then spiral back into earlier stages. Prochaska shows that many people benefit from learning the difference between a lapse and a total relapse, (a complete collapse back into the old way). Being prepared to recognize a lapse and take immediate action can save the effort and self-criticism.

> **COACHING NOTE**
> The wellness coach can play a vital role of support and accountability here. Often the client has never been successful at maintaining a change by themselves. Having a true ally in their coach, their chances of success improve dramatically. When the client spirals back to an earlier stage of a particular behavior, the coach can follow this process and help the client to re-set their goals based on the stage they are now in.

Recycling—back to one of the previous stages. *Changing for Good* shows that it is entirely possible for a person to fail at one stage or another, only to make a second or subsequent attempts that succeed.

6. Termination. The behavior has become a regular part of the person's life. Without much effort or thought, they naturally, and regularly engage in the new behavior. Depending on the desired change and the person, total termination of the problem behavior may not occur. Instead, there may be a lifetime of careful maintenance. In other cases, the problem is conquered and temptation to renew the poor behavior ceases. The Prochaska, et.al., state that the confidence that one has really succeeded peaks after a year but that temptation continues for two or three years.

> **COACHING NOTE**
>
> The coaching process helps the person to know when they have achieved their goal. The coach helps the client make distinctions between termination and on-going maintenance. The coaching process helps the client focus on other behaviors they are working on and/or helps them become clear about what they want to work on next. Coaching helps the client work towards independence and self-sufficiency and the termination of coaching as well.

How the Coach-approach Honors Level of Readiness for Change

When you combine the wellness coach mindset with the readiness for change concept, you find that the coaching principles of asking permission, the wisdom of the client, and co-creation serve the client beautifully in the coaching process. In order to truly match the readiness-for-change stage where the client is with the coaching you do, you continually ask permission to explore into new areas. You respect the wisdom of the client, knowing that the answers lie within them, and they know what they are ready for much better than you do. Together you co-create a way to mutually explore a behavior and which one of the six stages of readiness for change they are in.

Three Steps for Coaching for Readiness For Change

1. Help your client recognize the stage of readiness they are in for specific behaviors.
2. Coach for completion of the client's current stage.
3. Coach the client toward the next step in the spiral model of change.

Desire is the starting point of all achievement, not a hope, not a wish, but a keen pulsating desire which transcends everything.

—Napoleon Hill

Achieving Buy-In and Commitment with Your Client

I've often told people that I like to work with clients who are ready, willing and able. Now for the willing part, what makes a person ready? Fully equipped, map in hand, guide at your side, what is it that allows clients, perhaps even urges them, to take that first step on the mountain's path? Contrary to some people's approach, giving your client a shove in the back is probably not a good idea. That first step has to come from within.

So what sells a client on lifestyle change? How and why do they buy-in to this notion? How does the notion become a commitment? How does lifestyle improvement become a genuine desire on the part of the client?

Perhaps some of the answers lie in whether your clients value themselves. As we stated briefly in Chapter Three (The Ten Tenets of Wellness), self-esteem is a critical factor in wellness. A person will do little for self if they do not care very much about themselves. If your client's feelings of self-worth are extremely low, they may benefit from counseling or therapy. For most everyone though, accessing that desire to live a better, more rewarding life comes from that reservoir of good feelings they have about themselves.

You will most likely not be able to help your client work through all of their self-worth/self-esteem issues before you begin implementing a wellness program. We all have to start somewhere. Sometimes a person has to begin by "acting as if," and that can be perfectly OK.

The client needs to see the benefits of the self-improvement efforts. "What's in it for me?" is the main question. A health educator would list the many good reasons for lifestyle improvement for a client, while the coach asks the client to come up with the answers themselves, and explores it with the client. If your client sees no particular benefits, or isn't aware of any, you might seek an agreement with them to research the area, or you might prime the pump by suggesting some benefits that you are aware of from wellness and medical research.

James Prochaska promotes the idea that when people see the benefits of a behavior, the barriers to that behavior are lowered. He believes that one way we stay stuck in the contemplative stage of change is that we underestimate the value of a particular behavior (like exercise) and overestimate the cost (time, effort, expense, etc.) of the change. By challenging your client to really look at a contemplated behavior change, in realistic detail, you may have a very productive coaching session where your client begins to see that the change is worth it. You can also strategize with them to lower the costs by coming up with ways of completing their goals that are easier and still very effective.

When you are being an effective coach you walk a very delicate and thin line between facilitating change and growth, and convincing someone of the benefits of growth. Remember, you are not in sales. A pull to become the salesperson is probably a tip that you are not honoring the principles and the stage of readiness of your client. An athletic coach can challenge a young woman or man to bring out a better game from the abilities that the coach sees and believes they have. However, the coach cannot make the player love the game and want to be out there on the field or court, playing with heart.

Keep all of your wellness coaching in the context of personal growth and development. When your client begins to see that their lifestyle changes are not just burdensome tasks, but instead, are ways of actualizing their own potential, motivation shifts into a completely different, and higher, gear. As I've seen clients become turned on to their own personal growth journey their excitement fuels a true passion to learn, to experiment and, ultimately, to grow! They become hungry for more information about what they can do to live richer, fuller lives. Their level of self-efficacy reaches an all-time high.

Early on, the wellness field grew out of the human potential/self-actualization movement. As the field has evolved some of us have become caught up in the wonderful world of research and statistics, etc., and forgotten what we can use that good data for. Your clients benefit the most when your coaching mindset is grounded in the values of personal growth. Let yourself wonder, "What if Abe Maslow had known about coaching?"

Wellness Mapping 360° Accountability & Support

There is more to accountability and support than first meets the eye. Here is the real roll up the sleeves part of wellness coaching. All the best-laid wellness plans will not produce results effortlessly. Add value to the coaching experience of your client by working shoulder to shoulder with them on core issues such as motivation, self-permission, and self-defeating thinking. Be ready with tools and ideas for them to try out that help them to work through whatever is in the way of a successful wellness journey.

Motivation: Fear Based and Development Based

My first job as a counselor, after I got my Master's degree, was to be a caseworker in a residential treatment facility for emotionally disturbed adolescents. I found out then and there something that would prove to be true everywhere in life. I can't make anybody do anything. All I can do is invite.

As a wellness coach, remember that you cannot motivate anyone. You can, however, help them to find the motivation that resides inside of them. You can invite. You can help create the container, the situation of support. You can provide the presence of the conditions needed to facilitate personal growth. You can celebrate and reinforce when motivation shows up.

While there can be some value to the fake it until you make it approach, I would rather listen to Wayne Dyer talk about "You'll see it when you believe it." That brilliant little twist and play on words really does drive home the message that our internal beliefs shape our reality.

So, how do we coach people to discover their own motivation to be well? Public health campaigns, health educators, teachers, preachers, and parents have all tried very hard to convince us all to be healthy.

We've seen programs and campaigns based on scaring us to be well (e.g., pictures of diseased lungs). We've been lured with incentives, cajoled by peer norms, shamed, blamed, ridiculed, seduced, tempted and much more. Some of it has worked. Some of it got us started, but not nearly enough of it was effective enough to sustain our lifestyle changes for most of us. Most of industrialized western society is still faced with lifestyle choice-related health concerns that statistically, at least, seem out of control.

Looking at the field of wellness and health-promotion, the work of Abraham Maslow (*Self-Actualization Theory*), Jay Kimiecik (*The Intrinsic Exerciser*), Gerry Jampolsky (*Love Is The Answer*), cancer-survivor Greg Anderson, and others, we can gain much wisdom about human motivation and behavior change. With this perspective in mind, let's consider basically two types of motivation: fear based and development based.

Frankly, helping people find the joy or passion in movement is what's missing from most . . . programs . . . Intrinsic motivation— performing a task primarily for its own sake— is the most powerful way to change behavior . . .

—**Jay Kimiecik,** *The Intrinsic Exerciser*

Motivation—Intrinsic & Extrinsic

FEAR-BASED

Type 1: Deficiency-based
Comes from a perception of lack; operates on a sense of what is missing in life.

Internal Sourced

Need fulfillment—deficiency needs (Maslow)

Trying not to die—overcome the deficiency of lost health

Shoulds—internal pressure we put on ourselves

Identified regulation—sheer self-discipline we impose

External Sourced (Extrinsic)

Socio-cultural learnings

Norms, myths we are affected by

Identified regulation—doing it because you are supposed to, possibly even under agreement with a trainer/coach

Type 2: Threat-Based

Known threats

Unknown threats

Illness Avoidance

Environmental threats

DEVELOPMENT-BASED

Personal Growth-Based

Need fulfillment—being needs (Maslow)

Self-actualization

Human Potential

Internal drive to be more

Integration—seeking wholeness/completion

Love-Based

Movement to express love

Movement to protect that which is loved

Movement to receive love

Extrinsic or External Sourced

Positive peer health norms

Positive environmental conditions (safe, clean, friendly neighborhood, smoke-free public and workplaces)

Intrinsic or Internal Sourced

Inside-Out (Kimiecik) Motivation is from the inside first.

Joy/Pleasure

Satisfaction

Desire

Stimulation—It just feels good!

What Motivates Us?

There are two types of fear-based motivation. Deficiency-based and threat-based. Deficiency-based motivation comes from a perception of lack, or what is missing in life. With the modern emphasis on youth, we see millions of people striving for ways to reclaim their youthful appearances. There is a widespread fear of the natural aging process. The anti-aging marketplace is enormous. Can a fear of growing old, or at least looking old, motivate a wellness lifestyle successfully?

Is wellness simply the postponement of morbidity? According to this point of view we're all mortal and will die someday, and since the human body does break down over time, being healthy as much as we can, for as long as we can, is all we can do!

Deficiency-based motivation shows up in shoulds. "I should exercise today because if I don't I'll lose my figure." "I should eat this horrible tasting stuff because I've made an agreement with my coach to eat it five times a week!" Yes, even coaching can become part of this army of shoulds that a person experiences. This is what Jay Kimiecik calls identified regulation. The person is not doing something because they truly want to do it, but because they've set up an external source of pressure, which the coaching relationship could unfortunately be a part of.

When your client speaks in imperative terms—"I have to . . ." or "I should . . ."—you might challenge them to ask themselves, "Who says?" Where is the message coming from that they should look a certain way, act a certain way, etc.? This might help them discover and discuss with you the pressures they feel from their family, their workplace, their subculture, their ethnic culture, etc. to be a certain way. Help them examine this and decide how they want to respond to this pressure from outside sources. Help them move from the imperative to the volitional. A large part of coaching is reminding people that they have choices.

Threat-based motivations can propel us to take action. These fall into the categories of known threats, unknown threats, illness avoidance and environmental threats. When we look for motivation for lifestyle changes, doing something to avoid pain, disability or illness would seem obvious enough. People who smoke know that the risks of cancer and heart disease are high. People who eat at fast-food restaurants several times every week and pile on the fatty-greasy-salty-sweet diet usually know that it is not good for them. These are known threats, backed up by tons of research. Threats can be where the people involved often know other people who have died of lung cancer or other diseases directly related to their behavior. Clearly, just knowing about the threat is often not enough.

One of the weaknesses of fear-based motivation is that human beings are remarkable at exercising ways to dodge it. Most of it is called denial and minimization. I like to say that many of us, when we do this dance of denial, like to use a little voodoo to insure our safety. We say magic phrases like "It will never happen to me." Or, "It will be all right." We are playing the probabilities here aren't we? Everyone seems to know or have known some person who lived a reckless life of smoking, drinking, overeating or being a couch potato, and lived to a ripe old age and enjoyed much of it. When we say "Oh, one more won't hurt me." how well are we really keeping track?

Old school health education programs tried the fear-based approach. We found that frightening people away from risky behavior does not work well over all. While fear-based motivation may get you started, it does not do well at sustaining change over time. We often witness this when someone has a teachable moment in the doctor's office. They receive a diagnosis and a dire warning. They listen. It gets their attention and the person takes some action to change their health behavior. The bigger challenge is continuing to behave in the healthier new way.

Sometimes your client may be motivated by the fear of developing a life-threatening illness. "I don't want to die young of heart disease like my Dad did." "I don't want to come down with diabetes like my Mom did." That fear may motivate them to lace up their walking shoes, or jump into the swimming pool more often. If it is working for your client, there may be no need to challenge it. Will it be enough over the long haul?

In wellness coaching we are usually not working with the people who succeed on their own at lifestyle change. We are more often working with people who have tried and failed, tried and failed a number of times by themselves. They need something new and different. Instead of someone reminding them to take their medicine, do their sit-ups, and eat their oat bran so they won't die sooner, how about an ally who helps them discover how living well is about joy, more energy, and more fulfillment?

Development-based Motivation

Development-based motivation is really personal-growth motivation. Here we look beyond the deficiency needs that Maslow described in his theories—motivation and self-actualization. Now we look at what he called being needs. This is a view of human behavior that rests on the theory that all of us have within us a need to actualize our potential. When you see your clients removing the blocks that hold them back in their lives, they bloom. They flower into the amazing human beings they really are. Life coaches have long recognized this as the ultimate outcome of successful coaching. As a wellness coach, you support your clients in the same expression of self-actualization, on a whole-person, mind-body-spirit scale.

While all of this sounds rather idealistic and grand, it is also very concrete and practical in approach. The external sources of this motivation come, to a large extent, from the peer health norms that surround our client. As we described this concept briefly in The Ten Tenets of Wellness (Chapter 3), positive peer health norms can reinforce healthy behavior and can, in fact, open the doors for us to behave that way to begin with.

Coaching our clients to build strong and positive support systems made up of people who reinforce a healthy lifestyle can be some of our most valuable work. Every week our client's peers are around them much more than we are! It is so much easier to be active physically when our friends like to live that way too. Our clients can adopt new healthy behaviors more easily when they are surrounded by at least a few peers who already behave that way. Helping our clients expand connectedness in their lives may insure the adoption of, and the continuation of, healthy behaviors.

Another external, positive motivator can be the environment the person lives and works in. Living in a crowded, polluted, unsafe neighborhood can be a real threat to one's health, and make it difficult to engage in healthy new behaviors. On the other hand, a friendly, safe, clean neighborhood where there is access to healthy resources can make the adoption of new healthy lifestyle behaviors much easier.

Jay Kimiecik, in his book *The Intrinsic Exerciser*, contends that some of our best motivation comes from the inside-out. It is an outer expression of an inner motivation...that internal drive to be more of who we truly are . . . that seeking of expression of our wholeness and completeness. It is the intrinsic reward that is right there in the experience of the activity itself.

Why do you dance? Well, one person's answer might be: "I dance when I have to, like at a relative's wedding." Why do you play golf? Someone might answer: "I play golf because it's how I can build business relationships." Contrast that with the people who answer: "I dance because I love the feeling of movement! I love to move to the music! It's fun!" "I play golf because there is sheer joy when I hit a shot just right down that beautiful green fairway. I get so much satisfaction and relaxation out of it."

The first two people are operating on the external shoulds and real extrinsic deficiency motivation. The second pair are dancing and playing golf because they love it! Their motivation is intrinsic.

People with no experience of wilderness canoeing are sometimes baffled as to why my son, his best friends, and I, love to go deep into the northcountry on canoeing and fishing trips. When they hear our stories they pick up on the hardships of long days paddling, heavy packs and canoes on portages, mosquitoes, sleeping on the ground, etc. The pictures we bring back of big fish we've caught don't appear to be worth the sacrifice. What they can't know until they have experienced it are the more intrinsic rewards: the feel of the canoe slicing through still water, driven by only our own muscle power; the deep tranquility that can be found on the motorless lakes that we travel into; the amazing sense of brotherhood (or sisterhood) and self-sufficiency that we attain when we rely on each other and carry everything we need together.

So many unhealthy behaviors have immediate reinforcement! Nicotine imparts its effect on the smoker almost at once. Sugar tastes great as soon as the taste buds can perform their task. The tug of the couch into lethargy is pulling us down . . . now! The benefits of many healthy behaviors (e.g. exercise, good diet, etc.) are experienced further down the road. Our challenge in wellness coaching is to help our clients to have faith that the effort will be worth it. We reinforce immediately the desired behaviors, or help them set up ways of reinforcing it in the present. We also strongly support them in their vision of a healthy and vibrant life for them and help them hold that vision in their hearts and minds.

In effective wellness coaching, motivation is not about intellectually convincing someone of the benefits of a particular behavior, and then expecting them to agree and do! Wellness lifestyles may have an intellectual component, but wellness lifestyles are not often built simply on intellectual decisions. Clients benefit from looking deeper into their own motivation and trying methods that facilitate their own desire.

Kimiecik shares some research from a Canadian study, done by the Canadian Fitness and Lifestyle Research Institute, that found people who exercise regularly look to four primary sources of motivation:

- Fun, enjoyment, stimulation

- A feeling of accomplishment

- The pleasure of learning

- A concrete benefit, such as sleeping better and feeling calmer.

Help your client to explore a new behavior from the inside out. What is their experience in doing the behavior? What do they imagine it will be like to do that behavior when their body is more used to it, or they are more familiar with it? Help them discover the intrinsic joys in movement, in the sense of taste (help them find healthy foods they actually love the taste of), in their feeling of accomplishment. Help them find healthy lifestyle behaviors that pay off now in benefits they can feel, see, taste, hear, smell and touch.

Love or Fear

An ancient piece of wisdom that is often quoted by Gerry Jampolsky (*Love Is The Answer*) is that "everything we do comes either from love or from fear." A moment of reflection shows us what a truism this is. Think about an experience you may have had where a person was snobbish towards you. What were they afraid of? They certainly didn't appear afraid. Well, a snob is trying to be very selective about who and what they experience in their world. They are trying to make their world very small. How safe do they really feel? Their snobbish behavior said more about them than it did about you.

We've looked at lifestyle motivation that is based in fear. What about lifestyle motivation that is based in love? Some of our attempts to improve our lifestyles may come from our love for others. The grandparent who swims four times a week because they want to be around for their grandchildren (and take them swimming!). The couple who stopped smoking because their pet dog developed a lung problem from their second-hand smoke!

Coach your clients to explore who else would benefit from their improved lifestyle. Have them list their loved ones, friends and associates, and write down how these people would gain from them being healthier, more accessible, more active and vibrant! The airline steward/stewardess speech "put the oxygen mask on yourself first, and then assist others" is always a good reminder of one of the very best reasons to take care of yourself first; so you can be there, healthy and well, for others as well as for yourself.

Jay Kimiecik points out how as we develop mastery in a new exercise-related skill, we achieve a sense of accomplishment. That feeling of mastery bolsters our self-confidence and self-esteem. It feels wonderful to hit the ball down the middle of the fairway. It feels great to flow from one dance move gracefully into another. It feels great to run your first non-stop mile! This sense of accomplishment can be viewed as another form of self-love.

Self-love is once again what we are back to. Our client may start out at a place where they are willing to work their wellness plan for the sake of others, while they would not do it just for themselves. Hey! It's a start. As their health improves their feelings about themselves are likely to improve as well.

The Non-negotiable Law of Developmental Motivation

Greg Andersen, a cancer-survivor and author, reminds us of a truth that helps us understand this quest for self-improvement and self-actualization better. Instead of constantly striving and never arriving consider the following.

The essence of the law is this: I am complete but not finished. This is a statement of powerful truth. You are complete, whole, and fully alive right now! You need no more for life to be happy. You can be completely fulfilled with what is, now.

We are complete now, yet our natural development calls for further growth. This shift in thinking is critical. Lack becomes impossible. When we can see the inevitability of growth and change, we begin to become motivated by our dreams, not our deficiencies.

> *Satisfied needs, be they physical, psychological, or spiritual,*
> *do not motivate. Only unsatisfied hungers move people.*
> *This is one of the most powerful understandings we can have*
> *of ourselves and of others.*
>
> —Greg Anderson

Wellness coaching works best when we truly become allies with our clients and help them find motivation in development-based approaches. Exploring and listing all the ways in which the desired lifestyle changes fit into this approach provides motivation for change.

Coaching for Greater Self-care/Self-permission

As a wellness coach you may at times become very puzzled at the difficulty your client finds in behaving in new ways that are healthy for them. While they are completely equipped with knowledge, insight, awareness, accessibility, affordability, environmental support, and even a really good coach like you, they still won't give themselves permission to engage in the new behavior! In attempting to answer our golden question of coaching and wellness, "Why don't people do what they know they need to do for themselves?" self-permission is a indispensable concept.

Sitting in the shoes of that very puzzled coach I have asked my clients, "How do you hold yourself back from doing what you said you wanted to do this week?" They often say something like the following: "I don't know. I just forgot about it completely once we talked about it." "I had the time written down, just like we talked about, to go and workout, and then I thought I'd better get more housework done first." "Whenever I take the time to workout it feels like I'm taking time away from somebody else, like my kids, my partner, my job." "I feel really guilty when I just sit there and relax,—like I'm not getting anything done!" "My family always taught us to get all of our work done first before we could have fun, but now, as an adult, the work is endless!" "Are you kidding? Men (women) in my culture just don't do stuff like that!"

On one level or another, the client is denying himself or herself permission to exercise, relax, have fun, and express themselves, etc. They honestly don't feel all right doing these wonderful self-care, life-style-enhancing behaviors that they have intellectually concluded are good and important for them to do for their health. They are buying into a belief system, which may deny them needed gratification in any of a number of important areas of their lives. They may deny themselves adequate sleep, exercise, nutrition, contact with others, creative self-expression, and just plain enjoyment of life.

At times we need to help a client go back into the area of self-exploration and develop some understanding of where these powerful injunctions (as the Transactional Analysis theorists call them) come from. The roots for this may go deep. They tend to stretch back to four primary areas:

1. Self-esteem

2. Values, beliefs, and cultural norms

3. History of the person and their family

4. Myths and magical/irrational thinking

Self-permission and self-esteem beg the question, "Am I worth it?" The client debates with themselves "Am I worth the time? Shouldn't I be doing something for someone else (who is more worthy than I) instead?" As stated before, if the client's self-worth is extremely low, if self-hatred is more the issue, then, by all means refer this client to the help they need in a counselor's office.

For many clients gaining some insight about how they have adopted, without much examination and conscious choice, a set of values and beliefs that were expressed in the norms of their family, their culture, and subculture can be very freeing. And yet we are not talking about a deep analysis of every bio-socio-cultural contributor to one's life. Instead, help your client to realize and acknowledge some of the historical factors that have made them who they are today, and then help them experiment with being different today. If repeated experiments (such as those you will see demonstrated in the case below) go nowhere in increasing self-permission it may be a hint to the client that there are old wounds that need counseling and therapy. It may be more about healing than coaching.

All-Work and No-Play

I have had numerous clients teach me great lessons about self-permission and self-denial. One client was a woman who grew up in a hard-working family from the Great Plains. Her pioneer grandparents and great-grandparents had set the tone for self-denial and self-sacrifice as a survival strategy. Their religious practices had reinforced and glorified this. Admittedly this way of living may have been quite realistic in the years that helped them make it through the great drought of the dust bowl years, and the economics of the Great Depression. However, for her parents and for her, this severe way of living did not mesh with the abundant, yet fast-moving and high-stress world that they found themselves in.

This client was a self-employed businesswoman who found herself living a life of all-work and no-play. She was extremely stressed, significantly overweight, and, despite a hard-working life of service to others, was both personally miserable and struggling with the viability of her business.

As we coached together and our alliance grew into one of sincere trust, I challenged her to do more self-care. Her level of self-denial was so great that it had been literally more than fifteen years since she had taken a vacation of any kind, and she could not remember the last live concert she had been to, despite absolutely loving music. She did not exercise at all, but I knew that this was not the first place to start.

Her first suggested coaching homework was to research the schedule of a concert venue within an easy drive of her home (about fifty prairie miles). She came to our next session excited to report that the Beach Boys were actually doing a reunion tour and stopping there. I challenged her to take the extreme (to her) act of buying tickets for her and her husband and go to it! Rocking at that concert was like pushing a wedge in the slightly opened door of self-care for her. Little by little she began to do more for herself.

Eventually she found that her neighbor had a Golden Retriever that wasn't getting enough exercise. She asked the neighbor if she could take the dog out walking regularly. This helped her give herself permission to take so much time for something so "unproductive" as walking. The neighbor was thrilled. She and the Retriever became good buddies and daily walks of at least an hour ensued. This combined with a self-initiated participation in a dietary-support group helped the weight fall off of her.

Doing things for self, especially just for recreation and mere enjoyment felt really foreign to her at first. This was very incongruent with her view of herself and the world. To do even a little for herself she had to think in extremes and doing so helped her to grow!

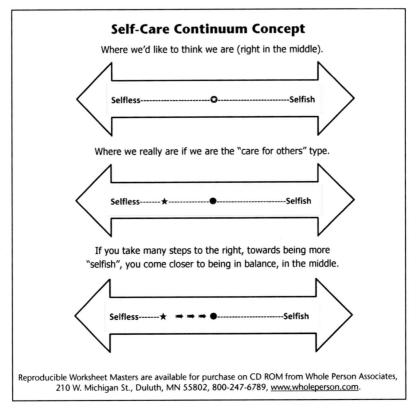

FIGURE 8.1

Myths and Magical/Irrational Thinking

Some of what we learn in our families and in our communities and cultures as we grow up are really myths, yet we take them on as truth. Some are self-limiting beliefs that the group (family, peers, community) somehow taught as truisms. These falsehoods become seen as "just the way life is." This is the view of the world where there is a sense that we are powerless to prevent the inevitable, be it poverty, illness, misfortune or unhappiness.

In the economically depressed area where I grew up there was an unspoken message that a young person should not think that they are anyone special. It was OK to be OK, but not OK to be great! To strive for excellence was seen as an attempt to raise yourself above your peers and that was considered narcissistic. At least, that is how I came to interpret my experience and observations there. I saw my best friend, who I always thought was just as intelligent as me, if not more so in some areas, succumb to the message from his family not to see education as a vehicle to greater success or happiness. He was directly told to not even consider college. A job, the military…these were his only options. While no one but him can judge his own happiness and how it all worked out, I still wonder, "What if?"

Health myths in some families abound. "None of the men in our family live long." "All of the women in our family are overweight, it's just the way we are." This type of insidious programming takes place with a very low level of awareness of the consequences. In an attempt to protect us from the bitter disappointments of life, our families set us up to expect certain health outcomes as inevitable. This gives the whole family permission to behave in ways that probably usher in exactly what we fear. Why bother to exercise and eat right when we're going to die before fifty anyway?

The work of philosopher Sam Keen (*Your Mythic Journey*) is a valuable resource for understanding what he calls our own personal mythology. Understanding the myths that we live and die by is one of his valuable contributions to wellness.

Coach for possibility thinking with your client. Help them become conscious and aware of myths like those we have described above. Encourage to have them to talk with a number of friends and relations who may have received the same messages and see how everyone dealt with them in their own way.

> *Think impossible and dreams get discarded, projects get abandoned, and hope for wellness is torpedoed.*
> *But let someone yell the words, "It's possible," and resources we hadn't been aware of come rushing in to assist us in our quest.*

—Greg Anderson

Affirming the Positive

Most of us tend to overlook what we are doing right. We take for granted all the good things that we did during the course of the day. We take for granted our strengths, talents, and abilities. So seldom do we take time to honor what we are blessed with, or to honor what we have accomplished.

As coaches, part of honoring our client is to jump on the opportunity to affirm the positive when we see it in evidence. Clients need to hear it. They need to hear what a good job they are doing, even if, to them, they are just doing their job.

Affirmations made by the client can be powerful statements that take them closer and closer to their goal. By affirming that they are whole and complete they realize how that is true. By repetitively affirming that they are lovable and attractive, they become so to the rest of the world.

Author Ilan Shamir has developed an outstanding program that brings this affirming positive approach to both individuals and to corporate/organizational programs that he explains in his book and program titled *A Thousand Things Went Right Today*. Coaches can study this material and expand their awareness of the positive in everyday life and help their clients to develop the same valuable skill.

Wellness Coaching and the
Inner Critic or Gremlin

One of the greatest ways that we dis-empower ourselves is through allowing the inner-critic to rule. Each of us has a part of our thought patterns that we refer to as the inner-critic or the gremlin. Operating out of fear, this part of us vehemently holds to the status quo and fights change—even change that is good for us.

Some people say the inner-critic is just trying to protect us. Its idea of protection is like this. Think of a high-school age boy who goes to a dance. His number one fear is being rejected. So the inner-critic/ gremlin protects him by insuring he will not be rejected. He never asks anyone to dance. Mission accomplished. No rejection. No dancing either!

The inner-critic is our inner-voice that speaks to our self-doubt and fear. When we listen to it we hear voices from the past that we have taken in, that tell us we aren't good enough, beautiful enough, smart enough, etc. The inner-critic tells us we don't belong out there being successful. The inner-critic destroys our confidence and causes us to withdraw from opportunities, or at least to perform poorly. At worst the inner-critic triggers all our negative feelings about ourselves, even self-loathing.

The key in gremlin fighting is to catch yourself early and not give the gremlin your ear. As you listen to it, it grows. Soon all you can hear is your voice of self-doubt and negativity. The other thing to remember about your inner critic is that you cannot kill it! It is really a part of you and will always make its attempt to gain your attention.

I worked with a professional golfer and helped him improve his game by silencing his inner-critic. Whenever he made a bad shot on the course his gremlin would attack him savagely! He would get so angry with himself that his next shot was almost guaranteed to be just as bad or worse. After great work on his part through our coaching he thought he had finally vanquished his cognitive nemesis and was appalled when it raised it's ugly head again on the course. "Wait a minute!" I said to him. "Are you waiting for the day when the gremlin doesn't come on the course with you?" "Well, yeah…" he replied. I had to tell him that that day would not come. The gremlin will always show up. Your challenge is to immediately recognize it, and silence it. You can do that effectively, but yes, it will always try. Giving yourself a hard time for not keeping your inner critic/gremlin in line is what I call advanced gremlin activity.

Rick Carson, author of *Taming Your Gremlin*, says that we are best off when we realize that the gremlin does not have our best interest at heart. We have to recognize when we are listening to the self-doubter within, and quickly silence it. Here is one method for doing just that.

Five "R" Process for Gremlin Fighting

1. RECOGNIZE when what you are saying to yourself is gremlin-talk.
   a. Know ahead of time what are some of your Gremlin's favorite lines are.
   b. Distinguish between gremlin talk and good problem-solving reflection.
   c. Identify if this is a particularly gremlin-vulnerable time for you. Use the H.A.L.T. Self-Quiz (below)
2. REFUTE the gremlin talk.
   a. "This is *not* true. What's true for me is . . ."
   b. Don't get into a debate with your gremlin.
3. REMOVE the gremlin from your experience.
   a. Use your own favorite gremlin-removing fantasy (gag 'em, bind 'em, throw 'em in the dungeon and lock them up again!)
   b. Don't let the gremlin travel with you. Throw them out of the car, out of your workplace, or wherever you are.
4. REGAIN your self-confidence. Remember how you have been successful in the past and affirm your abilities and talents.
5. RETURN to the present. Focus on the here and now.

You will notice that one of the "Rs" of gremlin fighting is *not* reassure. Some clients like to believe that the gremlin is really their own inner hurt child who is always fearful and needs kindness, gentleness and reassurance. There is an important distinction to draw here. Your gremlin or inner-critic is not your inner child, it is the accumulation of lies and distortions of reality that frighten and weaken your inner child. The inner-critic is just that—a critic! It constantly criticizes our actions, decisions and even our feelings and labels them not as just ineffective, but as wrong and stupid.

When we engage in conversation with our gremlin, even if we think we are making peace or reassuring it that all is and/or will be OK, we give it attention, and it grows. When we really realize that the inner-critic bases its FEAR campaign on False Evidence Appearing Real, we realize that we are engaging in debate, conversation and relationship with a pack of lies.

A valuable little tool that I believe was originated in work from the addictions field is the H.A.L.T. Self-Quiz.

Whenever you have identified your Gremlin, or Inner-Critic as being active, or you seem to be starting the process of reviewing your entire life in retrospect. Ask yourself, am I:

Hungry?

Angry?

Lonely?

Tired?

If so . . . HALT! Stop the self-review process until you are no longer hungry, angry, lonely, or tired. It's not a good time to look back on your whole life.

One of the best ways that a wellness coach can continue to be of value to a client is to help them spot the gremlin when it shows up. Gently challenge your client to examine something that they have just said. "Could what you are saying be gremlin-talk"? "Does that sound like your inner-critic?"

There is amazing power in simply noticing. Awareness opens eyes, doorways, and lives. It is the automatic pilot style living of habit that dulls our awareness and limits our lives. It is the subtle way we begin listening to the old tape recordings of our inner-critic that brings out our fears and causes us to grind growth and progress to a frightened halt.

When we notice, when we sharpen our awareness to catch the gremlin in action and then employ the Five "R" process above, we shut it down early, before it can gain strength. Have a zero tolerance of the gremlin's presence. No negotiations with a pack of lies that masquerades as self-talk in our own heads.

As your client progresses through the stages of change the gremlin will grudgingly take the journey with them, complaining and attempting to sabotage progress all the way. In fact some of the ways I've been most helpful to my clients is when I've helped them see how it is often their very success that triggers the self-doubt, self-worth questions of the inner-critic. The gremlin gets really scared when you are being successful at change!

Your client may struggle with this concept of the inner-critic or gremlin. Recommend that they read the extremely insightful and entertaining little book by Richard Carson, *Taming Your Gremlin*. Have some coaching conversations around what they've learned and how it applies to them.

I free myself not by trying to be free, but by simply noticing how I am imprisoning myself in the very moment I am imprisoning myself.

—**Rick Carson,** *Taming Your Gremlin*

Working With What Works

Coaching brings to the field of wellness many effective and practical methods to help our wellness coaching clients find success in behavioral change. Here are some very concrete ways to work with your clients to help them make lifestyle improvements that last.

Structures

Adopting new habits that are healthy requires continual reminders. Our wellness consciousness can be stimulated by a variety of physical things coaches call structures. Structures are any kind of visible device that reminds us (or our clients) of our wellness vision, goals, or tasks.

Some good insightful work by a client of mine once produced the awareness that she was taking life much too seriously and that the lack of joy in her life really was affecting her stress-level and consequently her health and well-being. She vowed to adopt an attitude of lightness and to seek to see the humor, irony, and the up side of her daily events.

She knew that the workplace was her biggest challenge for this. I explored with her the type of image that always brightened her thoughts and feelings and found she loved clowns. While some people actually are frightened of clowns, they always brought a smile to her face. I asked if she had any small clown statuettes. She did and I asked her to select one and bring it to her desk at work.

Whenever she noticed the clown figure on her desk she was to immediately take a deep breath, and if possible at that moment, lighten her thoughts. As simple as it was, it worked! To ensure that it would continue to be effective I encouraged her to move the location of the structure on and around her desk area, or to bring in another different figure of a clown. This would freshen up the structure and stimulate her memory of her commitment to shift her consciousness to a lighter and brighter view.

Structures can include: photos or magazine clippings of places and events that are in line with one's wellness vision (such as an older person who still climbs mountains or a dream vacation destination that you want to be in shape for); photos of loved ones you want to be healthy enough to enjoy being with; little pieces of nature (rocks, seashells, etc.) that remind you of the active things you like to do in the natural world (such as hiking or snorkeling); photos or magazine clippings that show someone doing the activity or displaying the emotions or behaviors you want to emulate; something that to you (or your client) represents an important metaphor that was arrived at in a great coaching session. Unrealistic or perfectionistic images (such as supermodel photos) don't work well as structures. Get creative with your client and brainstorm what would work for them.

Journaling

We spoke of journaling in Chapter 7, referring to it as a tool for exploration. It, and coaching itself, can help your client explore in ways beyond their own thinking.

Our own personal reflection has value, but it is limited, both in viewpoint (which always includes blind spots), and in what it brings forth. Talking with you, the coach (as well as others), allows for the power of relationship and requires your client to put their thoughts into words in order to be understood. This vastly different cognitive process allows them to synthesize their thinking and often yields entirely new perspectives and insights.

Writing their thoughts out on paper (or typing them onto our computer), draws upon yet another process that takes their reflections deeper and often in new directions that mere sitting and thinking would not reach. Journaling is another tool of elicitation. Engaging in the journaling process helps your client understand that all of this wellness/lifestyle improvement work is really about personal growth. Journaling helps them stay on task—the task of actualizing their potential and expressing their true nature.

Help your clients feel more attracted to journaling by urging them to do it their own way. Some people feel very intimidated by journaling. They sometimes think they have to journal like Henry David Thoreau. Support them in giving themselves permission to journal any way they find effective. Draw outside the lines. Be sloppy, be neat, it's up to them. They can use a structured, published journal or just write consistently in an inexpensive spiral notebook.

Journals need not be a simple chronology of events. They may at times just be a stream of consciousness. At other times they may be a gratitude list, or a list of action steps that were taken. Support your client in making their journal work for them, not the other way around.

Urge your clients to give their journal top security. A really secure journal allows them to say what they really need to say and express themselves. A password protected electronic journal works well for this. Keep paper journals reliably secure and confidential.

Make journaling part of the coaching process by securing a commitment as to how often they will journal each week. A commitment to journaling seven days a week is usually a setup for failure. Go for four or five—maybe even three entries to start with. Challenge the client who suggests only once or twice a week.

Urge your client to have only one rule about their journaling . . . that they write it by themselves, with no help from their gremlin! The inner-critic will attempt to seize this opportunity too. Beware and be forewarned! Urge your client to identify when their thoughts are slipping into gremlin talk" and do what it takes to silence it. Also, urge your client to observe and be patient as they go through the change process.

Tracking

Many of the behaviors that our clients seek to change can be tracked very easily. Frequency, intensity, duration and the nature of exercise can be written down, preferably each day it happens. Your client can gain much by writing down everything that they eat in a week. Most fitness programs provide charts for writing down both what you plan to eat and then what you actually do eat everyday. This is a very helpful process to teach a client the reality of their eating patterns, and then to improve them. There are also a number of commercial sites on the web that feature online diet journaling. Some of these are quite sophisticated and may appeal to some clients.

Simpler is better for some clients. One of the most effective tracking devices ever invented is the wall calendar. By having a wall calendar displayed in a frequently visible place in the client's home or workplace, they can quickly see their identified wellness behavior (or lack thereof) by marking on it with a heavy pen or marker.

The task of tracking raises awareness. It brings new consciousness to the process of change and helps the person be more accountable to themselves. It helps the person to see their improvements in black and white and celebrate them. It reduces self-deception and increases self-efficacy. It also allows the coach and client to know when goals are being reached and when they remain elusive.

Realistic Goal Setting

Even though we have spoken about clients often being goal phobic, here are some guidelines for coaching around goals and goal setting.

Goals contain three qualities:

- The content of the goal—what will be done?

- The degree of the goal—how much will be done?

- The duration of the goal—how often and how long it will occur?

Clients sometimes are very good at goal setting. Other times they may set their sights either too high, or too low. For a wellness plan to have a chance, the goals have to be:

- Realistic and obtainable. (Can your client make these behavioral changes in a realistic and timely manner?)

- Short enough in terms of completion time for success to have a sufficiently timely reinforcing effect. (Quicker success = greater reinforcement. Take baby steps)

- Imperative enough that the person really wants to succeed in this area.

- Imaginable. Your client has to be ready and able to see themselves succeeding in that area.

- Specific. Keep it simple, to the point, and, as the British say, "Spot on!"

- Client generated. The goal has to be the client's goal for themselves, not the coach's goal for the client.

- Challenging. Difficult enough to bring out the best in your client but not so challenging that it works against your client.

Obtaining Loophole-Free Accountability

Once goals are set, how does the client follow through on them? Coaching is distinguished by its emphasis on accountability and providing the methodologies that help a client to attain high levels of it. When a coach holds a client accountable, they are really helping the client to be accountable to themselves. The coach works for the client, not the opposite. In your role as wellness coach you are there to co-create with the client agreements of accountability that serve that client well. I've found it critical to a client's acceptance of the accountability concept that they understand that they are not accountable to you. They are accountable to *themselves*.

The part of your client that is afraid of change will search for loopholes—ways out—contained in your agreements for accountability. Your client's gremlin or inner critic will be on alarm status as you co-create your agreements because it knows that accountability is serious stuff! It gets results!

For loophole-free accountability follow these guidelines.

1. Start with good goals (using the guidelines above).

2. Match the degree of accountability to the client, the situation, and what they are asking for. Simply reporting back verbally at the next session may be entirely adequate for a specific goal with one client. Another goal in another situation, or with a very different client may require very stringent accountability. Ascertain what degree of accountability a client usually wants and needs in your foundation session with them, then keep observing and experimenting and see what really works.

3. Keep closing the escape routes. When a client is vague about when or how they will report back to you, require them to clarify it and nail it down. Help your client explore their "Yes, but…" excuses and see how valid they really are.

4. If they are having trouble committing ask your client what you should do if you don't hear from them by when they agreed. "What if I don't get your e-mail by the end of the day on Monday. What should I do?" Keep What if-ing them until you get a clear response.

5. Offer to connect but keep the responsibility on the client. "OK, if I don't get a response to my reminder-e-mail that I've sent back to you, what should I do?"

Wellness Mapping 360°
Evaluation & Measurement

We've come a long way with our client on their wellness journey. As their success in making lifestyle improvements has continued they have ventured into previously unknown lands. Evaluation provides feedback. It asks "Are we on the right path? How are we doing?" Good coaching is always examining the road traveled and the results. We ask and we measure. We constantly seek to find the value in what we have done.

Self-Report Data

Check in with your client on a regular basis to process the process. Examine the coaching relationship and the coaching process at regular intervals. You both may have wandered off the trail you thought you were on or coaching may have become less effective and less satisfying even though nothing has been said about it.

Refer back to the wellness plan originally developed. Are you both in alignment on this process and moving towards these goals? Explore how your client feels about it, no matter what the numbers say.

One-to-ten self-ratings are very helpful. Asking a client to rate their progress on a particular behavior from a low-effectiveness of one, to a high-effectiveness of ten. This can itself be a tool of elicitation and uncover important material to discuss.

Biometrics and Measurements

Here again, wellness coaching works with many outcomes that we can measure concretely. Our clients can record their number of hours of sleep. They can work with their physician and other health-care providers to attain physiological measures that let us know whether we're on the right path, or not.

The biometric feedback that clients receive will always have a psychological effect. What the effect is, from jubilation to depression depends on our client and their belief system. Be sure to explore the feeling-impact of test results, physiological measurements of any kind. Evaluation on these variables can produce results that are encouraging or discouraging. Exploration of their impact on your client's motivation will be key. Talk about it and explore it, but also observe how your client responds behaviorally to it over the following weeks.

Using Inventories Again

One of the easiest ways to assess progress is to have the client re-take the particular wellness instrument that they took at the beginning of coaching. The Wellness Inventory and TestWell, and even regular HRAs are very well-suited for this. They produce well-organized data that can be used to re-set the course of coaching.

Figure-Ground

As we attain a sense of completion in one area of focus it seems to lose energy and fades from our attention. What once was paramount and so important now recedes into the background. What to work on next becomes the big coaching question. An informal review of the wellness plan will help, but it may be most helpful for the coach to be sensitive to the shifts in energy, interest and excitement that they see in their client as they review new areas on to work. Follow the energy. What seems most pressing now and what is there motivation to work on? Looking at what is now primary in the person's life may help reset the course of wellness coaching for the client.

> *Overt action without insight is likely to lead to temporary change.*
>
> —**James Prochaska,** *Changing For Good*

Wellness Mapping 360°
Clear Measurable Outcomes

How can our clients know when they have arrived at their destination? How can they answer the classic question from the back seat of the automobile "Are we there yet?"? When we may have never been there before, how can we know what the X-marks-the-spot on our pirate's wellness treasure map for a specific outcome looks like?

Hopefully, at the onset of our quest, the destination was adequately described. The more measurable goals, like percentage of body fat reduction, are easy to determine. The more elusive destinations that depend on subjective self-assessment, may be just as valid, but now both the client and the coach may discover they are a bit foggy or tougher to recognize. To bolster your client's confidence and help them recognize success, lobby for at least some clear measurable outcomes in the wellness plan to begin with.

Maintaining Success & Managing Stress

When do we know that a new behavior has been integrated as part of the client's lifestyle? How will they know? Many improvements in lifestyle behavior relapse under stress. A smoker has kicked the habit until a project deadline at work coincides with the filing date for their taxes and the birthday of their child. An unexpected surgery means starting an exercise program all over again. Life happens!

Prochaska addresses the maintenance stage of change very well in *Changing For Good*. He points out how stress triggers the re-emergence of old behaviors (usually exactly the ones we've been working on changing), and so argues that we should build into our wellness plan some aspects of stress management.

Coach your client to develop the skills they need to cope with the inevitable stress that will challenge their progress. Co-create a back-up plan of action to use during times of extra stress. Realize that this may occur after coaching has already concluded, so your client needs to be self-sufficient in stress management strategies and skills.

Weekly Wellness Tracker

Name _____ Date _____

Focus Area – Desired Health Outcome _____

Action Steps	Check-in Plan	Monday	Tuesday	Wednesday	Thursday	Friday	Saturday	Sundqy
1.								
Duration								
Comments								
2.								
Duration								
Comments								
3.								
Duration								
Comments								
4.								
Duration								
Comments								

What relaxation method did you use? (*circle one*) Nature • Music • Deep Breathing • Meditation • Yoga/Tai Chi • Guided Imagery • Other

How did you sleep this week? (*circle one*) Good • OK • Not well •   Comments _____

How did you take care of yourself this week? _____   What disappointed you this week? _____

On a scale of 1-10 (10 being the best) how well did you do this week?   What encouraged you this week? _____
1 • 2 • 3 • 4 • 5 • 6 • 7 • 8 • 9 • 10

What do you want to remember to talk over with your coach? _____

Reproducible Worksheet Masters are available for purchase on CD ROM from Whole Person Associates, 210 W. Michigan St., Duluth, MN 55802, 800-247-6789, www.wholeperson.com.

FIGURE 8.2

The Power of Habit

Many times I've worked with clients who have made up their minds to change. They have determined that a change is needed and they have decided to change an old habit of their behavior that has been around for a long time (such as overeating, being sedentary or smoking). They appear motivated to change and vow to stop a certain behavior from occurring any more.

Before long they are disappointed that the behavior that they decided to end had resurfaced once again. Often the client would be disappointed not only that the behavior was back, but disappointed in their own lack of will power. They had thought, contrary to what we've seen Prochaska teach us, that change was an event (a decision) not a process. They made it about strength of character and gave their own inner critic plenty to berate them with.

Don't underestimate the power of habit! Once we have adopted a new behavior there are actually neural pathways set up in our nervous system related to this behavior. Our habits are part psycho-physiological! Our bodies, as well as our minds, are in the habit of reacting a certain way, so no wonder changing a habit is not as simple as making a resolution.

Urge your client to consider these quick tips for changing habits.

1. Practice patience. Research tells us that it takes as many as 180 days to truly drop an old habit and adopt a new one. So stay with it.

2. No beating yourself up! Don't put yourself down because you find yourself engaged in the old habit. Be compassionate with yourself instead.

3. Celebrate catching yourself! Take the repetitions in stride. Realize that despite the old habit showing up again, you are committed to changing the habit. Instead of putting yourself down ("There I go again!"), celebrate the fact that you managed to catch yourself and become aware of it. As you catch yourself earlier in the practice of the old habit, you'll have even more to celebrate!

4. Use structures, as discussed on page 150, to help remind you of the new habits you want to adopt. Structures are little physical reminders that help you remember your goals. They may be little signs you print up for yourself

reminding yourself to: "Wait to answer the call after 2 rings, not sooner!"; "Breathe!"; "Call a friend today!"; "30 min. of writing every day." Another hint about structures—move them around, change the look of them so they don't start blending in with the background again (out of habit!).

5. Involve others in your goals. Let co-workers, friends and family know what you are working on changing. Enlist their support and possibly their awareness and feedback to help you stay engaged in the habit changing process.

6. Get a coach! Working with a coach gives you someone to help you get clear about what behaviors you really want to change; give you support in the process and/or hold you accountable to do what you say you will do to change the habits.

Every man is more than just himself; he also represents the unique, the very special and always significant and remarkable point at which the world's phenomena intersect, only once in this way and never again.

—Hermann Hesse

Every person's path to and through change will be unique. As we strive to develop ways to help people make the lifestyle changes that will maximize their wellness we must remember that they are all just offerings we make for each person to examine for themselves.

Chapter 9

Choosing, Living, Loving, Being: Coaching The Strategic, Lifestyle, Interpersonal, and Intrapersonal Aspects of Effective Change

Whatever course you decide upon, there is always someone to tell you you are wrong. There are always difficulties arising which tempt you to believe that your critics are right. To map out a course of action and follow it to the end, requires some of the same courage which a soldier needs.

—Ralph Waldo Emerson

It's a big world out there. Before your coaching client lies so many possibilities! There are so many aspects to the journey that it may be overwhelming at times. There is a path to be found and chosen, there are things to explore and goals to set. So many choices to make that at some point an organizing process may assist us proceed.

Imagine your client is struggling to find direction, feels unclear about what to do next, and is wandering in circles from one topic to the next. They are committed enough to the journey of change so they are working with you, yet they don't know where to start. Perhaps they are afraid to even take that first step. To return to our coach-as-mountain-guide analogy, do you simply follow your client patiently around through the trackless thick trees at the base of a mountain range? How can you best serve them as a coach, as a guide?

Throughout this book we've continually talked about the benefits of a holistic approach to growth and development. Yet, does holistic mean an inclusion of everything? You need an organizing methodology. As a coach, one way you can best serve your client is to have enough knowledge of change theory and development to offer a variety of ways that your client can look at the change process, embrace it and begin their journey with you by their side. You do this by keeping this knowledge in the back of your mind to guide you as you guide them. As a coach it helps you think on your feet and gives you a sense of what needs to be included in the work you are doing with the client.

One great contribution that coaching has made to the growth and development process or movement is that it is so focused and practical. It is not about the geological history of the mountains in front of you, it is about choosing a peak to climb, getting in shape for the challenge, loading your pack and having someone to climb with!

Just like your client's challenge of where to start, you are faced with a similar question of what views of health, wellness, growth and development to draw upon in your work as a coach. Here is one methodology to consider.

Coaching for Strategic Lifestyle Change

Choosing Strategic	Living Lifestyle	Loving Interpersonal	Being Intrapersonal
Strategic Thinking	Environment	Love or Fear	Internal Aspects
Strategizing	Breathing	Conflict Skills	Belief Systems
Conscious Living	Moving	Conflict Resolution	Cognitive Thinking
Awareness	Eating	Communication Skills	Spiritual
Delegation	Centering &Relaxation	Connectedness	Self Talk
Values	Yoga	Support	Gremlin Fighting
Goal Clarification	Tai Chi	Inclusion	Self Worth
Priorities	Meditation	Camaradarie	Self Esteem
Thrive Not Survive	Exercise	Family	Self Expression
Re-owning		History	Play
Urgent/Important			
Travel Time			

TABLE 9.1

Choosing: Coaching the Strategic Aspects of Life

Strategic Thinking	True Priorities
Strategizing	Urgent / Important
Conscious Living	Thrive, don't just survive
Delegation	Re-owning
Values and Goals Clarification	

Our big brains seem to often be a liability when we believe that our intellect is the only guide to follow. However, effective use of that huge cerebral cortex that has allowed us, as a species, to adapt and survive, even thrive. We all problem solve, integrate, synthesize and process information. We deduce, assume, presume, construe, infer and conclude many things. We are, at times, our own worst enemy and our own savior. Like many human gifts the intellect seem to shine when we engage with others in our quest.

Coaching is an expedient process that allows our clients to find what will be most advantageous in less time. Through engaging with your client in strategic thinking you can help them to actualize and put into operation the goals they are pursuing. We have rightly emphasized motivation throughout this book. An equal number of failed attempts to reach the summit of the mountain can be attributed to poor planning and execution. Strategic thinking with your client is the practical, roll-up-the-sleeves part of coaching that is really fun! Your client's energy and excitement will be a boon to their progress and good strategic thinking can stimulate it.

Goal Selection Based On True Priorities

The order to the steps your client uses to move towards a wellness lifestyle may not seem so important, but they are. Certainly someone can improve their diet, gain sleep and develop and stick to an exercise routine at the same time. For most people the wellness to do list can be imposing and even impractical. People have so many good wellness ideas and intentions and so little time.

Priorities can guide us in our selection of where to put our energy (time, attention, effort, resources). However, not everything can be a priority. You might say that part of the definition of a priority is that

161

there aren't very many of them! So what are our true priorities? They are the ones rooted most deeply into our core beliefs and values. Our true priorities serve us best when they are centered in compassion for others and for self as well. Coaching can help us to distinguish what really is important to us, and how urgent it really is.

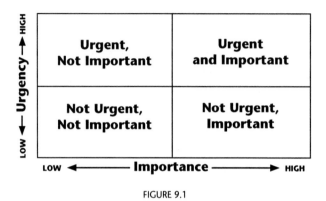

FIGURE 9.1

Help your client process the items from their wellness to do list through this matrix. You will see that not everything is of high importance and/or urgent. If your client feels like everything belongs at the highest level, it's time to spend more processing time with your coach!

Important

A good hard look at what really IS important, what truly matters to us will sometimes open our eyes. Coach your client to help them clarify their values. Help them to seek alignment with their own values. Have your client ask himself or herself, "How does this serve me, others and the world around me?" "Is this an expression of who I am?" "Am I being true to myself?" Help them experiment with perspective by asking themselves "How will this serve me in the future or in the long run?"

Urgent

Over the years I've found myself advising clients to "never make a decision just to relieve anxiety." If you are worried and highly anxious about something, deal with the anxiety first. Relax and center yourself first. Work on the feelings first rather than seeking a quick fix from a not-so-well-thought-out decision.

Conscious Living

As mentioned before, part of your job as a wellness coach is to remind people that they have choices! Good strategies are well thought out and consciously deployed and employed. When your client seems to encounter obstacles help them distinguish between real circumstance and ones of their own making. Obstacles of real circumstance can usually be seen as challenges to be overcome and a way can usually be found. If not, it's time to go back to the drawing board and rework the goal.

Obstacles of our own making can be more feeling based. If your client says, "Well, I can't go and do my exercise workout there because I don't know anybody." help them examine this conclusion. Could they find a place to workout where they know people? They may begin to see how they are creating ways of holding themselves back and may need to talk about their fears of rejection, and their feelings of isolation. As an effective coach we need to be able to address both partners, the head and the heart.

Drawing Distinctions

When we use the urgent/important matrix we are drawing distinctions. Distinctions are one of the primary tools in the masterful coach's tool box. When clients do not distinguish between urgent and important they feel constantly overwhelmed. As a coach you can ask powerful questions to challenge your client to explore different perspectives on key concepts that seem to be guiding their lives and determining the course of immediate action. I've always found that this is where many of the "Ah-ha!" moments are for my clients. The insights they gain from examining distinctions open up their options and often correct the course they are on.

Looking at such distinctions as: can't vs. won't; hope vs. faith; adjusting to vs. tolerating; and surrender vs. accept, etc., can spawn stimulating and insightful explorations. You can either suggest to your client the distinction to be drawn, "Do you believe this is a matter of wishing and hoping or of having faith?" Or, you can ask them to create and draw the distinction themselves, "What are you really looking at here? Is it a matter of trying harder, or is it something else?"

Thomas Leonard was extremely fond of this process and made it a foundational technique of the coaching he taught. His fascination with words and lists drew him to develop a *Distinctionary of Concepts* that serves as a great resource for coaches. (http://coachville.com/tl/distinctionary//dixpdf.pdf)

Delegation

Most every book on success implores us to delegate, delegate, delegate. It is another classic "Sure, I know to do it, but I don't." scenario. A client who wants to live a high-level wellness lifestyle will always be challenged with finding the time for it and with managing stress. Delegation sounds like a simple and fantastic solution. Where possible just hand some of the work to others who can help. Wow! Sounds great! However even where the work force of helpers is actually there, all too often delegation is not employed. My clients have often felt overwhelmed by work at home or in the workplace when able-bodied spouses, children, co-workers and employees were available to help.

Coach your client around delegation by having them ask themselves these powerful questions:

1. WHO do I actually (truly) have available to delegate to?
2. Have I TRAINED them to receive delegation from me or not?
3. Do I TRUST their competency? (Have I trained them to be competent?)
4. Do I make delegation PERSONAL when it really isn't?
5. What am I AFRAID of when I consider delegating?

It is astonishing sometimes how emotionally laden delegation can be. If it weren't the simple, logical and practical decision to delegate would be easier and occur more often. I've even had clients who own their own business reluctant to delegate to employees the very tasks they were hired to do! To my client it felt like their employee who was hired to file the office files was doing her a personal favor instead of her job.

Finding the way out of this emotional mine field is difficult. Together you and your client can explore delegation, set up experiments and then explore the results, both in terms of practical satisfaction, and the emotional component. Effective delegation creates the freedom to be more efficient and effective at work and at home creating the freedom to include more self-care and wellness in life.

Conscious Calendarizing

As simple as it sounds, urge your clients to be more realistic about time. The pace of life in the modern (especially urban) world has accelerated creating a time famine. When I presented about wellness and stress management in Thailand, I was astonished to hear urban Thais describing an exhausting lifestyle filled with traffic jams, excessive office work loads, and not enough time! Even in a land famous for massage and meditation, people were not using what was available to them and were experiencing many of the same stressors and stress related disorders we see elsewhere in the world.

Coach your client to be more conscious about time by:

1. Exploring their experience and perception of time.
2. Experimenting with putting everything on a calendar.

Make calendarizing a new term. Not everyone has an accountant-like affinity for writing everything down, so you will have to strategize with your client and develop custom-made ways that will work for her or him. Experiment with putting both work and wellness self-care items on the calendar. Help your client to recognize and operate again from true priorities, acknowledging the paramount importance of their own health.

Avoiding Action Evaporation

"Life happens!" Ah yes, the universal excuse (and sometimes very legitimate one) for not getting committed actions completed, especially wellness/self-care items. Life does indeed happen, so how do you help your client regroup when it does? An effective method I've developed to help avoid time evaporation is the following:

1. Calendarize as much as possible; make commitments to take action and designate the time to do so. Set up a designated start and stop day for the week (demarcating the calendar week).
2. When a unit of time (an hour, half-hour, etc.) set aside for a committed action is passed over (not used for that purpose) take note of it.
3. Reassign that unit of time to another time within that same calendar week.

4. Make a commitment to completing this committed action within the same week. Do not allow it to escape the week and evaporate.

5. Keep track of any unit of time that is not used for committed action completion in the week and put it onto a list entitled "Self-deception Units" or "B.S. Units."

6. Set up coaching accountability and coaching agreements around all of this.

The possibilities for coaching the strategic aspects of living a healthy lifestyle are only as limited as you think they are! Have fun exploring and experimenting with your clients. Co-creating strategies that really work are some of the fun parts of wellness coaching.

Living: Lifestyle Improvement Coaching

Nourishing/Moving /Centering	Centering & Relaxation Methods
Environment	Yoga
Breathing	Tai Chi
Moving	Meditation
Eating	

The second realm in our view of wellness is what we refer to as living. Coaching for lifestyle improvement involves many things, but here we will focus on some of the actions that are practical and affect our health directly. Let us bring some structure to our wellness coaching here by looking at how we nourish, move and center ourselves.

Environmental Nourishment

The environment around us either nourishes us or denies us nourishment. We are nourished by clean air, clean water, nutritious food, and safe surroundings where energy can flow into us and out of us efficiently. An important and often overlooked part of living a wellness lifestyle is conscious awareness of our environment. What aspects of our environment can we affect directly (e.g. using less air conditioning, learning and using Feng Shui principles), and what can we affect in concert with others (e.g. help establish a local bike trail, lobby for safer lighting in our neighborhood, support candidates devoted to clean environments)? What aspects are we unable to control, short of re-locating?

In the Wheel of Life illustrated earlier in this book a person is asked to visually show their level of satisfaction with their environment. They are invited to demonstrate how satisfied they are with where they live and work and how their wellness options are limited or enhanced by where they live.

Some communities have abundant resources for safe outdoor exercise such as walking and bicycle trails, tennis and basketball courts, swimming pools or clean lakes. Some communities do not. The city I live by today is a dreamscape of outdoor and public recreation options: parks, playgrounds, public swimming pools, an ice arena, and an extensive network of bicycle trails and wide streets that include bicycle lanes. My old hometown has zero parks, tennis courts, public paths or trails, its streets and highways have virtually no room for bicycles, and this was one of the reasons I moved. Your client may benefit from looking at their community and the area where they live with a critical eye for built-in wellness recreation resources, or the lack thereof.

As you coach your client on various areas of focus you will undoubtedly encounter environmental aspects to their wellness goals. They may feel fortunate to have a lot of opportunities easily available. They may feel blocked from being as healthy as they would like to be because of lack of opportunity. As they become more and more conscious of their own way of living and how it affects their health, they may begin to realize the toll that factors such as noise, crowding, polluted air (both indoor and outdoor), and stressful long commutes are taking. Their sense of connectedness to the natural world is also important to examine. Time in nature refreshes mind, body and spirit. A sense of perspective is regained and our experience of ourselves is deepened. A U.S. Forest Service study confirmed that one third of the visitors to National Forests went there primarily for spiritual purposes. Your wellness coaching may involve more strategizing with your client on how they can make the best use of their environment to get the nourishment they need.

Nourishing The Body/Mind

The body is nourished by air, water and earth. Air is often considered the breath of life and Prana, the life force that we breathe in. Air quality is the first level of awareness and it is important to improve it. How we breathe is the next. The more anxious we are the more our breath is short and shallow. Conscious awareness of our breath allows us to relax and to take in more of what we need to nourish ourselves. There are many ways in which our clients can benefit from learning breathing techniques and methodologies. Reclaiming our breath after surgery and/or illness is often a very important part of the recovery process.

Water nourishes us on a deeply cellular level. It flushes toxins away and restores homeostasis in our bodies. The effects of dehydration, either chronic or acute, can be truly amazing, ranging from kidney disorders to temporary mental derangement. Clearly we need good clean water and plenty of it.

Our wellness clients can benefit from good health information about the purity of the water they are drinking. Many municipal water sources are questionable in quality and when tested by a reputable firm show unwanted toxic content. Be safe by being aware. Most effective weight loss programs also find that there is greater success when people adequately hydrate their bodies.

The earth nourishes us in many ways, but of course it is the source of the food we eat . . . all of it! Healthy food starts at the source with clean soil and clean water, with limited or no chemicals. As I once heard the late Paul Knoop, an inspirational Audubon Society naturalist, say "Absolutely everything comes from a green leaf." Once the quality of our food is established the great quandary and great debate begins over what to choose to eat!

We come back to the word nourishing. Does the food I am eating truly nourish me? Is it what I (as a unique human being) need? Food is far more than calories of energy to burn. It supplies us with chemicals that our bodies need on many levels. Some of these we are aware of and some we are only beginning to discover. Whole foods supply us with both our known and unknown requirements, as long as we are eating a rich variety of good quality foods. Wellness coaching clients may have any of a number of unique food considerations. We can encourage them to factor in (perhaps with the help of professional nutritionists) their body composition goals, metabolic rate, allergies and sensitivities, hormones, and the requirements that their unique health challenges may impose.

As stated in our earlier section on motivation, eating is a behavior. It is a topic that only begins with health information. Most of our clients know basically what and how much they need to eat to be well (whether they are doing it or not). Wellness coaching regarding nourishing the body is not just straightforward hard science. It crosses over quickly into the so-called soft sciences of psychology, sociology and even anthropology. Eating behavior is multi-causal. It is a result of emotions, self-beliefs, culture and sub-culture. Media, peer health norms, traditions and accessibility influence our eating behavior. The job of a coach is to help our client become conscious of their eating behavior and to develop effective ways of improving it.

As tempting as it is to teach and preach about the benefits of making certain food choices, and eating in certain ways, we come back once again to coaching. Here we challenge our clients to become more and more conscious of their eating behavior. Conscious awareness is a very powerful antidote to the thoughtless eating behavior that operates on automatic pilot and steers us into self-defeating choices. Tracking techniques such as conscious meal planning and recording can help tremendously. Becoming our client's ally and support system in whatever healthy eating plan they choose and develop for themselves is one of the best ways we can serve them. The accountability methods of coaching can help your clients be consistent enough for them to experience success.

Keep yourself informed and aware of current information about all the diets that become popular. We see diets come and go, some achieving acceptance as healthy and beneficial, and others discredited and eventually abandoned. This is truly the arena of "If it sounds too good to be true, it probably is!" Encourage your client to check into the validity of a particular diet they are attracted to. Become familiar with qualified nutritionists in your area and refer to them often.

Moving the Body/Mind

*The only way to make sense out of change is to plunge into
it, move with it, and join the dance.*

—Alan Watts

We are designed to move. When there is flow, there is life. The enemy
of health is blockage of flow. That blockage can be either outside of
us or inside. An external blockage will be something we tend to strain
against. If we do not succeed in moving the blockage we may get discouraged, give up or possibly find a way to adapt. Internal blockage
may hinder our effort to move. Emotional paralysis, like its physical
counterpart, is truly tragic. One often leads to the other.

Whether we are looking at ancient Taoist texts, manuals for Chinese medicine, or John Travis's energy flow model for wellness, we
are talking about flow. Unimpeded flow of energy is often expressed
in movement of one type or another. The result of such flow is a state
of good health . . . wellness!

Challenging all of our clients (and ourselves!) is a world where
conditions have increased the sedentary factor in life. The more sedentary we are the more sedated we become. Working with data all day,
driving and riding almost everywhere, the rise of sedentary recreation,
all combine to numb us into a lack of awareness and a loss of health.
We now recognize sedentary lifestyles as a major health risk.

Wellness is often mistakenly equated solely with our level of physical fitness. Think of a wellness program and you picture a gym type
of setting with people working out. For some of our clients the word
exercise is loaded with negative memories and connotations. Yet, most
wellness-coaching clients know that being more physically fit is indeed a vital part of living well. Most of our clients want the results of
exercise yet it may not be a part of their lives. Like dieting, the world
of exercise often means memories of failed attempts at establishing
plans that did not work. It may even bring up painful memories of gym
classes and social situations where being less than a perfect athlete led
to embarrassment and shame. This is where the coach approach is so
critical to success.

We start with the mindset shift from the prescriptive to the coach-like. Instead of coming up with a person's ideal workout routine or having them buy into a specific exercise method, we coach, we provide an ally for them to explore their options and create experiments where we will provide continuous support. We may not be out there physically moving on the bike path or the swimming pool, with them, but through our coaching process of exploration, support and accountability we are with them.

Just as in the area of nutrition, you need to be a coach, not the expert. Again you join the client in the exploration of creating and/or choosing a wellness plan that works for them. Expanding the concept to movement makes it easier for the client to see ways to improve in this area. Much of your work regarding this area will be around motivation and all the excuses not to exercise.

You may not want to talk about exercise at all. Encourage your client to simply increase movement in their lives. Make a fun project out of helping them discover everyday ways that they can move more. Conscious awareness is our ally here. One client of mine had a profound revelation when she realized that she had engineered her life to minimize movement. She used this realization to flip her thinking around into more and more creative ways to move more in everyday life. This progressed from parking further away, taking the stairs and doing more errands on foot herself, to actually signing up for a vigorous dance class and even dusting off her long-abandoned treadmill and using it!

As a wellness coach you will help your client:

- Explore their beliefs, myths, self-defeating behaviors and patterns around movement/exercise (the internal blockages).

- Strategize practical ways to find/create time to exercise.

- Be more realistic and commit to doing less, and at times challenge them to commit to doing more.

- Gain accurate information about ways to exercise.

- Find outside resources (such as fitness trainers, yoga or Tai Chi teachers).

Just as we stated about the area of eating, the more knowledge of leading wellness information that you have about movement the better. If you are up-to-date in this area you can turn clients on to new methods that might be just right for them to try.

Healthy physical movement includes three major areas:

- Cardio-vascular fitness—endurance

- Strength

- Flexibility

Help your client to find a balance of all three elements. Help them explore their ways of avoidance in one physical movement area and coach them towards balance. (See the Wheel of Physical Satisfaction on page 101.)

A special note. As the baby boom generation ages, we are finding them to be the most physically active of any generation in history. They desire an active life and if they have a history of exercising regularly, may want coaching assistance to adjust to the physical realities of aging. Many runners are now seeking kinder and gentler ways of moving that don't stress the joints as much. Shifting into more balanced movement can help immensely. Flexibility is especially important as we age. Helping your clients explore new ways to stretch the aging muscles will be beneficial. They can try areas that may be new to them, or old passions that were abandoned and now wait to be rediscovered, like dance! Also, we live in a time when the aging joints are being replaced and the client may need your assistance adapting. Urge your clients to get the medical assessments they need and then be their ally in creating and committing to new ways of moving.

The dance is a poem of which each movement is a word.

—Mata Hari

Centered Body—Centered Mind

How we move through life may be just as important as moving itself. Achieving unblocked flow of energy is vital to health. When we describe our lives as being out of balance we are often talking about excessive stress and often much futile effort. What we seek is a centered way to move through life.

You may not be a martial artist, a trained mediator, or a practitioner of Tai Chi. You may not be a trained athlete whose performance depends on how balanced they are on a ski slope or an ice rink. You may not be a professional dancer whose moves reflect what appears to be effortless grace. So you may not be familiar with the term centering.

Be centered. Center yourself. Come from center. Move from center. Return to center. Centering practice. Unless you are watching Kung Fu movies or remember what Obi Wan Kanobi was saying about The Force in Star Wars, you might not hear phrases like this. Yet this concept, once understood and applied, can dramatically improve your life.

You have experienced what I am referring to as being centered and did not even know it. When you made a decision without anxiety, which was true to yourself, that was being centered. When you sank a long putt, a three-point shot, or hit a solid line drive, that was being centered. When you twirled on the dance floor beautifully, carved your best run on a snowboard, or made the perfect cast with your fishing rod that was being centered. You were in the zone. When you found a poem or piece of expressive writing just flowing out of you like liquid, that was experiencing a centered state. When you ended a relationship, not to relieve anxiety or fear, but because you knew, with calm certainty, that it was the best and right thing to do, that too was being centered.

Think of how different your life can be when you realize that being centered is always an option you have in every situation. Think of the effectiveness of decision-making and creativity of effort that can result from operating more from a centered state.

How do we become centered? Instead of it being a magical and elusive state that is hard to recreate, what if centering was a skill that you developed and practiced? What if knowing how to center yourself was accessible information that you could draw upon in conflict, in emergencies, and in opportunities that demand peak performance?

A centered body centers the mind. Centering has a physical aspect to it as well as mental/emotional aspects. They affect each other and you can start in either domain.

Quieting your thoughts will relax your body. Nervous and fearful self-talk can produce muscle tension, increased heart rate, blood pressure, stomach acid production, and more. Quieting the internal chatter and soothing yourself with more positive and calm self-talk, or enhancing it with mental images of tranquil and safe, even idyllic settings has just the opposite effect on the body.

Centering Mind and Body Experience

Physically center yourself by focusing on your breath, changing your posture, lowering your center of gravity and movement, broadening your stance, becoming more in balance. Breathe slower on each breath, and a little deeper. Close your eyes for a moment, perhaps. Sit up straight, or stand with your feet further apart, your knees slightly bent, your weight equally distributed on both feet. As you do this, and breathe in and out slowly and consciously, you'll notice that your mind is slowing down and you are focusing more on the present moment.

Move from center. Place your right index finger in your naval . . . yes, your belly button! Now take your first three fingers of your left hand and place them across your belly right below your right index finger. At that level on your belly where the third finger rests imagine the point that is half-way between your belly and the skin on your back. That spot right in the center of you is what the Chinese call "Tan Tien." The Japanese call it the "Hara" center. Imagine that this is where your body moves from, not up higher somewhere.

Stand like you have just mounted an invisible horse. This is the horse riding stance that you see martial artists assume in martial arts movies and demonstrations. Keep your back relaxed but nice and straight. Look straight ahead. Now flex your knees and shift your weight back and forth from one leg to the other while keeping your feet flat on the ground. Feel very connected to the ground you are standing on. Take small steps with one foot while leaving the other one planted." Move so "Tan Tien" is just floating at the same level all the time.

Experiment with how movement feels in this stance and by moving in this way. Continue to breathe fully and completely. Practice this for five or ten minutes several times a week.

Like the muscular concept of *optimal tonus* what we are looking for here is neither deep relaxation nor rigid tightness. The horse-riding stance is one in which you can feel very solid. Someone who is centered in this stance is no push over. It is a stance from which you can move quickly and in which you are very flexible. No energy is being wasted on muscles that are not involved in holding the posture itself.

Those unused muscles are at rest. Movement comes from your true center.

The next time you need to make an important decision, or deal with a challenging situation, just adopt this stance. When the others around you stop laughing the conflict will be over. Yes, I am kidding! Getting yourself centered physically can really help though, so try less obvious methods like the following.

Centering In Action

Breathe. A good, long, slow, deep breath can do wonders. It cues your mind to come out of a tendency toward overwhelm or panic, and allows you to take in more immediate information about the situation. Sit up or stand very straight, with your feet firmly planted on the floor or ground.

Now the mental part! Think of this "Tan Tien" center in your body and adopt the ancient Samurai notion of expect nothing, be prepared for anything. Be aware of everything around you where you are, right here and right now in the present moment. Let the past and future evaporate. Focus on the present.

Bring your thoughts to an observation of the present situation without letting your past biases influence it. Take what the moment brings you without judgment. Then from that calm, centered place make a distinction between your choices, based on the values that are true to you.

Coach a Centered Life

There are real benefits to engaging in a formally trained centering practice. The tremendous rise in popularity of meditation, Yoga and Tai Chi worldwide is evidence of this. Your coaching clients may find activities like this to be an ideal complement to the more vigorous fitness activities they engage in.

There are activities that we can participate in to deeply relax, bringing out the psycho-physiological response we call the relaxation response (parasympathetic nervous system arousal) such as relaxation training, biofeedback, meditation, self-hypnosis, etc. There are also ways that we relax that are less intense but very important to us. Likewise there are probably favorite activities that your clients engage in that produce in them, to some degree, this experience of centering. They are usually activities that are very healthy, that give them per-

175

spective, that refresh and renew them. They may be as simple as a walk in the park, a hike in someplace a bit wild, throwing pottery, gardening, or just getting together with good friends with no agenda or expectations.

1. Suggest to your client that they create a list of activities of what centers them in their lives.
2. Have them indicate when they last engaged in those activities.
3. Explore their thoughts and feelings about the activity and the lack of it.
4. Explore how ready they are to take some action to do some of the activities that help them center again.
5. Secure a coaching agreement for either preparation or action and include timing.

Loving: Coaching the Interpersonal Aspects of Life

Love or Fear	Community
Conflict Skills	Support
Conflict Resolution	Inclusion
Communication Skills	Camaraderie/Friendship
Connectedness	Play

Coaching sage Thomas Leonard would extol coaches to help their clients to succeed in life by eliminating tolerations and getting their needs met. Some of our most near and dear needs are interpersonal. We all have needs for inclusion and belonging, to nurture and be nurtured. When we look at health statistics its clear we just don't do well alone. Partnered people live longer and have better health. People with pets do even better!

How connected or isolated our clients are in their lives seems to be a huge determinant not only of their overall health, but their likelihood of success in adopting new lifestyle improving behaviors. As they strive to improve the way they move, eat and manage stress, it all has interpersonal impacts. There is the need for support and for positive peer health norms. This is an opportunity for conflict. Our clients need approval from the people around them—for people to get on board with the changes they are making rather than people who resist their changes.

We certainly train people in how to treat us, not through workshops or seminars, but in our everyday lives. Co-workers may come to expect our client to do all the busy work. What happens when they become more assertive and demand that the busy work be distributed fairly? The experience of re-training others and their response to our client's efforts may become an important part of coaching.

What happens when our client decides to reduce and eventually eliminate red meat from the family dinner menu? What happens in a partnership or family when a new diagnosis means our client radically alters the way they eat? Wellness becomes a very interpersonal issue.

Coach for Connectedness

During the coaching process you become an ally for your client, accompanying them on their wellness journey. A lot of the effectiveness of coaching seems linked to the support our client receives from their relationship with us. What's next? Not only will we not be coaching them forever, we are not physically around after our brief meeting each week. Who picks up the slack, both now, and in the future?

Coaching the building and bolstering of support systems may be the single most important work we do with our clients. Introduce the concept of connectedness and community early in your coaching. Check out their current level of isolation/connectedness (See The Wellness Mapping 360° Connectedness Scale, Figure 9.2) and the nature and extent of their interpersonal support systems during the foundation session.

There are many sociological factors contributing to the epidemic of loneliness, depression and isolation that we are seeing in the modern world. Robert D. Putnam, in Bowling Alone: The Collapse and Revival of American Community, highlights some of these:

- One in five Americans moves once a year.

- Two in five Americans expect to move in five years.

- In 1950 single person households were less than 10% of the U.S. population; one of every three households created in the

1990s was a single person household.

- There are more single person households—33.6% than there are households of couples with children—33.1%.

- Increasingly, corporate employees work more with data more and less with people.

- More people in the United States are self-employed (which often has an isolating effect) today than at any time since the Industrial Revolution began.

A new study of social isolation (Smith-Lovin, L., McPherson, M., Brashers, M. "Social Isolation in America: Changes in Core Discus-

Connectedness Scale

Please rate the truth of the question as it relates to you. Circle the appropriate number.

1= Not true   2= Hardly ever true   3 = Sometimes true   4 = True most of the time   5 = True

Connectedness to self					
1. I enjoy spending time alone.	1	2	3	4	5
2. I have enough time alone.	1	2	3	4	5
3. I understand my feelings.	1	2	3	4	5
4. I like who I am as a person.	1	2	3	4	5
5. I like my body.	1	2	3	4	5
Connectedness to nature and my environment					
1. My living space is comfortable and suites me.	1	2	3	4	5
2. I spend quality time in nature.	1	2	3	4	5
3. I have a place I go for refuge or to recharge.	1	2	3	4	5
4. My workplace is comfortable and suites me.	1	2	3	4	5
5. I know my neighbors.	1	2	3	4	5
Connectedness to family					
1. I have a supportive family.	1	2	3	4	5
2. I enjoy spending time with my family.	1	2	3	4	5
3. I spend enough time with my family.	1	2	3	4	5
4. I feel connected to my family.	1	2	3	4	5
5. I feel a connection to those who came before me.	1	2	3	4	5
Social connectedness					
1. I spend enough time doing activities I enjoy.	1	2	3	4	5
2. I spend enough time with friends.	1	2	3	4	5
3. I belong to a supportive community.	1	2	3	4	5
4. I have someone I can share most everything with.	1	2	3	4	5
5. I enjoy intimacy.	1	2	3	4	5
Spiritual connectedness					
1. I feel connected to something greater than my self.	1	2	3	4	5
2. I spend time in a spiritual practice.	1	2	3	4	5
3. I feel a sense of purpose in my life.	1	2	3	4	5
4. I belong to a spiritual group.	1	2	3	4	5
5. I am a spiritual being.	1	2	3	4	5
Connectedness at work					
1. I get along well with my co-workers.	1	2	3	4	5
2. I feel respected in the work I do.	1	2	3	4	5
3. I am part of a team at work.	1	2	3	4	5
4. I have adequate contact with others in the work I do.	1	2	3	4	5
5. My colleagues and I trust one another.	1	2	3	4	5

Reproducible Worksheet Masters are available for purchase on CD ROM from Whole Person Associates, 210 W. Michigan St., Duluth, MN 55802, 800-247-6789, www.wholeperson.com.

FIGURE 9.2

sion Networks Over Two Decades" *American Sociological Review* 71:3, 2006) concluded that in 1985 the average American had three people in his or her closest intimate circles—people in whom they confide matters important to them. In 2004 the number has dropped to only *one!* They also found that 25% of Americans have no one to confide in at all. As a wellness coach, you may have a profound role in helping your clients build social support systems and to become less isolated.

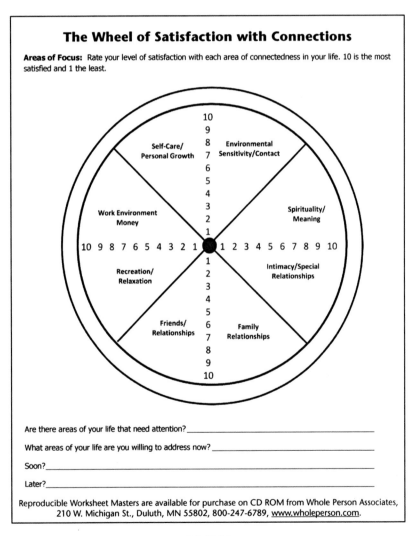

The Wheel of Satisfaction with Connections

Areas of Focus: Rate your level of satisfaction with each area of connectedness in your life. 10 is the most satisfied and 1 the least.

Are there areas of your life that need attention?_____

What areas of your life are you willing to address now? _____

Soon?_____

Later?_____

Reproducible Worksheet Masters are available for purchase on CD ROM from Whole Person Associates, 210 W. Michigan St., Duluth, MN 55802, 800-247-6789, www.wholeperson.com.

FIGURE 9.3

You may be your client's first experience with a trusted ally. A psychiatrist I used to work with would often say that a client needed a "corrective emotional experience." What she often meant was that by trusting a counselor (or in this case, a coach) the client learned to trust. Do not underestimate the power of the coaching relationship. Sometimes the anchor our clients have with us allows them to feel safe enough to take the risk and reach out to others.

As you coach, continually check in with your client about the involvement of others in their wellness goals. Help them explore the fears that may hold them back from seeking more support. Are they ashamed to need help? Do they see asking for support as a sign of weakness? Are they afraid of rejection? Does it go against the norms of their family, culture, or sub-culture to invite someone in or to change specific behavior? Have they been refused support before? Do they truly have non-supportive people surrounding them, or are they too isolated?

Help your client to see securing support as a key to maintaining lifestyle improvements they have made. At the close of your coaching relationship it is most likely that the change process and the continued adoption of new health behaviors will not be complete. Who can help them follow through what Prochaska calls the sixth stage of change—termination—to give the new behavior the time needed to habituate?

Coach for Community and Support

Keeping in mind the findings of Smith-Lovin, McPherson and Brashears (pgs. 180, 181), we should consider the following points as we coach our clients.

- Build sources of support right into the Wellness Plan.

- As new action steps emerge see if there is a connectedness component to be included.

- Ask permission to explore your clients fears about connection with others. Explore the value they see (or don't see) in community.

- Explore how their thinking (and inner-critic activity) affects their efforts at connecting with others.

- Strategize with your client how they can build greater community into their life.

- As the termination of coaching approaches, increase the emphasis on building support systems that will continue to help the client to grow and maintain the success they've achieved.

No one is to be called an enemy, all are your benefactors, and no one does you harm. You have no enemy except yourselves.

—St. Francis of Assisi

Being: Coaching the Intrapersonal Self

The Internal Aspects	Meaning—Purpose
Belief System Cognitive—Spiritual	Self-worth—Self-esteem
Self-talk	Self-expression
Gremlin Fighting	Play

It is not the mountain we conquer but ourselves.

—Edmund Hillary

I'm a long-time fan of Johnny Hart's strip "B.C." A recurrent theme in the strip is to have a character climb a steep mountain peak and ask the wise old man with the long white beard what the meaning of life really is. There is always some satirical comment that makes us laugh. The humor always hits home because we are laughing at ourselves. Don't we spend way too much time and energy in our lives looking for the answers outside of ourselves? Finding meaning, living a life on purpose, and understanding our reality is like a perpetual quest. Is that the real Holy Grail that everyone from the creators of the Monty Python movies, to author Tom Brown (*The Davinci Code*), to philosophers and Popes all talk about?

*The Creator gathered all of Creation and said, "I want to
hide something from the humans until they are ready for
it. It is the realization that they create their own reality."
The eagle said, "Give it to me, I will take it to the moon."
The Creator said, "No. One day they will go there and find
it." The salmon said, "I will bury it on the bottom of the
ocean." "No. They will go there too." The buffalo said, "I will
bury it on the Great Plains." The Creator said, "They will
cut into the skin of the Earth and find it even there."*

*Grandmother Mole, who lives in the breast of Mother Earth,
and who has no physical eyes but sees with spiritual eyes,
said, "Put it inside of them." And the Creator said,
"It is done."*

—A Sioux Creation Myth

Wellness author Don Ardell has long contended that we will
achieve better results in our efforts to help people accomplish lasting lifestyle change if we tie it in to the quest for meaning in life. He
proposes that we encourage people to think of meaning, purpose and
happiness in four structured parts:

1. The ground floor of meaning is subsistence/safety and
   security seeking. For most this is the orientation that gets
   attention throughout life. It means your job, career, and all
   that connects with securing the means to get by, preferably
   in a little style and comfort.

2. Meaning at the leisure level. This entails some concern
   for living wisely, agreeably and well (a phrase attributed
   to John Maynard Keynes). Maslow called this level
   belongingness in his famous hierarchy of needs construct.

3. Meaning found in the development, refinement and
   expression of talents, gifts and uniqueness. It entails self-
   fulfillment and earned self-esteem.

4. Meaning from reaching out and being of service. This
   could entail meeting needs of others, or the pursuit of
   knowledge for the betterment of society.

Ardell, D (2003) HENROD conference April 24, 2003.
Newark, Delaware @ Used by permission.

The internal aspects of wellness seem like a limitless universe of topics, ideas, concepts, wonderings, and wanderings. Again, how do we help our clients to tread in this territory without getting lost in space? I think Ardell's four structures ground the topic of meaning very practically. While you may never have a conversation directly about "the meaning of life" with your client (perhaps those are best left for spiritual retreats, campfires and starlit nights), you can usually tell when a client has work to do in this realm.

We often see it in a lack of motivation or a real inconsistency in motivation. There is a lack or ambivalence of energy to take action. Without meaning and purpose we see those that Thoreau wrote about when he said, "Most men lead lives of quiet desperation." It is really living a life lacking in vision. It is wandering through life, even with a map and a compass, but nowhere to go. You need a map of your own design, not one someone assigned to you. You need your own internal compass and the decision of a destination, above all else, needs to be yours. You are the author of our own life story, and the only true authority on your life.

Much of what we have looked at in this book has been about the internal aspects of wellness. The work on belief systems, thought patterns, self-perceptions, intrinsic and extrinsic motivation, gremlin fighting and more, all contribute to our way of approaching the world and set up what works for us and against us as we seek to give expression to our growth. As you coach your clients you will draw upon this myriad of information from many sources as well as all you have learned in your life about human behavior.

Again and again you will see how the way a person feels about themselves, and what they continually say to themselves about themselves will be a huge determinant of their lifestyle behavior and consequently, of their health. Focusing on self-esteem, self-worth, identity and self-concept are not endeavors necessarily requiring advanced degrees in psychoanalysis. Instead, bring these concepts down to earth with your clients. Put legs under them. Use your coaching skills. Listen deeply. Say what is.

- Let your client know what you are observing, and feed it back to them without judgment. "I see that each time we talk about the goal you said you wanted to work on this week, you change the subject."

- Ask powerful questions. "So, what would happen if you did step forward and ask for what you really want?" Remember that the least powerful question you can ask is "Why?"

- Encourage your client to grant themselves greater permission for self-care, and creative self-expression. Explore what this would actually look like in their life. Help them create experiments around these themes. As they engage more in these two areas, progress will emerge in the way they feel about themselves. As we have said earlier, self-esteem and motivation for change are intimately connected.

A client of mine was a profitable business owner who usually did an excellent job of managing his investments and running his busy agency. Part of what made him so successful was that he truly valued balance. He applied the principle of balance to the way he spread his money around and the way he lived his personal life as well. One of the things he realized as being vital to not only his health and well being, but to his business success as well, was creative self-expression.

My client knew from experience, that when he denied himself his outlets for creative self-expression he felt more stressed, anxious and less confident. He knew that he was far less creative in his work and that his customers were not as attracted to him and to doing more business with him. When he devoted adequate time to his pursuit of creative photography and developed his skills as a potter, then life, health, and business all were better.

Creative self-expression became a primary focus of our coaching and for several months he looked to coaching to help him be accountable to himself in this area. Even when life and work's busy-ness seemed far too pressing, he found value in the coaching process as it helped him center himself more and express himself creatively.

Coaching for Connectedness On the Intrapersonal Level

One Sunday in my teen-age youth, I experienced a profound sermon that was really about connectedness. The minister, who at the time was probably using terms like sin and unforgivable, was actually talking about how the worst state of being a person could be in was that of complete disconnection from their spirituality. I remember being deeply impacted by that message. It rang true for me, and still does.

Our sense of meaning and purpose actually connects us to all the rest of life. The expression of our true self grounds us in the world. How aware we are of our experience is an indication of our connection to all that is within and without. Are we in harmony with all that is around us and inside us? When that harmony is broken, and it will be, how do we regain it quickly? What is your harmony recovery time?

Wellness coaching clients thrive on self-awareness and connectedness. We usually think of connectedness as being equivalent to the experience of social support. We may even take a more ecological focus and talk about our connection to the natural world. There is an internal connectedness that our clients benefit from cultivating as well. How can we help them to turn this soil?

> *Wherever you are, whatever you do, you can always come back to this marvelous sense of stillness, the feeling of yourself, very, very much here. This is your reference point: this is your stability. This is your life force that gives you balance. This is your home you carry around with you wherever you are. This is your powerhouse, your reservoir, your endless inexhaustible resource . . .*
>
> **—Al Huang**
> *Embrace Tiger, Return to Mountain—the Essence of T'ai Chi,*
> speaking about being centered

Internal connectedness is much more possible when we slow down the pace of our lives, if only temporarily. It is more possible when we are not distracting ourselves from our own experience of the present moment. When we coach for intrinsic motivation we have our clients notice more. We have them notice what they are aware of in their own bodies as they move and exercise. We help them discover the intrinsic rewards in the activity itself, and in doing so, discover the joy as well.

When we ask powerful questions for our clients to reflect upon their experience in the present moment (yes even in the present moment of the coaching appointment), we are helping them to connect with their experience. When we help our clients eliminate clutter from their lives we are helping them reduce distraction so they can focus on the here and now. Help your client discover ways to bring him or herself into the present moment.

Connection to self, to source, to the oneness that we all seek in our own way, is a natural state. It is mostly about removing the things – the behaviors that get in the way. We simply have to get out of our own way. Restoring that natural state of connection may be where some of our best wellness work lies.

Trust the river, but keep the paddle in your hands

Life is like a river, that flows along infinitely. We do not control where the river goes. We do not control the flow of the river, not its crashing rapids nor its quiet still pools. We don't know where the fork on the left goes, or the fork on the right.

We are not driftwood. We are not helplessly being pushed down the river by the current, smashing into the rocks, or stuck in circling eddies.

It is like we are in a canoe, with a paddle in our hands. Sitting high in our seat, our eyes wide open, looking ahead we scan for signs of white water. Our ears alert, we listen for the roar of rapids and waterfalls.

We decide whether to take the fork to the left or the one to the right and we decide whether to run the rapids, or to put ashore and portage around, putting our craft back in the water when it is safe.

Going with the flow of the river we learn to navigate with the current, not against it.

We learn to trust the river, but remember the paddle in our hands. We remember the power of choice we have and know that we did not create the river, but we choose how to live with what it brings us.

Chapter 10

Health and Medical Coaching —Coaching People with Health Challenges

It is natural to resist change—for better or worse. This resistance to change is called homeostasis . . . your body has billions of feedback loops that keep your physiological functions within a narrow, normal equilibrium. And it's a good thing, or you might die . . . The same is true on the emotional and spiritual levels. We tend not to question our beliefs, our perceptions, and our patterns of behavior, even when they are causing problems for us.
The same homeostasis that protects us from change also makes it more difficult for us to transform even when it's in our best interest to do so.

—**Dean Ornish, M.D.,** *Eat More, Weigh Less*

Facing the Health Challenge

Health challenges can take on many forms. We are all faced with the challenge of living well in a world that doesn't always support healthy lifestyle choices. There are times in our lives, however, when the challenge might be much greater. The news of a close relative dying of a genetically linked disease, or a diagnosis of heart disease, cancer, diabetes, osteoporosis or arthritis, just to name a few, really changes people's lives. How we speak of and view these health challenges is important right from the start.

In coaching vernacular problems are translated into challenges. We are not always doomed by our problems, conditions, and diagnoses. It is extremely easy to lose hope and feel victimized by a lab result if we take such news as a final condemnation. Instead, we can shift our mindset and view the problem as a challenge that we must face. Then the possibility of meeting and overcoming the challenge and emerging as a stronger, deeper person becomes possible.

Speaking of a cancer diagnosis as a challenge is not to diminish its seriousness. We had better take it seriously! We know, however, that the people who face their fears and their diagnosis tap into their will to live and be well. When they don't have to do it alone, they often conquer more than just their own fears. A challenge engages a person to do what they can, and then do more. As a coach you have the honor of being a person's ally through this process.

Where Do You Fit In? Coaching and Coaching Skills

For many of you who are attracted to wellness coaching, people who have health challenges are not new, you work with them all the time. As a medical professional you continuously face the challenge when working with your patients: when to stay focused on the treatment methodology and when to recognize that what you are dealing with has crossed over into the world of behavior.

For medical professionals, using the mindset shift to coaching is a huge advantage when addressing behavioral issues. The coaching mindset coupled with coaching skills allows you to support people as they change their lifestyle behavior. As we have said frequently in this book, most wellness and medical personnel discover that just telling people what to do seldom works. Whether you plan to become a full time wellness coach or are a medical professional, training in coaching skills and the recognition of the coaching mindset will serve you and your clients/patients well. For the healthcare worker already inside the medical system coaching skills can transform the way you do one-on-one work. For the wellness coach seeking entry into the system it is a matter of finding forward thinking programs.

Coaching People with Health Challenges

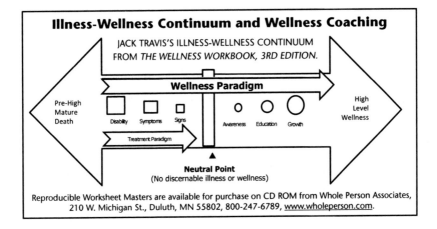

FIGURE 10.1

A careful examination of Travis's Wellness/Illness Continuum reveals that the work of wellness begins long before a person becomes ill. Preventing the onset of detectable disease is always preferable. When treatment is needed, the work of wellness and the wellness coach is most beneficial when it engages a person early in the treatment process, either as soon as an issue has been identified through a Health Risk Assessment or early in treatment. The ideal is a scenario where the coach supports a person's behavioral compliance with treatment and the enhancement of the body/mind's own systems for healing through the practice of a healthy lifestyle. This speeds and insures greater probability of treatment success and reduces present or possible risk factors. In addition to the internal healing process, it is important for medical professionals engaged in the treatment methodology to work hand-in-hand with behavioral change specialists to bring an ill person back to the midpoint, the point of no discernable illness. The Wellness Coach can be a vital part of this process.

Coaching for Prevention After a Warning Signal

There is an old saying that "heart attacks usually don't just happen overnight." Progressive diseases such as coronary artery disease are slow in development and sometimes go unnoticed until a serious condition has developed. Often though, for many health challenges there are some warnings that show up earlier.

In my stress management seminars I would often have people imagine driving a car down a highway and have them look at the gauges on the car's dashboard. I would ask them to imagine seeing the temperature gauge cause the red warning light to come on, and then ask them "What do you do?" Most people would say, "Pull off the road and check it out!" but others would humorously, but honestly admit they would just keep on driving! Unfortunately this same approach applies when it comes to the red lights on our own control panel of health.

In working for years with people with stress-related disorders I saw that stress had a way of sending its warning messages. If the low-level messages like insomnia and headache were ignored, then stress had a way of upping the ante, that is, increasing the stakes. The next round of warnings could be much more serious and include things like the onset of symptoms of physical conditions and disease processes such as gastrointestinal disorders, debilitating headaches or high blood pressure.

Many health conditions respond well to lifestyle improvement alone, if the lifestyle changes are early and sufficient enough. The role of wellness coaching in this level of prevention can be very valuable. Wellness programs have long sought to identify people who are at risk earlier and earlier. Once identified, there is something that wellness coaches can actually do to change clients' risks beyond just giving them more information. You can give the client an ally to help insure that they make the lifestyle changes that will address the health warning they have received. In many ways wellness coaching helps a person make use of the information they have and what they know.

Target potential clients who are in this early warning category. If they are ready to take their situation seriously enough, such clients can make great progress unencumbered by the fear and discouragement that comes with fully developed health challenges.

Coaching for Medical Compliance

As we have discussed before, there is a huge behavioral component to medical compliance. This fact has been recognized by the medical field for quite some time, but what to do about it has been another quandary. One increasingly common approach, especially used by corporations who self-insure, is to seek ways to increase medical compliance. This type of compliance can be measured on limited variables by using blood tests, blood pressure readings, etc. When employee/patients comply, they receive a discount on their share of their health insurance premiums.

To aid in this medical compliance, systems of coaching are gaining popularity. One of the most direct forms of wellness coaching has been systems and services that call patients once a month or so for five or ten minutes, check in with them, and ask if they have been taking their medications and doing their own self-testing/self-treatment properly. This has been a helpful process for some patients. The infrequency of the calls and the severe time limit for questions and/or building an alliance with the coach can, however, handicap this method.

The other aspect of medical compliance is behavioral lifestyle compliance. This is compliance with a lifestyle prescription. In addition to urging compliance with the pharmaceutical prescription and prescribed self-testing/self-treatment directives, there is often a directive to make certain lifestyle improvements—all of which are behavioral. Here, too, the coaches involved in such programs report real benefits to using a coach-approach. They find they are better equipped to establish a trusting relationship, focus the conversation to zero in on key issues (vital with severe time limits), and hold clients accountable in a better way. This is where expanded wellness coaching models and methods step further into the picture. When the coach has more contact time, professional training, and has set up a coaching alliance with their client, a broader range of behavior can be addressed.

We need to look at the effect of having a coaching ally who will address adherence to both treatment programs and the lifestyle prescriptions that accompany them. If over half of what determines our health is our lifestyle, how can we afford not to develop the best systems possible to support people in lasting lifestyle behavioral change?

Coaching On the Comeback Trail

Compassion and empathy with someone who is facing a serious health challenge takes courage. As a wellness coach you have to be willing to feel. You have to be willing to get close enough to your client's experience to realize that it could be you. That with a change in the winds of fate, karma, joss, or whatever you might call it, it could be you. Imagine you are flat on your back in a hospital bed. You have just completed a surgical procedure that felt like a train wreck with you right in the middle of it. Once you become aware enough of what is around you, the first thing you want is contact with other human beings. People often feel lost, sad, and lonely and want connectedness right now! Human contact, human touch—to know that you are not alone means the world to you.

It starts with loved ones who may or may not have been around, or with the kind and caring touch of the hospital staff. Little by little progress is made from that excruciatingly long first walk to the bathroom to sitting in a recliner with oxygen, to cranking up the speed on the treadmill in rehabilitation therapy. Fears are faced continually along the way. There is a yearning for more information about what is normal in the recovery process. Side effects of new medications range from bothersome to terrifying. Fears exaggerate every little physical difficulty.

Not so many years ago cardiac rehabilitation took an approach of rest not exercise. Then the medical field realized that movement was good, even vital to the healing and recovery process. Lifestyle improvement is now seen as an essential component of practically all recovery processes. Journeying out of the land of fear and reclaiming our health, our confidence and our independence is often a long hard walk. Traveling with the support and companionship of others makes the journey easier and helps the person arrive more surely at their successful destination.

Coaching the Re-integration of Work, Family and Self-care

The field of coaching has long specialized in helping people to achieve their goals in their careers and their businesses. Coaches help entrepreneurs to work smarter and more profitably. Coaches help people develop their careers to higher and more satisfying levels. When a person goes through a major health challenge, such as heart surgery, and eventually both needs and wants to return to work, a well-trained wellness coach is in a position to help them do this in a way that is both productive and healthy.

We've all heard stories about remarkable people who, for example, suffered heart attacks and didn't change their lifestyles or way of working one bit. I remember hearing of a high school principal who had an impressive reputation as a hard-charging, high stress, get-things-done-now kind of guy. After his heart attack, at about age 45, he returned to work almost immediately and absolutely reveled in showing everyone how little he had been affected by this blow to his health. He told everyone that the key to success in life was to work hard and when trouble arose, just work harder. He died within a year or two of yet another heart attack. Take a look at the 1979 movie *All That Jazz!*, for an amazing dramatization of this kind of approach to life.

As part of everyone's rehabilitation process there is a very large behavior change dimension. Compliance with a treatment program means taking medications, doing tests and following up with doctor visits in an effective manner. It also means, in most cases, lots of recommendations for lifestyle change. New diets, new exercise regimens, breathing exercises, relaxation training, using stress management strategies, are all behaviors. In addition to the usual challenge of how to fit these behaviors into a busy life, your client also has to find a way to do more behavioral self-care than ever before. At the same time the client must re-integrate themselves back into the world of work, and to the demands and dynamics of their families. What seemed like a tricky balancing act before may feel like a juggling act in a circus now!

If your client has suddenly been given a shocking message about their health such as we've described here, how they deal with it will depend largely on what stage of readiness for change they are at. It would be easy to assume, as many health care professionals do, that the seriousness of the diagnosis would prompt immediate action yielding all the needed behavioral change. Ah, if it were only true all the time! Astonishingly, some people do not take action.

Your client may have come to you when they are still motivated by their frightful health news. Or they may be at a point where the fire is out, but the health challenge remains. A client's readiness for change and their feelings of grief and loss when looking at their health challenge may all play a complicated role in the individual's motivation to make true changes. A concept that needs to be understood is found in the work of Elizabeth Kubler-Ross (*On Death and Dying*). What we perceive as loss—is loss. The perceived loss of our health activates the same process of grieving that we experience with other losses. The coaching work you do with your client will benefit from integrating what we know about the grieving process with what we know about readiness for change.

Rx LIFESTYLE PRESCRIPTION

Dear Health Care Provider:

Your patient is working with a Certified Wellness Coach to improve their life style. Please make your behavior related improvements known to your patient below.

Patients Name: _____   Date: _____

To improve your health I am recommending the following lifestyle behavior improvements:

Restrictions (if any):

I give permission for lifestyle related medical information to be shared with my wellness coach.

_____   _____
Name of Wellness Coach   Patient Signature

Reproducible Worksheet Masters are available for purchase on CD ROM from Whole Person Associates, 210 W. Michigan St., Duluth, MN 55802, 800-247-6789, www.wholeperson.com.

FIGURE 10.3

Readiness for Change, Grief, and Wellness Coaching

The Five Stages of Grieving and the Loss of Health

1. Denial, Shock and Isolation. The first reaction to learning of illness or death is to deny the reality of the situation. It is a normal reaction to rationalize overwhelming emotions. It is a defense mechanism that buffers the immediate shock. We block out the words and hide from the facts. This is a temporary response that carries us through the first wave of pain. The reality of a health issue has not yet been accepted by the person. He or she feels stunned and bewildered as if everything is "unreal."

2. Anger. As the masking effects of denial and isolation begin to wear, reality and its pain re-emerge. We are not ready. The intense emotion is deflected from our vulnerable core, redirected and expressed instead as anger. The anger may be aimed at inanimate objects, complete strangers, friends or family. Anger may be directed at our loved ones or our God. Rationally, we know they are not to be blamed. Emotionally, however, we may resent God for causing us pain. We feel guilty for being angry, and this makes us more angry. The grief stricken person often lashes out at family, friends, themselves, God, or the world in general. Bereaved people will also experience feelings of guilt or fear during this stage.

3. Bargaining. The normal reaction to feelings of helplessness and vulnerability is often a need to regain control. If only we had sought medical attention sooner. If only we had gotten a second opinion from another doctor. If we changed our diet, maybe we would have gotten well. In this stage, the bereaved asks for a deal or reward from either God, the doctor, or the clergy. Comments like "I'll go to Church every day, if only my health will come back to me" are common.

4. Depression. Depression occurs as a reaction to the changed way of life created by the loss. The bereaved person feels intensely sad, hopeless, drained and helpless. The way we used to view ourselves is missed and thought about constantly. Our reaction relates to the practical implications connected to the change. Sadness and regret predominate. We worry about the cost of treatment and the effect the illness will have on our lives and on those we love. We worry that, in our grief, we have spent less time with others that depend on us. This phase may be eased by simple clarification and reassurance. We may need a bit of helpful cooperation and a few kind words.

5. Acceptance. Acceptance comes when the changes brought upon the person by the loss are stabilized into a new lifestyle. It is not necessarily a mark of bravery to resist the inevitable and to deny ourselves the opportunity to make our peace. This phase is marked by withdrawal and calm. This is not a period of happiness and must be distinguished from depression. Usually, children recover more quickly, while the elderly take the longest. This is a time of integrating new information into a lifestyle or way of being in the world that works for the person.

A Story of Empathy With Loss

While in graduate school an older woman who was a fellow student in the doctoral program told a story about her most profound experience with attempting to empathize with another person. Betty was visiting a dear friend in the hospital who had just had her leg amputated due to her diabetes. Betty was in such pain seeing her friend lying there in misery. She felt the connection with her friend very deeply and searched for something to say. The best she could come forth with was "I know just how you feel."

Her friend's eyes narrowed, anger welled up inside of her and she yelled at Betty "How can you stand there on two good legs and know just how I feel?" Betty felt hit by a cannonball and had regretted her own statement as soon as it had left her mouth. Her heart went down to her feet but then somehow bounced back up, and recovering her sensitivity once again, Betty said, "There is no way I can know what it is like to lose a leg. But I do know what loss, deep loss, is like." Her friend understood Betty's botched initial attempt at empathy, and now felt the true empathy that Betty was showing her. They embraced and cried together.

You may find that it is not unusual to be coaching someone whose spouse, or other loved one, is facing a serious health challenge, even a terminal diagnosis. Be a source of support for your client. Help them expand their other sources of support, friends, family and community resources like hospice. Check out the tremendously useful contributions in this area made by Stephen Levine, author of *Who Dies?: An Investigation of Conscious Living and Conscious Dying*. Recommend his book to your clients. Help your client to practice extreme self-care right when they may feel all they can do is give to their loved one. If they empty their own reserves of health they will have even less available to help their loved one.

Prevention takes on a new dimension once a health challenge arises. Instead of exercising to feel better and to prevent the onset of some health challenge in the future, self-care behaviors need to be done now, or there may be much more immediate losses. Lung capacity may not return unless certain breathing exercises are done regularly. Muscle atrophy may increase, joint flexibility may be lost, stamina may not return if the prescribed movement program is not maintained. Blood sugar levels need to be stabilized through consistent and proper diet and exercise or insulin levels will shift the person into immediate and negative consequences.

Perhaps a more insidious situation occurs when your client can return to their old lifestyle patterns and seem to get away with it for a while. There are no immediately apparent consequences, so there is a natural tendency to return to business (and life) as usual. Even though your client may have been told that they will pay later for not changing their lifestyle behavior, the old habits are most likely to return.

Work/life balance takes on new and even deeper meaning when your client is recovering from surgery and/or dealing with a new and major health challenge. Very often a major contributor to the health challenge they face is the former strategy of sacrificing one's health for one's job, or for the benefit of others and not taking enough care of themselves. A pattern of letting self-care go in order to have more time for work, family, and community may have become deeply ingrained and socially reinforced. Now the sudden realization that self-care behaviors are more critical than ever may or may not produce the needed change.

Every client will have a unique experience when it comes time to begin re-integrating themselves back into their world of work. Self-employed people make up a larger portion of the population than ever before. When they don't work, there is, of course, little income. The same may be true for many blue-collar workers as well. Not everyone has disability insurance, qualifies for worker's compensation, or has solid company or union benefits behind them. In addition to the obvious pressure to restore income, there are a variety of both external and internal pressures.

Pressures to Return to Work and Resume Previous Ways	
External Pressures	**Internal Pressures**
• Restore Income—both realistically and pressure from family to do so • Return to former style of work-priority over self-care priority • Resume former pace of work and catch up on projects • Resume former levels of performance	• Regain self-respect and perceived respect of others • "Prove" to self that "it's not that bad" • Reassure self that all is not lost (abilities, etc.) • Identifying heavily with work as defining self and self-worth • Fend off fear of death by regaining a sense of control

TABLE 10.1

Coaching Your Client to Respond to Internal and External Pressures

As you can see in Table 10.1, the internal pressures affecting your client's return to work are not all intrinsically negative. Restoring income and self-respect are certainly wonderful things. The more negative internal forces are largely found around fear and sense of self. This is why we have emphasized more work on internal wellness. There is real value in the exploration of the self, and the deeper work on self that we have referred to here.

Be sensitive to the possibility that your clients will push themselves too hard and too fast to return to work and resume previous workloads and performance standards. Look for signs of desperation and an excessive sense of urgency. Help them gain some insights and self-understanding. Ask them powerful questions to challenge their perceptions of deadlines and expectations, which they may be attributing to outside sources, but are really within themselves.

There are times when there is a great deal of external pressure and not all of it may be healthy, or at least not in the best interests of your client's health. There are certainly workplaces that care very much about employees and value them, just as there are those that do not. Pressures can come from supervisors and from co-workers.

Some of your most valuable wellness coaching may really be about assertiveness. Help your client to be in touch with their own self-worth, to value their own health and well-being as a true priority. To protect this they may have to forge new boundaries that were not in place before. Your client may have to re-train other people in how to treat them. The do anything for others person may have to quit putting their own needs last and develop the fine art of saying no more often. Coach your client through this process. Help them experiment with new behavior in this area and help them process their experience as they attempt to put it in place.

Coach your client through the emotions of dealing with new physical limitations—and dealing realistically with them. They may simply not have the strength or endurance they had before. They may have to tread in what is for them new territory, and ask for help more often. Help them develop the essential skill of strategic delegation and coach them through the experience of implementing that skill. As always, be their ally as they explore what is now a new way of being in the world.

Health Challenge Specialization

In your healthcare work, or as a special niche in the wellness coaching you choose to do, you may be working with people with particular health challenges. In the United States the statistics on the occurrence of obesity, cancer, heart disease and diabetes (with it's epidemic numbers) are an indication of the tremendous need.

You may or may not have personal experience with one of these challenges yourself. Frequently the wellness coaching classes and trainings I have led have included coaches and healthcare workers whose interest in health and wellness was initiated by their own personal experience. We discovered years ago in the addictions field, you don't have to be a recovered drug addict or alcoholic to be an effective counselor to someone with that current challenge. Having experience in the area does help though, to establish trust, inspire hope, set intrinsic empathy, and familiarize the coach with the life of a person with that health challenge.

As a wellness coach with or without first-hand experience with a particular health challenge, you need to familiarize yourself with what your clients have as their personal and medical experience. When coaching a post-heart surgery client, you might benefit greatly from knowing what someone goes through with blood thinning medications. Find out what their medication is, what the generic name for it is, how it works, how blood levels are tested, what that testing is called, what scores they have been told to shoot for, what the most common side effects are, etc. That may sound like a lot of detail, but, for example, when your client begins talking with you about how they are working with a nutritionist to eat healthy, yet reduce their vitamin K (which increases the clotting factor in the blood) it would be good if you knew what they were talking about! Your specialized knowledge is not there for you to make any treatment decisions (unless that is your qualified healthcare job). It is there to provide empathy and understanding and increase trust. I'm more likely to trust a coach who understands my cholesterol score, or blood sugar level numbers in light of my treatment goals than one to whom I have to explain something so basic.

Let the Other Pros Help Too

The approach to coaching in this book and the Wellness Mapping 360° approach are based on the concept that much of what you do with any person with a health challenge will follow the same effective methods of good coaching. Support your client and the (other) healthcare professionals in what they do, and be a great coach!

Your client most likely has available to them a whole host of professional services that can help them with their health challenge, major surgery rehabilitation and even their return to work. Rehabilitation therapists, occupational therapists, job counselors, and social workers are among those who may be available for your client's needs. Your client may need assistance navigating the system to find the help they need. If you are specializing in coaching people with health challenges, become very familiar with the professional options available in your community, or, if you are coaching remotely, coach your client through the process of discovering for themselves what assets are available. Again, be their coaching ally and refer often to other professionals who can help your client.

Wellness Mapping 360° in Health Coaching —A Case Example

A part of the *Mindset Shift* is to understand that you are stepping out of the expert role and into the support or ally role. You are always coaching your client toward understanding or developing what they need. You support the client to find the information and resources they need. You help the client develop their personal visions and create the map that will guide them there. The Wellness Mapping 360° model gives both the coach and the client the environment for this to occur.

Here is an example of what a completed Wellness Map might look like for a client who is facing a health challenge. In this example we will talk about the experience of a man in his mid-fifties who has undergone successful heart surgery for mitral valve repair. This fictitious case is based partly on my own experience, and also, in part, upon the experience of others I have known.

Client Description: 56 year old male whom we will call Ken Black. He is remarried, with children and stepchildren who are grown and on their own, but remain nearby the small town he lives in. His wife is very supportive and understanding. Ken is a college biology professor who successfully underwent mitral valve repair surgery five months ago. This open-heart procedure was preceded by an experience with congestive heart failure where his lungs were filling with fluid, threatening his life. Ken was in very good health before the surgery and exercised regularly and enjoyed hiking and many outdoor activities.

Thirty-six sessions of cardiac rehabilitation (CR) were very beneficial for Ken. He completed this program recently and has been having a hard time maintaining the progress and regularity he achieved physically while attending the CR session three times a week. Ken is also finding that returning to work is not as easy as he thought it would be. The new school year brought its usual stress and accelerated pace for which he was not ready.

Ken is looking to your coaching help adjust to his full-time work, and to balance it with an adequate program of healthy self-care that will aid with his recovery.

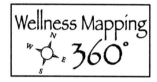

My Wellness Map—Life Vision and Focus Tool
KEN BLACK

1. Life Vision—Either on your own or working with your coach, arrive at a statement that sums up your idea of what it would look like to be living your life to the fullest and functioning at your best. Be realistic and yet, inspiring!

My Life's Wellness Vision:
I want to regain my health and vitality so I can return to the active outdoor lifestyle I love and continue to be there for the ones I love. I see myself as an older man who is still able to hike, camp, swim, fish, and even do wilderness canoe trips when I'm old enough to take my (future) grandchildren along with me!

2. Current Life Status—Summarize what your current life is like. Do not be discouraged or judgmental with yourself—just be honest.

I've got to say that despite all I've been through this year, that life is pretty good. I enjoy wonderful support from my wife and children, and from friends as well. I've been recovering well, but still am working at regaining my former strength and endurance. I still get winded going uphill, more than before. I still fret over any little thing that goes wrong, like feeling light-headed, gaining weight suddenly, etc. I'm still fifteen pounds heavier than before I went in for surgery.

Returning to work has been tough. The small college I work at is under-funded and in our department the chairwoman seems to be more worried about how many students we attract and retain than about delivering a quality education. I wanted a reduced number of classes to teach but didn't get it. There seems to be little accommodation for my health by my chair, and my colleagues. The students are great, but there's just too many of them! And now I have to do all this exercising, taking time to rest and so forth. I feel like I don't have time for all of it.

Take a deep breath, relax and ask yourself "What would have to change for me to achieve my life vision?"

I need to get some consistency. I'm afraid of losing ground already on what I achieved in rehab. I want to get my lungs back! I think that I've got to find a way to handle work better, not stress over it so much, and take care of myself better.

3. Areas of Focus—To make my life vision a reality I choose to focus on the following areas of my life. For maximum success, prioritize no more than five areas and make those areas the ones you are most ready to address. Suggested lifestyle improvements from healthcare providers and results from wellness assessments or health risk assessments can also be listed. You might want to work together with your coach to determine these areas.

1. Balancing work demands and self-care activities

2. Exercising

3. Managing stress

4. Following through on all medical appointments and taking meds on schedule

 **Areas of Focus Sheet**

Area of Focus One—To make my vision real I want to focus on the following area. Choose an area from #3 of the Life Vision and Focus Page that you are most ready to work on or because you feel you need it the most, or because it is easy and you just want to get the ball rolling.

Focus area: Balancing work demands and self-care activities

A. Desires: What do you want or how would you like it to be? Write in your own words, "What are your stated desires for this area of focus in your life?"
This is good to state as both an immediate action your want to see happen (for example, I want to lose ten pounds) and in

a longer-term, more motivational action (for example, I want to be able to go on a very physically active vacation this summer).

I want to schedule my day and week with self-care a priority over work.

I want to meet my work obligations while taking excellent care of myself.

B. Current Location: Where do you see yourself currently in this area of your life?

Right now this is where I'm at regarding this area of focus: (List whatever describes your present situation. For example you could list your current percent body fat; number of hours of sleep/night; 1-10 scale self-ratings of situations or levels of conditioning, etc.)

Currently I am exercising too little and not getting enough rest to improve my physical condition. I have gained five pounds since ending cardiac rehab classes and am not increasing my stamina. I am feeling very stressed by a demanding workload. My requests for some consideration of my recovery are not being responded to. I feel very unsupported at work and under pressure.

C. The Path: What do you need to do? What do you need to do or what needs to change in your life for you to realize your desire for this area in your life?

Describe what needs to change in this area of your life for you to attain your desires. State the changes needed as specifically as you can.

1. I need to make my health and self-care my #1 priority. I need to believe that myself and hold it in mind first every day.

2. I need to increase the amount of self-care activities that I do, and be very consistent.

3. I need to get more understanding and support from my department for my health recovery.

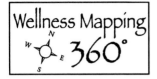

**Areas of Focus Sheet
Page Two**

D. Committed Course: What are you making a commitment to do? Work with your coach to create realistic and attainable action steps that will move you towards the desired outcome for your chosen life area. Choose an initial step to make that will get you moving. Like a map, chart your course to your chosen change. Once again being specific is important. Write down what you will do, when it will be completed by, and how you will communicate the accomplishment to your coach. Work with your coach to arrive at strategies that are challenging enough without being too much.

What You Will Do	Duration	When	Check in Method
Step 1. I will write down my planned self-care activities (exercise, rest, etc.) and what I actually did.	For one month and then review with my coach	Each AM and each PM	I will e-mail my coach each Monday and Friday and will also discuss this during my coaching appointments
Step 2. I will keep a wellness journal. There I will write down what I am experiencing with seeking balance between work and increased self-care.	For one month and then review with my coach	Five days a week	I will report in on how the journaling is going and any insights I gain during my weekly coaching session
Step 3. I will gather my courage and have a very honest conversation with my chairperson about my recovery and my need to prioritize my health	Once, or more times if needed	As soon as the schedule of my chairperson permits	I will e-mail my coach within one week and report on scheduling progress. I will prepare for the meeting in my coaching appt. and report on the meeting in my next coaching appt.

TABLE 10.2

Brainstorm here:

Be assertive about getting on Chair's schedule. Push for talking with her within one week. Don't let it wait. Keep a wellness journal on my personal computer, include pictures, etc. to make it more fun and positive.

E. Challenges: What are you up against? List what obstacles are in your way or what you believe could prevent you from reaching your desired destination.

High stress environment in my department. With the new school year starting there has been little accommodation for my recovery in terms of work load, and there has been resentment expressed by both chairperson and colleagues regarding the time I take to exercise and rest.

On my side, I don't like to feel like I am not pulling my weight, my fair share of the work when we are all under pressure. I want to help my department face its larger challenges of lack of funding, etc. At times I fear losing my job when that realistically is not likely to happen.

Go back and forth from periods of too much self-care neglect (where I end of feeling fatigued, and make little recovery progress), to periods of inadequate attention to my work.

F. Strategies To Meet The Challenges: Ways to overcome the hurdles. With your coach develop strategies that you can use to make adjustments in your life to overcome or get around things that hold you back from your committed course of action. (For example: when under a work deadline I will make my exercise session briefer, but not skip it.)

1. Increasing communication with my chair and others in the department. Most of them know little if anything about valve surgery and expect me to recuperate just as fast as someone they know who had by-pass surgery, which is significantly different. Have more formal and informal conversations with all in my department.

2. Ask for the support I need. Tell others what I need and very specifically how they can be of help.

3. Using my calendar more to plan ahead of time for my self-care activities instead of just fitting them in where I can, when I think of it. Journaling about the work/life balance and keeping track of it. Keeping work/life/recovery balance a central area of focus for my coaching.

G. Sources of Support: Who can share this journey with you or support your journey? State specifically who or what your sources of support, encouragement, and accountability are as you follow this area of focus on your wellness map into new territory.

1. Talk more with my wife about all of this. She can handle it, and is very supportive. She is also a great source of ideas.

2. One colleague, Bill, has been through some serious health challenges of his own, including the onset of diabetes. He seems to exercise quite religiously. I will reach out to him too.

3. My friends outside of the university department are very positive. I will avoid complaining to them about my struggles for support in the department and will do more to enjoy our friendships.

This same process would then be completed with each area of focus that Ken indicated (exercise, managing stress, following through on all medical appointments and taking meds on schedule).

The coach would then meet at the designated times with Ken and review his progress and explore what gets in the way. Once the Wellness Map is set up it is easy to see when the client accomplishes what they set out to do and this is a time to celebrate.

We are what we think. All that we are arises with our thoughts. With our thoughts, we make the world.

—**Siddhartha Gautama**, *The Buddha*

Chapter 11

Wellness Coaching In Action

Today, almost 95 percent of the things we spend our money on—which most of us think of as necessities—were not seen around when many of us were born: television sets, airline travel, Disneyland vacations, high-fashion clothing, stereos, DVDs, air conditioners, personal computers, day care, movies, fast-food restaurants, dry cleaning, Internet access, to name a few. The same will happen with wellness.

—Paul Zane Pilzer
The Wellness Revolution, p. 47

Wellness Coaching: Destination Unknown—Possibilities Endless

Closely observing and actively participating in the wellness field since 1979 has been a joy. Watching it go through it's own metamorphosis has been at once interesting, puzzling, astonishing, and continually surprising. I've seen it labeled a dream, a temporary trend, a wave, and even a tidal wave. It's been called essential, superfluous, vital, unnecessary, flakey, evidence-based, touchy-feely, and the only way we're ever going to make an impact on healthcare costs. I've spoken around the world on wellness and found that it is here to stay.

Wellness programming works! The effectiveness of wellness programs in reducing health risks and affecting the bottom line are now substantially documented. An exhaustive review of the evidence appears in Larry Chapman's book Proof Positive: The Practitioner's Guide To ROI and Program Development, published by The Wellness Councils of America (WELCOA). Chapman sees wellness programs as being capable of both quick and long-term positive returns on investment. As more coaching components are added to wellness programs gathering data on their effectiveness is essential.

The visibility of wellness coaching seems to be increasing rapidly in recent times. The services that are being called wellness coaching come in many shapes and sizes. Just as in the coaching field when managers became coaches and merely did what they always did and just changed their title, some wellness professionals take on the new title of coach and continue to do individual work as best they can. Others pursue coach training vigorously and find great benefit in it. The upside is that people in corporate wellness programs, many medical fields, insurance companies and individuals as well, see the value of wellness coaching. It's almost like there are many chefs out there who are having tremendous creative fun combining the two ingredients of wellness and coaching in ways never thought of before!

The trend toward the individualization of wellness is clear. As more wellness professionals bring more one-on-one focus into their work they are turning consulting and educating into coaching. Also, coaches with an interest in the health and wellness fields are discovering ways to apply their coach training to the wellness arena. A thorough overview of this ever-changing field is like describing a sunset or perhaps a sunrise that is constantly changing before your eyes. Instead, in this final chapter I would like to speak about some of the applications of wellness coaching we see today.

Hospital and Medical Institutions

The medical field is now a vast system of health care companies that provide a variety of services through different methods of delivery. A wide variety of medical companies are looking at ways they can be more effective in holding down healthcare costs. Fortunately a number of them are looking to wellness strategies for the answer and when

210

they find a program that works they often reach out beyond their own employee and patient (customer) base and offer wellness services to their communities.

Madonna Rehabilitation Hospital and the Madonna ProActive Health & Fitness Center in Lincoln, Nebraska have long been involved in wellness programming through their rehabilitation hospital. As they expanded their programming to include not only employees and patients, they developed a model for providing services to the Lincoln community. They have constructed a new state-of-the-art medical fitness facility (ProActive), and have discovered the value of training staff in wellness coaching. A small number of staff went through ICF accredited training to become coaches with a specialization in wellness coaching. A consultation on how to fit the wellness coaching model into their new ProActive center helped them design effective ways to deliver wellness coaching to their customers. They have not only integrated wellness coaching skills into their staff training, but also into the clinical programming at ProActive. They have weight management, cardiac rehabilitation, and general health management programs that all use coaching constructs to help clients achieve their wellness goals. The Health Psychologist at ProActive, Dr. Todd Fleischer, also developed a wellness measure called the ProActive Wellness Assessment (PWA) that assists in helping clients develop wellness goals. The PWA measures Bill Hettler's six dimensions of wellness as well as stages of change and the attitudinal barriers that can impair the adoption of healthy behaviors. They have proven the significance of this measure on over 1,200 members. Members have been able to develop and track their comprehensive wellness goals using this measure. Training for ProActive and hospital personnel in what wellness coaching is, how to be more coach-like in their own wellness work, and how to refer to staff wellness coaches, has expanded awareness of the new model and helped in the mindset shift that we have spoken of in this book.

Other hospitals are seeking ways to increase the effectiveness of their wellness programming by including wellness coaching and by helping staff become more coach-like. Recognizing that the lifestyle components of healing, recovery, and prevention are truly behavioral issues, they are looking for ways to shift the approach taken by not

211

only wellness educators, but by personnel such as diabetes educators, cardiac rehabilitation therapists, nurses, nutritionists, physical therapists, and others to an approach that is more coach-like.

Sutter Connect, a Sutter Health affiliate, is a leading healthcare management and administrative services company based in California. They have had the vision to see the connection between wellness and cost containment. To help maximize the benefits of this connection they have identified a need for disease management coaching for the people they serve who have diabetes. Hiring professional coaches from ICF accredited programs, they developed telephonic services to help their clients manage their disease process better through greater medical compliance and healthier lifestyles. Brian Marsh championed the cause to increase the effectiveness of the disease management staff by seeking out specific training in wellness coaching.

Disease management coaches became wellness coaches and despite a very time-limited coaching format, patients benefited greatly from this further training. The Wellness Mapping 360° training model extends over a period of time, allowing the coaches to really apply their learning. Brian and the staff began to see the tremendous value of helping their clients create community and more connectedness to others who support their health journey. They began to see that helping clients increase support for healthy lifestyle changes was one of the best things they could do in a limited time model. Their dynamic staff is continually examining how they can be even more wellness- and coaching-oriented with their clients.

Corporate Applications

Wellness coaching is beginning to find a home in the corporate world in organizations that understand the connection between wellness and productivity. Most large companies have had some form of wellness program for many years. With increasing emphasis on one-on-one services some are looking for ways to go beyond what they have done in the past and experiment with new ways to increase effectiveness.

Expanding the HRA paradigm

In Chapter Seven we spoke at length about health risk appraisals and the various ways they are used to help people take charge of their own wellness. Certainly one of the most common wellness programming scenarios is when an HRA instrument is applied widely to an employee population and the results are shared in some form of feedback process. In this setting wellness coaching could be put into action allowing the employee with a health risk to work in multiple sessions with a well-trained wellness coach. Here are some suggestions to consider for making HRAs and wellness coaching a positive piece of the company's wellness program:

- Hire companies with well-trained wellness/health coaches who process HRA results with employees either in-person, or on the telephone.

- Another option is to train your in-house staff who work with HRA's in wellness coaching.

- Give employees more than one session. Multiple sessions allow true coaching to take place with opportunity for change, accountability, and the value of the coaching alliance.

- Make coaching sessions as long and as often as feasible.

- Take "Readiness for Change" into consideration as you develop your program.

In-house and Outsourced Wellness Coaches

Many corporations have instituted and valued executive coaching programs, sometimes hiring coaches as employees, and sometimes contracting with coaches outside of their system. Now we are starting to see some emergence of on-staff coaches with a health and wellness emphasis. These coaches may work with especially valuable employees to help prevent burnout and retain them as healthy employees longer. They may be assigned to work with employees identified as being at high-risk medically in an attempt to curtail the usage of a high percentage of healthcare costs by high-risk individuals. Or they may take the approach that it is less expensive to keep healthy employees healthy by the preventative power of living healthier wellness lifestyles.

As an in-house wellness coach you may have the opportunity to work face-to-face more often with your clients. This model works well

213

for large companies who are centrally located. For companies with sites in many geographic locations telephone-based coaching is a good alternative. This can be achieved either through on-staff coaches or through contracting with independent coaches or coaching services.

Organizations may also find that it may be more cost-effective for them to outsource wellness coaching services rather than have the added expenses of full-time employees and providing them benefits packages, etc. If the teleconference style of coaching is likely to be the norm the coaches can be anywhere and still connect with the employee who needs coaching.

Taking It Directly to the Consumer

Most wellness work in the past has been done though contexts such as employee wellness programs. As we review the incredible growth in all aspects of the wellness industry described in economist Paul Pilzer's book, The Wellness Revolution, it appears the time may be right for taking it directly to the consumer.

Demographics rule much of the wellness field. When we look at the epidemiological factors of illness and the sociological factors influencing behavioral change we see that who, what and where are big questions to answer. In the United States the sheer numbers of the baby boom generation are astounding. We must remember that World War Two did not have this same effect everywhere else in the world. Much of Europe experienced great loss of life while we were booming. The bulge in the population that the boomers push up in the U.S. is absent in these countries.

The baby-boom generation is having an enormous impact on healthcare in America and is putting tremendous stress on the medical system. In addition to remedial care demands, the desire for more and more health and wellness-related products is skyrocketing. "The economic impact of the baby boomers on wellness is even stronger than their numbers suggest—because this group is behaving differently than any prior generation. Boomers are refusing to passively accept the aging process." (Pilzer, The Wellness Revolution, p. 42)

Among the customers in the fitness center, alongside the trim younger bodies are women with long grey hair down over their shoulders and men whose hair, what they have left of it, is also turning more and more silver. You see it everywhere. Boomers on the bike paths, out dancing, filling the Yoga classes, and snatching up all the copies of health, fitness, and spa magazines. Vitamins fly off the shelf, while demand for organic and natural foods continues to amaze us all. And, the demand is coming not only from the aging baby-boom generation, but from younger minds who see the value in living a wellness lifestyle, being active and are more at ease about self-pampering in spas, etc.

Pilzer exhorts us to look at the abundant opportunities not only in providing personal services in the wellness field, but also in sales and distribution of wellness products. His economic prediction, made in 2002, which doesn't seem to have anyone contradicting it yet, is that the goods and services of the wellness field are the next trillion-dollar industry in America.

Elsewhere in the world there is also tremendous interest in wellness. As we see in the U.S., there are overlaps between alternative medicine (a.k.a. complimentary medicine, integrative medicine), holistic health, and wellness. From spas in Thailand and Brazil to wellness resource websites in Poland, we see expanding application of new ideas in wellness and more and more interest in wellness coaching.

Many coaches are self-employed. By either applying previously gained knowledge from the world of business, or by rapidly learning the ropes of entrepreneurship, coaches can bring many good ideas to the wellness industry. The question is: how can you position your services to attract people interested in wellness.

Many coaches find that their clients connect with them because they have seen them speak or present somewhere. There has been some kind of personal exposure that is far more powerful and more trust building than any printed or electronic marketing can create.

One way to attract the wellness consumer directly is by creating attractive wellness-oriented retreats, workshops or *play-shops*. Make the experience fun, practical, relaxing, and even pampering. Teach people extreme self-care by allowing them to experience some of it. Experiment with the format and find what works for you and your clientele. Half-day, whole day, or weekend resort "get-away" types of retreats may work for your focus clientele. Create the experience around attractive themes and ones the consumer can relate to. Perhaps partner with a colleague or with a professional event planner and do it right!

215

The workshop itself is providing a great service. If people find they can connect with you and are attracted to you as a coach new clients will result. Think of reaching out with your services beyond your local area. It's a big world out there!

Some Self-Employed Wellness Coaching Business Tips

- Grow your coaching business (not "practice") as you can. Consider starting part-time while you gain traction.

- Call it what it is. Name your business something that people understand right way. Avoid the temptation to go with your favorite, but esoteric, name.

- Say it clear, say it now. Be able to articulate with laser-like ability exactly what services you offer, how people benefit from them and what sets you apart.

- Keep the door open. Answering machine messages should clearly state your own name, the name of your business, and be a combination of professional, warm, and inviting. Put your business phone number on the home page of your website where potential clients can find it effortlessly. Don't come across like you are more concerned with your own privacy than you are about being of service.

- Diversify. You are not just a coach. You are bringing all that YOU are to the world. What other skills and talents do you have to offer? Training, consultation, speaking, etc., bring in much needed income and also drive clients to your coaching services. Offer products to the public in ways that do not conflict ethically with your work with clients.

- Learn the business of business. You can do a lot on your own, but also consider courses in coaching attraction/marketing offered by professional coaching schools, and services of private marketing experts and teachers (for example: www.helpingthehelper.com).

- Do what you are best at. Determine when it just isn't worth it for you to do it yourself. Instead of sitting at home learning how to build websites and program HTML, get out and promote yourself in public. Hire others to handle time consuming tasks or ones where someone else's expertise would give you better results.

- Create your own team. Hire a mentor coach. Have great business resources available such as a good webmaster, accountant, a reliable place for your printing, etc. Have great resources available for your own self-care (now needed more than ever): massage therapist, holistic healthcare providers, fitness facilities/resources, spa access, etc.

- Co-create mutual alliances. Develop a network of helping professionals that you refer your clients to (fitness trainers, nutritionists, physicians, psychotherapists, career counselors, acupuncturists, etc.), and develop relationships with them where they are referring to you as well. Don't do business with people who don't want to do business!

- Remember that you are not your work. You are not your cash flow! You own the business, don't let it own you. Avoid over-identifying with your business. Focus and work smart, but have a life—preferably one with fun, grace, and adventure! It all makes you more attractive as a coach anyway.

- Custom fit to your clientele. Consider new and different ways to size, shape, package and custom-fit your services to the people you serve. Experiment with modifying the old standard times and dates for appointment times.

The Wellness Revolution Rolls On

As new scientific breakthroughs continue to show us the importance of our lifestyle on our health and well-being, the demand for wellness products and services will continue to grow. "Until now, most people were told to accept their wellness deficiencies as part of the aging process, as though there were nothing they could do about them." (Pilzer, p. 57) Now people are quicker to question this assumption and to seek out ways to live their lives with more health and vitality.

Our wellness coaching challenge is not that of "marketing," but of "market development." We market products and services people are already familiar with. We have to do market development to educate consumers as to what our products and services are and how they can benefit them. We are poised to ride an immense economic wave, but the public has to be aware of what we have to offer them.

Positioning wellness coaching is the challenge we all share.

- Position wellness coaching as the resource for lasting lifestyle improvement.

- Demonstrate that wellness coaching has the kinds of results that show that taking wellness one-on-one is highly effective.

- Provide quality services, collect sound statistics, and get the message out to those who need to know.

New Venues!

Get creative with your wellness coaching marketing development. Go where no coach has gone before! Look for potential places to attract clients or cultivate referrals. Through alliances the wellness coach becomes part of a team. Consider these new venues for wellness coaching:

- Fitness facilities. Workout clubs of all kinds abound. Some of them may be open to having you do a free talk for their members. You may be able to connect with fitness trainers there for mutual referrals. You may even be able to sell the idea of wellness coaching as a service that can be effortlessly added by the facility.

- Health stores. Natural foods stores are growing in superstore proportion. Many have public education programs and even training/presentation rooms available.

- Public athletic clubs. Outdoors clubs.

- Senior citizen centers where public programs happen all the time. Many active seniors are great business/medical contacts.

- Spas and day-spas. The huge public interest in "all things spa" can be capitalized on. Many spas are limited in their services and see themselves primarily as hospitality (hotel) businesses. It is worth exploring how open they are to wellness services for their clients. When they do buy in, they are inexpensively adding your out-sourced service to their clients for very little, if any, expense to themselves. Many of the internationally famous "big name" spas already have full time staff who do wellness coaching. While getting hired there is a long shot, many hundreds of other spas are worth checking out and having conversations with.

Finding the Niche Within the Niche

No matter how you pronounce it, niche marketing can be highly effective. While "wellness" coaching might be considered a niche, how can you set yourself apart even within this very broad area of lifestyle improvement? The challenge here is to be focused without eliminating too many potential clients. Who is your market? Your market may not just be people you are absolutely comfortable with, identify with, or can relate to. While all of that is nice to have in a client, can you really afford to be that restrictive? Perhaps a little stretching and growing would be a good thing for you as a coach, and as a person. Ask yourself, "What holds me back from coaching this variety of client?

It's fine to go with the strength of your own experience, just be vigilant at keeping your story and your client's separate. Your "story" in life can be an advantage. My fifty-five year old friend who coaches people about "retiring well," both personally and financially, will probably get more trusting clients than a twenty-five year old trying to reach the same market. Many of the coaches I've trained have been attracted to wellness coaching from their own experiences with their own health challenges. Cancer survivors, coaches who are diabetic, who have been through heart surgery, who have been successful with weight loss issues, etc., can carry those experiences into developing a coaching niche where knowledge and empathy are very high.

Choose your niche based upon a combination of it really and truly being something you are passionate about and one where there really is a market for it. Does society value what you have to offer? Are there ways I can reach a sufficient number of people to serve who need what I offer in this niche? In short, is the niche big enough? What we know for sure is that wellness coaching is becoming an important part of our world as people and businesses strive to become healthier and to reduce the cost of health care.

> *A non-doer is very often a critic-that is, someone who sits back and watches doers, and then waxes philosophically about how the doers are doing. It's easy to be a critic, but being a doer requires effort, risk, and change.*
>
> **—Wayne Dyer**

Afterword: Quantum Soup

This is truly a new batch of soup we are creating in the merger of wellness and coaching. Lasting lifestyle behavioral change is the taste we are trying to attain. No one is sure of the recipe, except that it should have lots of mindset shift, quite a few cups of coaching competencies and a broth that is rich in wellness foundational principles. This is a soup that will come out of every kitchen a bit different, with flavors from bland to spicy. Predicting all the variations would be like trying to predict the future. It is very exciting to anticipate all that will be created. My hope is that it will all be very nourishing.

In *The New Physics for the Twenty-First Century*, edited by Gordon Fraser, it is said that the Universe was a tiny bowl of Quantum Soup until a fraction of a second after the Big Bang. Well, it may be a bit pretentious to compare our fledgling wellness field with the creation of the universe, but have fun and think about it. The desire for greater levels of health in the world is met with the staggering illness statistics we see despite incredible efforts to make a difference. Two forces in separate orbits, like the medical world and the behavioral world, finally intersect like never before, and BANG! We can only hope the new creation will serve us all well.

Behavioral medicine has been around for a long time. As a psychologist I felt very gratified by the progress I saw in clients that I helped with stress-related disorders. Biofeedback, relaxation training, psychotherapy and other approaches all helped. In hospitals psychologists and other behavioral experts continue to make enormous and valuable contributions. What wellness coaching is doing is making the competencies of behavioral change available to more people who are in a variety of helping capacities. We have found ways to extract essential elements of behavioral change, which, combined with a growth-oriented way of practicing yields lifestyle changing results.

It reminds me of days long ago in graduate school when I saw how Robert Carkhuff and Bernard Berenson (*Beyond Counseling and Therapy*) expanded the work of Carl Rogers. They identified three nec-

221

essary and sufficient conditions that are related to a positive outcome in therapy: acceptance of the client, accurate empathy and congruence on the therapist's part. Perhaps we are evolving a set of competencies through coaching that can serve us the same way in the wellness field.

You are presented with a world of tremendous opportunity. Those feeling the drudgery of illness care are being reinvigorated by both a growth-oriented way of doing healthcare, and a growth-oriented way of living. There will always be a need for remedial care, to say the very least. It is just so exciting to see us going further "upstream" into the land of prevention. It is an inside-out job. As you work on your own personal growth, mind, body, spirit and the connectedness to your environment, you become a person who can help others to grow as well.

Post Script

My own wellness journey, like that of most of us, has included many twists and turns. The day after I sent the first draft of the manuscript for this book to my editor, I left to keynote on wellness coaching in London. The keynote and workshop were very well received, but the next day I seemed to be coming down with a severe chest cold. A couple of days later, as we began some touring, a doctor in Wales told me that yes, I probably had an upper respiratory infection, and by the way, had anyone ever told me that I had a heart murmur? My stamina diminished day by day and soon I was in a hospital emergency ward having difficulty breathing. Six days in a British hospital and the conclusion was finally reached that my mitral valve had sprung loose and blood was backing up into the upper chamber. My lungs were filling with fluid.

I managed to return home to Colorado and have the surgery there as I began going into congestive heart failure. When they did a heart catheterization the day before surgery, the technician told me that my arteries were clean as a whistle! No heart disease at all. All that good wellness lifestyle effort had not been in vain!

In earlier years I had been through other major surgeries. With all of this behind me I thought I knew what surgery felt like. Open heart surgery is a whole different experience, it's more like a train wreck.

While not as common as bypass surgery, valve surgery is just as severe, and sometimes more so. The chest is opened by splitting the sternum and the wall of the heart is sliced into. I was very fortunate. I had no heart disease. I had no diabetes. I was in very good physical condition to start with…and, instead of valve replacement, my gifted surgeon was able to repair the existing valve.

As I lay in my hospital bed with a view of the Front Range foothills, a nurse began saying how my good physical condition had been a distinct advantage for me. I asked her to look out the window at Greyrock Mountain on the Rocky Mountain skyline. "You see Greyrock? A month ago I climbed that." She was astonished. We both paused and reflected on the unpredictability of life. Now, months later, after weeks in cardiac rehabilitation, and tremendous support from my wife Deborah, friends and family, I am recuperating well and on the way back to good health.

I've always been a believer in experiential education, but this may have been taking it too far! I have always had great ability to empathize with another's experience, but what an intimate and total way to know what major health challenges are really all about! The power of the last year has taught me many things on a deeper level than ever before. Patience, faith, tenacity, and the importance of connectedness.

I've seen myself go from where the distance from bed to bathroom was a challenge, to where walking around the block was a daunting task, to where I'm walking all-day hikes with great stamina. I've gone from a weight lifting limit of less than five pounds to where I'm pressing over seventy pounds on a chest press. Working out in cardiac rehab while the speakers played Van Halen and Santana was something I had never envisioned!

More than anything, though, I am so thankful I didn't have to go through this experience alone. That is one thing I can't imagine, and would not wish for anyone. "Connection is the currency of wellness," is what my friend Jack Travis likes to say. Lack of it has to be the worst kind of impoverishment.

In the British hospital I shared a wardroom with five other men. One was bedridden, three could sit beside their beds only, and another chap and I were able to walk about for short distances. It was like a scene from *The English Patient,* or *For Whom The Bell Tolls.* In the bed beside me, a kind, but tough, old fellow was battling emphysema with bulldog determination, swearing that he'd danced with the devil a few times, but he wasn't going to get him yet! Across the way, the bedridden man, who was deaf and mute, was visited everyday by family members who signed to him and did what they could. All around me nurses, nurses aids, cleaning ladies, and doctors showed the most amazing compassion and dedication.

As I watched the men of the ward, I thought of those Hemingway-type scenes and how we justly honor the soldiers who have been wounded, as heroes. No less heroic are the efforts of all of these men, their families, the staff, and all the patients and those who care for them around the world. They summon the courage to sit up, to draw deep for that breath, and to heal as they are able. Their caregivers look past the things that would frighten and repel, or at least discourage, many of us, past the smells, the messes, and the expressions of pain, to connect with this fellow human in front of them and show them love.

I was given inspiration by the tenderness, mercy, strength and courage I saw on that ward, and in my own Colorado hospital. I was reminded of the many expressions of caring and connection shown to me, my loved ones and others throughout my life. In hospitals, funeral homes, schools, counseling centers, and treatment facilities of all kinds, and in day-to-day life, wherever that acknowledgement is made that we were all given each other to help one another, we see the power of connection.

Appendix I
Coaching Core Competencies*

The following eleven core coaching competencies were developed to support greater understanding about the skills and approaches used within today's coaching profession as defined by the International Coaching Federation (ICF). They will also support you in calibrating the level of alignment between the coach-specific training expected and the training you have experienced.

These competencies were used as the foundation for the ICF Credentialing process examination. The core competencies are grouped into four clusters according to those that fit together logically based on common ways of looking at the competencies in each group. The groupings and individual competencies are not weighted—they do not represent any kind of priority in that they are all core or critical for any competent coach to demonstrate.

A. Setting the Foundation

1. **Meeting Ethical Guidelines and Professional Standards—** Ability to understand coaching ethics and standards to apply them appropriately in all coaching situations

   a. Understands and exhibits in own behaviors the ICF Standards of Conduct (see list)

   b. Understands and follows all ICF Ethical Guidelines (see list)

   c. Clearly communicates the distinctions between coaching, consulting, psychotherapy, and other support professions

   d. Refers client to another support professional as needed, knowing when this is needed and the available resources

2. **Establishing the Coaching Agreement—** Ability to understand what is required in the specific coaching

---

*Taken from the International Coaching Fereration's *Professional Coaching Core Competencies*

interaction and to come to agreement with the prospective and new client about the coaching process and relationship

   a. Understands and effectively discusses with the client the guidelines and specific parameters of the coaching relationship (e.g., logistics, fees, scheduling, inclusion of others if appropriate)

   b. Reaches agreement about what is appropriate in the relationship and what is not, what is and is not being offered, and about the client's and coach's responsibilities

   c. Determines whether there is an effective match between his/her coaching method and the needs of the prospective client

B. Co-Creating the Relationship

3. Establishing Trust and Intimacy with the Client—
Ability to create a safe, supportive environment that produces ongoing mutual respect and trust

   a. Shows genuine concern for the client's welfare and future

   b. Continuously demonstrates personal integrity, honesty, and sincerity

   c. Establishes clear agreements and keeps promises

   d. Demonstrates respect for client's perceptions, learning style, personal being

   e. Provides ongoing support for and champions new behaviors and actions, including those involving risk taking and fear of failure

   f. Asks permission to coach client in sensitive, new areas

4. Coaching Presence—
Ability to be fully conscious of and to create spontaneous

relationship with the client, employing a style that is open, flexible and confident

   a. Is present and flexible during the coaching process, dancing in the moment

   b. Accesses own intuition and trusts one's inner knowing—goes with the gut

   c. Is open to not knowing and willing to take risks

   d. Sees many ways to work with the client, and chooses what is most effective in the moment

   e. Uses humor effectively to create lightness and energy

   f. Confidently shifts perspectives and experiments with new possibilities for own action

   g. Demonstrates confidence in working with strong emotions; can self-manage and not be overpowered or enmeshed by client's emotions.

C. Communicating Effectively

5. Active Listening—

Ability to focus completely on what the client is saying or is not saying, to understand the meaning of what is said in the context of the client's desires, and to support client self-expression

   a. Attends to the client and the client's agenda, and not to the coach's agenda for the client

   b. Hears the client's concerns, goals, values, and beliefs about what is and is not possible

   c. Distinguishes between the words, the tone of voice, and the body language

   d. Summarizes, paraphrases, reiterates, mirrors back what client has said to ensure clarity and understanding

e. Encourages, accepts, explores and reinforces the client's expression of feelings, perceptions, concerns, beliefs, suggestions, etc.

f. Integrates and builds on client's ideas and suggestions

g. Bottom-lines or understands the essence of the client's communication and helps the client get there rather than engaging in long descriptive stories

h. Allows the client to vent or clear the situation without judgment or attachment in order to move on to next steps

6. Powerful Questioning—
Ability to ask questions that reveal the information needed for maximum benefit to the coaching relationship and the client

a. Asks questions that reflect active listening and an understanding of the client's perspective

b. Asks questions that evoke discovery, insight, commitment or action (e.g., those that challenge the client's assumptions)

c. Asks open-ended questions that create greater clarity, possibility, or new learning direction. Asks questions that move the client towards what they desire, not questions that ask for the client to justify or look backwards

7. Direct Communication—
Ability to communicate effectively during coaching sessions, and to use language that has the greatest positive impact on the client

a. Is clear, articulate, and direct in sharing and providing feedback

b. Reframes and articulates to help the client understand from another perspective what he/she wants or is uncertain about

c. Clearly states coaching objectives, meeting agenda, purpose of techniques or exercises

d. Uses language appropriate and respectful to the client (e.g., non-sexist, non-racist, non-technical, non-jargon)

e. Uses metaphor and analogy to help to illustrate a point or paint a verbal picture

D. Facilitating Learning and Results

8. Creating Awareness—
Ability to integrate and accurately evaluate multiple sources of information, and to make interpretations that help the client to gain awareness and thereby achieve agreed-upon results

a. Goes beyond what is said in assessing client's concerns, not getting hooked by the client's description

  b. Invokes inquiry for greater understanding, awareness and clarity

  c. Identifies for the client his/her underlying concerns, typical and fixed ways of perceiving himself/herself and the world, differences between the facts and the interpretation, disparities between thoughts, feelings and action

  d. Helps clients to discover for themselves the new thoughts, beliefs, perceptions, emotions, moods, etc. that strengthen their ability to take action and achieve what is important to them

  e. Communicates broader perspectives to clients and inspires commitment to shift their viewpoints and find new possibilities for action

  f Helps clients to see the different, interrelated factors that affect them and their behaviors (e.g., thoughts, emotions, body, background)

231

g. Expresses insights to clients in ways that are useful and meaningful for the client

h. Identifies major strengths vs. major areas for learning and growth, and what is most important to address during coaching

i. Asks the client to distinguish between trivial and significant issues, situational vs. recurring behaviors, when detecting a separation between what is being stated and what is being done

9. Designing Actions—
Ability to create with the client opportunities for ongoing learning, during coaching, and in work/life situations, and for taking new actions that will most effectively lead to agreed-upon coaching results

a. Brainstorms and assists the client to define actions that will enable the client to demonstrate, practice and deepen new learning,

b. Helps the client to focus on and systematically explore specific concerns and opportunities that are central to agreed-upon coaching goals,

c. Engages the client to explore alternative ideas and solutions, to evaluate options, and to make related decisions,

d. Promotes active experimentation and self-discovery, to facilitate the client's ability to apply what has been discussed and learned during sessions immediately afterwards in his/her work or life setting,

e. Celebrates client successes and capabilities for future growth

f. Challenges client's assumptions and perspectives to provoke new ideas and find new possibilities for action

g. Advocates or brings forward points of view that are aligned with client goals and, without attachment, engages the client to consider them

h. Helps the client "Do It Now" during the coaching session, providing immediate support

i. Encourages, stretches, and challenges client's learning pace while recognizing and accepting their comfort level

10. Planning and Goal Setting—
Ability to develop and maintain an effective coaching plan with the client

   a. Consolidates collected information and establishes a coaching plan and development of goals with the client that address concerns and major areas for learning and development

   b. Creates a plan with results that are attainable, measurable, specific, and have target dates

   c. Makes plan adjustments as warranted by the coaching process and by changes in the situation

   d. Helps the client identify and access different resources for learning (e.g., books, other professionals)

   e. Identifies and targets early successes that are important to the client

11. Managing Progress and Accountability—
Ability to hold attention on what is important for the client, and to leave responsibility with the client to take action

   a. Clearly requests client actions that will move the client toward their stated goals

   b. Demonstrates follow through by asking the client about those actions that the client committed to during the previous session(s)

c. Acknowledges the client for what they have done, not done, learned or become aware of since the previous coaching session(s)

d. Effectively prepares, organizes, and reviews information obtained during sessions with client

e. Keeps the client on track between sessions by focusing attention on the coaching plan and outcomes, agreed-upon courses of action, and topics for future session(s)

f. Focuses on the coaching plan while being open to adjusting behaviors and actions based on the coaching process and shifts in direction during sessions

g. Moves back and forth between the big picture of where the client is heading, setting a context for what is being discussed, where the client wishes to go, and where the client is at that session

h. Promotes client's self-discipline and holds the client accountable for what they say they are going to do, for the results of an intended action, or for a specific plan with related time frames

i. Develops the client's ability to make decisions, address key concerns, and develop himself/herself (to get feedback, to determine priorities, and set the pace of learning, to reflect on and learn from experiences)

j. Positively confronts the client when he/she did not take agreed-upon actions

Appendix II
Wellness Mapping 360° Welcome Packet

Personal Information

(Completely confidential)

LAST NAME _____

FIRST NAME _____

NAME YOU LIKE TO BE CALLED _____

MAILING ADDRESS

    STREET, RR, ETC. _____

    CITY _____ STATE _____

    ZIP CODE _____ COUNTRY _____

PHONE INFO *(Please put a check mark by the phone # you want to be primarily called at)*

    HOME TELEPHONE (_____) _____

    WORK TELEPHONE (_____) _____

    MESSAGE OR MOBILE PHONE (_____) _____

    FAX NUMBER (_____) _____

E-MAIL ADDRESS _____

OCCUPATION/NATURE OF BUSINESS _____

_____

EMPLOYER NAME (OR NAME OF YOUR BUSINESS) _____

ADDRESS OF SAME _____

DATE OF BIRTH _____ MARITAL STATUS _____

SIGNIFICANT OTHERS NAME _____

NAME(S) OF CHILD(REN)/STEPCHILD(REN) AND THEIR AGE(S) (LIST BELOW AND ON BACK IF NEEDED)

_____

Please write a brief description of:

Your Education History: colleges attended, degrees, majors, etc., other trainings.

_____

_____

_____

_____

_____

Your Work History: basics of the type of work/career areas you have experienced, and for how long.

_____

_____

_____

_____

Your Relationship History: chronicle your marriage(s), long-term relationships, etc.

_____

_____

_____

_____

Thank you very much! This information helps me be the very best coach for you!

Focusing Your Choices

An aspect of the coaching process is to assist you in clarifying your direction in your life style choices. This exercise will add clarity to the primary areas you want to focus on in coaching. Please describe the five areas you would like to change or improve in your way of living. How will it look when you accomplish your goals?

1. What I would like to change or improve is . . .

_____

_____

How will your life/health change when this is improved or changed?

_____

_____

2. What I would like to change or improve is . . .

_____

_____

How will your life/health change when this is improved or changed?

_____

_____

3. What I would like to change or improve is . . .

_____

_____

How will your life/health change when this is improved or changed?

_____

_____

4. What I would like to change or improve is . . .

_____

_____

How will your life/health change when this is improved or changed?

_____

_____

5. What I would like to change or improve is . . .

_____

_____

How will your life/health change when this is improved or changed?

_____

_____

10 Things You Want Me to Know About You

1. _____
_____
_____

2. _____
_____
_____

3. _____
_____
_____

4. _____
_____
_____

5. _____
_____
_____

6. _____
_____
_____

7. _____
_____
_____

8. _____
_____
_____

9. _____
_____
_____

10. _____
_____

Laying the Foundation for Coaching

As your coach, it's important for me to understand how you view the world in general, yourself, your family and your job or career. Each person comes from a unique place in their thinking and their interaction with the world around them.

Answering these questions clearly and thoughtfully, will serve both you and me. The questions may help you clarify perceptions about yourself and the direction of your life. These are "pondering" type questions, designed to stimulate your thinking in a way that will make our work together more productive. Take your time answering them. If they are not complete by our first (foundation) session, bring what you have completed and finish the rest later. These answers will be treated with complete professional confidentiality.

Occupation / nature of business: _____

_____

Employers or Business Name: _____

Date of birth: _____ Marital status: _____

Do you have children? _____

Do your children live with you? _____

Coaching

1. What do want to get from the coaching relationship?

_____

_____

2. What is the best way for me to coach you most effectively, what tips would you give to me about what would work best?

_____

_____

3. Do you have any apprehension or preconceived ideas of coaching?

_____

_____

239

Job/Career
1. What do you want from your job/career?

_____

_____

2. What projects or tasks are you involved in currently or regularly?

_____

_____

3. What are your key job/career goals currently?

_____

_____

4. What skills or knowledge are you developing? How are you gaining this knowledge?

_____

_____

5. How do your job/career goals support or fit with your personal goals or sense of purpose?

_____

_____

6. In what ways does your job affect your level of stress and your health?

_____

_____

Personal
1. What accomplishments or events must, in your opinion, occur during your lifetime to consider your life satisfying and well-lived?

_____

_____

2. What is (or might be) a secret passion in your life? Something you may or may not have allowed yourself to do so far, but you would really love to do.

_____

_____

3. What unique gift or knowledge do you have to contribute?

_____

_____

4. What is your spiritual base or belief system? How do your draw upon your spiritual beliefs for support and to help you with moving forward with your life?

_____

_____

5. Please describe what gives you a sense of purpose in life? What activities have meaning or heart for you?

_____

_____

6. What's missing in your life, the presence of which would make your life be more fulfilling?

_____

_____

7. What do you do when you are really stressed, and feel up against the wall?

_____

_____

8. What two steps could you take immediately that would make the greatest difference in your current situation?

_____

_____

9. What else would you like your coach to know about you?

_____

_____

Health & Wellness Information

As your coach, my job is not to treat you, but to be your ally and your resource. When it comes to health and wellness issues I will help you discover steps you may choose to take towards greater health and higher levels of wellness.

241

As your ally, I may refer you to medical, psychological, nutritional and other health-related services for more information and to seek treatment in these areas. I can be a source of support and accountability, helping you to follow through with any treatment plans that you devise with these other professionals.

Please share with me information about your health and wellness so that I may more fully understand your health challenges and aspirations for higher levels of wellness.

1. Please describe your lifestyle and what you do to be healthy and well.

_____

_____

2. Please describe any health challenges that you currently experience (including not only major concerns, but problems like headaches, insomnia, etc.)

_____

_____

3. Are you currently on any medications? If so what is the name of the medication and the intended impact of the medication?

_____

_____

4. Please list any lifestyle changes/recommendations that have recently been made to you by a healthcare professional.

_____

_____

5. What do you do to reduce stress in your life, or to counter-act the effect of stress in your life?

_____

_____

6. Please describe a typical week in terms of diet and exercise.

_____

_____

242

7. What do you do in your life that brings you happiness and joy? How often do you do this?

_____

_____

8. What gets in the way of you doing what brings you joy and health in the world?

_____

_____

9. Please list the behaviors you'd like to change and then rate your readiness to make changes on each of the identified behaviors you listed.

 1 = Haven't even thought of changing this

 2 = Have given it some thought

 3 = Have started preparing to change (have looked up information, talked with others about it, etc.)

 4 = Am already taking some action to change in this area

 5 = Have already made the change and want help maintaining my progress

WHAT BEHAVIORS RELATED TO YOUR LIFE STYLE DO YOU WANT TO CHANGE?	RATE READI-NESS 1–5	COMMENTS

10. How can a coach be of assistance in helping you make the lifestyle changes you'd like to make?

_____

_____

11. What else would you like to add about your wellness goals?

_____

_____

Please take the time to think about the different areas of your life reflected in the Wheel of Life Below. Rate yourself in each category.

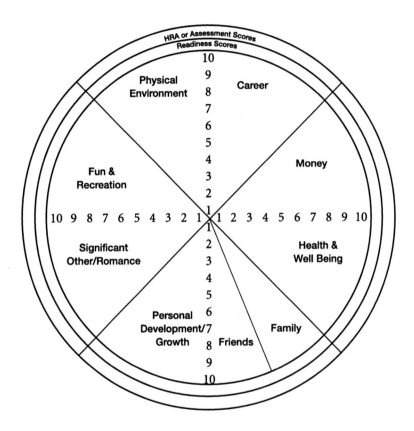

The nine sections in the Wheel of Life represent fulfillment and balance. Rank your level of satisfaction in each life area by marking the number and drawing a line in each section to create a new outer edge of the wheel. The closer you are to a 10, the more fulfilled you are. The new perimeter of the circle you draw represents your Wheel of Life. How bumpy would the ride be if this were a real wheel? "The Wheel of Life", a simple pie chart, is a commonly used tool in the health and wellness fields and is public domain property. Please copy it, and use it.

Bibliography and Resources

Ardell, D. (1982). *14 Days to a Wellness Lifestyle*. Mill Valley, CA: Whatever Publishing, Inc.

Ardell, D. (1981). *High Level Wellness: An Alternative to Doctors, Drugs, and Disease*. New York: Bantam Books.

Ardell, D. (1996). *The Book of Wellness: A Secular Approach to Spirit, Meaning, & Purpose*. Amherst, NY: Prometheus Books.

Arloski, M. (1994) "The Ten Tenets of Wellness". *Wellness Management*. The National Wellness Institute. Spring. http://www.realbalance.com

Arloski, M. (1999). "Coaching for Wellness". *Wellness Management*. The National Wellness Institute, Winter.

Arloski, M. (2002). "Simply Centered". http://www.realbalance.com

Arloski, M. (2002). "The Power of Habit". http://www.realbalance.com

Arloski, M. (2003). "Lasting Lifestyle Change Through Wellness Coaching". *Wellness Management*. Spring 2003

Arloski, M. (2004). "The Wellness Coach: Lifestyle Prescriptions Filled Here". *Tomorrow's Life Coach*. January, Volume 3, Issue 1.

Arloski, M. (2006). "New Mindset, New Model: From Prescribe and Treat, or Educate and Implore, to Advocate and Inspire—The Coach Approach". *Coach, The Magazine of Coaching and Mentoring International*. March/April.

Carlson, R. (2003). *Taming Your Gremlin: A surprisingly Simple Method for Getting Out of Your Own Way*. Rev. Ed. New York: Quill/Harper Collins.

Cashman, K. (2000). *Leadership from the Inside Out: Becoming a Leader for Life*. Provo, UT: Executive Excellence Publishing.

Chapman, Larry (2002). *Proof Positive: The Practitioner's Guide to ROI and Program Development*. 5th Ed. Omaha, NE: Welcoa.

Chodron, P. (2000). *When Things Fall Apart: Heart Advice for Difficult Times*. Boston, London: Shambhala Classics.

Covey, Stephen (1989). *The Seven Habits of Highly Effective People*. New York: Simon & Schuester, Inc.

Crum, T. (1987). *The Magic of Conflict: Turning A Life of Work into a Work of Art*. New York: Touchstone/Simon & Schuster, Inc.

Czimbal, B & Zadikov, M. (2005). *Kindred Spirits: The Quest for Love and Friendship*. Portland, OR: Open Book Publishers & The Abundance Co.

Czimbal, B & Zadikov, M. (1999). *Vitamin T–A Guide to Healthy Touch*. Portland, OR: Open Book Publishers.

Donaldson, F. (1993). *Playing by Heart: The Vision & Practice of Belonging*. Deerfield Beach, FL: Health Communications, Inc.

Ellis, D. (2000). *Falling Awake*. Rapid City, SD: Breakthrough Enterprises.

Ellis, D. (1998). *Life Coaching: A New Career for Helping Professionals*. Rapid City, SD: Breakthrough Enterprises.

Ellis, D. (2000). *Falling Awake*. Rapid City, SD: Breakthrough Enterprises.

Flaherty, J. (1999). *Coaching: Evoking Excellence in Others*. Boston: Butterworth & Heinemann.

Giesen, G. (2001). *Creating Authenticity: 200 Meaningful Questions for Meaningful Moments*. Highlands Ranch, CO: Greg Giesen & Associates, Inc.

Giesen, G. (2003). *Creating Authenticity: Meaningful Questions for the Minds & Souls of Today's Leaders*. Denver: GGA, Inc.

Hargrove, R. (1995). *Masterful Coaching*. San Diego: Pfeiffer.

Jampolsky, G. (2004). *Love is Letting go of Fear*. 25th Ed. Berkley/Toronto: Celestial Arts.

Kimiecik, J. (2002). *The Intrinsic Exerciser: Discovering the Joy of Exercise*. Boston/New York: Houghton Mifflin Co.

Kimsey-House, H., Sandahl, P., & Whitworth, L. (1998). *Co-Active Coaching: New Skills for Coaching People Toward Success in Work and Life*. Palo Alto, CA: Davies-Black.

Leonard, T. (1998). *The Portable Coach: 28 Surefire Strategies for Business and Personal Success*. New York: Scribner.

Levine, S. (1989). *Who Dies? An Investigation of Conscious Living and Conscious Dying*. New York: Doubleday.

Lowery, S. & Menendez, D. (1997). *Discovering Your Best Self Through the Art of Coaching*. Houston: Nexus Point/Enterprise.

Lusk, J. (1992). *30 Scripts for Relaxation, Imagery & Inner Healing*. Duluth, MN: Whole Person Associates.

247

Lusk, J. (1993). *30 Scripts for Relaxation, Imagery & Inner Healing Vol. II.* Duluth, MN: Whole Person Associates.

Lusk, J. (1998) *Desktop Yoga: The Anytime, Anywhere Relaxation Program for Office Slaves, Internet Addicts, and Stress-Out Students.* New York: Perigee.

Smith-Lovin, L., McPherson, M. & Brashers, M. (2006). "Social Isolation in America: Changes in Core Discussion Networks Over Two Decades". *American Sociological Review.* Vol. 71:3.

Maslow, A. (1962). *Toward A Psychology of Being.* Princeton, NJ: Van Nostrand.

Moore, T. (1992). *Care of the Soul: A Guide for Cultivating Depth and Sacredness in Everyday Life.* New York: Harper Perennial.

Patterson, K., Grenny, J., McMillian, R., & Switzler, A. (2002). *Crucial Conversations: Tools for Talking When Stakes are High.* New York: McGraw-Hill.

Phillips, B. (1999). *Body for Life: 12 Weeks to Mental and Physical Strength.* New York: Harper Collins.

Prochaska, J., Norcross, J. & Diclemente, C. (1994). *Changing for Good.* New York: Harper Collins/Quill.

Pilzer, P. (2002). *The Wellness Revolution.* Hoboken, NY: John Wiley & Sons.

Putnam, R. (2001). *Bowling Alone: The Collapse and Revival of American Community.* Rev. Ed. New York: Simon & Schuster.

Richardson, C. (1998). *Take Time for Your Life: A Personal Coach's Seven Step Program for Creating The Life You Want.* New York: Broadway.

Ruiz, D. (1997). *The Four Agreements: A Toltec Wisdom Book.* San Rafael, CA: Amber-Allen Publishing, Inc.

Seaward, B. (1997). *Managing Stress: Principles and Strategies for Health and Well-Being.* 2nd Ed. Sudbury, MA: Jones and Bartlett Publishers.

Travis, J., & Ryan R. (2004). *Wellness Workbook: How to Achieve Enduring Health and Vitality.* 3rd Ed. Berkeley, Toronto: Celestial Arts.

Wellness Councils of America (2002). "The Coaching Connection—Special Edition". *Absolute Advantage: The Workplace Wellness Magazine.* October. Vol. 1, No. 10. Omaha, NE: Welcoa.

Whitmore, J. (1995). *Coaching for Performance*. Sonoma, CA: Nicholas Brealey.

Williams, P., & Anderson, S. (2006). *Law & Ethics in Coaching: How to Solve and Avoid Difficult Problems in Your Practice*. Hoboken, NJ: John Wiley & Sons, Inc.

Williams, P. (2004). "Coaching and the Wellness Industry: A New Gateway for Consumer Awareness". *Choice*. Vol. 2, Issue 2.

Williams, P. & Davis, D. (2002). *Therapist as Life Coach: Transforming Your Practice*. New York: W.W. Norton & Co.

Williams, P. & Thomas, L. (2004). *Total Life Coaching: A Compendium of Resources*. New York: W.W. Norton & Co.

Institutes and Organizations

American Cancer Society: www.cancer.org

American Diabetes Association: www.diabetes.org

American Heart Association: Cholesterol levels. www.americanheart.org

American Holistic Health Association: www.ahha.org

The Institute for Life Coach Training: www.lifecoachtraining.com

The International Coaches Federation: www.coachfederation.org

National Wellness Institute/Conference: www.nationalwellness.org

Wellcoaches Corporation: www.wellcoaches.com

Other Good Web References

Abundance Company/Bob Czimbal: Great handouts on wellness, humor and connectedness: www.abundancecompany.com/free_handouts.htm

Body For Life: Fitness and diet program: www.bodyforlife.com

E-diets—Central clearing house for online diets and diet services: www.ediets.com

HealthWorld Online: Endless wellness/health information, articles, speakers, and medline searches: Jim Strohecker & The Wellness Inventory: www.healthy.net

My Food Diary—subscriber-based online food journal: www.myfooddiary.com

OncoLink: Large web resource about cancer: www.oncolink.upenn.edu/types/

PubMed—The National Library of Medicine/National Institutes of Health. Great resource for journal articles, etc: www.ncbi.nlm.nih.gov/entrez/query.fcgi?db=PubMed

Real Age—Simple, free, online HRA type instrument: www.realage.com

Real Balance Global Wellness Services: Resources and information about lasting lifestyle change. Training, speaking, wellness coaching, products, newsletter: www.realbalance.com

Sacred Passage and The Way of Nature Fellowship/John P. Milton: Contemporary vsion Quests, meditation retreats, Qi Gong and T'ai Chi Training, study of ancient Shamanic practices, and Traditional Vision Quests: www.sacredpassage.com/

TestWell : Division of The National Wellness Institute: www.testwell.org

Whole Person Associates: Publishers of a wide variety of wellness and stress management books, tools and resources: www.wholeperson.com

Your True Nature/Ilan Shamir: A Thousand Things Went Right Today; Advice From a Tree; many products for connection with nature and positive wellness programs: www.yourtruenature.com/

The Wellness Inventory: www.mywellnesstest.com

Wholesome Resources/Julie Lusk: Yoga, meditation guided imagery, affirmations, stress relief and wellness: www. relaxationstation.com

CPSIA information can be obtained at www.ICGtesting.com
Printed in the USA
BVOW020059060613

322577BV00008B/18/P